PHOENIX
RISING

PHOENIX RISING

JOHN J. NANCE

CROWN PUBLISHERS, INC. / NEW YORK

Published by Crown Publishers, Inc., 201 East 50th Street, New York, New York 10022. Member of the Crown Publishing Group.

Random House, Inc. New York, Toronto, London, Sydney, Auckland

CROWN is a trademark of Crown Publishers, Inc.

This is a work of fiction. All characters, events, and dialogue are imagined and not intended to represent real people, living or dead.

Manufactured in the U.S.A.

Design by Jennifer Harper

Library of Congress Cataloging-in-Publication Data

Nance, John J.
    Phoenix rising / by John J. Nance. — 1st ed.
        p.   cm.
    1. Airlines—United States—Officials and employees—Fiction.
    2. Commercial crimes—United States—Fiction. I. Title.
    PS3564.A546P48   1994
    813'.54—dc20
    93-31528
    CIP

ISBN 0-517-58566-9

10 9 8 7 6 5 4 3 2 1

First Edition

There are many invincible, intelligent women in this world who, like Elizabeth Sterling, have survived terrible adversity with both their dignity and femininity intact.
This work is dedicated to two of them:

Patricia Ann Davenport,
my long-time business partner and executive assistant,

and

Mary Carolyn Carmichael,
my sister, and a fellow Texas lawyer.

ACKNOWLEDGMENTS

The research for this novel cut a wide swath from Hong Kong through London, Amsterdam, Inverness, New York, Vancouver, and many American cities, as fellow airline people, financiers, government representatives, and those from a host of other professions unselfishly helped in a thousand ways, and I thank them all.

There are some people, however, whose contributions were particularly indispensable and appreciated:

- My many friends and acquaintances with the Boeing Company, whose superlative products I have flown and trusted for thirty years;

- Clark Stahl, pilot of KIRO-TV's Chopper-7, who was brave enough to give this fixed-wing pilot some stick time in his Jet Ranger in order to validate Eric Knox's flying technique;

- Charlie Gibson, co-host of ABC's "Good Morning America," who helped impose some economic discipline on the model of my resurrected Pan Am;

- My executive assistant, Patricia Davenport (to whom this book is dedicated), and to my wife, Bunny, for their invaluable editing throughout the project;

- My editor at Crown, Jim Wade, for his steady hand, sage advice, and periodic citation of Ockham's Razor;

. . . and,

- My literary agents, George Wieser and Olga Wieser of New York.

PHOENIX
RISING

PROLOGUE
Tuesday, February 14, St. Valentine's Day

Elizabeth Sterling woke in a panic with her heart racing and the distant roar of surf in her ears. In the darkness she grasped frantically for the fading image before her, trying to hold on to the tranquil feeling that had enveloped her so completely mere seconds before.

But the warmth was slipping away rapidly—and so was he, the man who had been with her on the beach. She watched him race away, recognizing slowly that he was only a fleeting character in a disturbingly sensual dream that evaporated with the suddenness of a slammed door, leaving her alone and empty again.

Surrounded by darkness, she fought to clear the mental cobwebs and locate reality. In his place now was only the same background roar that sounded like surf, tinged with the rich aroma of new and expensive fabrics. She was in a comfortable bed—alone. That much was clear. But where *was* that bed?

"Mom? Are you awake?"

Kelly's sleepy voice floated in from somewhere above in the darkness, bringing Elizabeth's memory with it.

That background roar wasn't surf, she realized. It was high-speed air passing just outside their window.

"Cover your eyes."

Elizabeth groped for a switch, flooding the lower regions of their small cubicle with light as Kelly lay unseen above in the upper bunk. Squinting, Elizabeth tried to read the tiny, numberless dial on her watch. Although the small hands seemed to show a few minutes past 2:00 A.M., she felt as if she'd been asleep much longer. Her subconscious had been lulled by the sounds of the slipstream at 39,000 feet as their airborne bedroom sped through the night toward the mainland of the United States.

"Where are we?" Kelly asked.

"Over the Pacific and at least seven hours out." They were supposed to arrive in Seattle, she recalled, at 9:30 A.M.

"Were you having another nightmare, Mom?"

"No." Elizabeth remembered the man on the beach and smiled to herself. It definitely hadn't been a nightmare.

"You've been real tense, Mom, and that's when you get them."

"I'm fine, Kelly. Are you okay, though?"

"I think I was having one of your bad dreams. I woke up falling."

"Try to get back to sleep, honey."

There was a singular murmur of assent from her fourteen-year-old daughter and, within a few minutes, the sound of gentle snoring from overhead. Elizabeth smiled and leaned back on one elbow, trying to recapture the feelings of pleasure she'd felt when she snuggled into this gilded cocoon after takeoff, luxuriating in the opulence of the compartment and stretching her legs against the crisp percale sheets with the Pan Am logo.

I'd better wake up. I promised Ron Lamb I'd meet him at 3:00 A.M. Seattle time, in the upper lounge.

The mattress was seven feet long—more than enough for her five-foot-six-inch height—and three feet wide, with an identical bed just above. The compartment itself was eighteen inches wider than the beds—just enough extra room for the occupant to stand comfortably between the sliding compartment door and the edges of the beds at night—each of which had privacy curtains. During the day, the upper bed retracted neatly into the ceiling while the lower one split into two plush, first-class seats facing each other in the private compartment.

Unlike the railroad Pullman cars of decades past, which featured beds separated from an open corridor by curtains, each of the roomettes was separated from the adjacent aisle by a wall of space-age glass that could be turned electronically opaque with the flick of a switch.

Not since the days of propeller transports had an airline embraced the concept of private airborne compartments for sleeping and sitting, but the startling new Pan Am design had garnered worldwide attention—and full bookings. Equipped with television, air-to-ground telephone, and an intercom, the compartment's only flaw was a traditional one: the communal bathroom and airborne showers were located where the first-class galley used to be, at the foot of the circular stairway leading to the upper deck.

A small concession at worst, Elizabeth figured, as she pulled on the gold-monogrammed terrycloth robe Pan Am had supplied, and opened the sliding door, intent on padding barefoot down the plush carpet to the bathroom. It was, indeed, the only way to fly—and Elizabeth felt a flash of pride that she had been a part of making it happen.

She glanced again at her watch.

Oh Lord, it's not two, it's after four! I'm late!

◆ ◆ ◆

A raven-haired senior flight attendant was waiting for Elizabeth when she emerged from the gold-trimmed bathroom fifteen minutes later and rushed back to her compartment to dress. The inaugural flight of Pan Am's Seattle-Tokyo route was filled with expensively dressed guests and dignitaries, but in terms of importance to the airline, Elizabeth Sterling and her daughter were at the top of the list. The flight attendant recognized her instantly. Pan Am had flown them nonstop from New York to Tokyo on a competing carrier just to attend the inaugural party and join the flight back.

"Ms. Sterling?"

Elizabeth felt somewhat embarrassed to have been cornered in a bathrobe, even talking to another woman.

"Yes?"

"Mr. Lamb's waiting for you on the upper deck."

"I know, I know. I overslept." Elizabeth rolled her eyes toward the ceiling as she fumbled with a plastic bag filled with toiletries.

Ron Lamb, president of the newly created airline using the venerable name of Pan American, was well known to her. After the gala party in Tokyo, she had seen him only briefly before departure from Narita Airport, and he had asked her to set an alarm and meet him when they both presumed the party in the upper lounge would be over. Something important was up, and considering the immense amount of money involved in restarting worldwide operations, it couldn't be good news. Elizabeth had felt a shiver of apprehension telegraph itself down her spine, the same little announcement of fear she'd felt for the entire eighteen months it had taken to construct the billion-dollar start-up package from her office in New York. It hadn't seemed possible to do what she'd done.

The flight attendant was waiting quietly for a message.

"Please tell Mr. Lamb I'm embarrassed, but the compartment was too comfortable and I didn't hear the alarm. Tell him I'll join him upstairs in a few minutes, as soon as I get myself together."

◆ ◆ ◆

Ron Lamb was waiting for Elizabeth when she topped the circular stairway, still feeling like a dried prune from the low in-flight humidity, despite a liberal application of skin moisturizer and several glasses of water. She marveled at the thought that flight crews could tolerate such environments for an entire career.

The upper lounge was breathtaking. Extending back from the cockpit door some forty feet, the new Pan Am design had converted the upper deck area into a luxurious club of leather and chrome, teakwood and indirect lighting, with couches and huge swivel chairs that could be moved in various directions on hidden rails. Movable tables were set at intervals. A quiet track from an album by Seattle's own Kenny G blended in the background with the soft sound of the slipstream at 39,000 feet.

Ron Lamb greeted Elizabeth with a warm smile. He looked tired and worried, but if he was upset at her lateness, he was trying to hide it. He was of average height with silver hair, sparkling eyes, and a perpetual smile that made the small mustache he wore look slightly silly. Elizabeth had enjoyed working with him from the day Lamb and his delegation of hopeful entrepreneurs had walked into the offices of Silverman, Knox, and Bryson in New York to pitch their outlandish idea. Since he was the former CEO of two substantial airlines and, at fifty-eight, a thirty-year airline veteran, even a wild idea from Ron Lamb was worth listening to.

But his idea had turned out to be far from crazy.

That had been just under three years ago, and now—with a year of highly successful operations under their belt—it looked as if "Pan Am: The Sequel" was going to make it. But with so much money at stake, not to mention her reputation with the financial community, it seemed like a continuous high-wire act without a net.

"Ron, I'm very sorry to keep you waiting."

He smiled. "I'm just glad you're here—on the inaugural, I mean."

The senior flight attendant materialized with a freshly brewed pot of gourmet coffee from Starbuck's specialty house in Seattle on a silver tray that also held a variety of pastries. Elizabeth followed Ron to a couple of leather chairs with a small table in between.

"You slept well, then? You like the accommodations?" He asked it with a proud air as he sat opposite her, placing his cup and saucer on the highly polished teak tabletop.

Elizabeth smiled. "Too much so."

They talked about the magnificent interior for a few minutes, and the galvanizing effect Pan Am's bold new ideas were having on the big carriers. But she ran out of superlatives as Lamb ran out of polite questions, and an awkward silence filled the lounge before they both spoke in unison.

"So . . ."

"I wanted to . . ."

"You first." Elizabeth laughed. "You've been waiting up all night for me. What's up? Are we in trouble?"

Ron Lamb leaned over and pulled a sheaf of papers from a battered brown leather briefcase, placing them on the small table, slightly under the edge of the pastry tray.

"I've got the latest financial results and projections here for you to study. The good news is we're still ahead of schedule and gaining traffic."

"And the bad news?"

"William Hayes has resigned as chief financial officer."

"I hadn't heard," Elizabeth replied. She had worked with Hayes, and found him secretive and not terribly sharp, but his departure shocked her.

"Well, it was sudden, and so is this," Ron Lamb was saying. "We want to hire *you* for the job. *I* want you, the board unanimously agrees, and the airline you helped to create needs you. I know it would mean resigning from your partnership. I know it would mean moving to Seattle and uprooting your life and your daughter's life."

"To say the least. I'm not opposed to the idea of a change, but . . ."

I mustn't let him know I'm sick of Wall Street! she cautioned herself.

Lamb was almost sputtering, his hand moving higher in her visual range. "Okay, consider this, please. If you accept and come aboard, this position will give you your very first full executive position in a publicly held corporation, *and,* to our benefit, you could be of immense assistance in nurturing this company through the formative years. And remember, Elizabeth, we wouldn't even exist if you hadn't kept at it. You're the wizard who built this financial structure, and you're the one to bring it to maturity."

Some of the flattery and awe drained away with that, and she looked hard at him. "Why, then, Ron," she began, "have you been fooling around with the debt structure? I'm aware you renegotiated several of the credit lines I sweated blood to arrange. Several friends alerted me. I didn't think it was my place to say anything, since neither you nor Bill Hayes asked my advice at that point, but—"

"Elizabeth, I know." Lamb was moving closer across the table, earnestly, his hands gesturing in symmetry with his words. "I apologize for leaving you out of the loop. But that's precisely why we no longer have the CFO we started with. He screwed around with your structure, and lied to me and the board about it. We thought he had coordinated with you. After all, you're still our investment banker.''

"He sure didn't.''

"I know that—*now*! That's why I need you. *We* need you.''

She sat in silence, searching his eyes for hidden meanings.

"How much can you tell me?'' she asked at last.

"Until you're legally a corporate officer, only what's in this report.'' He patted the stack of papers on the edge of the table. "But I promise you can handle it, and the compensation package I've arranged includes a new condo in downtown Seattle, moving expenses, signing bonus, parachute, and stock options.'' Ron Lamb smiled and leaned back, looking at Elizabeth with what he hoped was a slightly envious and appreciative look, and being very, very careful not to betray the anxiety that had gripped him the last few days.

"Think about *this*, Elizabeth. You'll be making more than I do!''

Friday, February 17
La Guardia Airport, New York

The ground dropped away beneath Elizabeth Sterling with stomach-churning suddenness as the helicopter leapt off the western end of the overcrowded airport like a startled cat, clawing for altitude over the Grand Central Parkway as it headed toward the south end of Manhattan Island. The leaden sky above was an Impressionist painting of impending snow set off by wild swirls of alto-stratus clouds, nature's brushstrokes of winter on the gray canvas of a high overcast, framed by leaf-whipping winds.

"Good grief!" The words were half-muttered as her senses rebelled at the acrophobic recognition that only the raw power of the Jet Ranger's turbine engine was holding them aloft. Elizabeth was a low-time, fixed-wing private pilot, and to her the lack of *forward* airspeed was unsettling.

Eric Knox was grinning at her behind the microphone boom of his headset, fully aware she had a death grip on the arm rests. One of the senior partners of Elizabeth's investment banking firm and worth many tens of millions now, Eric could afford to commute by helicopter. Forty-two and single, he owned a mansion on eastern Long Island equipped with its own airfield, and spent his spare time indulging a grand passion for flight. With the retirement of his father, *he* was now the Knox in the highly respected investment banking firm of Silverman, Knox, and Bryson.

"Wait'll you see what's ahead, Elizabeth! Only the worst weather days can force me to take the train. I love coming to work in Cinemascope and Surround Sound!"

They reached five hundred feet and began moving forward faster toward the East River as Eric gently banked the Ranger twenty degrees left toward the heliport by the South Ferry dock near their office building.

Elizabeth's eyes scanned the magnificent cityscape ahead, her apprehension draining away as the chopper accelerated and began to behave like a traditional air machine—as if someone had finally equipped it with some visible means of support, such as wings.

How could twelve years have passed so fast? She had been utterly thrilled to move to New York. The day she first drove into the city, even from the cluttered perspective of the Triboro Bridge, she'd luxuriated in the intimidating visage of Manhattan's skyline, drinking it in with the wide-eyed excitement of a cat in an aviary. The years in Harvard Business School had been nothing short of brutal, especially for a widowed mother going through the lonely trials of raising a baby daughter alone. She had fallen in love with a fellow MBA candidate—an ex–Air Force pilot named Brian Murphy—whom Kelly had begun to regard as her father. But Brian had had six months to go to his degree and couldn't accompany them to the big city as Elizabeth began her new job.

Nevertheless, New York had taken her in and hugged her those first few weeks. First she had had the amazing good fortune of finding an affordable flat in Greenwich Village, a flat, she reminded herself, owned by Hilda Biggersford, a somewhat lonely, retired schoolteacher. Mrs. Biggersford began helping with baby-sitting chores in the first few months. She grew protective of Kelly and Elizabeth over the following year, and disapproved sternly when an unmarried male named Brian moved in with mother and daughter just before Christmas.

Slowly, with Elizabeth and Brian both working, Mrs. Biggersford became four-year-old Kelly's nanny. When Brian left them to fly for a start-up airline in Phoenix four years later, Kelly had turned to Mrs. Biggersford in her inconsolable grief of losing the only father she had ever known.

The memory caused her smile to fade, but Eric hadn't noticed. In the distance, Elizabeth could see the buildings near Washington Square where Mrs. Biggersford had been run down by a delivery truck on Kelly's eleventh birthday. The elderly woman had lingered for weeks in pain, and Kelly's tearful vigil had shocked Elizabeth to the depths of her being. She'd had no idea how strong the bond had become between Kelly and Mrs. Biggersford in recent years. As the kindhearted woman lingered at death's door, there was nothing to be said about Kelly's grief, or about the sinking reality that Elizabeth had all but lost her daughter to the endless nights and weekends on the job.

After the funeral, Elizabeth had changed her lifestyle completely, arranging to stay home each morning until Kelly had been picked up by her car pool, and making sure a newly hired housekeeper was there when Kelly came home each day, to bridge the ninety-minute gap until her mother, the successful investment banker, returned from Wall Street. Elizabeth learned to work late at night from home, using computers and fax machines after Kelly had gone to bed. She was there at each basketball game and school play, aggressively making time for the two of them as she fought back the tears at Kelly's continuing rejection. For nearly two years an angry and rebellious Kelly withheld a significant part of her love as she continued to punish her mother, not quite able to trust the change in her. But, gradually, Elizabeth's love and determination to make up for lost time won Kelly over. By the time she entered junior high school at the age of thirteen, a precocious and rapidly blooming Kelly discovered that she had a smart and successful mother who loved her deeply. With that realization, the defensiveness dissolved at last.

The helicopter turned south now, the bustling urban squalor of Little Italy and Delancey Street visible to the right.

Elizabeth's own metamorphosis into a blasé New Yorker had come all too fast. Within a few years she had more or less crusted over with a veneer of suspended appreciation for Manhattan—a façade that sophisticated New Yorkers seem to adopt as they use the city without admitting to loving it.

During the last few years, the selfishness and pointlessness of her job had begun to gnaw away at the linings of her conscience. Every new stock issue, debt exchange, or junk-bond package was publicly hailed as a benefit for the corporations involved, but she knew better—and lying to herself had never worked. What she did for a living, she had finally admitted to herself, was similar to a financial shell game: she thought up ways to magically change the ownership of hard-earned corporate profits. With that recognition, a hard edge of cynicism had begun to overtake her.

But then the Pan Am project had come along, fraught with the opportunity to create new employment and new, productive wealth. She had believed in it and fought for it and ultimately succeeded brilliantly. But afterward, everything had snapped back to the same pointless routine.

Kelly had noticed her growing distress, but her associates had not.

I'm scared to leave, she admitted to herself, *and I'm scared to stay.*

The helicopter ballooned suddenly on a gust of wind, the blades slapping the air for a few seconds with a different sound. Eric grinned again and steadied his ship, watching Elizabeth's wide-eyed reaction in his peripheral vision.

"Why would you leave this behind, Elizabeth?" Eric's voice cut through the noise again, paring her thoughts with spooky timing as the sweep of his left hand took in most of Manhattan. "Seattle's pretty, but it's a backwater. Hell, it's *under* water most of the time, with the rain. This is your home, and we're your professional family. Support Pan Am, for chrissakes, but don't marry the bastards."

"I haven't decided yet."

"Well, decide now. Decide no," he countered.

"I'm thinking about it."

As deftly as he had handled the departure, Eric slowed and maneuvered the Jet Ranger with precision, kissing skids to concrete in a perfect touchdown despite a troublesome crosswind, and appreciating the fact that Elizabeth had been impressed.

The short walk to Old Slip Street and their building was taken at double time. Elizabeth smiled at the receptionist as she breezed through the double glass doors and headed for her office with Eric in hot pursuit. She stood before the floor-length window by her desk, her eyes scanning the same cityscape from a slightly safer aerial perspective, her thoughts suddenly far away as Eric sat on the couch and studied her, wondering for the thousandth time what her body was like beneath those elegant clothes.

Eric Knox had toyed for years with the fantasy of linking his life outside the office with Elizabeth. There were times he even ached for her, but she had always kept him at a distance—which he had never really minded, since there was always tomorrow.

But now she might be leaving, and in the throes of wondering what he should do, he had made an amazing discovery: he *liked* being single.

Eric watched her carefully as she stood with her back to him, her amber-blond hair cascading gently over her sculpted shoulders, the broad angles of her face turned from him but etched in his mind. In heels, she was almost as tall as he was, and he liked that fact. Her nose was perfect, diminutive and slightly upturned, in symphonic balance with her broad mouth, set off by laugh lines. She had to work to look stern or unhappy; the edges of her mouth did not naturally turn down, they had to be forced, and sometimes the effect was more comical than threatening.

But as Eric had discovered with secret pride years before—after hiring Elizabeth Sterling as much for her looks as for her professional qualifications—any male that mistook her gentle female image for weakness rapidly slammed into a brick wall of confidence and determination. Her captivating femininity cloaked a confident, capable businessperson who had all the toughness necessary to make gender irrelevant.

"Elizabeth?"

"Um-hmm." She was still looking out the window, still deep in thought, her right hand absently tugging at a gold loop earring.

"If you'll stay, we'll change the masthead for you."

She turned, surprised. Eric's father had been adamant that the firm name always stay the same, regardless of how many partners they had.

"Silverman, Knox, Bryson, and *Sterling*?" Her voice was tinged with incredulity. "Your dad would kill you!"

"I'll even change it to *Sterling*, Silverman, Knox, if you'll stay."

Elizabeth searched his eyes and smiled slowly. "Sure you will, Eric."

"This new Pan Am could fail miserably, you know."

"I'll have a golden parachute."

"But you won't have *us*."

"I know," she said, softly. That part would be hard.

◆ ◆ ◆

The day was brutal, with all the problems and phone calls held at bay during Elizabeth's quick trip to Tokyo now crashing through the dam of secretaries to overwhelm her. Nevertheless, she managed a constant barrage of outbound calls as well, calls about Pan Am to friends and contacts from Manhattan to London, as she absorbed the responses with equal speed.

"Be careful, Elizabeth. They're a bright hope, but they've got a ways to go to full viability."

"Take it, babe! Check the parachute first, but take it and run. You can always write your ticket back on the Street if they crash."

"Elizabeth, they're making some bold moves, and if you're a name in the annual report when they really succeed, well, you'll hang your star."

And one odd response from the most negative curmudgeon she had ever known, Stanley Mossler of Salomon Brothers. She had expected Stanley to tell her to forget it. He advised her instead to take it, but with a strange caution:

"Elizabeth, they're upsetting some very powerful people. Be careful."

At 4:45 P.M. she put down the phone, closed her briefcase, and headed for the ladies' room, anxious to get back to her apartment. Kelly would already be home from school.

She was in the process of touching up her lipstick when the soft voice of Linda Wright wafted out of one of the stalls behind her as Linda herself appeared in the mirror, straightening her skirt.

"You've never looked better, Mizz Sterling!"

Elizabeth turned to face her, reminded suddenly of the mousy woman in oversized glasses she had "discovered" years before in a sales position, a female who knew more about the sale and feeding of junk bonds in the post-Milken period than anyone else on the Street. With Elizabeth as her mentor, she had flowered. A statuesque redhead who had finally learned to wear feminine clothes and makeup, she was now bond manager.

"When I heard you might be leaving," Linda continued, "I realized I'd never told you how much I've always admired the way you balance things. You know, businesslike and ladylike too."

"*Lady*like?" Elizabeth tried to look incredulous.

"Well-l-l . . . I mean . . . oh hell, *sexy*, okay? Sexy but in charge and no nonsense."

Elizabeth looked down and shook her head, trying to keep from laughing. "Thanks, Linda . . . I *think!*" She looked at her watch with obvious intent, and inclined her head toward the door. "Linda, I've got to run."

"No problem. I'll walk with you. I take the same train."

They headed for the elevators and the street, with Elizabeth trying to guide the conversation to more comfortable territory. She had never felt secure with overt compliments. She had been raised to pity vain people. She *refused* to be vain.

Elizabeth set a brisk pace as they left the building and walked toward the subway. Linda, refusing to be sidetracked, launched in again, recalling their first meeting and how it had shocked her to find a woman so effortlessly penetrating the firm's male exclusiveness.

"You didn't hide yourself the way I did, Elizabeth. You remember? I used to wear tweed suits and glasses and pull my hair back, scared they'd figure out I was female—until you came."

"You were always attractive, Linda." Elizabeth had to jump sideways to avoid an onrushing formation of dark-suited men charging in the opposite direction toward some urgent purpose, briefcases flapping in the breeze. Linda followed in tight formation.

"Yeah. *Now* I look okay. Before, whenever I'd dress like a woman I'd get plenty of dates and no sales. When I wore pants, I'd spend my evenings alone, but I could sell bonds, boy.

"I remember going to dinner with a client once in this little cocktail dress with my hair down. I'd decided to wear girl clothes for a change," Linda continued. "When I showed up, this guy was stunned. He hadn't seen a *woman* at the office, he'd seen a suit with a high voice, so suddenly it wasn't a business meeting, it was a date. I spent the evening studying his prospectus while *he* spent it talking to my chest. It was a disaster.''

They found the stairway together to the Rector Street station and descended, the dank smell of stale air carrying the faint stench of urine as the rolling thunder of a passing train rumbled up the filthy concrete steps from the bowels of the station.

"Anyway, after that experience, I went back to business suits. It took another year and your arrival to convince me to look like a female again on the job. I'll miss you, Elizabeth.''

"I haven't left yet. I haven't decided.''

The doors of the uptown A train opened. The two of them stepped aboard automatically, amid the motley collection of rush-hour commuters and other passengers. There were no empty seats and no chivalrous males aboard the subway car, so they both grabbed handholds and braced themselves as the train lurched forward.

"So what does your number-one daughter think of this prospective job change?" Linda asked, several stops later.

Elizabeth smiled and sighed, gesturing toward her street, two stops away, and hoping Kelly had remembered to give their housekeeper the packet of instructions Elizabeth had prepared.

"I'm taking Kelly to our Cape Cod place in the morning. The beaches are unbelievably beautiful this time of year, and sometimes we get snow covering the dunes. We're going to pig out on crab at the Lobster Pot in Provincetown, walk the beach, and hopefully make a decision.''

"Sounds idyllic!" Linda said.

"Going up there was *her* choice. She was very definite that I couldn't decide this without sand between my toes, even if it *is* the middle of winter.''

Saturday, February 18, evening
Provincetown, Massachusetts

Saturday blew in on a freezing east wind accompanied by a full moon hung in a frosty indigo sky. Provincetown, no longer awash with the tide of tourists that normally ebbed and flowed through the narrow streets in the summer, had an intimate atmosphere, even in the cold. Elizabeth was glad she'd succumbed to Kelly's wishes, though the beaches adopted a strange and ethereal character in the pristine frostiness of a maritime winter.

It was eleven by the time Elizabeth and Kelly returned to the cottage from their evening of seafood. Kelly had already decided what her mother should do, and with a seriousness beyond her years she had sat Elizabeth down at the small kitchen table and paced like a worried adult as she restated the obvious in order to announce her conclusion.

"Mom, as long as we keep this place, moving is the right thing to do."

Elizabeth looked at her daughter with pride, realizing what a beauty Kelly was becoming. Her clear blue eyes and shoulder-length auburn hair were already attracting the attention of the awkward boys in her class. Kelly tossed her hair and smiled an odd little smile that made her look just like her father. Elizabeth felt herself weaken for a moment as she thought of Ted and how much he would have loved their daughter. She seldom thought about the drunk driver who had killed him, leaving a pregnant young wife with nothing.

Elizabeth shook off the memories and smiled back at Kelly. "You're sure you're happy with the idea?"

Kelly was trying unsuccessfully to suppress a smile and look introspective. She loved her grandmother, who lived in Bellingham, Washington, less than two hours north of Seattle by highway and three thousand miles closer than New York. The move was an exciting change. The idea of the free passes Elizabeth could get as a Pan Am officer had filled Kelly's head with visions of endless trips to exotic destinations. Kelly nodded, running her long fingers through her hair and trying hard to act as mature as her fourteen-year-old body was becoming. "I'm sure."

But Elizabeth was still in agonizing doubt.

When Kelly was asleep, Elizabeth pulled on a parka and slipped outside to brave the wind and think. She had grown up walking on beaches. Usually it had been the inland sea known as Puget Sound that had kept her company on introspective evenings, a calmer body of water than the wild Atlantic or the blue Pacific. But she knew the ocean as well. Her parents had spent summers on the beach in Ocean Shores, Washington, a moderately developed stretch of beachfront on the Pacific Ocean, only four hours from Bellingham. The crash of surf was more than music to her ears; it had been the soundtrack to her soul.

How do I feel?

Elizabeth recalled friends in New York—good friends—and years of building a network of contacts, as well as a considerable professional momentum and reputation. And, she had to admit, she was worried about what Ron Lamb probably *wasn't* telling her.

Money was not the issue. Cashing out her partnership interest would leave her with a considerable sum of money, probably over a million after taxes. And with her track record, she could come back. Maybe not to Silverman, Knox, and Bryson, but somewhere. So even if Pan Am flopped, she would be safe. What else was there to worry about?

Elizabeth sat for a moment on a driftwood log, listening to the relaxing crash of the surf as she realized the decision had already been made.

In the distance, across the moonlit bay, lights sparkled and danced over the waves, reflecting softly in an occasional breaker. Somewhere out of sight over the far shoreline was Boston and the Old North Church, which had held the lanterns that had signaled Paul Revere. She had read about that church as a little girl, and always wanted to visit it.

Perhaps the next time we're back here, she thought. *Whenever in the world that might be.*

Ron Lamb replaced the receiver and sat back uncomfortably in his elaborate desk chair, fighting once more to keep the increasingly familiar feeling of panic from parading across his face like a Times Square advertisement.

It was 9:50 A.M. in Seattle and 12:50 P.M. in New York, and already four different stock analysts had called for reassurance that all was well with Pan Am—even as the new airline's stock sank on the market, indicating otherwise.

"Rumors!" Ron had roared at each of them with what he hoped appeared to be unshakable confidence.

The origins of the rumors were unimportant for the moment, but they would force him to stage a show-and-tell meeting for the airline analysts within a few days in New York, in a frantic attempt to calm them down. Already the black financial crêpe of impending doom and lowered bond prices had been hung around the cornices of Pan Am's credit rating. Once such rumors began having an effect, they could become self-fulfilling prophecies.

The decision to base the new Pan Am headquarters in Seattle instead of near Wall Street now began to seem very naive. If they were sitting in New York, such things would be easier to control.

"We've gotta stop this, Ron." Joseph Taylor, chairman of the board, was staring at him from the seriously strained Argentine leather office couch across from the CEO's white oak desk.

"I know it." Ron tried to mouth the words with confidence as he checked his watch again. Elizabeth Sterling was supposed to call in another ten minutes.

The chairman wasn't finished.

"Ron, what's going on with the FAA? Are they after our ass, or what?"

Taylor, an imposing lump of a man at over 280 pounds, had made a fortune creating an international chain of warehouse clubs. His considerable bank account and a lifelong devotion to the original Pan American Airways had made him the engine—and the chairman—of the corporation they had formed to re-fly the Pan Am name. But Taylor needed help finding airports, and knew nothing of what went on there. For the most part, Joe Taylor had stayed out of Ron Lamb's way. But now that the corporate ship was under fire, Taylor had rumbled in at dawn and insisted on occupying the bridge—along with the invited members of the impromptu war council consisting of the four senior vice-presidents now arrayed in front of Lamb's desk.

Taylor's little round eyes were boring holes in Ron Lamb's, searching for a barometer with which to measure the danger they were in. Taylor could be abrupt and undiplomatic at times, but he was a smart businessman with an iron grasp of basic corporate finance.

Ron Lamb inclined his head toward the vice-president of operations, Chad Jennings, who snapped to attention.

"Mr. Taylor, we don't think there's any sort of, uh, campaign on to nail us on violations, but as you may know, a team of FAA inspectors descended on our Denver maintenance station last week and found parts records missing. Yesterday they called and claimed we were using the wrong minimum-equipment lists on the 747s, and to brace for a large fine. They said they were responding to tips."

Taylor fired a barrage of questions at Jennings before refocusing on the CEO.

"Sounds like one of our competitors may be setting us up, Ron."

Ron Lamb's secretary appeared in the office doorway with a handful of newspaper articles and wire stories faxed in from New York, all of them painting gloomy pictures of Pan Am's future.

Ron had come around the desk to read with the others. He returned to his chair now, after slamming several of the pages onto the coffee table.

"Goddammit, we're profitable! We're *not* sinking! Where are these stories coming from?"

Ralph Basanji, senior vice-president of public affairs, leaned forward. "Ron, they're coming as a result of Bill Hayes's dismissal. They see us kick out our finance man suddenly, and several weeks go by without a new one, so these guys in Manhattan turn into fiction writers in order to explain it."

"It's that important? Having a current CFO, I mean?" Taylor asked Basanji, who nodded solemnly.

Ron Lamb felt his stomach tighten even more. What if Elizabeth turned him down? He hadn't even considered anyone else. He'd probably have to promote someone from within—fast. But the analysts would see through that in a second.

"Mr. Lamb?" His secretary's voice wafted over the desk from the built-in telephone intercom.

"Yes?"

"Miss Sterling on line two, sir. She's calling from Provincetown, Massachusetts."

Ron Lamb took an overtly ragged breath and picked up the receiver.

"Okay, Ron, I'll take it. You've got yourself a new CFO."

"How soon can you get here, Elizabeth? We need you yesterday."

He had already made the split-second decision not to deploy her to New York to work against the rumor mill. If she was in Cape Cod, she probably knew nothing of the rumors, and so much the better. There were things he needed to explain to her in person.

"Good Lord, Ron, I haven't resigned from Silverman, Knox yet."

"Well," Ron Lamb replied, "at least let us announce you're coming aboard. How much time do you need?"

"Two weeks." Her reply was instantaneous.

"Can you come out here tomorrow, just for a quick orientation?"

"Yes, I can do that."

"Good! I'll have first-class tickets for you on our early-afternoon flight out of Kennedy tomorrow. Bring Kelly if you like. Just give me one day to get you briefed and up to speed on some important items."

"Such as why the financial press thinks you're going belly-up?" She said the words in a breezy tone, but there was stunned silence from Seattle.

"Oh, I know that's nonsense, Ron. I read all the information you gave me. You were worried I'd back out, right?"

"Yeah . . . yeah, I was. We need you out here, y'know."

"Well, I'm a bit tougher than that."

♦ ♦ ♦

At the very moment Ron Lamb's office was emptying of Chairman Taylor and other Pan Am corporate officers in downtown Seattle, Pan Am's chief pilot, Brian Murphy, was engaged in a delicate balancing act: aligning his Boeing 767 for a tough approach to fog-shrouded

Anchorage, Alaska, while trying to figure out why his cellular phone was ringing.

A background irritation at first, the rapid chirping was causing the check captain in the right seat to flash worried looks at various corners of the cockpit in urgent search of the strangely non-Boeing-like noise. Nothing *seemed* wrong, yet there it was *again*, echoing this time like a frantic electronic canary in full warble, the tiny sound waves bouncing in confused abundance from every surface in the small technological capsule of instruments and lights.

With the final approach course comfortably tamed, the landing gear extended, and the invisible airport seven miles ahead of them (according to the moving map display), Captain Brian Murphy snapped on the auto-flight system and reached for his phone.

The voice in his ear was honeyed and familiar, but unrecognized in the distractions of the moment.

"Brian? Is that you?" The higher-than-masculine register conjured up instant images of things soft and feminine. Some deep recess of his brain assigned to deal with recognition finally located the right biochemical file, the find instantly triggering responses that rippled through his motor control centers like the initial shudder of a major earthquake. He lurched forward in his seat involuntarily.

"*Elizabeth?*"

"Yes, it's me. Where *are* you?"

"In the box . . . wait a minute."

Brian nodded at the check captain, who was pointing to a switch, which he now threw, freezing the ten-million-dollar flight simulator in theoretical flight four miles from the theoretical runway.

Brian pressed the small phone to his cheek and hunched over the control yoke, a broad smile bisecting his face and the check ride all but forgotten.

"Where are *you*? Are you here in Seattle?"

"No . . . Cape Cod . . . but I'm coming to Seattle."

"*Wonderful!* When? For how long?"

"Maybe forever, Brian."

"What do you mean, Elizabeth? You aren't teasing me, are you?" Brian's deep voice overrode the background hum of the electronic cooling fans, which normally filled the cockpit like audible cotton. The check captain in the right seat recognized instantly something intensely personal in his tone. Without a word, the man unstrapped and headed for the exit at the rear of the simulator's cockpit, leaving his boss in the privacy of a multimillion-dollar phone booth.

She told him then of the job offer, and her acceptance, and of the impending move. She had refrained from calling him on the return from Tokyo, not wanting to complicate her decision, and had tried to imagine life in Seattle without Brian's image imposing itself on every thought.

That attempt had failed. Despite all the years and the supposedly final choices they had made, she missed him. She missed him more than she had ever let herself admit.

"I'm coming in tomorrow for a quick orientation," she said.

"*Tomorrow?* Damn!"

"You're flying?"

"I've got no choice. I have to be in D.C. We've, ah, had a few problems with the FAA I've got to take care of."

The word *problems* didn't register. The fact that she wouldn't see him for a few more weeks did.

Suddenly, it seemed an eternity.

3

Jake Wallace turned the time card over again in complete confusion. The imprint that showed that he had already clocked in for the graveyard shift was still there in stark black and cream, the time of 9:54 P.M. showing clearly on the appropriate line.

Pan Am's luxurious new round-the-world service starts March twenty-What the hell?

Jake glanced around the interior hallway of the sparkling new hangar, searching for an explanation. There were twenty-two other mechanics on the graveyard, and he was their foreman. Obviously one of them had grabbed Jake's card by mistake.

He sighed and began looking through the time cards of his shift-mates, verifying the time stamp on each one until he had counted twenty-two properly clocked-in employees.

So much for the obvious explanation, he thought. He pocketed the time card and headed for Job Control.

Ed Washburn looked up from his computer screen with a characteristic grin as Jake walked in, but received no smile in return from the bearded mechanic. In fact, Ed thought, he had never seen Jake Wallace look so preoccupied. All the employees of Pan Am's Moses Lake facility were proud of their new hangar and their new airline and the beautiful fleet of refurbished 747s and 767s they were there to maintain. Most were veterans of bankrupt old-line airlines such as Braniff, Frontier, Eastern, and Pan Am, and all of them were grateful and excited to have been selected by the new Pan Am's recruiters, made instant stockholders, and given a chance to make airline history—even if they did end up moving to the remoteness of central Washington State.

Worried expressions, in other words, were rare in the Pan Am maintenance facility, and Jake's was a classic mask of distracted concern.

As two of his crew came in the door, Jake waved the offending time card in front of Ed and explained the problem.

Ray McCarthy, who had overheard, raised his index finger in response.

"That new man may have got hold of your card, Jake. He came in with me and clocked in just behind me. He seemed surprised his card was already there."

Jake Wallace looked at Ed Washburn, who looked back with the same expression Jake had worn seconds before. Simultaneously they turned toward McCarthy and spoke in stereo.

"*What* new man?"

He had worn the regulation white coveralls with the Pan Am logo, McCarthy explained, and introduced himself as Bill somebody-or-other before asking for directions to the Job Control office, which was just off the hangar floor. The last name sounded vaguely Norwegian. The man had come through the security door into the maintenance complex with McCarthy, and yes, it was Ray who had punched in the security code and opened the door for them both. Five-foot-ten and of medium build, the new man had a "forgettable face."

"No one checked through here, and I wasn't expecting anyone new," Ed Washburn told McCarthy. "Did he have an ID badge, Ray?"

Ray McCarthy felt his stomach tighten as he tried to call up a memory of the man's identification card. There had been something there clipped to his pocket, but in the darkness of the parking lot, he could have just assumed it was a Pan Am ID.

"I *thought* it was there."

They all stared quietly at each other, silently turning over the implications in their heads.

Washburn broke the silence.

"Whoever he is, we'd better find this guy before he hurts himself, or steals the coffee money. I wonder if someone in Seattle hired him and forgot to tell us."

The search began casually. After all, there was sure to be a logical explanation. But when a quick walk-through of the facility turned up neither an explanation nor a confused new-hire mechanic, Ed Washburn, as shift supervisor, began to get seriously concerned. With FAA regulations regarding security of commercial aircraft and the incessant cautions about potential terrorist acts now parading around his memory in accusatory profusion, Washburn stepped up the search and alerted his boss at home. Robert Chenowith, the general manager of the maintenance base, jumped in his car and arrived in Job Control within fifteen minutes, equally worried. By 11:00 P.M., Washburn and Chenowith were sure that whoever the man had been, he was not a new hire. That meant his presence had to be considered threatening, until they knew otherwise.

Two dozen mechanics now roamed the hangar and connecting buildings, looking for the intruder. Someone had invaded their space, and the group was determined to catch him. All other work had ceased.

At first the search had centered around the only aircraft in the facility, Ship 612, a sparkling 747-200 which squatted with impatient majesty in the middle of the giant hangar, bathed in sodium vapor lights and looking magnificent. Ship 612 was due to be flown back to Seattle the following morning, carrying the latest modifications to the Compartment Class and First Class sections, and would fly a trip the next evening. They had to get it out of the Moses Lake hangar on time.

Washburn had stationed Ray McCarthy in the door of Job Control. McCarthy looked thunderstruck, wide-eyed, and scared, his face a bloodless white. He had let the intruder in. All of this was occurring because he had failed to check the man's ID badge.

"When you last saw him, Ray, where was he heading?" Washburn asked on one circuit past the office.

By 11:30 P.M. it was obvious that whoever had crashed their gate was long gone. Every square inch of floor space, every closet, every aircraft compartment, and every broad space in the rafters had been checked and checked again in a well-coordinated effort.

But the intruder wasn't there.

They turned, then, to the more sinister question: Regardless of who he was, did the intruder *do* anything to our airplane?

Two dozen people now began crawling over Ship 612. There was a procedure in the manuals to be used to examine an aircraft grounded by a bomb threat. They opened to that section now, using hand-held checklists to comb the 747 meticulously from radome to rudder, looking for anything unusual. But by 2:00 A.M., with every type of tampering, sabotage, theft, or other mischief considered and probed, a shaky Ed Washburn declared Ship 612 to be clean. With Chenowith's permission, they terminated the search.

Chenowith now faced a dilemma of his own, his hand hovering over the telephone in Job Control as his mind calculated the percentages in alerting his vice-president of maintenance in Seattle. He would be getting the man out of bed, of course, but for what? What else could be done?

They *did* know that someone had been inside the perimeter, masquerading as a mechanic, and they *did* know the man had left. But whatever he had been doing in the meantime, it obviously couldn't have involved sabotage. There was virtually nothing he could have done to 612 that wouldn't already have been discovered.

Seattle had enough to do without worrying about some benign intrusion in Moses Lake. Perhaps it was nothing more than an episode of industrial espionage, he reasoned. Maybe the guy had been after pictures of the interior, especially the new tapestries and other changes they had just made. After all, he rationalized, the big carriers were more than a little unhappy about Pan Am's innovative cabins, and any of the big three could well afford to hire investigators—though it would be easier to buy a ticket.

Despite the nagging doubts, Ship 612 was clean. Now his people would have to drive themselves twice as hard during the remaining four hours of their shift to get the huge bird rolled out by 6:00 A.M. and ready to fly back to Seattle.

Industrial espionage. That was probably it.

Chenowith read 2:45 A.M. on the wall clock as he quietly replaced the receiver, his decision not to call already made.

◆ ◆ ◆

At the same moment, some two hundred miles to the west, Pan Am's president and CEO was sitting in the backseat of a rented limousine and rubbing his eyes, the heavy veil of sleepiness still wrapped around his head like a warm towel. Ron Lamb had presided over more expensive advertising campaigns in his years of airline leadership, but never one more critical than this. The multimillion-dollar advertising package he was supposed to help launch in little more than an hour was critical to Pan Am's success.

The gold lettering on the slick black folder trumpeted the slogan:
WE'RE AROUND AGAIN! AROUND THE WORLD, THAT IS!

The inauguration date for the new globe-circling service was three weeks away, Ron reminded himself, and yet there was still much left to do.

The dark mass of KOMO television's front wall slid into place, and with a practiced rush of opened doors and a refreshing puff of cool, damp air, heavy with early-morning fog, the limousine driver delivered the airline president to the care of a studio technician. The man seated him in the comfortable chair of a talk-show set and fussed over an earpiece as he clipped a tiny microphone to Ron's tie.

"Where do I look?" Ron asked.

"Right in the camera, Mr. Lamb. Charlie Gibson will be doing the interview," the floor director said, as he studied Ron Lamb's forehead and responded automatically, dabbing at a shiny spot with a cosmetic powder brush he'd seemingly produced from midair. "You won't be able to see Mr. Gibson," he continued, "but you'll hear him in your earpiece. Just imagine he's behind that lens, and please don't glance around the studio. We wouldn't want you to look shifty."

"I can't see him?"

"No, sir. We *could* hook up a monitor for you, but there's a delay of as much as a second between what you hear and what you see, and it drives people nuts. Trust me."

"No problem."

Ron glanced around the darkened studio. There were several bright studio lights shining in his eyes, but the house lights in the background were turned off. The empty gallery of bleacher seats lining one side of the huge room looked brooding and disapproving, heightening his sense of impending stage fright.

He began concentrating on the briefing paper provided by Ralph Basanji, and that triggered a mental review of the past week.

The meeting with the financial community in New York had been an inquisition, but he'd pulled it off—or so the feedback had confirmed. The rumors, which had been echoing like a gunshot in the Grand Canyon, had put the Street on alert. But since nothing had happened to validate those rumors, Ron's performance had quieted the waters for the moment. Elizabeth Sterling couldn't arrive a moment too soon, and Ron reminded himself that she'd be landing in Seattle this very evening to take over the financial reins at last.

"Mr. Lamb?"

The sudden voice in his ear caused him to jump slightly as Ron reminded himself that the technicians back east were probably looking at him by satellite through the lens of the camera that sat staring silently at him like a cyclops some fifteen feet away.

"This is the director in New York, Mr. Lamb. You hearing me okay?"

"Uh, yes. Can you hear *me*?"

"We can hear you and see you just fine, sir. We appreciate your getting up at such an early hour to be with us. We're going to run a taped report about your company, then we'll come back to the studio and to you, about six minutes from now."

"Okay." Ron tried to discipline himself to look at the lens as he realized his left hand was fussing with his left ear, pushing at the earpiece.

There were other sounds now, of microphones being adjusted on the set in New York, and of various voices talking back and forth.

The rest of his company was filled with happy, optimistic, proud, energized people. *So why am I feeling so damned negative?*

He closed his eyes for a second and felt the butterflies begin to alight, one by one.

The familiar theme music of "Good Morning America" filled his ear now, and the soothing voices of Joan Lunden and Charlie Gibson followed as Ron Lamb took a deep breath and prepared to pump sunshine into the hearts of the flying public.

Pan Am's luxurious new round-the-world service starts March twenty-seventh, and by damn, I'm gonna make them want it!

4

Wednesday, March 8, 8:07 P.M.
Seattle, Washington

Beneath the high overcast that covered Puget Sound by sunset, a wispy veil of stratus now floated like an afterthought at three thousand feet. The diaphanous layer gently enfolded the nighttime city of Seattle like the gossamer curtains of an Elizabethan bedchamber, enshrouding a region of mysterious beauty and twinkling lights in multicolor hues, all softened by the diffusive effects of the clouds. Along the waterfront, the wake of a late-departing ferry heading out into Elliott Bay flared brightly and briefly in the reflected luminescence of the downtown district—the phosphorescent trail followed instantly by the marveling eyes of many newly airborne passengers as Pan Am Flight 10 slipped into the sky over the West Seattle Bridge, making a lazy left turn toward Tokyo, some five thousand miles distant.

Within the space of five minutes, the huge Boeing jetliner—born of a giant assembly line some thirty miles to the north in Everett—lifted itself above the overcast, leaving the visage of Puget Sound below to memory. Within thirty minutes the 747-200 was essentially at sea, sailing seven miles above the waters, as the efficient silicon-based minds of the onboard computers aimed their giant client at the Japanese Archipelago, a quarter of a world away.

Wednesday, March 8, 8:40 P.M.
Pan Am Flight 10, in flight some 100 miles west of the Olympic
Peninsula, Washington

For the last few minutes there had been nothing but a soft electronic hum in the earpiece of the captain's lightweight headset. It changed now, suddenly, the businesslike voice of an air-traffic controller cutting through the void.

"Clipper Ten Heavy, say again your GUNNS estimate."

To Captain Jim Aaron, the radio channel had been quiet for so long that he'd begun to wonder if they'd lost contact with Seattle Center. But no, the controller was still with them, and wanting to know when the 747 crew expected to pass over the invisible checkpoint called GUNNS, an oceanic intersection some 360 miles west-northwest of the coastline of Washington State.

Judy Griffin, the copilot, raised her microphone to reply.

"Clipper Ten Heavy is estimating GUNNS at . . . ah . . ." Judy leaned to her left, her eyes searching the screen of the flight computer for the right number. ". . . zero-five-two-two-zulu, Seattle. We're level now at flight level three-five-zero."

There was a light rustling of papers in his ear as the flight engineer, Patrick Hogan, handed the fuel plan forward for the captain's approval. Patrick—he refused to let people shorten his name to Pat—was experienced and competent, and a longtime friend. He was also a fellow deregulatory refugee whose deceased airline had been the original Pan Am.

The fuel would be tight tonight. With the jetstream blowing down their throats part of the way, a nonstop flight from Seattle to Tokyo was just barely within legal range without a fuel stop in Anchorage.

Jim scribbled his initials on the log and handed it back. It would be the first step of a constant monitoring routine to make certain the fuel-burn curve didn't start diving away from the fuel-burn plan during the ten hours of flight time that stretched ahead of them.

He turned to Judy and then to Patrick.

"You two ready to rig for ocean running? Turn the house lights up, I mean?"

Night flying in a dark cockpit made everyone sleepy, and once over the ocean under positive control at high altitudes, there was no point in looking for other traffic.

They both nodded in unison and Jim reached up to the overhead panel to flood the cockpit with light.

Just in time, too, he thought. *I was about to get comfortable and drowsy in the dark.*

"Jim, you going to use the circadian room tonight?" Patrick Hogan was watching him for an answer. They were all eager to try the new section in the belly lounge, one deck beneath the main cabin floor, which was another popular Pan Am innovation. Reached by a small elevator, part of it was an exercise room that the passengers could use by appointment, and the other side a small cabin of seats surrounded by very bright light panels that provided the illusion of daylight. New research had discovered that an hour or so of such light exposure could reset the body's internal clock and almost erase jet lag. Pan Am had jumped at the chance to introduce what they had advertised as a bright idea long before the rest of the industry.

The captain had just opened his mouth to answer, when a soul-shaking *thud* thundered through the 747 cockpit.

♦ ♦ ♦

The cockpit voice recorder duly recorded the time as 04:46:08 GMT— 8:46 P.M. in Seattle.

♦ ♦ ♦

Captain Jim Aaron felt as if something large and hard had hit the plane at high speed. The combination of sound, orange light, vibration, and the sudden yawing of the 747 overwhelmed him.

Somewhere in his head, the words *What the hell was that?* tried to form, but with a river of adrenaline flowing into his bloodstream and time beginning to dilate instantly, seconds seemed like minutes, and the words wouldn't come.

In a split second Jim's eyes were scanning the instrument panel. The fact that a cold, foggy mist had suddenly formed in his cockpit registered, but in the immense confusion of the moment he was trying to grasp everything at once and could focus on nothing.

The 747 immediately began to yaw dangerously to the right as the left wing came up. Jim's hands flew to the yoke, pulling instinctively as he rolled the giant Boeing back to the left.

Maintain aircraft control! That was the prime directive. But the mist meant that . . .

''Rapid decompression!'' Judy was flailing at something on her right and trying to speak above the sound of a warning bell.

Rapid depressurization! We're depressurized! Jim Aaron understood instantly now. *Get your mask on, boy!* The voice of experience was echoing in his head suddenly, and the mist of a rapid decompression made lethal sense.

Jim clawed over his left shoulder with his right hand, flailing for his oxygen mask as he held the yoke with his left hand and fought for control.

He felt a fingernail on his right hand tear as he connected with the mask—a flash of pain he ignored. There were precious few seconds left before lack of oxygen would doom him to unconsciousness.

Finally his grasping right hand found the stem of the mask. He swept it over his head and into place with immense relief. For the next few seconds all his conscious energy flowed into the controls, trying to right the airplane. He knew Judy was fighting to pull her mask on in the right seat, but whether Patrick had grabbed his or not, he couldn't tell. The unspoken fear that the 747 might be coming apart in midair sat like a cold specter on his shoulders, unseen but omnipresent.

The controls felt mushy, and he found himself testing them, rolling the yoke left and right slightly to see if the airplane would respond.

Please don't let me lose the flight controls!

The plight of United Captain Al Haynes and his uncontrollable DC-10 over Sioux City years before flashed through his head. But no, the 747 *was* responding. There! When he rolled the yoke left, there was a response, however tepid. They were still flying, but they were obviously in trouble.

Now, what the hell had happened?

He held the control yoke severely to the left, opposing the roll, his left leg holding pressure on the left rudder pedal. There was nothing but blackness outside over the moonless Pacific.

Emergency descent! We've got to turn back! We're still headed out to sea!

His eyes scanned the center instrument panel—the zeroed readings on engine number three were all too obvious. Number four's instruments looked strange. He stared at them. It was hard to concentrate with all the noise.

Noise?

There was a loud, persistent ringing noise that had been there all along, he now realized! A bell.

Oh, jeez, a fire warning!

It had been ringing away unheard in the confusion. Now it commanded his full attention.

Judy was pointing excitedly to the illuminated fire handle for number three, the inboard engine on the right wing. He could see a bright orange glow out to the right over her shoulder, reflecting against the edges of the window frame. Jim fumbled for and found the intercom button, activating the small microphone in his oxygen mask. He punched it hard.

"Engine fire number three!"

Judy nodded vigorously, her head jerking to her right at intervals and coming back with wider eyes each time. Unable to locate her intercom button, she pulled her mask an inch away from her face for a second to yell in his direction.

"It's burning out there! Shut it . . . we need to shut it down!"

Jim nodded as he grabbed the number three fire handle and saw Judy nod in confirmation that he had the correct one. He pulled hard, instantly shutting off the fuel supply to the engine, then punched the fire-bottle-discharge button to send a small wave of fire-extinguishing foam into the surrounding cavities of the huge engine, before dropping his hand to the center pedestal to move the start lever to off.

Gotta get down!

He had to get the passengers to lower altitude, where everyone could breathe. The puny passenger oxygen masks were insufficient at 35,000 feet.

Only nineteen seconds had passed since the initial explosion, but in a court of law he would have sworn to three minutes.

"Emergency . . . ah . . . descent!" He couldn't seem to get the words out without a struggle, but Judy nodded again. He heard her voice on the overhead speakers as she pressed the transmit button to talk to Seattle Center, her voice straining against the constraints of the oxygen mask.

"Ah . . . Seattle . . . ah . . . Pan Am . . . ah, Clipper Ten . . . we have a problem up here. We're going to make an emergency descent . . . we're turning back . . . leaving flight level three-five-zero now, and, ah . . ." Judy glanced briefly at Jim before continuing and made an instant decision. He was too busy fighting the airplane. She would declare the emergency on her own.

". . . and declaring an emergency, squawking seventy-seven hundred this time."

The captain's eyes were on the forward panel as his hand closed around the four throttles. Without looking at the copilot, he was nodding his assent as she dialed the emergency code in the transponder, which would relay the information to the controller's radar screen.

Throttles idle, speed brake out, turn off course forty-five degrees, turn on continuous ignition, and get the checklist. The emergency memory items played in his mind as Jim Aaron pulled all four throttles and extended the speed brakes as he let the huge, 750,000-pound aircraft bank to the right and start down.

Gotta reach fourteen thousand feet in four minutes. That's what I want . . . wait a minute, how about structural integrity? Are we in one piece? It could be catastrophic to do a high-speed dive if we're structurally damaged! I'll keep the speed moderate until I know.

His mind was still racing in fifty directions at once, his concentration fragmented. He felt himself shaking inside.

The calm voice of the Seattle Center controller cut through the cockpit, a welcome sound of home. "Clipper Ten, roger, receiving your emergency squawk. You're cleared to descend pilot discretion to ten thousand, right turn to a heading of zero-nine-zero degrees for now. Say your intentions." The controller wanted to know what they wanted to do, but Jim couldn't focus on the question just now.

"Jim, number three's still burning!" Judy's voice penetrated his thoughts and he looked instantly back at the fire handle, which was still illuminated, meaning a fire was still in progress.

"Look out there." He asked her on the intercom, "What do you see?"

"I think I see flames!"

"Okay . . . ah, shoot the other bottle, Judy." He saw her hand react instantly, pressing the alternate fire-extinguisher button for the last fire bottle they carried in the right wing.

A firm hand on his right shoulder confused him for a second. It was Patrick, the flight engineer's muffled intercom voice ringing out over the cabin speakers above his head.

"Jim, we've lost some hydraulic systems, I, ah . . ." Jim glanced over his shoulder at the flight engineer, whose right hand was pointing to the hydraulic section of the huge sideways engineering panel. Even at first glance the needles looked wrong.

Judy's voice registered in his mind, distracting his mental effort to interpret the strange readings.

"We're through twenty-eight thousand now," she announced, "coming down."

Jim Aaron looked at the engineer's face and saw wide-eyed fright. Patrick met his gaze and leaned forward, pressing his interphone button again.

"I just talked to the lead flight attendant. Everyone's frightened, but they're hanging on."

Jim nodded a thank-you, the hydraulics momentarily forgotten as Judy's voice rang out again.

"Jim, you've turned past our assigned heading."

He swiveled instantly back toward the instrument panel as Judy continued, "You want zero-nine-zero degrees. You want to turn us back to the left now."

She was right. He had overshot. He immediately rolled the yoke left as far as he dared, leveling the wings and beginning a turn back to heading, thankful she had been watching out for their navigation. It was all he could do to hang on to the airplane and just keep it flying.

Jim focused on the unwinding altimeter. They were descending through 22,000 feet, the rate of descent more than eight thousand feet per minute. The steep nose-down angle of the 747 was frightening him as his sweaty hands strained to hang on to the control yoke, forcing it forward as the big Boeing dropped smartly toward the undercast that obscured the coastline many miles ahead.

Jim Aaron had always hated the feeling of being behind his airplane, being pulled along by events rather than controlling them, but that was exactly his circumstance now, as he struggled to control the chaotic situation around them.

Dear God, did we lose anyone down there? Do we have a hole like . . . like that United? The image of the United Airlines 747 that lost a cargo door at midnight south of Honolulu flitted across his memory. The accident had haunted all 747 pilots for years. Nine passengers had been pulled out with that door.

He pressed the intercom button. "Patrick, ask the flight attendants if they see anything wrong—holes or such—in the cabin.

He felt ill with revulsion at the thought that at least one passenger from that flight had been consumed by number-three engine. Here he had almost identical symptoms. *Oh my Lord, that must be it! We've lost our cargo door!*

"Jim, we ought to dump fuel if we're going back." The low, urgent voice came from behind him, so it had to be Patrick's.

Jim Aaron snapped his head around to look at the engineer's panel again. This time the four hydraulic systems registered with clarity, though what the gauges said made no real sense.

Where the hell are the hydraulics? I don't see pressure anywhere!

Jim looked forward again, remembering that the 747 was following his control inputs, even if sluggishly.

I have to have at least one hydraulic system left! I couldn't be flying if I didn't have at least one!

He stared again at Patrick's hydraulic gauges, counting the zeroed gauges. Only system one was working.

"Jim, I need to dump fuel!" Patrick repeated.

Suddenly fuel didn't seem very important. Hydraulics did. Patrick was waiting in vain for a response.

The controller's voice interrupted Jim's fragmented thoughts again. "Clipper Ten, Seattle. Come right now, to one-zero-zero degrees. State your intentions."

There was no answer from the left seat.

Judy looked at her captain and faced the reality that he was task saturated. She punched the transmit button on her own. "Seattle, ah, we want vectors directly back to Seatac for an emergency landing ... and we'll level at fourteen thousand."

Jim was still staring at the engineer's panel, trying to make the dead hydraulic systems live again through force of will. He punched the intercom button. "What ... what the hell's *wrong* here? We ... are we really down to one?"

Patrick looked back at the captain with genuine fear in his eyes and nodded. It was a short, staccato nod of one who knows the options have been reduced to a singularity.

"Systems two, three, and four are gone—no pressure and no fluid. Number two has fluid, but the pumps won't work, including the air pump. All we have left is hydraulic system one. We *will* be able to lower the gear and fly the plane, as long as nothing happens to the ... the last system, but I'll have to read you the other things we've lost ... with the other three hydraulic systems, I mean."

Jim Aaron had to fight to keep an even expression. He saw his engineer flick some switches on the far end of his panel, unstrap, pull off his oxygen mask, and disappear through the cockpit door to check on the cabin. He could feel himself physically struggling to keep the ship flying in a modified straight line, and he could see Judy working at high speed. But his mind was threatening to go off-line, a protective measure all pilots learn to suppress.

He pulled himself back to reality as fast as he had drifted and turned back to the forward panel.

Patrick was back within a minute, resuming his place at the engineer's panel. "No holes in the cabin, Jim. Everything looks normal down there."

Jim nodded a thank-you.

Okay, we're through sixteen thousand now, headed back east, he thought as he began to shallow the descent and level the huge aircraft. He pushed the power up on the three remaining engines, startled to feel heavy yawing to the right all over again as the engines on the left wing out-thrusted number-four engine on the right.

This damn thing flies like I've got two engines out on one wing! The thought triggered the need to verify something, but the sight of Judy pulling her oxygen mask off distracted him. *Right. We're low enough now,* he thought.

Jim Aaron pulled his mask off as well, and turned toward Patrick.

"Everybody can come off oxygen now. Patrick, tell the cabin."

The flight engineer nodded and reached for the PA, as Jim rolled in still more aileron to the left, shaken at how much it was taking to keep the wings even close to level.

The airspeed caught his eye. It was too low!

Something's wrong!

The readings were confusing. Something else he hadn't yet figured out was happening.

Jim Aaron pushed the throttles up as far as he dared, not wanting to overboost the remaining engines, but the yaw worsened instantly, and the airspeed kept dropping as he held the altitude constant at fourteen thousand feet.

"Judy"—he spoke without looking at her, his eyes riveted on the airspeed, his voice an anxious appeal of worry and urgency—"it feels like she's refusing to fly level at this altitude on three engines. I don't understand this. What's going on here?"

There was no way he should be having airspeed problems with three engines at full power!

Engines! Do I really have three? Is something else wrong?

His eyes snapped to the center engine instrument panel once more and bored in on the readings for engines three and four. Three, of course, was zeroed.

But so was four!

"What the hell?" Jim's words caused Judy to look to her left and follow his gaze to the panel.

"What?" she said.

"Number three *and* four . . . look like . . . I mean, they're *both* zero. Did we lose both?" Jim Aaron's face wore an incredulous expression as his eyes darted around the engine instruments searching for some mistake, some salvation from the nightmare of a two-engine loss.

There was none. Both engines on the right wing were useless.

Judy's head snapped to the right for a quick look at the wing, then back in the captain's direction.

"What's . . . what's out there?" Jim asked.

The back of Judy's head filled the copilot's window as she strained to see the engines. For several moments she tried to make sense of the flames now roaring around the right outboard engine.

"I think it's number *four* that's burning!" she said. "But we never got a fire warning!"

"We're out of fire bottles . . . we fired both of them on the right wing into number three." The voice was Patrick's.

"Patrick . . . go back again, and this time take a look out there at the right engines. See what we've got," Jim ordered.

The flight engineer took a large flashlight from his brain bag and rushed from the cockpit. He returned in two minutes.

"Boss, number three must have exploded! The engine looks to be gone and . . . and number four *is* burning, but it's going straight back from the engine. I don't think it's going to get the wing." Patrick reached up as he spoke, and pulled the engine-fire switch for number four without asking, an act that for a split second shocked and irritated Jim Aaron. He would deal with it later.

"Are we . . . together, otherwise?" Jim hated the tightness in his throat, but he could do nothing about it. He was scared, plain and simple.

"No damage I can see, but it sounds like . . . beneath the floor, you know . . . it sounds like something's punched a hole in us, and that's probably what dumped the cabin pressure. But everyone's still aboard and the cabin's intact."

"We *didn't* lose the cargo door?" He knew his voice sounded incredulous. He had convinced himself that was the problem.

"I don't think so," the engineer replied. He, too, was straining to see out the copilot's window now, his head and Judy's side by side.

Jim glanced back at the flight instruments, horrified to see the speed decaying through 180 knots and just above a stall. Engines one and two, the two powerplants on the left wing, were already just a hair below maximum power, yet he couldn't hold a safe flying speed and stay level at fourteen thousand feet. There was no choice but to keep on descending. With rising fear, he pushed the yoke forward.

Immediately the 747 picked up a healthy rate of descent as the wings resumed flying and the speed increased again, but the realization on Jim Aaron's part was now unavoidable: *We're too heavy to fly level with only two engines and whatever damage is out there. But . . . if we can't maintain fourteen thousand, what can we maintain? How low do I have to get this tub before we can level off?*

Patrick's warning about having too much fuel coalesced at last. They had enough fuel to get to Japan, and it was dragging them into the water.

Captain Jim Aaron turned to his flight engineer and fairly barked. "Start dumping!"

Patrick's eyes met his, and his answer was instantaneous. "I *am* dumping. You were distracted, so I started before I went downstairs."

Jim nodded in appreciation as Patrick furiously worked at pumping fuel from the right-wing tanks to the left-wing dump nozzle. He had made a terrible error in using the right-wing dump nozzle, however briefly. If that stream had caught fire from the burning engine . . .

"Jim?" Patrick's voice was strong but strained.

Jim Aaron had turned back to the instrument panel in front of him, but he looked back now at Patrick. "Yeah?"

"We can only dump out of the left wing. I can't use the right dump mast with number-four engine burning right next to it. That means . . . ah . . . our dump rate's one-half of normal. We're at six hundred eighty thousand pounds weight now and coming down, but I . . . I don't know about . . . altitude."

"Okay."

Jim turned back to the panel.

If we didn't have the damned overcast down there, I could see the coastline by now.

He dearly wanted to see something solidly connected with the ground. The thought of having this happen a thousand miles from the nearest land was terrifying.

As it was, only blackness filled the windscreen.

"We're through eight thousand," Judy intoned.

Jim knew the descent rate was slowing. They both did. But he still couldn't fly level.

"How . . . ah . . . how far out are we?" Jim asked.

Judy had been calling the controller without success.

"Fifty-two miles from Neah Bay," she replied. "But we've lost contact with Seattle Center. We're too low." Judy was responding automatically. Her eyes had been drawn again to the engine instruments. There had been a needle movement she had tried to ignore. Yet she thought it was starting again. Like a moviegoer who covers her eyes in a horror film, then peeks between her fingers, she had to face it.

There it was again! A flicker in the exhaust-gas temperature of number-two engine, the inboard engine on the *left* wing! She was already scared, and the thought of losing a third engine was simply unacceptable. Judy willed the gauge to return to normal and looked away, concluding that she had probably misread it anyway.

Jim Aaron let himself take a deep breath and straighten himself in the command chair. They were descending now through seven thousand feet and under control, but he wasn't doing it right. There were checklists to run and a thousand duties to perform, including speaking to the passengers, and here he was trying to play the game singlehandedly—the brave captain flying the airplane and giving the orders. Judy and Patrick had already saved his bacon several times over in the previous five minutes. Now it was time to act like a crew commander, not a self-sufficient fighter jock.

"Judy, it's stupid for me to try flying and thinking too. You take the airplane and keep us in the air while I work on the problems, okay?"

Her reply was instantaneous. "Roger, I've got it."

Judy took the yoke, astounded at the control pressures necessary to keep them going straight. Jim watched her for only a second, then turned to the flight engineer.

"Ah, okay, give me a reading, an assessment of what we've got."

Patrick pointed to the right side of the jumbo. "Apparently number-three engine exploded on us. Why, God only knows. Anyway, I'm sure it threw debris everywhere, and it probably peppered number four with shrapnel and threw pieces in the front of the engine as well. Number four just took a few more minutes to go, for some reason. I . . . my panel was confusing back here. Still is. It looks like we've got power from number three, and it's not even hanging on the engine strut anymore. I mean that sucker is *gone,* Jim."

"Why are we depressurized?"

"Well, I heard roaring below, as I told you. Number three . . . ah . . . probably machine-gunned turbine blades into our belly, you know, the air-conditioning systems, and maybe even the landing gear. We could have blown tires and brakes too. Somehow it breached the pressure vessel and blew our cork, but I don't think we're gonna come apart or anything."

"Air conditioning? But that's under the belly!"

"Yeah, well, boss, with that size explosion on number three, no telling where all the pieces went, or which engines ate parts."

The mere use of a plural sent a chill down Jim's back.

"God, are you saying it could have hurt the *left* engines *too*?"

Patrick heard the strain in Jim Aaron's voice. He could feel the fear. They might make it on two engines, but they would have to ditch if they went down to one. A nighttime ditching in a 747 would probably turn out to be unsurvivable.

Jim's head was throbbing with tension.

Jesus Christ, how'd this happen?

The feeling of being cornered pressed in on him.

We'd need exposure suits to ditch. We'd need three hundred exposure suits! No one can survive more than thirty minutes in waters as cold as these!

But there were no survival suits aboard.

Patrick interrupted the nightmare.

"Jim, about the hydraulics? You wanted to know what we had left?"

The captain nodded, and Patrick ran down the list.

We're hanging by number-one hydraulic system. That's all that's keeping us alive!

A mental diagram of number-one system's tubing played in his head, but an awful truth was coursing through all their conscious thoughts: even if he could keep them airborne, if they lost the last system, there would be virtually no way to control the ship.

In Sioux City, Al Haynes at least had an engine on each wing, Jim thought. *I don't even have that.*

Jim turned to the other two.

"Okay, we're already too low to fly over the Olympic Mountains. We're gonna have to follow the Strait of Juan de Fuca back in toward Seattle to keep clear of all terrain. I'll get the radar tuned up to follow the channel, 'cause with the undercast, we won't be able to see ..."

Judy had been staring at the forward panel while the captain talked. Suddenly her voice rang through his words.

"Jim?" Her tone was a rising alarm.

"Yeah?"

"Jim, we're losing number two!" Her left index finger was nervously tapping a small round gauge on the center panel, on which a tiny indicator needle was climbing into unacceptable temperature ranges.

"How in the hell ..." Jim caught himself before going further.

Raging at it won't help us! Think, dammit, think!

The needle was definitely climbing. There was something wrong with the hot section of number-two engine as well. Perhaps if he pulled the power back, they could keep it running at part power. Anything was better than the alternative.

He pulled the throttle for number two back about halfway.

"How much do we weigh now?"

The response was immediate. Patrick was monitoring the dump rate like a computer. "Six hundred forty-two thousand. I've checked the charts. With two engines and max power and a full dump rate, we should have been able to level at eight thousand. With one engine and half a dump rate, I . . . don't think we can stay in the air long enough to dump down . . . to . . . ah, flying weight, because . . ."

It was not necessary to finish the sentence. Jim Aaron and Judy Griffin understood perfectly. They were flying toward the intersection of two curves on an imaginary graph. One represented their diminishing gross weight as they dumped fuel overboard as fast as possible; the other was the rising curve representing the altitude the aircraft could maintain with the power they would have from one engine. Where those two lines intersected was where Clipper Ten could level off.

The fact that the point of intersection was still below sea level grew like a malignancy in his thoughts.

Jim Aaron straightened himself once again in the left seat and looked at his two companions. "Okay, we're not licked yet. If nothing else, we'll fly this ship *like* a ship in ground effect until we get rid of enough fuel to climb again."

Patrick was stunned. "We'll do *what?*"

"Ground effect! I've seen it done before over water."

Jim knew an airplane otherwise incapable of flight could hang above the surface at an altitude of up to half its wingspan on the very cushion of air it was compressing by the act of flying by.

"I'm guessing, but I think we have enough power. We're only sinking at three hundred feet per minute right now, and you're still dumping, right?"

"Right."

"Okay. Provided number-one hydraulic system holds, and engines one and two continue to run, and provided the fire on the right side doesn't get bigger and threaten the wing, and there aren't any large freighters in the way, I think we can get as far as Whidbey."

Jim Aaron had never landed at Whidbey Island Naval Air Station, but from ex-Navy friends he knew it was the only major Puget Sound airfield with a runway on the water. It was their only chance. Seattle was too far away, and every other airport within range was too high above sea level.

Patrick was leaning forward, holding the back of Jim Aaron's seat with his left hand and wearing an ashen expression.

"What if we get all the way down to the surface, intending to fly in ground effect, and she won't?" Patrick asked quietly.

Jim turned to Patrick and tried to smile, an effort that looked more like a wince and betrayed the fact that he was shaking inside.

"Then we ditch her, right then and there," Jim said. "That's the plan. We try to stay airborne, but if we have to ditch, so be it."

Patrick nodded solemnly.

"Not much of a plan, I'll admit," Jim said, "but it's all we've got at the moment." *And I'm not going to give up yet!*

5

The rhythms of the room had shifted, though to the eyes and ears of an uninitiated visitor, the subdued lights and quiet background noises that filled the cavernous interior of the Air Route Traffic Control Center were unaltered. The long rows of radar display screens mounted vertically on lengthwise consoles divided a work area occupied by a host of men and women wearing headsets and speaking quietly by radio to airborne pilots scattered all over the skies of the Pacific Northwest. The continuity seemed soothing and endless, promising to look exactly the same twenty-four hours a day.

But to the senses of a veteran air traffic controller, the atmosphere filling Seattle Center had suddenly become electric.

In a far corner, a small, solemn gathering could be seen standing behind the sector controller in charge of the airspace just west of the Olympic Peninsula—the northwestern corner of the continental United States. The man was punching his transmit button repeatedly, trying once again to raise Pan Am Flight 10, whose call sign was Clipper Ten Heavy.

Three minutes had elapsed since the last transmission from the Pan Am jumbo, though the radar signal and the aircraft's transponder were still strong. Five sets of highly trained eyes tracked the computer-generated radar return as it crawled across the screen eastbound toward the coastline of Washington State, but there was no answer from the occupants of the distant cockpit.

The controller's stomach was in a knot behind his polished mask of detachment. He knew there were several hundred people aboard that phosphorescent blip, all of them now dependent on the skill of the pilots he ached to contact once again—but couldn't. What in hell was happening out there?

There had been clear tension in the voice of the pilot working the radio as the flight descended and turned back, and he could hear the sounds of a voice laboring to talk around the constraints of an oxygen mask.

But it was a helpless and cold feeling to sit in a windowless room a hundred miles distant, devoid of radio contact, watching a sterile version of the drama unfold as the Boeing 747's transponder dutifully reported their sinking altitude back to the FAA computers in Auburn.

The controller glanced quickly at his shift supervisor, who had materialized by his side just after the Pan Am pilots had set their transponder to the emergency code of 7700—an act that set off an insistent alarm in the normally hushed warrens of Seattle Center.

"He's got a rapid depressurization and an engine loss of some sort, and an on-board fire, probably in the engine," the controller had reported. "I cleared him to fourteen thousand and then to five."

"But he's now at two thousand!" The supervisor's voice was incredulous. "Why is he down to two thousand? What's he doing that low over the water in a 747, for God's sake?"

The controller could only shake his head in frustration.

The supervisor's hand scooped up a telephone handset. Pan American's dispatch needed to know what was happening. If Clipper Ten's crew couldn't even reach the FAA's VHF antennas, which bristled from the top of a mountain near Neah Bay on the northwesternmost point in the continental United States, they sure as hell wouldn't be able to talk to their company's more distant radios, back in Seattle.

"Where does he want to go?" The supervisor held his hand over the mouthpiece of the telephone as he waited for the connection with Pan Am Dispatch. "Is he coming back to Seatac?"

The controller kept his eyes glued to the screen as he answered. "He didn't say. I'm ready to vector him wherever he wants . . . Victoria, Whidbey Naval Air Station, Paine Field, Seatac, wherever. But I've got to reach him first, and I've got to turn him. He's too low to go over the peninsula!"

"He may be hearing you, and not able to reply," the supervisor suggested. The controller punched his transmit button almost instantly, inwardly angered at himself that he hadn't reached the same conclusion.

"Clipper Ten Heavy, if you're hearing Seattle Center, change your squawk to 7600."

Seconds that felt like minutes crawled by as they watched the small data block on the screen. Finally the numbers changed to 7600.

"All right! He hears me!" The controller jabbed the transmit button again. "Clipper Ten Heavy, come left now to a heading of zero-six-zero degrees, vector heading to the north of Neah Bay and the Tatoosh VOR. I show you forty-two miles west of Tatoosh now."

The supervisor's voice was in his ear once again. "How about bringing him down in Port Angeles?"

The image of the Port Angeles airport popped into the controller's head. He flew small Cessnas on weekends and knew the area well. Port Angeles was on the north shoulder of the Olympic Peninsula, and the closest real airport to Clipper Ten if he planned to limp eastbound down the Strait of Juan de Fuca.

He turned to his supervisor. "That might do it. They've got a new overrun, and the runway is about sixty-three hundred feet. I think a 747 could get in there."

The supervisor turned to one of the other controllers watching the situation.

"Jerry, go call the Port Angeles manager's night number. Tell him what we've got. Can they handle it, especially if he can't get her stopped in the available concrete? Ask him, does he have enough people and equipment to deal with a crash as big as United 232 at Sioux City?"

The supervisor already knew the answer, but they had to try.

The small block of alphanumerics accompanying the blip that represented Clipper Ten was labeled PA10. Suddenly it blinked as the altitude readout changed again, from 2,000 feet to 1,800, a fact that registered instantly in the controller's mind.

Oh Lord, he thought, *they're still descending!*

9:15 P.M.
Seatac Airport

Thoroughly disgusted, Pan American's vice-president of operations, Chad Jennings, shot out of the crowded underground shuttle and dashed up the escalator two steps at a time. It was a short subterranean ride from Seatac's main terminal to the north satellite. Because he was late, the laconic gaggle of passengers ahead had left him dangerously steamed.

Jennings checked his watch again. He hated being behind schedule, and yet he might just make it after all. Elizabeth Sterling and her daughter were coming to town again, this time for good. He had met her two weeks before, when she came in from New York to finalize her new position. Elizabeth had technically become an officer two days ago, a senior vice-president like him, but with a seat on the board—something he didn't rate as yet. Meeting her flight was a courtesy—and a smart idea in the corporate hierarchy of things—but being late was not.

The flight's ETA was 9:25 P.M., but the flight crew had made it in a few minutes early. They were just nosing the 767 into the terminal as Chad covered the last few hundred feet to gate N-4. As he watched the jetway being moved toward the aircraft, his cellular phone began to chirp.

Chad pulled the diminutive portable out of his inside coat pocket and punched it on, instantly recognizing the voice on the other end as that of a TV newsman from Seattle's Channel 7.

"Mr. Jennings, we know that your Flight Ten has had some sort of explosion off the coast and is coming back. We know they've declared an emergency, and we're told he may be on fire, and that there are engine problems, and that he's way, way down in altitude for some reason. Can you tell us anything more?"

Jennings was stunned. He had heard nothing. The image of their beautifully refurbished 747 in flames and in trouble flitted across his mind like the movie trailer to a horror flick as he pumped the newsman for information. The reporter relayed all he knew. The 747 was some forty miles west of the coastline, and might come down somewhere other than Seatac airport. They were sending their news helicopter to wherever the captain decided to land. The betting in the newsroom was that it would be one of several other airports closer than Seatac. Would Jennings like a ride?

The sight of United's newly arrived passengers flowing out of the gate reached Chad's eyes, but not his consciousness. One of his airplanes was in trouble, and that had led to momentary confusion. What should an operations chief do? Should he go to the operations control center across the field?

Suddenly the urge to be as close as possible to the action overwhelmed him.

"You say you'd come pick me up?"

"Yes, sir, we could, depending on where you are."

"I'm at Seatac, the north satellite."

"Our pilot will be there in a few minutes. He's already airborne."

"Listen . . . ah . . . one stipulation, okay?"

"Tell me."

"I don't want to be on camera from the helicopter and interviewed in flight unless I okay it. Especially when I talk to the crew by radio, if I get to."

"Sure. Sure, that's fine. We'll honor that. As long as you'll give us on-camera interviews sometime tonight."

The helicopter would land north of the north satellite. He would have to find a United Airlines representative to get him out on the ramp. Chad had already turned and started walking the other way when he finally remembered what had brought him to the airport to begin with: Elizabeth Sterling, their new CFO.

♦ ♦ ♦

Elizabeth and Kelly had already left the jetway when Chad found them. He filled them in, his face a mask of ashen concern and his manner hurried.

"I'm going to meet a news station helicopter and try to be wherever our flight lands," Chad told Elizabeth. "I hate to say hello and goodbye, but I've got to run. I'll have to let you take a cab to your hotel."

"No."

Chad Jennings stopped cold, completely puzzled.

"No?"

"No. How big's the helicopter?"

"It's a Jet Ranger, I think, but—" Chad replied.

"Okay, then take us with you. Rangers carry five. Two seats in the front, three seats in the back. One pilot, one photographer, and three of us. We can get our bags later." Elizabeth turned to Kelly, who had been taking in the whole exchange in silence and nodded now with wide-eyed excitement.

9:20 P.M.

In flight, Clipper Ten

Captain Jim Aaron had pushed the throttle for number-two engine back up a bit, feeling the surge in power as the huge JT-9 Pratt and Whitney turbofan pulled forward on its pylon.

And just as quickly the exhaust gas temperature began climbing toward red-line limits. It was no use. Jim pulled it back to almost idle. It made sense to keep it running in case they needed a final surge of power, but it wasn't going to keep them in the air. Either they got enough fuel dumped in time to fly on one engine, or they would have to put Ship 612 in the water.

There! I faced it! he thought to himself. Once he knew the worst possible case, he could calm down. But there was one act of formalization necessary. He hated doing it, but he had no choice. Jim Aaron picked up the intercom handset and punched in the code for the lead flight attendant. Her voice filled his ear almost instantly.

"One right." The voice seemed shaky and strained, but determined.

"June, is that you?" Jim Aaron knew the answer. June Digby was perhaps the most experienced flight attendant to join the new Pan Am, a pro with file cabinets full of complimentary letters and over thirty-two years in the air.

"It's me. What's happening up there? I mean, Patrick has been keeping us informed, but what're you planning? We going to have to swim back to Seattle or what?" It was an anemic attempt at humor, but she had hoped for instant reassurance. Instead, she triggered the last thing she wanted to hear.

"June, I need you to get everybody ready for a possible ditching."

There was a soft groan from her end as Jim continued, "I don't think I'm going to have to make that choice, but we'd better be ready."

"How long? How much time do we have?"

"At worst, ten minutes. Maybe much more. If I have to do it, we'll come down as close to shore as possible."

There was a long, long pause.

"The water down there, Jim—it's very cold."

"I know," he replied. There wasn't much else to say. She was an avid scuba diver who knew well the short survival times in the waters of Puget Sound.

Jim Aaron replaced the handset and looked at his copilot. Judy was doing a magnificent job of holding the crippled 747 steady. The rate of descent was lessening, but they were through fourteen hundred feet now and still coming down at two hundred feet per minute.

"Clipper Ten Heavy, Seattle Center. How do you hear?"

Judy shook her head in disgust. "I've heard him for the last five minutes. I just can't talk to him! We're too low to reach his antennas with our radio, but *his* radio's powerful enough to get through to us."

Jim raised the microphone and replied once again, expecting nothing, and was startled when the controller's voice came back with open excitement.

"Clipper Ten Heavy, read you loud and clear. How are you doing out there? We show you at fifteen hundred . . . uh . . . fourteen hundred feet."

"The altitude checks, Seattle."

"Say your condition?"

Jim looked around at his flight engineer. Patrick was still engrossed in his panel, trying to find a way to restore more than one hydraulic system and working to keep the fuel balanced between the left and right wings. They were getting lighter bit by bit, but they were still sinking.

He took a deep breath and tried to sound calm and collected. "Okay, Seattle, please relay this to our company dispatch, too."

Patrick had been unable to raise Pan Am Dispatch on VHF radio frequencies, and there had been no time to use the satellite phone.

"Roger, Clipper Ten, we've got your dispatch on the line. They're listening to you."

Jim Aaron grabbed his microphone and filled in the details for the dispatcher before getting to the subject of altitude.

"I can't stay high enough to get over the terrain, so I'm going to fly over water the whole way. If you can see us on radar, I need you to coordinate with the Coast Guard ship-traffic control people in Seattle to keep us clear of ships. We may be that low."

"Coordinate with . . . with *whom*, Clipper Ten?" The incredulous tone of the FAA controller was not unexpected. The whole thing sounded like a bizarre joke, Jim realized. The FAA asking for clearance from the Coast Guard for an inbound airplane was ludicrous.

And in this case, he thought, critical.

Jim punched the button again. "I'm not kidding, Seattle. We may be flying in ground effect as low as fifty feet or so off the water. We're still too heavy to stay level, so we can't afford to get too close to any big ships, and only the Coast Guard traffic control center knows where they are. I've toured the place. It's in Seattle."

A long silence ensued. Just when he had concluded that they had lost radio contact with Seattle again, a very somber voice came back.

"Roger, Clipper Ten. Alter your course now to a vector of zero-four-five degrees. We're establishing contact with the Coast Guard now. All search-and-rescue forces in the area are scrambling as well. We're checking on Port Angeles International as a possibility . . . uh, for a usable airport."

"Port *Angeles*?" Jim knew he sounded shocked. He had never landed at Port Angeles. It sounded far too small an airport for a 747.

"Roger, Clipper Ten, they've got sixty-three hundred feet, with a thousand-foot overrun, and are stressed for a jumbo."

The statement was met by silence on both ends for a few seconds while Jim Aaron ran over the possibilities. It was the closest airport, all right, but . . .

"What's their field elevation?" he asked at last.

"Two hundred eighty-eight feet above sea level," the controller replied.

All three pilots looked simultaneously at the altimeters. They were under a thousand feet above the water now, and still descending at nearly two hundred feet per minute. Port Angeles was seventy miles away.

Jim Aaron punched the transmit button and held it while he took another deep breath, the inviting proximity of Port Angeles competing with the other truths he knew he needed to face.

"Get them ready, Seattle, but I'm not sure we can use it."

"Roger, Clipper Ten. What else can we do for you?"

Jim glanced at Judy, who shot back a thin little smile of attempted encouragement.

"Just stand by, Seattle. And a few small prayers would be in order, too."

Jim looked down at the navigation panel in front of him, the so-called HSI. The small numbers indicating the distance to the Tatoosh navigation radio near Neah Bay was down to twenty miles, and their altitude was now dipping under eight hundred feet.

"Unlike Port Angeles, which is at two hundred eighty-eight feet," Jim began slowly, "Whidbey Island . . ."

". . . is literally at sea level." Judy finished the thought.

He nodded.

"Jim, it's also a hundred twenty miles away."

"I know it," he said, simply.

9:35 P.M.
In flight, Chopper 7

Chad Jennings had borrowed a second cellular telephone from the cameraman aboard the TV news helicopter, and had been huddled in the left front seat of the Jet Ranger with a phone to each ear. At last he looked up and turned toward Elizabeth in the backseat as the magnificent backdrop of nighttime Seattle passed on their right, with Elliott Bay five hundred feet below them.

"Okay, here's where we are. They're vectoring him literally down the Strait of Juan de Fuca . . . he's just by Neah Bay now . . . and he's thinking of landing at Port Angeles. We're trying to coordinate . . ."

The pilot had removed the left lobe of his headset and leaned in Chad's direction with a loud "What? I didn't hear you."

Chad turned slightly in his direction. "Can you head for Port Angeles airport? That's where he may come down."

The pilot nodded and banked the chopper gently to the left, calculating a heading directly across Puget Sound.

They had climbed in at Seatac from the left, Chad taking the left front copilot's seat, Elizabeth the left rear seat. Kelly sat in the middle, next to the photographer, who was balancing his camera in the right rear, behind the chin-high barrier wall that separated the front and back seats. The pilot leaned to his left then, speaking to Chad, his voice a semi-shout. "That's about sixty miles from here. At top speed, it'll take us thirty to forty minutes. He'll beat us there by at least fifteen minutes, depending on his speed, but I'll do my best." The pilot hit one of his transmit buttons to talk to his assignment desk in Seattle as Chad turned back to Elizabeth, struggling to be heard over the noise of the rotor blades and the loud background whine of the Ranger's turbine engine.

"Port Angeles is small, Elizabeth, but it can handle a 747. The problem is, he's having trouble holding altitude."

"Who is he?" she asked. "Who's the captain?" The thought had occurred to her that it could be Brian, but she had been too embarrassed to ask. Chad was Brian Murphy's boss, and might know of their relationship. Besides, she reminded herself, Brian should be in Washington, D.C., tonight.

"Captain Jim Aaron. Braniff veteran. Excellent man. He . . . hasn't decided yet if he can make Port Angeles. They're also preparing for a ditching in case he can't keep her flying." He had already briefed her on the engine explosions, the rapid decompression, and the hanging question of what would happen—or wouldn't happen—when they tried to lower the landing gear.

Jennings turned to look out to the right through the Plexiglas bubble at the passing Space Needle, a faraway look in his eye that Elizabeth knew had to be an attempt to mask tension and emotion.

"Mr. Jennings?" The pilot was looking at Chad again.

"Yeah."

"I'm told we're going to be feeding both CBS and CNN live by satellite when we get there. We're going to do an in-flight report in a few minutes. Can I use what you just said?''

Chad nodded as the photographer changed places with Elizabeth in the back, taking the left rear seat, from where he could focus his camera on the pilot.

She glanced to her right then, noticing the fascinated expression on her daughter's face as Kelly watched the city go by on their right. Kelly turned and met her gaze momentarily. "It's beautiful, Mom. Can we see our condo?''

"Maybe." Elizabeth searched the passing cityscape and pointed to a high-rise on a bluff overlooking the waterfront.

"There . . . I think.''

Kelly nodded. "Cool!''

Elizabeth put her mouth close to Kelly's ear. "Honey, keep your voice way down. They're about to do a live interview, and remember the seriousness of what's happening.''

Kelly looked at her mother's sober face and nodded.

Elizabeth sat back and watched as the photographer focused his portable TV camera on the pilot, who began doing a live interview as he flew the chopper northwestward.

Her thoughts snapped back to something Chad Jennings had said while they waited for the helicopter to touch down at Seatac airport. Pan Am was being targeted by the FAA for a host of violations. He personally suspected that a dirty-tricks campaign might be behind each one of the FAA inspections that had turned up the problems they didn't know they had. Jennings had seemed very upset on the subject, and had assumed that as an incoming officer, she had already been told. She hadn't. The thought that something more than financial problems faced her new company was chilling.

Brian had said something about trouble with the FAA. What was it? *When* was it? She couldn't remember. But one thing hung in the back of her thoughts as a dark warning of trouble: Jennings's reaction. It was as if this emergency threatening Clipper Ten was merely the latest in a long string of operational problems, none of which Ron Lamb had mentioned.

9:40 P.M.
In flight, Clipper Ten

Somewhere north of Tatoosh Island—the ancestral home of the Makah Indians—a lone fishing boat suddenly heeled and turned in con-

fusion as its captain whipped the helm toward the east and throttled his engine to standby. In the biting cold of saltwater spray driven by a stiff breeze from the west, he had heard nothing but the wind and his engine until seconds ago. Now, with adrenaline pumping through his bloodstream in massive quantities, causing his hands to shake, he tried to sort out what had thundered by over his head. The sounds had accelerated to a crescendo thirty seconds before, and he had glanced over his shoulder as the specter of a huge aircraft bore down on him from the west at what seemed to be the level of his radio mast, its landing lights surreal against the dark sky, and the screaming of its engines assaulting the sanctity of his hearing as his ears clicked under a sudden wave of air pressure. He had expected, then, to see it crash into the water, but it had sailed away, still airborne, its twin white taillights now visible in the distance like the forlorn lantern on the caboose of a receding train.

What on earth was such a craft doing so low? Was it a military plane? Was it civilian? How could such a thing be possible? The man fumbled for his marine radio, desperate to tell someone what had just happened.

◆ ◆ ◆

The tension in the cockpit of Clipper Ten was mounting moment by moment, second by second.

"Don't let me get below seventy feet, or bank over fifteen degrees, Judy." Jim Aaron's eyes were riveted on the instrument panel, his vision taking in the radar altimeter, which now showed a mere eighty feet above the waters of the Strait of Juan de Fuca. Clipper Ten's wingspan was over two hundred feet, the fuselage nearly three hundred feet in length. Yet at their present weight, they couldn't fly any higher than seventy feet off the surface. Not yet, at least. Not until the left dump nozzle had spewed enough fuel into the night to lessen their weight and put the performance curves back into the range of normal flight.

Jim had pushed number-two engine up a bit, bringing its exhaust-gas temperature right to the red line. He was numb inside, and fully focused now on the job at hand. Life or death seemed a somewhat esoteric consideration. He had a job to do, and pushing number-two engine to the point of meltdown if necessary was part of it.

Number-two engine was stable, but barely. Everything was in a state of precarious balance: the rudder trim full left to compensate for the worst-possible-case thrust situation, a five-degree left bank cranked in to maintain a straight course as Seattle Center vectored them down the channel, and the fuel-jettison pumps throwing jet fuel out of the left dump nozzle as fast as possible.

They had already passed abeam of one oceangoing freighter, a ship with a superstructure tall enough to snag them out of the sky if they'd attempted to fly over it. The ship was fully lighted and had been visible for miles, but it had helped to know in advance it was there, thanks to Seattle Center's new liaison with the Coast Guard.

A Coast Guard Rescue C-130 had found them and joined up overhead now, matching their anemic 190-knot flying speed and acting as a radio relay station when they hit blank spots in Seattle Center's coverage. The passengers had been briefed and prepared, and the flight attendants had reviewed their procedures with the rafts. Everyone below crouched in a brace position. If he had to put it in the water, they were as ready as they would ever be.

Survival now depended on the skills and courage of the pilots of Clipper Ten to keep their ship flying in ground effect without dipping a wingtip in the water and cartwheeling everyone to their deaths. And, as the three of them knew well, an airborne 747 could cover the seventy feet to the surface in the blink of an eye, or the flick of a wrist.

"Position, Judy?" Jim dared not take his eyes off the radar altimeter. Even with the landing lights on and showing the waves and water ahead, they were far too close to the surface to fly visually.

"The INS shows us twenty-four miles from Port Angeles airport."

Patrick's voice followed immediately. "We're down to six hundred and eighteen thousand pounds now. If I'm figuring the charts right, in about twenty minutes we should be light enough to gain some altitude."

Jim Aaron quickly converted the twenty minutes to sixty-four nautical miles. It wasn't enough. They would have to fly in circles off Port Angeles until they were light enough to climb to the four hundred feet needed to use the Port Angeles airport. Banking the aircraft much in such perilous conditions was unthinkable. One circle could take in a diameter of twenty miles.

Judy saw Jim Aaron start to shake his head. Patrick noticed the gesture as well. The captain's eyes were on the instruments, but his head was moving in jerks left and right, ever more rapidly, as his mind compared the possibilities and faced the inevitable.

"We can't make Port Angeles." The words fairly exploded from the captain's mouth. He immediately glanced at his copilot with an apology on his face, noticing that she, too, had figured it out as well.

"We've ..." he began, "... we've got Whidbey dead ahead about eighty miles, we're aligned with the runway, and even if I can't gain ten feet, we can get her on the ground."

"Roger, I'll tell them." Judy's finger was already pressing the transmit button.

6

The full magnitude of what was happening finally began to sink in. For the past twenty minutes, Elizabeth Sterling's ears had been filled with technical facts of Clipper Ten Heavy's emergency somewhere out to the west, but it had all seemed rather impersonal.

Until now.

As they raced north from Seattle with the rotor blades slapping the air in a full-speed dash toward Whidbey Island Naval Air Station, the facts and images coalesced in her mind. She was now a corporate officer of Pan Am. That, in effect, was *her* crippled airplane out there, loaded with passengers who had trusted *her* airline. Suddenly it all became personal and frightening.

And then the presence of the TV camera became intimidating. This was no private airborne cocoon, it was a flying studio to the world. The drama was being played out before a worldwide television audience. Some of the pictures being broadcast by satellite out of Atlanta and around the world on CNN were originating from the small TV camera now bumping her left arm, as their pilot continued giving a running over-the-shoulder commentary.

The fact that whatever happened, Pan Am would now be seen as an airline with safety problems, sent more chills down her spine.

In flight, Clipper Ten

"PULL IT UP!" Judy's voice rang sharply through the cockpit as Jim Aaron pulled the yoke back quickly. The radar altimeter had dropped below fifty feet for a second, startling them. He felt the ship respond and gain a little altitude, then reach the crest of the pressure wave they were flying and begin to protest. *From here on,* it seemed to say, *it's altitude or airspeed, but you can't have both.*

Yet it seemed they were getting light enough to nudge higher, out of ground effect. Slowly he let the rate-of-climb needle start up as the radar altimeter cracked through a hundred feet for the first time in many long minutes: 120 feet; 140 feet; then mushing into 160 feet as the airspeed dropped to 180 knots and stabilized, a tiny rate of climb still showing on the instruments.

"Hallelujah! I think we're going to get out of here!" Jim's voice was cracked and hoarse.

"Thank God!" Judy said. "We've got to have at least a few hundred feet in the air approaching the runway threshold. Jim, when we lower the landing gear, we're gonna slow down big time and start sinking."

Judy watched Jim Aaron from the corner of her eye, waiting for a response.

There was none.

"Jim?" Judy's voice pierced his concentration.

"Yeah?"

"Could we discuss how we're going to handle this?"

A small breaker of shame rolled over him now. He had been flying solo again, making unilateral decisions and not even announcing them, let alone discussing them. This was a crew, right?

"I'm sorry. We need to be making these decisions together," he said, glancing around at Patrick. "All three of us."

He paused to check the altitude again. They were climbing again ever so slightly, edging foot by foot through two hundred feet off the water.

"Okay, let me tell you what I think we're facing. Then you two give me your opinions. I think we should take it straight in to Whidbey and land it with whatever we've got. When we put the gear down, we're going to slow down, so we can't lower it until the last possible moment. We've got to time it just right. Too soon and we sink into the shoreline or the water before getting to the runway, as you pointed out, Judy. Too late, and we touch down with the gear not fully extended. Same with flaps, if we even have time to use them. And, Judy, you'll have to bring them out with the alternate extension system."

Patrick leaned forward. "Boss, why don't we circle out here for a little while and keep dumping? Then we could get enough altitude to give us an edge."

Judy was shaking her head. "Patrick, number four's still burning out there, as far as I can tell. Not much, but some. I think we'd better get on the ground as quick as we can."

Patrick's voice came back strong and worried. "You're both being stampeded. I want to get this over with too, but, dammit, Jim, you said it yourself—we've got to time this just right. If we buy some extra time, maybe it won't be that critical."

"We've been overboosting number-one engine for nearly an hour," Judy said," and number two's barely above idle. Either could fail at any time." She turned now to look him in the face.

"Okay ... okay, look at this," Patrick said. "We come in at, say, three hundred feet. You put the gear down at two miles. Because of the reduced hydraulic capacity it doesn't come down fast enough, but it's already a speed brake, so we sink right onto the runway with all the main struts at odd angles and nothing locked—and we're still full of fuel!"

"We just have to time it right," Judy said.

"*How?* We can't practice it! I can only guess at it!"

Jim Aaron had listened quietly. Now he spoke up. "Good point, Patrick. If I could approach at five hundred feet, I'd feel a lot safer, but I'm equally worried about trusting number-one engine." He glanced at Judy. "Okay. Let's plan to make a wide circle as close to Whidbey as we can make it, out over the water. If number one goes, I'll firewall number two and let the sucker burn off the strut if necessary to get us to the runway. It may be damaged, but at least it could give us a controlled ditching."

"What would you think," Patrick said, "about my using the right-wing dump mast? It's far enough from number-four engine. I don't think the fuel stream will catch fire."

"But," Judy replied, "if you're wrong, won't the fuel catch on fire explosively, and we blow the wing off?"

"Not necessarily." Patrick's reply lacked conviction, but there it sat.

They both looked at the captain, and waited for his response.

"I say we try it," Jim said at last. "We need to get lighter fast. You violently object, Judy?"

She looked at the forward panel for a moment, then turned toward the captain and smiled thinly.

"Not violently."

Patrick nodded and immediately flipped the appropriate switch, doubling the fuel-dump rate to five thousand pounds per minute.

The sudden, unexpected sound of an engine fire warning bell rang through the cockpit almost immediately. Judy craned her head to the right, expecting new flames, but saw nothing, as Patrick fairly yelled, "It's number two! That's nothing to do with my fuel dump."

Jim Aaron hesitated, holding his hand up in a "stop" gesture, as much to slow himself down as to warn Judy and Patrick that he wasn't ready to shut down the engine yet.

"Is it really burning?" he asked. Patrick picked up the interphone handset and punched in the number of the aft flight attendant station as Judy scanned the engine instruments.

"Jim, it's not putting out much power."

Jim Aaron reached for the thrust lever and pushed it forward. The engine thrust remained the same. Only the fuel-flow and exhaust-gas temperatures were rising as Patrick heard a frightened report from the aft galley and relayed it.

"It's really on fire! They—one of the crew in the rear galley—says there's a plume of flame coming out!"

Jim shook his head. "If it was giving us any thrust . . ." He reached up and pulled the fire handle, and then punched the fire-extinguisher button as Judy and Patrick ran through the engine-fire checklist, watching then with relief when the fire light went out and another report from the aft galley confirmed there were no more flames.

There was also no more thrust from the inboard left engine. Almost instantly, Clipper Ten's airspeed began dropping, forcing Jim Aaron to push the nose over ever so slightly. With a sinking heart, he realized that number two had been giving the critical edge of thrust they needed to get out of ground effect. Now it was gone.

Reluctantly, he relaxed his back-pressure on the control yoke to let the big ship settle back down to an altitude of seventy feet—and back into ground effect.

One engine left, and no options.

Whidbey Island Naval Air Station

With little more than twenty minutes' notice, the duty officer had accomplished wonders. Rows of fire trucks and rescue equipment lined the taxiways in their appointed positions, pulsing a silent staccato symphony of flashing red beacons into the night. Base ambulances stood by, and more were coming, scrambled from nearby communities such as Oak Harbor, Anacortes, and Mount Vernon.

Three TV news helicopters were circling the naval base and staying in contact with approach control and each other to stay out of the way. More choppers—Army, Coast Guard, Air Force, and several private medical evacuation helicopters—were en route from various points.

Cars were screeching to a halt before base operations every few seconds as more and more members of the command element of Whidbey NAS arrived, all roused from their homes by last-minute phone calls. A line to Naval Operations at the Pentagon stood open as well, and a telephone alert chain had roused several high-ranking naval officers to the fact that their normally tranquil Puget Sound base was about to be the focal point of a world-watched drama.

In the control tower cab, the chief petty officer on duty lowered his field glasses and turned to his newly arrived commander, stabbing a finger at the western night sky.

"There, sir. Use the glasses here. You can see the beacons just coming in view, right on the surface."

Clipper Ten

The fire on number four eliminated the idea of circling. It was growing worse, and threatening to eat into the underside of the wing. The crew of Clipper Ten elected to head straight for the runway at Whidbey Island Naval Air Station, praying they could stay airborne that long.

Inch by inch, Jim Aaron had once again nudged Clipper Ten up to two hundred feet above the water on the power from a firewalled number-one engine alone as fuel continued to spew into the night from the two dump masts, lightening the aircraft's gross weight pound by pound as they clawed for more altitude, speed, power, and time.

"Clipper Ten, Whidbey Tower. Winds are one-six-zero at eight knots."

The runway lights were in view now, dead ahead. Jim wondered if they were forgetting anything.

Nine miles remained. The three pilots could see the red-over-red visual approach slope indicators as well, indicating they were dangerously below glide slope for a normal approach.

"Two hundred feet off the water, speed one-eighty-five." Judy's voice from the right. Her eyes were riveted on the instruments as Jim clawed for more altitude.

"Two hundred ten, speed one-eighty-five and holding. We're coming up!"

"Okay, Patrick, watch our timing." Jim said. "You tell me when."

Patrick had used the satellite phone in an unprecedented conference call, frantically trying to organize the collective thinking of Seattle maintenance and the Boeing company on exactly how long it would take to extend the gear and the flaps in their present condition.

"Remember," Patrick replied, "the gear figure's only good if there's no damage."

The captain nodded. "We'll land with whatever we have."

There was no possibility of a go-around. Clipper Ten was coming down one way or another as soon as the gear lever was moved to the down position.

"Two hundred twenty feet, speed dropping slightly to one-eighty knots."

Jim held the back-pressure. He needed three to four hundred. They would lower the landing gear first, then the flaps, but only to the five-degree position.

"Two hundred fifty feet, airspeed's dropping to one-seventy-five!"

He could take it only to 170. Jim nudged the yoke forward slightly, watching the rate of climb begin to drop.

Five miles.

"Clipper Ten, Whidbey Tower. You're cleared to land, sir. Emergency equipment is standing by." He could see the rows of flashing emergency equipment beacons ahead.

"Two hundred seventy feet, speed one-seventy. Don't get it any lower, Jim!"

"Roger, Whidbey. Thanks," Judy transmitted.

He would lower the gear at three miles, the flaps as soon as the gear was down. They had worked it out.

Four miles. Almost there. The ship had stopped climbing. He couldn't get more than 275 feet, but the speed was back up to 175 now and climbing slightly.

"There's three miles, Jim."

"I don't think we're high enough! I may cancel the flaps!" Jim said.

This is gonna work. We're gonna make it work! Jim's thoughts were whirling by.

"Stand by on the gear!" Patrick's voice was taut with tension as he calculated the remaining distance and time, and marked the proper moment.

"Gear down!" Patrick fairly yelled it, and Judy's hand reacted instantly. The sound of the nose gear and the shuddering of the wing and body gear assemblies coming off their uplocks after the gear doors opened radiated through his senses. *Something*, at least, was happening down there.

And predictably, the airspeed began dropping. Jim lowered the nose slightly, feeling the big ship shudder and begin to descend, trading precious altitude for airspeed as the landing gear acted like speed brakes.

"Nose gear down, body gear both sides down, but the right wing gear is not locked. Left one is down," Judy answered.

So, there *was* a gear problem after all.

"We'll live with it."

"Coming up on flap extension," Patrick announced.

"I'm not sure I want them," Jim said.

"Now or never!"

Jim traced through the possibilities, and decided yes.

"Flaps five!" he barked.

Judy's right hand moved the alternate flap switches at the same moment her left hand positioned the main flap handle to five degrees.

Less than two miles now, and sinking through two hundred feet, airspeed dropping to 160 as the flaps changed their minimum airspeed to a lesser value.

But the threshold of the runway began to climb slightly in the windscreen. They were sinking too much!

"No more flaps! We stay at five!" Jim said.

His hand pushed the number-one throttle, but it was already at maximum. With five degrees of flaps, he could slow only to 150 knots before the stall warning would start.

"One hundred fifty-five on speed, Jim!"

He was pulling more than he should on the yoke. They were through 150 feet now. He needed to cross the threshold of the runway at fifty feet, but they weren't going to be that high.

One mile to go, and they were settling through one hundred feet and slowing.

Oh God! We did it too soon! The cry echoed through his head as he bit his lip and tried to reinvent the laws of aerodynamics. Speed, altitude, airspeed.

Airspeed! He could cheat with more flaps!

"All the flaps you can give me. NOW!"

She complied instantly. It would be a race between conflicting curves.

Increasing drag against decreasing airspeed against increasing lift as the flaps slowly lumbered out on electrical motors against remaining distance to the runway buoyed by ...

Hold it! Hold it! Hold it!

His hand was coaxing the big ship to stay put at fifty feet, and she was complying. He had bought some time, but he could feel the airspeed decaying with the monstrous braking effect of the giant, triple-slotted flaps.

As the threshold lights slipped beneath the nose, the stall warning began, a small, eccentric motor that shook the yoke like a berserk vibrator. They were too slow!

Jim pulled ever so slightly, increasing the pitch, holding the altitude, praying his wheels were still above the surface of a runway which in truth was twenty-eight feet above sea level.

The airspeed was unreadable with the vibration coursing up to his eyeballs. He knew they were approaching a real stall, but there was nothing left but to hold and hope.

♦ ♦ ♦

No one aboard Clipper Ten felt the first contact between the rear pair of wheels on the left wing gear and the absolute edge of the runway overrun, but Jim Aaron heard the speed-brake handle deploying automatically with wheel spin-up, and knew they'd touched something.

The remaining tires of the extended main gear struts settled onto the hard surface one by one in rapid succession, all of them fully supporting the weight of the 747 before it left the overrun surface and rumbled onto the main runway.

Those in the emergency vehicles near the end of the runway had watched in stunned silence as Clipper Ten sank lower and lower, arresting the descent at what looked like mere inches above the surface. Now it had thundered over the shoreline like a nightmarish apparition of an accident about to happen, the wheels at more or less the exact elevation of the overrun surface.

But instead of flame and tumbling metal, there were aircraft wheels rolling across hard surfaces as they were designed to do.

"Jesus Christ, tower, he rolled it on! He didn't have an inch to spare!" was merely the first of the radioed comments.

When it was obvious his machine was on the ground, Jim lowered the nose as he made sure the speed-brake lever was fully back. He hit the brakes immediately as he pulled number one into reverse more or less simultaneously, but Ship 612 barely slowed as they continued to barrel down the runway toward the red lights which marked the far end.

All three of them watched, mesmerized, as the 747 ate the remaining concrete, the brakes seemingly ineffective though the pressure was good and Jim was pressing the pedals as far as his feet could push. They were willing it to slow now, mentally begging her to stop. The upward angle of the landscape on the other side of the runway was invisible in the dark, but they knew it was there.

Jim Aaron plunged his feet as far forward on the brakes as he could. At last he began to feel the big Boeing move decisively beneath him as the brakes began to grab.

The red lights marking the end, however, had all but disappeared under the nose.

Jim had pulled number-one engine into reverse idle. Now he pulled it into full reverse, feeling the effect as he fought to maintain directional control.

Agonizingly, Clipper Ten rolled off the runway and onto the overrun, its momentum dying, its nose gear finally coming to a halt less than a hundred yards from the absolute end.

The fire trucks raced for the still-burning number-four engine immediately, spurting a greeting of fire-suppressant foam.

Within ten minutes the passengers and crew of Clipper Ten had evacuated the airplane, using the emergency slides on the left side. The huge Boeing now sat bracketed by several portable searchlights as a convention of emergency vehicles ringed the scene. The TV cameras broadcast live feeds from the various reporters on hand. Several times loud applause and cheers broke out from the rescuers and the rescued alike as various members of the crew came down the slides after checking to make sure their passengers were all off. Captain Aaron slid to the ground last, watched live by well over eighty million viewers around the world. With the passengers gathered on the grass on the eastern side of the runway, the happy confusion of the scene was marked by what seemed a hundred firefly-like rotating beacons.

Jim Aaron and his crew then walked around their ship, noting the gaping absence of the right inboard engine, the scarred and peppered hulk of the right outboard engine, and the torn and jagged metal skin beneath the fuselage where shrapnel from the disintegrating engine number three had pierced the baggage compartment and damaged landing gear and hydraulic lines before flying to the left side of the 747 to be ingested by engine number two.

The right-wing landing gear was partially extended but had been held up by damaged tubing of some sort. It hung at a 45-degree angle now, its tires several feet above the pavement, with the aircraft supported nicely by the remaining three main landing-gear assemblies.

Jim Aaron returned to the side of number-one engine with Judy and Patrick at his side. The lead flight attendant appeared as well. Jim hugged her as Patrick reached up to pat the right outboard powerplant that had brought them back. The gesture was broadcast live, and the passengers broke out in applause and cheers once more.

On the western side of the runway, standing quietly by the empty Jet Ranger that had brought them there and holding her daughter's hand, Elizabeth Sterling watched the scene in shocked silence, awestruck by the size of the aircraft and the people who had been just numbers thirty minutes ago.

She was shaking slightly, but she wasn't cold. The suspense as they had hovered and watched the 747 limp the last few miles toward the runway had been almost unbearable. Looking up now at what the airliner pilots called ''The Whale''—remembering what it had just gone through—she suddenly felt very small. Very small and very out of place.

My God! This is what I've helped create!

There had been fleeting moments of terror during the years in New York, when she suddenly felt like a little girl awakening in an adult body in the midst of a hostile world. Those were momentary, fleeting episodes, but they would leave her shaken and introspective for days. *Do I really belong here? Do I really know what I'm doing? HAVE THEY FOUND OUT I DON'T HAVE A CLUE?* The little girl would torture the successful woman, and then scurry away to the lace-curtain recesses of her childhood memories, leaving Elizabeth to revalidate her adult self-confidence all by herself.

The same feeling now squeezed her middle, as never before, with the icy grip of pure anxiety. This was no paper company she was playing with. This . . . this *airline* . . . was people.

Elizabeth felt Kelly snuggle against her, and a different, more practical wave of guilt rose up in her throat.

I was so quick to bring us here. What if . . .

The looming shape of the 747 filled the night before her, but it could just as easily have been in pieces on the ground now, with broken bodies everywhere—and Kelly by her side to witness it. What kind of mother would chance that? Why hadn't she *thought* about the potential consequences?

"Mom? Are you cold? You're shivering." Kelly was looking up at her, obviously worried.

"A little."

"Let's get back in the helicopter."

"I shouldn't have brought us here—" she began.

"Mom?"

"Yes?"

"They did a good job, didn't they? The pilots, I mean."

Elizabeth turned her eyes back to the airplane. She could see the bright portable lights of several TV photographers illuminating the vice-president of operations. "Mr. Jennings used the word 'magnificent' after they stopped, Kelly. He should know. It looked pretty impressive to me."

Kelly took in the same scene without a word, a smile spreading across her face. "If you hadn't done the money work, they wouldn't have an airline, right?"

Elizabeth nodded slowly as Kelly smiled again and turned to open the door of the Ranger, reaching out to pull her mother inside, catching her eye as she closed the door.

"I'm real proud of you, Mom."

Moses Lake, Washington

Robert Chenowith watched the happy images from Whidbey Island Naval Air Station in pure shock. He had been tuned to a late-night sitcom when the first news flash broke. Within minutes it was apparent that the Boeing 747 that Pam Am's flight crew was trying to coax back to safety was none other than Flight 10. The new Pan Am was too small for the director of the Moses Lake facility not to know which ship was on which flight. That was Ship 612. The same one that had been sitting in his hangar the night before. The same one that had been exposed to an intruder.

And the same one he had declared free of sabotage.

With a long, ragged sigh, Chenowith came forward in his recliner and put his hand on the telephone. He had been so proud to land this position, it would be shattering to lose it, but he had no doubt that his decision the night before not to report the intruder to the vice-president of maintenance would be fatal to his career.

Apparently it had almost been fatal to Flight 10.

As he dialed the number in Seattle, he knew deep down that engine number three had not come apart by itself.

7

Thursday, March 9
Pan Am Corporate Headquarters, Seattle

Elizabeth had hidden her anger well, but it was becoming increasingly difficult. Making a good first impression with the staff and fellow executives of Pan Am was the prime directive for the moment, but she was aching for the opportunity to get Ron Lamb alone. He had some serious explaining to do.

She hated facing an important day with less than four hours' sleep, but by the time she and Kelly had picked up their bags, reached the new condo, and settled down the previous evening, it was 2:00 A.M. By 5:30 A.M., the continuous dreams revolving around the momentous events of the night before had made sleep impossible, and the memory of Clipper Ten staggering across the runway threshold was haunting her. She had given up trying to sleep and rummaged instead through the minimal stack of groceries they'd ordered in advance, finding coffee to brew and bread to toast. She took a shower then, and left a long list of chores for Kelly before clearing the door as soon as the new housekeeper arrived.

By seven-fifteen, Elizabeth was twenty blocks across the city on the fifty-sixth floor of the Columbia Center Building.

Her office was beautiful. She had picked the decor on the previous trip, and it had turned out even better than she had imagined. She stuck her head inside long enough to verify that everything was in place, left her briefcase on the edge of the mahogany desk, and set off in search of Chad Jennings. In the middle of the night she had seized on what Jennings had told her about the FAA. She had accepted it as if Pan Am were completely guiltless. But were they?

The executive offices had become a beehive of activity by 8:30 A.M., with two TV camera crews and various reporters calling or waiting in the reception area, emergency briefings, and a frantic crisis atmosphere as the headlines praised Pan Am's flight crew at the same time they flailed Pan Am for allowing the incident to happen in the first place.

By 9:00 A.M. she had briefed her assistant, her new secretary, the comptroller, and most of their people, in addition to touring the accounting offices and reassuring everyone that the only changes she would be making in the next few months were strategic ones at the corporate finance level.

"Everyone, breathe easy. I'm not here to fix something that isn't broken, and from what I see, the internal financial structure is well oiled."

The only glitch was her second-in-command, Staff Vice-President of Finance Fred Kinnen. It wasn't necessarily instant dislike, more a feeling of distrust that sounded an internal warning when she tried to talk to the man. Thin-lipped and intense, his answers irritated her, but she couldn't quite put her finger on why. He was correct and polite and well informed, but he made her feel uneasy and unwelcome.

At 10:15 A.M. the executive committee of the board was to meet. They had invited her, as a new board member, to attend. The agenda was urgent and worrisome, especially the news that yet another FAA inspection had been launched an hour before at the Seatac operations offices. Ralph Basanji, senior vice-president of public affairs, ran through the media damage from Clipper Ten, and minced no words.

"The conclusion," he said, "seems to be that we have the best pilots around who're able to do superhuman feats with a broken airframe, but that the broken airframe is somehow a result of our being, and I quote, 'struggling Pan Am,' end quote. The allusions to the long financial problems of the first Pan Am are being hung around our necks like an albatross, and I'm fighting to put a different spin on it, based on the fact that we're a new company. But I won't kid you, the ship has taken on some water this morning."

And finally, at long last, by half past eleven, Elizabeth was able to follow Ron Lamb into his office and close the door.

"Ron, I'm here now. What were the other things I needed to know?"

She had made up her mind in midmorning after getting a clearer picture from Chad Jennings. Pan Am's public image was in trouble, and it was affecting the markets. If Ron Lamb didn't level with her about the FAA pressures and other problems—if he tried to mislead or snow her on anything she now knew—the deal was off. She'd take Kelly, go back to New York, and file the damnedest lawsuit the airline world had ever seen.

Ron's eyes met hers across the desk, and he immediately sat forward, clasped his hands, and cleared his throat.

"Okay. Now I can brief you." He began by outlining the same scenario Chad Jennings had detailed, leaving nothing out, and added a new twist.

"Politically, we have a problem in Washington. Someone may be, shall we say, energizing the FAA to lean on us real hard. We're successful so far, and we're taking traffic from some of the big boys, so I suppose retaliation is understandable. We're not much of a threat, mind you, but we're a future threat, and they have a lot of muscle."

"Who's 'they'? You talking about American?"

"And United, and Delta, and Northwest, and the international carriers."

She must have looked shocked, though she was trying to keep her expression in check.

"They're smarter than that," Elizabeth said. "American in particular."

"I know it. But *someone* seems to be pushing the feds, and any of the airlines we just named would be much happier if the new Pan Am weren't around to bother their growing international route systems."

"How much trouble can the FAA cause?"

"Large fines, bad publicity, and a lot of internal embarrassment, plus building the perception in New York that we're losing it."

She nodded and looked out the window in thought. The effects of such things on the financial markets could be seismic. If she had to refinance . . .

She turned back to him suddenly.

"Ron, a month ago, flying in from Tokyo, you told me the previous CFO had misled you and the board about the new loan agreements. What exactly did you mean?"

He had been waiting for the question—dreading it, in fact. It took a half hour to tell her the story of how the previous financial officer, William Hayes, had effectively been seduced by the promise of a doubled credit line for less interest in exchange for sale and lease-back of the fleet.

"Essentially, we—the board and me—let ourselves be talked into accepting a risky agreement. As long as we were doing fine in the public eye, it really didn't bother me. But now we're getting pressure."

Elizabeth leaned forward, impatient with the vague references. "*What*, Ron? What's risky about the loans?"

He sat back and looked her in the eye in silence before replying, his mouth screwed up with distaste as if he'd bitten into a lemon.

"We gave the lenders—the consortium of banks and institutions who financed the package—what amounts to the right to call the loan if they ever felt threatened.''

"You *what?*" Her words echoed like a rifle shot around the office.

"We sold the fleet at the same time, and figured we'd always have enough cash in reserve so that it wouldn't be a problem. The provision limits their rights to calling the loan only if all consortium members agree that we have insufficient profits or assets to justify their continued trust that we can repay the loan, so we do have some control.''

He handed over a copy of the loan agreement, a several-hundred-page legal tome that had been opened and a particular paragraph marked with a paper clip. Elizabeth balanced it on her lap and began reading rapidly, going back and forth several times and following references to other sections before looking up again, completely shocked.

"Ron, what did your general counsel say?"

Ron Lamb looked down at his desk again. "Jack Rawly begged us not to sign this because he felt we were giving them the sole right to determine what constitutes profits and sufficient assets.''

"I agree with Rawly. This is dangerous as hell!''

Lamb's hand went up, palm out. "Now, mind you, I don't for a minute think this consortium would ever hurt us, because they'd be hurting their own investment if they did.''

"But they're already threatening, aren't they?'' she asked.

Lamb looked sick and stunned, the memory of yesterday's acrimonious conversation with a representative of the lead bank still ringing in his ears.

He nodded slowly. "Yes. They're worried about the media rumors.''

"Okay.'' Elizabeth was on her feet and moving toward the window. "We've got to get this paid off and get back to a normal loan agreement. The line I got you was for two hundred fifty million. This one's for five hundred million. How much have you borrowed on this?''

"Four hundred thirty million.''

Elizabeth felt her stomach sinking through the floor as she turned to face him, trying not to let her shoulders slump.

"*Already?*''

Lamb nodded sadly. "This time of year, you know, that's when we need it, with traffic light.''

"How about the equipment financing? Where did *that* money go?''

"That, too, has been a disaster. Hayes convinced us to sell the fleet of aircraft and lease them back, giving us considerable additional capital, but vast monthly payments. The capital should have been used in place of the revolving credit, and separate municipal bond issues sold to finance the Moses Lake operation. We felt we didn't have time, and there were political problems in issuing the bonds.''

"You paid *cash* for the Moses Lake facility?'' she asked.

He nodded.

"With the money from selling the fleet?''

Again he nodded, his eyes cast downward to the desk. "Most of it. We acquired a lot of land in the deal, too, but it would be difficult to sell it rapidly. That was a long-term investment. You know. As we grow, the Moses Lake area becomes a boomtown, and our land value goes through the roof.''

A few hours ago, Elizabeth thought, *I worried that I was in over my head. Now I find out I'm working with people who are in way over theirs! No way would I have made such a mistake!*

"Ron, I'm . . . I'm flabbergasted. You've snatched financial disaster from the jaws of solvency. I had this set up so your payments were low, your security was high, and you could ride out three years with heavy losses.''

"There's more, Elizabeth.''

How could there be! she thought. *I've already been nuked!* She had wanted him to level with her. Now she was almost sorry he had.

"What else?''

"If we're ever declared in default, the aircraft leases can be canceled.''

She sat down quietly, feeling sick to her stomach.

Ron Lamb held out his hand, palm up. "You, uh, see why I need you?''

Elizabeth searched Ron Lamb's eyes and saw a combination of desperation and contrition. He had most of his money in the company, and all of his reputation. He had made one gigantic mistake in trusting the wrong man as CFO, and now he wanted her to wave a magic wand and make it all better. *Two years of work shot to hell! Two years of wheedling and massaging and arranging, and they blow it all away. I should walk out of here. Fraud, deception, misrepresentation . . . no one could repair this!*

Only once before in her life had she felt so much like running. She had tried to teach an English class in a vocational school in Boston for extra money while working on her MBA. She had walked in planning on enjoying the attention and being a bit of a performer—and found instead a roomful of hopeful people who barely spoke the language and were looking for a miracle so they could be employable. She was to be the miracle worker, and she had run in fright from the awesome responsibility, resigning the first evening in an embarrassed rush of meaningless apologies. That memory was bitter. Never again, she had sworn, would she run from a frightening task. *But this—*

Ron's voice cut into her thoughts.

"Elizabeth, I . . . know . . . this is a gargantuan task. I know I made it seem rosier than it was. There are nearly two thousand people carrying our ID cards now, many of them people who have been tossed aside by aviation, yet were the best of the best. They've left other jobs and moved their families and pinned their hopes on us. That's why I need you. *We* need you! Please don't run."

Her eyes flashed toward his at the use of the word *run*, and she found herself nodding, and taking a deep, ragged breath. Her lips were as dry as a bone, and she wet them before replying.

"Okay, Ron. The first task is refinancing, and it's going to be a bear."

8

Thursday, March 9, 7:00 P.M.
Seatac Airport

lizabeth started to leave the ladies' room, then stopped once more and turned toward the mirror, adjusting her blouse and carefully coaxing a stray lock of hair back into place. She had spent more time deciding what to wear to greet Brian than she'd spent picking an outfit for her first day on the job—and Kelly had needled her unmercifully about it.

Kelly loved Brian. Plain and simple. Some of her earliest memories were intertwined with the warmth and humor and strength that the six-foot-one, square-jawed Irishman from Boston had brought to their tiny flat in Cambridge when she was just a baby and her newly widowed mother was falling in love with the ex–Air Force pilot. Elizabeth and Brian were both struggling MBA candidates almost clinging to each other, and Brian had accepted responsibilities for Kelly that bespoke a much deeper commitment. Elizabeth had tried to suppress the realization that her daughter considered Brian her father, yet Brian was the only father figure Kelly had ever known. They never agreed to marry, but when Brian followed Elizabeth to New York, then later decided to divorce the Big Apple and join an upstart airline in Phoenix as a line pilot, the sudden loss of his daily companionship was tough to take. It saddened Elizabeth, but her self-protective mechanisms for coping simply recategorized the separation as temporary and rejected all attempts to review the truth of that lovely myth.

But to Kelly, then age eight, Brian's departure had been the end of life as she knew it, and nothing short of a divorce. When her strong-willed mother had refused to chuck her Wall Street career and follow Brian to Phoenix, an inconsolable Kelly had blamed that mother—a wound that had never completely healed.

Brian was attentive over the years as best he could be from so far away, more so even to Kelly than to Elizabeth. After a year in Phoenix, he began dating a Spanish teacher—a woman who eventually moved in with him, but left five years later when all her hopes for marriage to Brian seemed to dead-end in his endless delaying tactics. He knew he should have been upset and distraught at her departure, but the only thing that bothered him was that losing her seemed inconsequential. Even then he didn't dare admit that the root cause of his inability to make a marriage commitment was his deep-seated, dormant love for Elizabeth.

For her part, there was no way Kelly was going to stay home and let her mother greet Brian Sean Murphy alone. And there was no way Kelly was going to be shy about the other major item on her agenda: marriage. Elizabeth was to marry Brian as fast as she could drag him to an altar. That was that. Her mother's feelings in the matter were immaterial. After all, Kelly had said, as flippantly as possible as they left the condo at 5:45 P.M., "You're the one who took the job offer. I merely follow as the faithful daughter. So, Mom, you made your bed, now get Brian into it!"

"Kelly!"

The conversation had gone much the same all the way to the airport, Kelly playing the picador, Elizabeth the shocked and somewhat scandalized mother who was secretly proud of the wit and maturity her offspring was displaying.

♦ ♦ ♦

Elizabeth found Kelly waiting in the concourse outside the restroom, and together they took the underground shuttle to the south satellite terminal and gate S-6. The blue and white 747 had already touched down, and they watched it taxi majestically into the ramp area and turn toward the gate. Elizabeth's thoughts drifted to Brian's first visit back to New York after leaving the financial world—and them—to become an airline pilot. He'd spent an entire evening spinning exciting tales of what it was like to complete each flight—each one a self-contained, challenging task that he could leave behind at the gate, a tiny jewel of accomplishment that could stand alone, and a task that would need no call-backs or follow-ups the next morning.

"There he is!" Kelly's voice interrupted the daydream momentarily. She had spotted Brian in the left seat as the 747 bore in on the gate.

Without warning Elizabeth's mind replayed again the sights and sounds and trauma of Clipper Ten, less than twenty-four hours ago, and a shiver worked its way up from the small of her back.

Brian had spotted them now, and waved enthusiastically from the cockpit as Kelly threatened to dislocate her shoulder waving back.

It took forever to get the passengers out of the way and the crew up the jetway, but finally Brian was there, calling to Kelly.

"Kelly! C'mere!" Kelly gave him a bear hug, hanging on with not a shred of dignity as he hugged her back. Smiling, Elizabeth moved to embrace him just as she noticed someone else waiting for the captain. She had spotted the man before, but thought nothing of his presence until it was obvious he was waiting for someone on the crew as well.

"Captain Murphy?" The man was younger than Brian by several years, short and stocky, and Brian obviously recognized him. Brian gave Elizabeth a quick hug and held her arm, massaging it lovingly with his thumb, as he turned a friendly expression to the man.

"Scott, what're you doing out here?"

The man held out a folder. "Mr. Jennings wanted this delivered to you on arrival, sir, and asked you to call him as soon as you could, on his portable or at home."

They began walking toward the escalator then, Brian with one arm around Kelly, who was pulling his wheeled flight bags, the other around Elizabeth, who was hating every second of the intrusion. She wanted to hold him and kiss him and talk to him, not get blind-sided by more business. Corporate officer or not, tonight she was all too aware that she and Brian were long-separated lovers.

"How did the inspection go?" Brian asked in a breezy fashion.

The man named Scott looked around nervously at Elizabeth and back at Brian, motioning to the folder.

"Captain, you might want to take a look at that right away."

Brian understood instantly, and introduced Elizabeth as the company's new CFO.

"So summarize what's in here, Scott."

"We've got some real problems, sir. There were a lot of records missing."

The entourage came to a halt as Brian stood stock-still and stared at him for several seconds, nearly causing an elderly couple to fall trying to get around them.

"*Our* records? *Pilot* records?"

"Yes, sir. The FAA is quite upset. Your secretary outlined it in a memo in there, and that's what Mr. Jennings wants to talk about."

Brian had already pulled his arms away from Elizabeth and Kelly and ripped open the envelope, scanning rapidly over the three-page memo, his features contorting in anger and tension.

At last he looked up at Scott. "Jesus Christ! This is not possible!"

"That's what *we* said, sir."

He stared at the paper again, and then at Scott, before speaking.

"Thanks. I'll take it from here."

"Yes, sir."

They waited until the man had disappeared down the escalator.

"What is it?" Elizabeth coaxed, snaking her arm through his.

He lowered the papers then, and Elizabeth could feel him slump slightly. When he looked up, it was with great fatigue and a long sigh.

"I've got to get over to the office. The FAA pulled an inspection of our records this morning."

"I heard, but—"

"If I can't find the missing ones, we may have to start grounding pilots instantly all over the system. We've got guys flying illegally, according to the FAA."

"But how?"

Brian looked at the far end of the concourse as a British Airways 747-400 lifted off bound for London, the muffled sound coursing through the terminal.

"I don't know. I'm a stickler for good records. This has to be an easily explained mistake. *Has* to be!"

They drove him to the operations center, where he'd left his car, and he got out with a promise to come downtown to the new condo as soon as he was through, whatever the hour. He hugged Kelly again and kissed Elizabeth before turning toward the building, then swiveled back around toward the car.

"I'm . . . I'm really overjoyed to see you both! I'm sorry about this getting in the way. I'll get there as quick as I can."

"Hey," Elizabeth said, forcing a smile, "we're on the same team now, kid. I expect you to work your tail off!" She wondered whether he'd thought about her rank in the company, and whether it would bother him. On the corporate ladder, he was chief pilot, but she was three rungs higher.

Brian leaned through the open window of Elizabeth's rental car and kissed her again, with greater depth and promise this time.

"If I don't get this straightened out, I'll be working for the Mrs. Grace L. Ferguson Airline and Storm Door Company instead of Pan Am."

The ride downtown was melancholy, and even Kelly's attempt to cheer them up fell flat.

"When he gets there, Mom?"

"Yeah?"

"I'll stay in my room so you two can, uh, have some privacy."

"If he gets there at all," Elizabeth said absently.

Thursday evening, March 9
Anacortes, Washington

Bill Conrad had arranged the meeting while driving the seventy miles north to Anacortes, which was connected by a single bridge to Whidbey Island. Jacob Lovesy, who went by "Jake," was the investigator in charge of the NTSB "go team" probing Clipper Ten's close call with oblivion. He had agreed to meet Pan Am's maintenance chief at a small restaurant in the diminutive harbor town at 9:45 P.M., responding to Conrad's insistence that it was a matter of substantial urgency. The pleasantries finished and the orders for dinner placed, Bill lowered his voice and leaned closer to the NTSB veteran.

"Jake, let me summarize this, in the interest of time. We have reason to believe our airplane, and number-three engine in particular, was sabotaged the night before, in our Moses Lake hangar, and with some sort of explosive device."

The NTSB man sat quietly for a moment, probing Bill Conrad's face. They were a study in contrasts, Lovesy a trim man in his early forties with a full head of sandy hair, a mustache, and a penchant for crisp suits and monogrammed shirts, Conrad a balding veteran approaching sixty, who always looked like he'd been sleeping in his clothes. Lovesy sat back now and cocked his head slightly.

"I know you by reputation, Bill. I know you were with Henson at Midway Airlines and ran a tight ship. I also know a fellow like you doesn't launch a statement like that without something to back it up."

Conrad nodded and glanced around, satisfied no one was targeting their conversation. Nevertheless he motioned Lovesy back toward the middle of the table as he leaned in again and related the embarrassing saga of the midnight intruder.

Jake Lovesy sat back again when the story was finished and twirled a swizzle stick in his alcohol-free Bloody Mary. When Bill Conrad had begun to wonder if he was ever going to look up, Lovesy spoke, still contemplating his drink.

"You've got an intruder with access, I'll grant you that. Your intruder was probably professional, and had a toolbox big enough to conceal some sort of device. I'll grant you that possibility as well. What you lack is motive and hard evidence that anything but internal failure seized and scattered that engine."

He looked up with a snap of his head suddenly, a gesture that Conrad knew meant trouble.

"That's a gap as big as China," he added.

"Jake, I've never seen a JT-9D do what this one did, not without help."

"Where's the evidence? Is there plastique residue on the shop floor? A blasting cap? Wire? *Something, anything?*" Lovesy's eyes were boring in now, and Bill didn't flinch as he shook his head.

"We've got nothing except a collection of broken parts about eighty miles off the coast, in several hundred feet of salt water. That would tell the tale."

Lovesy nodded.

Good, Bill thought. At least we agree on something.

"Look," Jake Lovesy said suddenly, shifting in his chair, "I agree this one flew apart with an unusual vengeance. I also promise we'll get the FBI in on this and comb the wing and what's left of the pylon for any evidence of explosives. We find any, I'll buy the idea. We don't find some hard evidence, all we can do is crank that into our thinking."

"Jake, I—"

"Bill, I've been around this business long enough to know that the publicity is already hurting you." Bill started to protest, but Lovesy's hand was already up. "I know. I know, man. You would never concoct something for that purpose. It's just that I can't go public with speculation on a bomb or sabotage without something more than what you've given me. Hell, I'm not supposed to go public with anything. Our board member does the platitudes and the leaking of facts, but only facts we're sure of."

"The publicity is hurting a little, but it'll get worse," Bill began. "At least don't defuse this possibility if the media should ask you—"

Lovesy was shaking his head at the mere mention of the media.

"Don't do it! Don't you guys run to the media with this story prematurely. You'll end up embarrassed. Go tell the camera about the highly unusual aspect of a 747 engine scattering like this if you want, talk about how damn good your maintenance is, talk about gremlins in flying saucers, but don't—repeat, *don't*—put the media in my face with questions about sabotage before we have hard evidence, or I'll leave you hanging."

As they parted in the parking lot after dinner, Lovesy walked back over to Bill's car before he could climb in.

"If it's on the structure of your airplane—the evidence of explosives, I mean—we'll find it. Meanwhile, go get that engine out of the water if there's any way you can do it. Go get someone to dive and photograph it, at least. Air traffic control will have the radar track, and I'll bet it's just like United 811's door, south of Honolulu. I'll bet we can locate the impact point from the tapes."

"Already have," Bill said, noticing with some satisfaction the look of surprise on Lovesy's face. "Friend of mine at Seattle Center spent hours today with the tapes, and he found a large radar return headed for the water just after the explosion. He's got the exact coordinates."

"Good. Go get the sucker."

Friday, March 10, midnight
Downtown Seattle

Kelly had succumbed to fatigue and sleep in the new condo when Brian phoned. Elizabeth read ten past twelve on her watch as she picked up the telephone.

"I'm sorry, Elizabeth, I'm going to be here all night, I think."

"You haven't found them?"

"Nothing. And I damn well know we're not negligent! Those files were there. I'm wondering something really bizarre. I'm wondering if the FAA is setting us up."

He sounded furious and bitter and exhausted.

"Brian, you've been awake since Tokyo. You can't think straight when you're that tired. Remember our fruitless attempts to pull all-nighters before exams back in Cambridge? You were worthless without sleep."

"So were you. Anyway, I gotta keep on looking."

"Go to bed. At least get some sleep on your couch in the office."

There was silence from the other end.

"Brian?"

A long sigh filled the phone, a resigned sound of someone about to admit partial defeat. "Okay. A few hours, then. Can we ... take a rain check tonight and spend tomorrow evening together?"

"Tonight's gone and tomorrow's not possible. I've got my mother coming to town, and you know what kind of portable thunderstorms she brings."

"She's a sweet lady, Elizabeth."

"She's Attila the Mother when we get on the subject of Kelly."

"Well then, don't—"

"Can't help it, Brian. She's coming to pick up Kelly for the weekend."

More silence, then a chuckle. "The weekend, huh? Even if I'm unemployed by Saturday, I can't pass this up. How about Saturday evening at your place, m'lady?"

"I thought the gentleman would never ask. Bring wine. Bring yourself."

9

Friday, March 10, morning

The tip had come into the newsroom of United Press International at around four on Thursday afternoon, and it took one of the editors an hour to track down their aviation specialist to deal with it.

By 1:00 A.M. Eastern Standard Time, the story was in motion and being picked up in early-morning news operations worldwide, including CNN.

By 9:00 A.M. in New York, the story had begun to depress the price of Pan Am stock, and at 9:15 Eastern—6:15 Seattle time—two stock analysts had issued an emergency sell recommendation on Pan Am as Elizabeth Sterling turned on her TV and saw the Pan Am logo hovering over the shoulder of the CNN anchor in Atlanta.

"The new Pan American Airlines, whose Seattle-Tokyo flight suffered a catastrophic multiple engine failure on Wednesday and had to make an emergency landing after a harrowing flight at wavetop level, is reported this morning to be the subject of a special investigation by the Federal Aviation Administration. Sources close to the FAA have told CNN that major fines in the millions of dollars are pending against the newly formed airline for alleged violation of training and other operational regulations, including serious maintenance violations. The National Transportation Safety Board has not commented on a cause of the accident Wednesday, but the investigation is said to be centering on past maintenance problems with the destroyed engine. There has been no comment from the troubled airline."

By the time Elizabeth arrived on the fifty-sixth floor of the Columbia Center, two TV crews were waiting. She brushed by at first, only to recognize the cameraman she had flown with to Whidbey Island. He shrugged as if to apologize, and came forward to shake her hand.

"We're hoping to snare your president. You wouldn't want to, uh . . ." He gestured to his camera.

"No!" She looked wide-eyed and laughed. "Ees not my yob, mon! I just got here. I know nothing."

She had entered the inner sanctum when Ron Lamb materialized from his office, a thoroughly panicked look on his face.

"Elizabeth—"

"I know, Ron, I saw them. I heard the story on TV a while ago."

He looked puzzled, she thought, and that was odd.

"Oh. Oh, those guys." Ron gestured to the reception area. "That's Ralph Basanji's problem. That's nothing."

"Nothing?"

Lamb stood stock-still for a second and searched her eyes before gesturing for her to follow him the few steps to his office. She entered and moved to one of the chairs opposite his desk as he carefully, almost conspiratorially, closed the door.

What on earth? she caught herself wondering.

There were papers spread across the usually neat desk, and Ron moved to them now and scooped up a couple before turning to Elizabeth.

He was breathing hard, she noticed.

"You all right, Ron?"

"No." He shook the papers, sat on the edge of his desk next to her, and studied his shoes. "I'm going to have to call an emergency board meeting on this, I think."

"What?"

"An hour ago I got a call from the lead bank of the revolving-credit-line consortium—the one you're going to try to replace."

"And?"

"They're panicked. They heard the news this morning, they saw the stories, and they've panicked."

"Okay, Ron, so they've panicked. What did they say?"

"They froze the revolving line at its current balance."

"Can they do that? Under that Byzantine agreement you signed, can they legally do it?"

"I don't think so. I really don't know, I've called in Jack Rawly, our general counsel. I think you've met him. But even if we get it changed, we've got a bond payment due on the twentieth of this month. We have to make that payment, and without the credit line, I don't know how we're going to find the money!''

Elizabeth let her mind race back over the complex details of the original financial package. They had sold several short-term debenture issues. It had to be one of those. The plan had been to redeem them through current accounts, revolving credit, or a combination of the two.

''I haven't had time to study the corporate payables. How much?''

''We owe, and must raise, eighty-five million dollars.''

''*What*? I didn't leave you any eighty-five-million balloon redemption!''

''No, we negotiated a delay of two other bond payments that came due last year, and let them all mature at the same time. We agreed to a slightly higher interest rate in return.''

Elizabeth sat back in the soft leather chair.

''Ron, I haven't had a physical for a while. I'm not sure my heart can take many more of these shocks.''

''I'm sorry, Elizabeth. This wasn't supposed to be a problem, but now it's a life-or-death rhubarb. We can't be declared in default.''

''How much do we have ... hell, that's *my* department.''

''This is your second day. I don't expect you to be up to speed yet. I checked with your assistant, and he tells me we've got about forty million in the accounts right now, but that's operational money. We spend that, we can't pay our bills.''

''And if we don't pay the debentures and someone in that crowd declares us in default, poof.''

''Yeah. Poof.''

Friday, March 10, 9:20 A.M.

Brian Murphy replaced the telephone handset and looked at his watch. He had made the appointment with Larry DePalma for 10:00 A.M. It was less than fifteen minutes' drive from Pan Am's Seatac base to the FAA's Northwestern Mountain Region headquarters nearby, but he preferred being early than late.

For what seemed like the fifteenth time, against all logic, he pulled his desk drawers out to see if by any chance the missing files could be hiding there. He was sure, now, that their disappearance wasn't an accident, but his instincts kept telling him that if he'd turn over just one more rock, or look behind one more stack of boxes, he'd find them all.

Nothing.

He got up, but hesitated by his desk, feeling the full weight of many sleepless hours. He looked sadly at the framed picture of Elizabeth and Kelly. Kelly would be miffed that he wouldn't get to spend time with her until next week, but the warm feeling that rushed over him when he thought of being alone with Elizabeth the next evening washed away any pangs of guilt.

♦ ♦ ♦

Larry DePalma's second-floor office was not hard to find in the new FAA headquarters of the Northwestern Mountain Region. Larry was waiting for him, but not alone. In the corner was Larry's boss, Ken Schaffer.

Afraid of meeting me alone, are you, Larry? Brian thought as he shook hands with DePalma and Schaffer and cautioned himself to stay gracious. They kept the small talk to a minimum, and within two minutes Brian had Larry DePalma's full attention across his desk.

"Larry, I'll say it plain and simple. Someone stole our files. Both my pilot files and the training files for the same people. You say you've got nine captains involved, and coincidentally they happen to be our most experienced and most important captains, all but one of them on the 747. But their training was completed correctly, and there is no way those files could have been misplaced accidentally. I mean, we've got the same information on the computer, and it shows everything's been done right."

DePalma looked down and sighed deeply before looking up again and meeting Brian's eyes.

"We had a tip, Brian. I told you that on the phone. The tip was that you folks had been short-changing the training. We were told that where your operations specifications require a full four hours of simulator time for the 747 captain recurrent training session, your check captains have been cutting it down to three hours."

"That's bullshit!" Brian shot back. "We did nothing of the sort! We fly exactly what's scheduled, and not a minute less."

DePalma leaned forward, elbows on his desk, and Brian could see the strain on the man's face. DePalma had never been their enemy, and he wasn't now.

But someone around here doesn't like us! The thought echoed through Brian's head.

"Okay," Larry continued, "so we organized an unannounced inspection, as you know, expecting that, at worst, we'd find we had a disagreement with you over interpretation of practice simulators, or something of the sort. Instead, when we did a routine check of the records for the only captains who've gone through the complained-about recurrent training in the last five months, we discovered the folders had been removed! We can't even check to see if the simulator rides were signed off properly because—guess what—the records aren't there!''

Brian could feel his jaw grinding around as he fought to contain his anger at the implication.

''We didn't pull those files, Larry, if that's what you're implying. That would be an act of idiocy. Besides, we didn't know you were coming, *and* the folders don't contain anything that would tell you the exact number of minutes spent in the simulator session. Your tip is ridiculous, and none of us have any knowledge what this *tipster* is talking about.'' Brian pronounced the word with visible distaste.

''I didn't say you did. I merely—''

''But your implication is clear. So let me ask you—let me ask both of you gentlemen—'' Brian turned to Schaffer with a sweeping gesture of inclusion. ''Since this looks suspicious to you—why the very records that would prove a violation aren't there to inspect—consider an alternate conclusion. Assume that someone wants to set Pan Am up for an embarrassing situation and destroy any trust between the FAA and Pan Am. Assume there is no discrepancy in training or the training records, or whatever the bastard who called alleged. Now, what better way for that someone to accomplish his goals than to phone in a tip to you, then go steal the very records the tip concerned? We can't prove we're innocent, because the records are gone, and on top of it, *we* end up looking like we're trying to hide something by apparently concealing the records!''

Larry DePalma shook his head and sat back, his right hand held up, his index finger extended as if about to give a downbeat to a band. ''Exactly the point I've made, Brian. Ken?'' DePalma turned to Ken Schaffer, his boss, who had been less than excited about attending the meeting to begin with.

That guy's look could kill, Brian thought. Schaffer was not happy to be suddenly in DePalma's spotlight.

''What?'' Schaffer said quietly.

DePalma had turned to his right in the compact office to look at Schaffer. ''I raised this issue with you two days ago, but . . .'' DePalma turned back to Brian. ''. . . but, Brian, we need hard evidence. And you guys are going to have to provide it. Otherwise we've got missing files, and airmen whose training now can't even be verified, and that's suspicious as all hell when viewed from back in D.C.''

Brian thought he could hear something catch in Schaffer's throat in the corner, or it could have been his imagination. DePalma could catch hell for revealing that Washington's scrutiny was involved, but it was just as Brian had suspected. It was someone back East who had it in for Pan Am.

"What are you saying?" Brian asked slowly, carefully, but with a metered amount of acid dripping from his words.

"I think you know what I'm saying, Brian. Either we find those records or some acceptable proof that those nine captains of yours have been trained in accordance with your training manual, or you've got to ground them and retrain them."

"That is ridiculous! I brought a complete computer printout showing that everything's been done properly, and if you want it, I'll have affidavits faxed in by all my captains by sundown. I'll—"

"Won't be acceptable, Captain Murphy." Schaffer's voice stabbed at him from the corner. "You haven't applied to us, nor have we approved, the use of your computer records in lieu of your hard-copy folders. That computer file could easily have been altered. Now, we'll let you reconstruct and recertify those hard-copy records if you can show us the independent proof upon which you're basing the reconstruction—simulator instructor logs, classroom logs, that sort of thing. But just asking your guys to call in and say, in effect, 'Hey, I'm legal'? Forget it."

Brian whirled on Schaffer. "You know damn well that'll take days, and in the meantime I'll have to ground all these guys worldwide."

Schaffer shrugged. "You're already in violation for not having the records in place for us to inspect. I would hope you wouldn't make it worse by using unqualified pilots."

Larry DePalma looked panicked. He could see the meeting was deteriorating to a contest of wills between Schaffer and Murphy, and that had been the last thing he intended.

"Mr. Schaffer!" Brian hissed, his eyes flaring as he fought to bring himself under control. "If someone out of our control has stolen those records, we are *not* in violation!"

"Well, Captain, I guess that's our determination, not yours. We could take it under consideration in terms of amount of fines and penalties or whatever, but that decision is ours alone. Besides, you said someone *out* of your control might have stolen those records, but someone *within* your control might have been involved, too. Someone could have misplaced them, or shredded them. Perhaps someone in your shop wanted to hide the records from you, someone who'd been cutting corners on simulator time without your knowledge, for instance.''

"That's a ridiculous suggestion.''

"Well, in my years of experience, it's not unusual for the boss to be unaware of something going on right beneath his nose.''

Brian Murphy sat quietly for a split second, rolling an explosive retort around in his mind, and deciding at last to fire it off.

"That cuts both ways, doesn't it, Mr. Schaffer? Are *you* aware of virtually everything your people do? I admit I don't know who removed our records, but the culprit's ID card could have the FAA's emblem on it as easily as Pan Am's.''

"Now, I resent that, dammit!'' Larry DePalma's voice shot across the desk. "We didn't take your damned records, Brian.''

Brian turned back toward the desk, slightly startled at the furious expression on DePalma's face.

"Neither did any of our people, Larry. Not . . . at least not . . .'' Brian found himself stumbling, a scary possibility flitting across his mind. ". . . not anyone with authorized access to those records.''

"I'll tell you one thing, Brian. Anger and accusations are going to get us nowhere. Frankly, I'm still pretty upset at being chewed on by your vice-president of operations yesterday afternoon.''

Brian let that drop. He would question DePalma in private later. Not that he could control Chad Jennings, but he hated hearing that Jennings had let his temper get the best of him again, leaving yet another mess for Brian to clean up.

Well, Brian thought, *I guess we understand the hostility here. They don't like Jennings, therefore they don't like Pan Am.*

Brian glanced over at Schaffer, then back at DePalma.

"I need some relief, gentlemen. I need forty-eight hours with no violations for letting my people continue to fly while we're trying to prove to you that we're guiltless in this.''

Larry DePalma was looking down again—a bad sign. He wasn't going to take the heat, certainly not with Schaffer in the room. Brian looked over at Schaffer, who met his gaze with a neutral expression and a single word.

"No.''

"No? Why not?''

"Again, Captain, you're already in violation. We can't suspend the rules.''

The hell you can't! Brian thought, stopping short of a spoken retort.
"So what do I do?" Brian asked in a more subdued tone.
"I think," Larry replied, "we've already outlined the answer to that."

♦ ♦ ♦

Brian Murphy had been gone from the office for a full minute—the
sound of the elevator door closing in the hallway encapsulating his departure—before either DePalma or Schaffer spoke.

"You were pretty hard on him, Ken," Larry DePalma said.

Schaffer shrugged again as he got to his feet. "He's a goddamned
hothead."

Larry was shaking his head. "No, he's not. His *boss*, Chad Jennings,
is a certified hothead. No, Ken, what you've got there in Brian Murphy is
an honest, frustrated chief pilot who's being royally screwed by someone."

Schaffer paused at the door. "He's going to be even more frustrated
in another hour or so. Headquarters is announcing that Pan Am is going
to be fined big-time."

♦ ♦ ♦

Brian Murphy worked hard at self-control. With his height and build,
he had long since learned that he could be physically intimidating when
he meant nothing of the sort. Self-control in aggravating circumstances
was vital, and he practiced it now all the way to the FAA parking lot. He
climbed calmly behind the wheel, closed the door, and finally permitted
himself to slam his fist into the padded dashboard.

"Goddammit!"

There was a cellular phone in the car, and he turned to it now, dialing
his secretary to trigger the action he had hoped to avoid. All nine of the
affected captains would have to be pulled off the line. One was in Hong
Kong, another in Tokyo, and several more in offshore locations, which
meant that other captains would have to be sent out unproductively as
passengers and positioned to each station to replace the grounded captains.
The possibility of delayed flights was very high, a fact he had avoided
facing until now.

Brian accelerated away to regain Interstate 405 for the short ride
back to Seatac. Something was nagging at the back of his head, something that had flitted across his mind earlier in the meeting with De-
Palma and Schaffer. *You haven't been focusing on the obvious, have you,
Brian?* he thought. *The question is not how or why the records got taken,*

but by whom. Who had access? Who may have left a trail? If I can find out who, I can find out why.

He began picturing the file cabinets at the office, wondering how to breach the security precautions they had taken.

And that was, in itself, a revelation. There were very few precautions. The file cabinets were locked at night with a combination kept by several people, but they were open during the day. They were even left open at lunch, but there was always at least one secretary around as a barrier, wasn't there? And at night and on weekends, the windowless room the file cabinets occupied was locked with a key.

Is there any way to figure out when this was done? he wondered. *Wait a minute! One of the guys was in the simulator just a few days ago. The last date of entry in the computer could tell us something.*

Brian realized he was sitting forward against the steering wheel, anxious to get back. If there was a trail, he was going to find it! He pressed the accelerator even harder, a firm resolve causing a thin, mean smile to play around the corners of his mouth.

If I catch the bastard who did this to us . . .

3:30 P.M.
Pan Am Headquarters

The fallout from the network deathwatch suddenly sparked by the FAA's announcement had already rolled through the fifty-sixth floor, leaving everyone stunned. Elizabeth had spent the day on the phone, it seemed, bypassing the need to learn the ropes of the financial structure in her new company in order to deal with the life-or-death crisis of the credit line and bond payments. She had called Eric Knox in addition to a dozen other friends on the Street in an initial search for the soft underbelly of the money market, preparing the way to find eighty-five million dollars by the twentieth. Eric had been out, but now her former partner was on the line from his home, and Elizabeth asked him to hold while she closed her office door, a precaution that seemed rather curious when she thought about it consciously.

"Eric. Hi! It's very good to hear your voice!"

"Hello, beautiful former partner in the boondocks. Ready to come home now?"

"That's not funny, Eric. This ship's in a lot of trouble."

"The ship's sunk, if you ask me. What the hell's happening out there? You're there two days, and the place flies apart. Such talent!"

"Seriously, Eric, cut it out. I'm in the middle of a real-life corporate crisis, and much of it's sitting on my shoulders. And . . . and it's a bit frightening."

His voice changed timbre and tone immediately.

"Can I help?"

"I don't know," she said slowly. There was a barrier between them now that had never been there before, a fiduciary barrier that prevented open discussion of sensitive corporate information. She had to tiptoe through the minefield and decide what could be said. It was too new a position to be comfortable.

She told him about the loan she needed to arrange, asking for help and guidance if possible, without telling him *why* it was needed so fast. Eric, however, had been at the game a long time.

"You've got some hellacious note due, or bond payments, or something. Don't answer. I'm just saying I understand."

They talked for half an hour professionally, Eric promising to do what he could, before the conversation dropped back to the personal level they had always enjoyed.

"Elizabeth, technically you're still a partner."

"Eric, I can't."

"Yes, you can. You've triggered your parachute. I read it over, remember? They didn't tell you everything they could have told you, and you're entitled. We'll get our lawyers on it. They're too weak to fight."

She realized the shaking of her head couldn't be seen in New York.

"Eric, you know me better than that. I made a commitment . . . I *have* a commitment. I can't walk out on these people, even if they did gloss it up a bit. Lord, we've done the same thing a hundred times and held our breath on various underwritings."

He chuckled on the other end. "No comment. I didn't hear that, and neither did the Securities and Exchange Commission wiretapper."

"I wish I were back there, but—"

"Think about it. I'll pigeonhole the partnership sale papers for a few weeks. Call me night or day. I miss you."

"You'll call about the other stuff?"

"In the morning. Without fail."

They disconnected then, as Elizabeth looked around her bright new office, which so effectively exuded professionalism and success. The spectacular view of Seattle and Elliott Bay underlined the heights to which she'd climbed, yet she felt like running and hiding.

Those same feelings again.

Dictating the same solution.

Elizabeth got to her feet and closed her briefcase. Seattle was a very walkable city, almost like a miniature New York in some respects. A good, fast, mind-numbing walk was what she needed. After all, she reminded herself, her mother was due in shortly, and she would need all her strength to deal with the latest chapter in her mother's never-ending criticism of Kelly's upbringing.

10

Friday, March 10, night
Denver Airport

What struck Captain Dale Silverman most about the new Denver airport was how empty it seemed. Even now, at midnight, as he and his copilot taxied one of Pan Am's two 767s, Ship 102, toward one of the jetways, the place looked like a thoroughly modern ghost town.

Of course, Silverman reminded himself, *we're on the Columbia Airlines concourse. There's nobody home because they're still dead.*

The variation on an old "Saturday Night Live" gag caused him to chuckle out loud. Pan Am had been "still dead" too, until Ron Lamb and company had breathed new life into the name.

Dale Silverman had struggled through many years as a pilot with the original Pan American as it took a decade to die a slow and painful death.

A lone figure wearing white coveralls appeared beneath the docking lights with a pair of lighted wands and waved them in. Silverman wondered if the man was a recycled Columbia Air employee. Ever since mighty Columbia Airlines had collapsed in bankruptcy and utter ruin the previous year, their people had run into great difficulty finding new jobs in the airline business.

♦ ♦ ♦

By the time Dale Silverman remembered his reading glasses, his crew and all their baggage had been loaded into the hotel van. He hated to admit he needed glasses, but without them he'd be too blind to deal with flight paperwork in the morning.

"You guys go on and get checked in and send the driver back for me. I left something on board." After eight hours' rest, Silverman and crew were scheduled to fly a tour group back to Seattle—an urgent replacement, he had been told, for another charter operator who had come up short on aircraft to fulfill his contract.

Getting back through security was the usual idiotic hassle, as if an airline crewmember with a valid ID might be planning to hijack an airplane. He was forced to shed his coat with the metal buttons and empty his pockets before being waved on, all the time mentally muttering his usual litany of anger.

Not one recorded case of an airline pilot hijacking an airliner, and they put us through this crap so the FAA can lie and say it's done something of value for safety!

It was so incredibly stupid.

As he passed through the boarding lounge, headed for the jetway, he noticed through the window that the lights of the cockpit had been turned back up to full bright, which was curious.

A mechanic he had never seen before greeted him from the door of the cockpit as he approached the front of the 767. The man was wearing the same color coveralls and insignia of the individual who had blocked them in, but his face and build were different, Dale noted.

"Hello, Captain. Forget something?" the mechanic said breezily.

"My glasses," Dale replied. "Be out of your way in a second."

He squeezed past the mechanic, who seemed rooted to the spot.

"No hurry, sir," the man said. "I'm just waiting for the fuelers."

That explains the cockpit lights, Dale thought. *He's going to refuel her tonight.* He hadn't recognized the small company logo on the man's coveralls. Probably the logo of yet another tiny contract service outfit, he supposed, hired to take care of the occasional charter flight for carriers that didn't normally serve Denver.

Silverman entered the cockpit and reached over the left seat, relieved to find his glasses still sitting where he'd left them, right by his flight bag—which still appeared to be there.

What the hell?

He'd already put his flight bag on the bus with the rest of the crew—hadn't he?

Now that would be a great sign of advancing senility! Like I'm going into Alzheimer's, or something.

That corner of the cockpit was shaded by the seat, and he had to look closely to see what was there. It wasn't his flight bag. It was the mechanic's tool kit, along with two rack-mounted electronic black boxes apparently destined for his airplane.

Oh, good! he thought. *So I'm not losing my mind.*

"What're the boxes for?" Dale asked as he left the cockpit.

"Routine swap-out for one of the computer components. Your people back in Seattle requested it."

"Okay. Sorry to hold you up." Dale smiled at the mechanic and left.

He was halfway back to the hotel before the mechanic's words coalesced in his mind. Why would Pan Am order components swapped at a station without Pan Am maintenance, unless there had been an open maintenance writeup in the log he'd failed to notice.

He resolved to ask the copilot about it in the morning.

Saturday, March 11, afternoon
Downtown Seattle

Elizabeth looked at her mother, tracking the latest wrinkles around her eyes, and feeling guilty. Brian was right, of course. She was a sweet lady, and one who had always stood by her daughter and granddaughter, no matter what—even if she did have the ability to drive Elizabeth to distraction over Elizabeth's methods of mothering Kelly. After all, this was the woman who left her home to move to a tiny flat in Massachusetts to help her daughter through the first eleven months of her granddaughter's life when Elizabeth was struggling to get started in Harvard Business School.

I guess she deserved a more loyal child than she got in me, Elizabeth thought. *I haven't been very supportive of her.*

"You sure you two have everything?" Elizabeth asked, almost wistfully. She had hovered around the door of the condo for the last two trips as her mother and Kelly loaded the minivan downstairs. She found herself wishing she could take time to go, too.

The fact that Brian would be coming through the same door in a few hours entered her thoughts as well, and a slow flush of warmth began a secret and sensuous ripple through her body. She felt transparent and a bit embarrassed when she realized her mother was standing in front of her, as if her thoughts could be seen.

Virginia Sterling stopped in the doorway with two bulging pillowcases pressed into use as impromptu bags, one for Kelly's dirty clothes, the other stuffed with odds and ends—the result of the decision they'd made together last night. Kelly would attend public school classes in Bellingham until early June, and enroll in a private school in Seattle the following autumn. Elizabeth had bristled at first at the suggestion. Here was her mother once again trying to alter every decision she made regarding Kelly. But the logic was irrefutable. She knew deep down that the Pan Am battles ahead of her would once again leave Kelly a work-orphan, this time in Seattle. With her mother so close, that made little sense—as Virginia had pointed out.

Virginia smiled and rolled her eyes. In her full-length camel's-hair coat and with her hair perfectly coiffed, the image was as incongruous as Mrs. Howell of "Gilligan's Island" carrying a pig.

"This is almost like having you back in undergraduate days," she said, inclining her head toward the laundry bag. "Only this time, your mom has to come *get* the laundry. Usually you'd at least bring it *to* me to wash."

At fifty-nine she was still the glamorous woman Elizabeth had always known, trim, blond, feminine, and attractive. She had dated a few times since the death of Elizabeth's father, a decade ago, but if she had a love life, her daughter was unaware of it. Elizabeth worried about her being alone, but if loneliness bothered Virginia Sterling, she never let it show.

Virginia had disappeared down the hallway with the load as Kelly came back for one more, bubbling with excitement.

Elizabeth caught herself being distracted by the television again. The TV had been turned to CNN all morning as she watched for more on Pan Am and tried to assess the damage from the tsunami of bad press that had washed over them in the past two days.

"Well, I think we're ready." Her mother was standing at the door with Kelly, and Elizabeth snapped off the television, piqued at herself for getting lost in the news again.

"Okay, Mom. I'm sorry I can't go with you."

Virginia looked at Elizabeth quietly for a second.

"That was a good talk last night, wasn't it, honey? I didn't get upset, you didn't get upset, and we carved out a better course, I think."

"It was, Mom. The best in a long time. I'd gotten used to running for cover whenever we . . . well, you know . . ."

"I do know. I've been too quick to fire at you all these years." She gestured to her granddaughter. "Gotta admit, you haven't done too badly."

Elizabeth hugged her energetically. "I do love you, Mom."

"And I love you, Elizabeth. I appreciate your listening to me this time. I really do. Starting Kelly in that private school with only two months left was a noble idea, but not a good one."

"I just had no idea this job was going to be an instant marathon the second I got here."

"Kelly would have been shifting for herself."

"I thought we'd have plenty of time, but—"

"You will—later. You've got too much to worry about in the next few months. You take care of those problems, and I'll take care of this one." She gestured with her thumb in Kelly's direction, as Kelly rolled her eyes in response.

Kelly gave Elizabeth a final hug at curbside, and waved to her from the passenger seat as the van disappeared into Seattle traffic.

Elizabeth found herself standing there for a few minutes deep in thought, the light cotton dress she was wearing feeling suddenly very good on what had become an unusual and almost balmy Seattle day. Usually, March brought showers and cold weather in Puget Sound, but the unseasonable warmth had caused more than a few weathermen to wonder whether global warming was kicking in at last.

A small breeze ruffled Elizabeth's skirt, teased her sandaled feet, and mussed her hair a bit. The windows of a passing bus gave her a brief glimpse of herself standing there, looking fresh and lithe and windblown. If it had been five degrees warmer, it would have been exactly the type of day she usually loved, the type of day that seemed to demand a barefoot run through a grassy field. She never felt more feminine and attractive and . . . well . . . sexy, than she did on days like this.

So why did none of those delicious feelings course through her now?

Brian was due in two hours, at 5:00 P.M. She had just enough time to bathe and freshen up as she tried to get her mind off Pan Am's troubles—and on its chief pilot.

Saturday, March 11, 3:00 P.M.

Pan Am's maintenance chief had been home for only a few hours' sleep each night since Clipper Ten's close brush with oblivion. The fatigue showed on his face now as he stepped through the cramped doorway of the salvage barge and back into the sunlight of a Saturday afternoon. The large, unshaven owner followed him out, clanging the door closed behind them as he adjusted the unlit cigar he had been masticating since Bill Conrad arrived. The man patted his enormous beer belly and smiled, and Conrad could well understand why he didn't dare light the cigar: he reeked of diesel fuel, but not sufficiently to mask what could be referred to charitably as the pervading bouquet of a man who apparently perspired more than he bathed.

"I could have her on site in about two days, Mr. Conrad. But the support equipment, the divers, the sonar equipment, and all that—we'll have to get that elsewhere, as I said. Once they find it, I can haul it up."

Bill thanked him, shook the greasy paw the man offered in parting, and returned to his car, wondering if he had a towel in his trunk to wipe off his hand. He had run the gamut now from the professional and neatly run salvage firms to the other extreme, and they all charged the same.

He punched the number of Operations Vice-President Chad Jennings into his car phone as he backed through the maze of rusting industrial marine equipment in the unkempt waterfront yard and turned around, heading back to the Interstate.

There was one more possibility for reaching the drowned engine. A research vessel he knew of docked in Tacoma. The captain of that vessel was to meet him in an hour.

Jennings was on his new sailboat in the middle of Puget Sound when he answered his maintenance chief's call on *his* cellular, a hand-held model. Jennings sounded distracted, and possibly a bit drunk, as Conrad filled him in on the bottom line: finding the sunken engine and bringing it up was going to cost a minimum of fifty thousand dollars, and probably a lot more.

There was an attempt at a soft whistle from Jennings's end.

"So do I have your authorization, Chad?" Conrad asked.

There was a pause.

"For what?" Jennings asked.

"To contract for a salvage operation that's going to cost that much," Conrad prompted, heading his car east onto the West Seattle bridge.

"Tell me again why we need it?" Jennings asked.

Bill Conrad shook his head in silent disgust. Somehow the idea of Jennings sailing around and enjoying the day while the prospects of his company were in peril seemed wrong and repugnant.

Pay attention, man, you're supposed to be the executive in charge!

He explained it again: the refusal of the NTSB to pay for such a mission; the refusal of the NTSB even to admit publicly that sabotage was a possibility, despite the intruder in the Moses Lake hangar; and the growing holocaust of publicity pointing fingers at the competence of Pan Am maintenance, and therefore the safety of the airline in general.

"I don't know, Bill, that's an awful lot of money."

Conrad could hear ice cubes tinkling against a glass in the background and the murmur of a feminine voice saying something low near the mouthpiece. "Just a second," Jennings said, and the sound of a hand brushing the mouthpiece in an ineffective attempt to cut off the sound reached Conrad's ears. Jennings, he knew, was newly divorced and showing, at age forty-two, all the signs of a midlife crisis resolved at the expense of his family. Bill Conrad had tried to avoid the gossip about Jennings, but at fifty-eight, with a stable and happy thirty-three-year marriage, he couldn't help but be put off by the rumors about the younger man. Chad Jennings had supposedly walked out on a wife and four children in Dallas and paid incredible sums to some high-priced legal talent who had successfully manipulated the court into leaving him with most of the assets, and his family with nearly nothing.

Conrad negotiated the on-ramp to southbound Interstate 5 as the sounds of Jennings's partially covered phone came through the speaker in his car.

The mouthpiece was suddenly uncovered. "Okay, Bill, sorry. Something came up."

There were more giggles in the background.

"You were asking for money? No, you were asking for authorization to spend up to fifty thousand, right?"

"At least."

"Okay. Go ahead, you got it. Call me back on Monday."

The phone rang again almost immediately, and Conrad punched it on, fully expecting to hear Chad Jennings's voice with second thoughts.

Instead, a Seattle newspaper reporter introduced himself and asked for an interview on the NTSB's search for answers to Clipper Ten's accident.

"No," was Bill Conrad's reply.

"Okay, I know this is out of the blue, but—"

"If you'd like, I'll give you the number of our public-relations department, and you can—"

"Already talked to them."

"Well, then, I can't help you."

Several seconds ticked by as his car moved south on I-5, Boeing Field passing on the right. A row of multicolored 747-400s lined the northern end of the airport, each with a different airline logo.

"I know about the sabotage, Mr. Conrad." The words echoed around the car before Bill Conrad was able to compose an answer.

This is dangerous! He's guessing, or fishing!

"We had a tip that someone broke into your 747 at Seatac the night before the accident and fooled with the engine."

"I've heard no such rumor regarding Seatac," he said, walking the razor edge of the truth.

"Okay, but I've heard you're urging the NTSB investigators to look into sabotage, and the FBI's been seen working on your aircraft at Whidbey. Now talk to me, Mr. Conrad. You're the maintenance chief."

"And not the PR man, which is why I have nothing to say."

"If you change your mind," the reporter said, "my name, again, is Adrian Kirsch, K-I-R-S-C-H, and here's my number. Please write it down."

It was a useless gesture, Bill told himself, to take down the number; he had virtually no intention of using it.

But he did it anyway. He rehashed the conversation mentally during the remainder of the trip to Tacoma. How had the reporter found out? Who had tipped him? How did they know about the FBI? What had the FBI found, if anything? Jake Lovesy and he had talked Friday night, and there was nothing new. They still weren't going to mention sabotage as a possibility, Jake had said, until there was at least one piece of hard evidence.

So who the hell is leaking? Bill wondered.

Deep down he wished that Kirsch or someone else *would* tell the public that all the bad press was nothing but a rush to judgment.

Pan Am maintenance wasn't at fault!

Or so he hoped.

Saturday, March 11, 5:00 P.M.
Downtown Seattle

Brian was early, and Elizabeth was ready, greeting him at the door with a long, sensuous kiss, wearing only a silky Hawaiian print shift that was little more than a negligee with flowers.

Both of them had been through so much tension the previous two days, they were determined to put their problems behind them for a few hours and enjoy this evening.

They had closed the door and were gravitating toward the couch when the phone rang.

Eric Knox had called as promised during the morning and asked to postpone a more lengthy report until late afternoon. Elizabeth had forgotten until now that he was planning to call back.

Reluctantly she disentangled herself from what had become an increasingly impassioned embrace and answered the call, sinking to the couch with a hastily retrieved notepad as Brian took the bottle of wine he'd brought to the kitchen and tried to busy himself with mundane duties, while his thoughts kept migrating back to the couch, and to her.

"It's a tough sell, Elizabeth, I won't kid you," Eric was saying. "Pan Am's reputation on the Street took a harpoon in the middle yesterday, and I was almost laughed at by a number of our old friends when I pitched the need for a short-term loan."

"We'll find the security to back it, Eric."

"Oh, I'm sure of it. I'm just looking for basic willingness, and I've got several people outside our firm looking and spreading the word that you're interested. You may have to call in some markers on this one, Elizabeth. I think you need to get your lovely tail back here tomorrow and be ready to hit the bricks Monday morning."

"*That* hard a sell?"

"Indeed it will be. Bring your ideas for security, and best have your legal department standing by to jump through any hoops anyone raises before you."

"Okay. Okay, I'll come in Sunday."

"Elizabeth, you may not win this one. Just . . . just be prepared."

She replaced the receiver as Brian materialized beside her with two crystal goblets of cold Zinfandel wine—her favorite. He held his glass with his left hand, then, sipping at the wine and lightly running his right hand through her hair as she told him about the call and the hurricane of problems she had confronted since arriving in Seattle—carefully avoiding a specific mention of the ticking bomb, the eighty-five-million-dollar payment that could doom the company. He was chief pilot, but he wasn't a corporate officer, and there were certain things she couldn't tell him.

She didn't notice the faraway look in his eyes until he spoke suddenly, interrupting her litany, his mind obviously on other thoughts.

"I've missed you, Elizabeth," he said, his eyes tracking the cascading mane her amber-blond hair had become under the teasing of her hair dryer a few minutes before he arrived. She knew he liked it that way. The "Farrah Fawcett in an open cockpit" look, he had dubbed it.

She stopped talking about Pan Am and smiled at him, remembering the warm security of being enfolded in his arms. He had carried her emotionally through a thousand doubts and terrors in those early years. Whatever battles she had faced by day, whatever heartless torpedoes had been fired at her self-esteem, she could always escape in his embrace and know everything would work out.

Elizabeth chuckled quietly and shook her head as she let her eyes drop to his chest, extending her hand to touch him the way she used to—unbuttoning a single button on his shirt and lightly caressing his skin with the tip of her finger.

She looked up at him then, getting lost in his eyes.

"I've missed you so much," she said. "I could never let myself dwell on it, because . . ."

"I know. Me too," Brian replied. She felt his large hand brush her cheek as he worked absently to push back her hair and arrange it just so. His hand brought with it the aroma of a woody cologne, and she turned to nuzzle it, kissing his palm and enclosing the back of his hand in hers before turning to him with a smile and a nod toward the kitchen.

"Come on, my long-lost lover, and let me feed you."

The aromas from the ample kitchen in the two-story condo had already commanded his attention and approval. She had always been an incredible cook, trained by her mother, who was equally adept at producing a multi-course meal out of almost nothing.

"Remember the MRE?" he asked, as he watched her effortlessly prepare a sauce for the beef bourgignon main course.

"The what?"

"Meals-ready-to-eat. Friend of mine gave me one from the Army, and I brought it to you on that visit to New York, what was it—four years ago?"

"Oh yeah." She smiled at the memory, knowing what he was going to say and loving it.

"You took that barely edible stuff and made a gourmet meal out of it, how I'll never understand. The deal was, you couldn't use anything but spices and bouillon cubes and a few tomatoes."

"It wasn't hard."

"Yeah. You're saying that to a guy who can burn water."

"Five more minutes," she announced, leading him out on the balcony.

The sun was still swimming above the horizon beyond Elliott Bay, backlighting the Olympic Mountains on the Olympic Peninsula fifty miles distant, its low angle creating a softened light that painted a warm glow on their faces as they stood holding hands, watching the Bremerton ferry churning away to the west.

"Beautiful, isn't it?" she asked, as Brian turned his head to look at her.

"Incredibly beautiful," he said, "and the scenery out there's nice too."

"Brian! Honestly!" She turned to him. "What am I going to do with you?"

There was a definite twinkle in his eyes as he stood there grinning at her.

Elizabeth took his hand and slowly intertwined her fingers with his, her eyes focused on the effort. "I . . . think . . . we'd . . ." She looked up suddenly. ". . . better eat first."

There would be no more shop talk, they agreed. Not tonight. He had thoroughly compartmentalized the complex troubles that had greeted him Thursday night, and if he could put impending personal disaster out of mind for one night, so could she.

Though she had agreed, Brian could sense a part of her holding back.

Dinner was magnificent, just as she had planned it, and just as he had known it would be. With the usual Puget Sound evening chill in the air after sundown, they built the inaugural fire in the new condo's fireplace and settled back together on the white leather couch, talking of Cambridge, New York, Phoenix, and flying, and the strange twist of fate that had never let either of them find another to permanently fill the void.

"I never thought we'd ever live in the same area again," he said. "I never thought we could ever make it work again."

"Can we now?" she asked, instantly upset at herself for the suddenness of the question.

We haven't even been together one whole evening, she chided herself, *and already I sound like I'm pushing for commitment!*

Fortunately he smiled, and the smile expanded and grew to a chuckle and then a laugh. The laugh ended and he shook his head then, side to side, as his eyes became preoccupied once more with her hair.

"Oh, honey," he said, "if you only knew the thoughts that have been going through my head these last few weeks since you called."

His right hand had moved around to cup the back of her head, and she felt herself being drawn forward gently as he leaned to kiss her.

She eagerly met his embrace, lighting a flame in both of them as she nibbled his lips and drew his tongue inside, rising on her knees to his height, her breasts feeling the hard, masculine wall of his chest. Her hands climbed his back, feeling the cropped hair on the back of his neck as she moved to cradle his head and hold him even tighter against her.

She was powerfully aroused now—as was he, she knew. Their kiss had become an impassioned tangle of lips and tongues when the ringing of the phone cut through the moment like a fire hose. Elizabeth began to disengage, finding Brian unwilling to stop.

"Don't answer it!" he said somewhat breathlessly, while nibbling her lips. "Please!"

"I have to."

"No ... no, you don't." He was smiling and so was she, but the phone was on its third ring.

"Don't you have an answering machine?" he asked.

"Yes, but—"

"Let the machine earn its keep. We're busy." His mouth closed on hers again as the machine snapped on, playing its recorded announcement to the unheard caller. She tried to surrender again, loving the feeling of his strong hands on her back, but the message had ended and she realized a large part of her mind was waiting for the tiny machine to broadcast the voice of the caller through the room.

"Elizabeth, this is Ron Lamb," the message began. He sounded exhausted and beaten, and Elizabeth instantly felt compassion for the agony he was going through. "Uh ... I've been on the phone with some of the bond holders, people I know, trying to work something out in principle."

The message continued on, somewhat rambling. It was obvious he was losing hope even before his new CFO had had the chance to look for a rabbit—let alone pull one out of her hat.

And it was obvious to Elizabeth that if Ron Lamb went too far with the phone calls on his own, he could prejudice her efforts.

Brian's embrace slackened a bit. He could feel her drifting away. They kept nuzzling each other, but even Elizabeth's eyes, he noticed, were looking toward the machine.

Patience! Brian cautioned himself as he pulled back.

Elizabeth turned back to him suddenly, caressing the back of his head. "Brian, I need to talk to him."

He smiled and nodded, letting her twist over the back of the couch to retrieve the phone.

"Ron? Elizabeth. I just came in and heard your voice."

There was a grateful response on the other end, and she sat back down on her ankles in the same position as before, concentrating on the conversation, and not noticing that Brian had moved around behind her with a mischievous grin.

"Who did you talk to?" she asked, concentrating on Ron Lamb's reply.

Brian could hear the company president's voice as a series of electronic squawks through the earpiece as he bent over to kiss her neckline, and slowly reached down with both hands along her thighs, grabbing the hem of the gown and working it back up toward her hips. She seemed oblivious to his efforts, even when he hugged her from behind, letting his hands slide under the gown and around to softly cup her breasts for a minute. She merely patted one of his hands and kept on talking.

"Ron, I really don't think it's a good idea to keep on calling these people over the weekend," she was saying, as she automatically raised her right arm for Brian to pull the gown free and over her head.

"No, Ron. No, I don't. I need time to work on this next week in New York. You alert too many people, and we will have a confidence crash."

She cradled the phone between her bare shoulder and her face for a second as she pulled her left arm through the sleeve, then resumed holding the receiver in her left hand, apparently unaware that she was completely naked.

He gasped to himself. She was even more beautiful than he had remembered, her breasts still firm and substantial, the flickering orange from the fire bathing her in thermal light.

Elizabeth nodded her head to something Ron Lamb was saying.

"That's right. I don't think any of them has a need to know unless we're sure we can't work a deal."

There was another long soliloquy from Ron Lamb's side of the conversation as Brian moved around to the other end of the couch to face her.

He thought about slipping out of his clothes as well, but she seemed almost oblivious to what he was up to and it would be more fun to see how much she could take without having to end the phone call.

"Why? Because, Ron, that's the way it has to work. Let me explain what I'm planning to do."

As she launched into a detailed analysis of her game plan, Brian leaned forward and nuzzled the soft valley between her breasts before brushing his lips over her left nipple. Her hand stroked his head in response, but there was no break in the meter of her voice, until one of her routine murmurs of acknowledgement—what had been intended as an "um-hum"—became an extended "um-m-m-m-m!" and he felt her hand tighten on the back of his head as she promptly added, "Okay, I see, Ron."

Brian looked up at her, grinning, as she looked down and flared her eyebrows in mock anger while swatting at him gently and mouthing the word "No."

Which was exactly what he had wanted to see. He turned his full attention to her breasts now, massaging and kissing them, feeling her responses become more pronounced as he slowly pulled more and more of her consciousness away from the conversation.

When he knew she could no longer tune out what he was doing, Brian began gliding his tongue slowly, sensuously, down her stomach and abdomen, as his finger traced a feather-light path down her right side. He felt her shudder in response as she swatted him again in mild protest. The infrared heat from the fire had warmed her skin, and his face was fully flushed and hot as he kissed her lightly now, brushing his lips against her in a dozen places, leaving a sparkling trail of exciting sensations, and pressing a hand to each thigh, feeling her tense suddenly as her body and mind anticipated the next caress, knowing where his experienced tongue was headed.

There was no way she could concentrate on what Ron Lamb was saying.

"Ron . . ."

She took a deep and somewhat ragged breath.

"I . . . ah . . . better call you back in a few minutes. I've . . . got to take care of something."

He felt her reach to replace the phone. She would come to him now, her eyes glazed and her head in the clouds.

That was what he expected. That was the Elizabeth he knew, sensuous and responsive and hungry once they reached a certain point.

But instead, she reached out to stop him, gently pulling his head up. "Honey, I need to concentrate."

"I want you to concentrate, too, but on us."

Elizabeth sat up and pulled Brian to her, kissing him deeply.

"No business tonight, remember? We agreed."

"I *have* to do this, Brian. Duty calls. I have to call the man back."

"You can't solve anything tonight, Elizabeth."

She patted his face. "It won't take long. We've got all night."

Brian struggled with himself, fighting down irritation as she re-placed the call to Ron Lamb and tried her best to keep it short, while Brian kept his distance. But Lamb was in an inconsolable mood, and it was twenty minutes before she hung up. When she turned back to Brian at last, her preoccupation was as deep as his rising frustration, and when he gathered her in his arms and kissed her, something was missing.

Brian carried her effortlessly up the spiral staircase to the bedroom with the lights of nighttime Seattle sparkling behind them through the fifteen-foot-high picture windows. He laid her gently on the bed and kissed her in a long and lingering promise before excusing himself for a minute. She heard the door to the bathroom click just before Ron Lamb called again.

Distracted and burning with desire for Brian, she only wanted to finish the conversation with Lamb. She was angry with herself for answering, but he already knew she was in. She had to get off before Brian emerged from the bathroom, and she was doing just that when Ron Lamb mentioned the name of Irwin Fairchild.

"Ron . . . what did you say? What was that name?"

"Irwin Fairchild. Of the old Bankers Trust, now with Lassen Associates. He's an acquaintance who's been helpful with advice over the last year or so."

"Who introduced you?" she asked, already suspecting what the answer would be.

"I don't know, Elizabeth, is it important? Oh, wait. It was our previous CFO, Bill Hayes."

Ron Lamb heard silence on the other end.

"Why does that interest you, Elizabeth?"

She heard the sound of the bathroom light being turned off as Brian opened the door.

"Nothing. I'll tell you later. I've got to go."

"Okay. Sorry to bother you again. Good night."

She murmured good night and replaced the receiver, but it was too late. Brian had already seen her, and his face showed puzzlement.

"Lamb again?"

"Yes, but I got rid of him. Come here, lover."

He smiled and came to her, conscious immediately that she was trying too hard, her attention riveted elsewhere.

For nearly an hour, with increasing frustration, he tried everything he knew that had ever turned her on, and though she tried to react, her mind was racing with the implications of Ron Lamb having been influenced by Irwin Fairchild. There was no way that could be an accident! William Hayes had been something more than a poor financial officer. He had been an instrument for someone else's purpose.

But what purpose, and to what end?

"Goddammit, Elizabeth!"

Brian had sat up suddenly, immensely frustrated. The only edge either of them seemed to be going over was distraction. She was enjoying what he was doing only in the background, and he'd had enough.

Brian threw off the covers and sat on the edge of the bed, looking at her. "I don't know where you are tonight, but you're not with me."

"Yes, I am."

"What did Lamb say to you this time?"

She started to tell him, and stopped. It was just a suspicion that was consuming her.

She started to lie, then, and say it was nothing, but he would see through that as well.

"He mentioned the name of a man who's a notorious manipulator of greenmail and other nefarious activities on Wall Street. It's a name I know well. A major deal I put together was destroyed by this guy."

"So?"

"So, well . . ." She sat up and pulled her legs up, hugging her knees, missing his touch as he sat angrily a few feet away and brushed his hair back. "If this man is involved with Pan Am, we could be in even more trouble than I thought."

He leaped to his feet and started pacing the floor.

"Elizabeth, dammit, can't you compartmentalize? Can't you put away business for a while? You *used* to be able to do it, but now"—he swept his arm through the air in disgust—"now I get to play second fiddle to phone calls and corporate concerns on the first evening we've had together in years, with . . . with all the promise of a future for us, and—"

"Brian." A hard edge had crept into her voice. "I'm trying to save your job, too."

"Well, thank you, ma'am, but kindly do it on Monday, okay? You have any idea how demeaning it is to be ignored in bed?"

"I wasn't ignoring you! I'm in a fiduciary position with respect to—"

"Don't give me that formal crap, Elizabeth!"

"Brian, *listen* to me!" She wanted to cry, but anger was overwhelming her. How could he be so childish? "You're grossly overreacting. We've got all night, and if I'm a little preoccupied right now—"

He whirled on her.

"A *little*? What I was just doing used to send you over the edge two or three times. You're oblivious! I might as well be trying to make love to an inflatable woman."

The phrase *That could be arranged!* formed in her mind, but she suppressed it with great difficulty.

"Brian, come back to bed. Come hold me."

He continued pacing. "What, exactly, is the financial problem you've got to solve next week?"

"I . . . really shouldn't go into it."

"Bull."

"Really, I can't tell you."

Brian stopped and looked at her suspiciously.

"Why not?"

"Well . . . there are things that are, more or less, privileged information, and—"

"From me?"

"Brian, I'm a corporate officer."

He looked at her with an expression she had never seen before, a combination of hurt, anger, and frustration—as if she had just turned into something frightening, threatening his being.

"And I'm just a peon, right? A stupid working stiff."

"Brian, cut it out!"

"No, I hadn't paid any attention to the rank difference. I didn't think you would, either. I didn't think you'd ever forget we came up together, Miss High and Mighty. But you obviously have."

"Brian—"

♦ ♦ ♦

She couldn't sleep after he'd left, angry with herself for a thousand things not said and not done. He was right and he was wrong. She should have shouted at him and thrown him out, and she should have apologized to him. Back and forth the recriminations echoed through her head, until she found herself crying uncontrollably and calling his phone without success. He had apparently disconnected even the answering machine.

She dressed at 4:00 A.M. and drove to his house, across Lake Washington in Bellevue, relieved to see his car in the driveway.

Sullen and bleary-eyed, he let his guard down and answered the door, surprised that she'd come.

They talked for an hour, never touching, and she told him everything she had refused to reveal earlier.

They parted at his door in a sad, passionless embrace.

"Elizabeth, I'm sorry," he said at last. "I love you. I always have. But I don't know if I can live with you—or you with me."

Sunday, March 12
Tacoma, Washington

Bill Conrad collapsed the antenna of the cordless phone and fairly slammed the instrument back in its cradle.

"Goddamn bureaucrats!" he muttered, grabbing his coffee cup from the counter and leaving a small tidal wave of the liquid behind. He ignored the spill and paced off instead in the direction of the fireplace. Bill had paced the floor most of the afternoon and evening. The dark clouds of an advancing cold front, which had rolled in around dusk, matched his mood, and not even the slow emergence of the twinkling city lights of Tacoma across Commencement Bay from his Brown's Point home could bolster his spirits.

On the coffee table behind him, faxed copies of a half-dozen clippings from as many Sunday newspapers lay in haphazard profusion, some of them merely hinting at potential Pan American maintenance incompetence, others actually raising the issue of how safe Pan Am really was—with a Monty Pythonesque wink-wink, nudge-nudge.

He had called Jake Lovesy again after reading the last one, begging him at least to tell the media about the intrusion at Moses Lake. But it was painfully clear that the NTSB was not going to publicly acknowledge the possibility of sabotage—even though Lovesy hinted broadly that the FBI might already have found something "interesting."

Lovesy, once again, had counseled patience.

"Patience, my ass!" Bill Conrad muttered.

There was an underlying nervousness—an apprehension—eating away at his conscience, a chilling realization that Pan Am was still in danger. If what had happened to Ship 612 was sabotage, and if it was a professional job, as Jake Lovesy had suggested, there was no reason to believe that the saboteur had gone away—or given up. And next time the crew might not be able to bend the laws of aerodynamics and get themselves back on the ground safely. He was beginning to feel like the proverbial Dutch boy with his finger in the dike, his voice of alarm lost on the wind.

No one else, though, seemed to see the urgency. Chad Jennings was only mildly alarmed, and had even questioned the extra money for the added security precautions his director of maintenance had ordered throughout the system. He had approached the president as well, but even Ron Lamb wouldn't believe it until the NTSB formally agreed that someone had purposefully monkeyed with a Pan Am airplane.

No, no one was listening, so it was up to him to force the issue.

He charged back across the room suddenly and grabbed the phone once more, fumbling for the small scrap of paper that held the number he had decided to call. He was drumming his fingers restlessly as the last ring was replaced by the voice of a *Seattle Chronicle* reporter.

"Adrian Kirsch."

"Mr. Kirsch? This is Bill Conrad, of Pan Am."

Monday, March 13, morning
New York City

Elizabeth pushed through a gaggle of commuters blocking the subway exit, and maneuvered into the filthy corridor beneath Vanderbilt Avenue, checking her watch as she walked. Fifteen minutes to go. The crowd between her and Grand Central's main atrium was heavy, but not unmanageable. Long ago she'd learned to handle the challenges of an appointment in midtown during rush hour.

Eric's lengthy memo had been hopeful, and she needed hope. He'd obviously spent most of Saturday putting together a list of the sources most likely to let themselves be persuaded to loan Pan Am eighty-five million dollars, and had precontacted several of them, leaving a list of their home phone numbers for her to reach Sunday night from Eric's loaned condo.

In typical fashion, Eric had left the papers on a bedside table in the Victorian-decorated mini-mansion, along with a bottle of Dom Perignon champagne with a tiny sticky note reading, "In case of success, break seal."

And, true to form, he'd left his token sexual overture as well, a gilt-edged handwritten note just beneath the covers, saying, "Wish I were here!"

The incredible noise and echo of Grand Central's main concourse now surrounded her like a dowdy old friend as Elizabeth accelerated toward the east exit to Lexington Avenue. She had paused to buy a copy of *The New York Times* on boarding the subway, but had yet to open it. The dossier on Harold Hudgins—her first appointment—was more important reading. He was one of the principals in a consortium of investors consisting mostly of U.S. banks, and for them, eighty-five million would be a drop in the bucket.

And he'd indicated to Eric that Pan Am was not an unwelcome applicant.

She pushed through the heavy doors to Park Avenue and turned left, northward, letting her thin leather briefcase flop slightly against the side of her full-length coat, a black cashmere meant for slightly colder weather, but fashionable in the big city. There was a gray overcast above with the temperature in the fifties, and the winds were whipping through the canyons of Manhattan from the north, blowing discarded scraps of paper in the air and requiring Elizabeth to keep her coat firmly buttoned over the tailored hunter-green dress she had chosen to wear.

As she moved toward the target building on East Forty-fourth, she forced herself to avoid looking up at the renamed building once owned by Pan Am. It towered like a specter on her left, and she was acutely aware of its presence. Most New Yorkers who loved aviation had thought the sale of the building in the seventies the final indignity for Pan Am. Then came the bankruptcy and shutdown. But the ultimate desecration of the airline had been the removal of those huge blue letters. At least it had been a tombstone, and now even that had been kicked over.

The building's presence seemed to loom over her confidence as well as her person, an exclamation point made of steel, a cynical reminder that even the mightiest of companies can fail—a contemptuous monolith of scorn for someone who would seek to raise the dead.

Who is this little girl, it seemed to glower, who would challenge the mighty tide of Wall Street common wisdom?

She closed her eyes and shivered for a split second to exorcise the demons of doubt, and found herself crossing on a red light.

A bank of television screens swam into her peripheral vision in a corner electronics shop as she hurried past, hardly noticing, but for some reason she glanced in that direction, startled to see her company's logo filling each set.

She came to an instant halt and pressed her nose to the storefront, a small shiver of apprehension flashing through her as she wondered what had happened now. The logo receded to an over-the-shoulder box as one of the morning-show hosts began a story she couldn't hear.

Elizabeth quickly pushed through the door of the shop and found the volume control on one of the sets.

"... Conrad, director of maintenance for the newly restarted airline, has revealed that the National Transportation Safety Board is investigating the possibility of sabotage in last week's near disaster involving a Pan Am 747."

She had heard Conrad's name, but had not met the man. His face looked haggard as he appeared now, live from a Seattle TV studio. The word *sabotage* caught her cold. No one, not even Ron Lamb, had mentioned such a possibility, nor had anyone told her about the intruder at the Moses Lake facility.

Who would want to sabotage us? she wondered.

Conrad answered the first few questions cautiously, but when asked why the NTSB had yet to confirm such suspicions, he seemed to explode, leaving a clear impression that he thought the NTSB was engaged in a coverup. Conrad vigorously defended Pan Am maintenance, but when asked how an intruder could have gotten into a Pan Am hangar in the first place, and whether their security was competent, he stumbled badly. It was obvious that Bill Conrad hadn't thought about the implications of his argument. If Pan Am *was* sabotaged, that would prove that Pan Am had failed to provide adequate security for their airplanes. Either way, Pan Am looked guilty, sloppy, and perhaps less than safe. After all, he was claiming that Pan Am was still an active target of someone who hadn't succeeded on the first try.

♦ ♦ ♦

When she was ushered into his office, Elizabeth was relieved to find that Harold Hudgins had apparently not seen either the interview or the story she had just found in her copy of the *Times* as she waited in his outer office. At least he didn't mention it.

As they went through the usual pleasantries, she found herself wondering if Mr. Conrad had given the interviews without clearing them through the corporate public affairs department. If so, the man was in deep trouble.

It took an exhausting two hours of discussion and explanation, but Elizabeth hit Park Avenue around 11:00 A.M. with real hope coursing through her veins. Hudgins would, he promised, spend the rest of the day on the loan and have an answer for her in the morning. His words had rung like sunshine through the mist: "I think we've got a deal here, I just need to cement it together."

The pain of trying to walk in high heels the twenty blocks to her next appointment finally reached her consciousness and she gave up and hailed a cab, feeling a pang of hunger at the same moment. The sight of a restaurant made it worse, but there simply wasn't time for food.

She'd been out of contact all morning on purpose, but now she opened her briefcase and pushed the "power on" button on the small cellular phone Ron Lamb had obtained for her in Seattle.

A chirping sound erupted from the phone almost immediately, signifying an incoming call with the company president on the other end.

The corporate office was a madhouse of reporters and reacting executives. As she had expected, everyone was ready to kill Bill Conrad, and the chairman of the NTSB had been on the phone for thirty minutes, warning a room full of Pan Am executives headed by Ron Lamb that such outbursts were going to backfire.

"He's holding a press conference in a little while to try to counter what Conrad did, and Conrad's already called and apologized to the man."

She reported the progress in the first meeting before asking why no one had bothered to tell her about the sabotage possibility.

"Elizabeth, *I* didn't even know until Thursday, when Conrad told us, and *he* hadn't known the details until that morning."

In the back of her mind, though, as Ron answered, another question burned to be answered. Had Brian known about this? Had he known about it Saturday night when he was so angry with her over questions of corporate rank and responsibility? Even when she'd chased him home to Bellevue and told him everything she shouldn't have, he had said nothing about sabotage, or any intrusion in Moses Lake. Why? If he *had* known, what kind of game was he playing?

The question started to form on her lips, but she suppressed it. Her interest in what Brian knew and when he knew it was personal. *Very* personal.

The memory of Brian's infuriated speculation that someone had "sabotaged" their training files began to merge with Conrad's statements, and suddenly she felt a bit dizzy.

"Call me, Elizabeth, day or night, if you make any progress. I'm not sleeping anyway," Ron said as he rang off.

There had been an intrusion at Moses Lake, stolen files in the Seatac operations center, the suspicion of sabotage on their 747—which would constitute attempted mass murder—and something else. Oh yes! The anonymous tipster with a penchant for calling FAA headquarters in Washington. Like an arsonist who keeps tipping off the fire department to his own handiwork, Brian had growled.

This isn't bad luck, it's all part of a pattern!

The abrupt insight left her feeling cold and shaken.

The next banker she was going to see had been alerted to upcoming coverage of the news conference on CNN. He had a TV in his office and had it tuned up as he showed her in. They watched together as a distinguished man approached the podium and introduced himself as Joe Wallingford, chairman of the NTSB.

"The impression was left this morning on national television that the NTSB might have access to certain information regarding the Pan American Flight Ten incident last week, information suggesting possible sabotage, and yet might be sweeping it under the rug or otherwise hiding it. Not only is that totally untrue, the gentleman who left that impression, Bill Conrad, director of maintenance for Pan Am, assured me by phone a little while ago that he never intended to imply any such thing."

Wallingford characterized it as an honest difference of opinion on whether the NTSB should speak in public about the unproven details of an ongoing investigation. Generously, graciously, the NTSB chief defused the controversy, leaving both the NTSB and Pan Am relatively intact—and Elizabeth impressed.

The NTSB chairman, still commanding the camera, paused and looked around at his staff before holding aloft a small manila envelope.

"It so happens that as Mr. Conrad was speaking this morning, the FBI's crime lab was delivering to us a report that indicates, and I quote . . ."

Wallingford put on a pair of half-frame reading glasses and peered at the paper he had taken out.

". . . residue removed from the lower right wing of the subject aircraft by FBI personnel under NTSB supervision and labeled item 482, has been found to be of a metallic nature foreign to any metallic alloys used in the construction of either the subject aircraft or the subject aircraft engine.''

He removed the glasses and let it sink in.

''In other words, folks, the small shard of metal found impaled in the underside of the wing did not originally come from Boeing or Pratt and Whitney, and that raises a real possibility of sabotage. When we have more information of the exact alloy, and so on, we'll release it. The FBI remains fully involved in this case.''

Elizabeth was shocked. That *was* confirmation of sabotage, wasn't it? Surely that would help her win over someone in the financial quarter.

But the banker had been looking for an excuse to declare Pan Am too hot to handle, and with rolled eyes and a reference to the volatility of the market—as well as the prospects of an airline that had someone out to get them—he now had it. It was nice to see her and all that, say hello to Eric Knox, and by the way, good luck, but don't even think of asking for money here.

''We saw the name change on that building once,'' he said, motioning uptown to the old Pan Am tower, now owned by Met Life. ''And that's enough of a warning about putting money in airlines.''

There were meetings with Chemical Bank and another investment house in the early afternoon, followed by a dozen hurried phone calls and two more late-afternoon exploratory meetings in the financial district, but by five-thirty in the afternoon, starved and somewhat numb, it was obvious to Elizabeth that Hudgins was the only viable possibility so far. Every other institution, banks and investment houses in particular, were unconvinced that Pan Am could make it—and none of them wanted to end up someday having to liquidate pledged security located somewhere in the middle of the state of Washington.

Okay, I'll have faith that it's a go from Hudgins in the morning, and I'll get a good night's sleep without worrying, and . . . who am I kidding?

The light changed to DON'T WALK in front of her yet again, and Elizabeth realized she had been standing in deep thought through at least two cycles.

Heels or no heels, she started walking. The subway had carried her back to Eric's neighborhood, and that was only a short distance from her own.

The eight blocks back to the condo went quickly. She shucked her shoes and settled down with the phone to call Kelly and her mother.

"We're fine, dear, but you mentioned those passes?"

"On Pan Am? Sure. Where do you want to go?"

Elizabeth realized she was only half listening, most of her mind still preoccupied with how she was going to handle the next day. She tried to focus on what her mother was saying, but her thoughts kept snapping back to the frustration of having been a part of the New York financial world for so long, and yet having so much trouble with a simple corporate loan.

"I'm not sure, Elizabeth, but Kelly doesn't have to be in school until next Monday, so I thought I'd fly her somewhere."

That got her attention. It would be far less lonely if they were in town.

"How about coming out here to New York, Mom?"

"Well, maybe. I've got a Pan Am schedule. Let me see what Kelly wants."

"Call my secretary when you're ready. I'll tell her to give you first-class passes wherever you go, but just don't forget to get back in time, and if you're thinking of anywhere overseas, check on visas and let me know."

Smiling, Elizabeth promised to call the next evening, then dialed Ron Lamb's office in Seattle.

He answered on the first ring.

The day had been a constant battle, he told her, with little good news to report. In fact, a new problem had begun to show up in late afternoon. Scores of reservations were evaporating, presumably at the hands of frightened passengers. It wasn't yet a trend, but it had made an otherwise terrible day even worse.

"Maybe I'll have some good news in the morning," she told him.

"Praise the Lord and pass the money," he replied, a tired chuckle in his voice.

"You're showing your southern roots, Ron."

"*Texas* roots, ma'am. That comes from one of our colorful governors, W. Lee "Pass the Biscuits, Pappy" O'Daniel, in 1939."

"Ron, is someone trying to ruin this airline?"

She hadn't planned the question, but it tumbled out suddenly and lay there between them. She heard Ron Lamb clear his throat before replying, "Why . . . do you ask?"

"Suspicions, Ron. Flight Ten, Moses Lake, the FAA actions, the missing files in Brian Murphy's shop . . ." She spun the verbal web of industrial sabotage—a paranoid delusion, to be sure—expecting to hear his easy laugh as he swept it aside.

Instead there was silence.

"Ron?"

"Yeah. Well, I've had the same thoughts, Elizabeth. But who the hell would do such things as a planned campaign? Who? We have no enemies, as far as I know. Unless there's some very sick nut out there, avenging the old Pan Am or something. Flight Ten may be genuine tampering, but the rest of it has to be coincidence."

There was one other call she had been waiting to make, but she hesitated, half dreading it. It was just after 6:00 P.M. in Seattle, and Brian would probably still be at his office, too. She longed to talk to him, but was afraid she'd hear that same cold edge in his voice.

Fatigue was making her foggy. She wobbled into the bedroom, set the alarm for midnight New York time, and decided to take a nap.

Then she would call Brian.

Brian Murphy sat down heavily behind his desk and rubbed his eyes before squinting at the wall clock. It was 9:10 P.M., and the duty to get a decent night's sleep before report time at eleven in the morning was pressuring him almost as much as the hunt for the thief who had stolen the pilot files.

There was no way he wanted to pilot a Boeing 767 to Frankfurt and back in the middle of a crisis, but with nine captains grounded and recertification of their training records still a day away at best, it was either step in and take the flight or let crew scheduling cancel it for lack of 767 pilots, costing the company tens of thousands in revenue and leaving him with yet another black eye.

He hadn't slept much Sunday night, and what little rest he did get was on his office couch.

And Saturday night, of course, had been a red-eyed disaster.

For the umpteenth time he thought of calling Elizabeth and decided to wait a while. What could he say to her anyway that he hadn't already said in the early hours of Sunday morning? He had acted like a spoiled brat, a stupid idiot, and a male chauvinist piglet all rolled into one.

He decided to call and check on Kelly at her grandmother's in Bellingham, glad she didn't know what had happened. Her plans for getting her mother and him to marry were anything but subtle, and, sure enough, two sentences into the conversation, she brought up the subject.

"Okay, I left town so you and Mom could be alone. Have you proposed yet?"

"Kelly! Stop pushing. Things take time."

"I can't wait!" she said, sounding wounded. "I'm growing up! You guys wait any longer, I'll be finished with college and married myself."

"You're fourteen, young lady. Slow down."

He was surprised when Elizabeth's mother joined them on an extension and asked for suggestions on where she and Kelly should fly. Brian hadn't known Kelly would have the better part of a week before she had to be in school.

"Well, look, I have to fly a trip to Frankfurt tomorrow as captain, and I've got a two-day layover there. If we've got seats left on the flight and you've both got your passports, why not come along with me on that one?"

"Frankfurt? I haven't been there in years," Virginia Sterling said. "And don't worry about the passports, Brian. I always keep mine up, and so do Elizabeth and Kelly. Kelly's is right here."

"That's great! We stay in a hotel on the Rhine in Mainz, Germany, not far from the city, and we catch a train to Mainz in the basement of the airport. It's fascinating, and I can show you the area in two days. We'll rent a car and go down the Mosel Valley."

The prospect of playing tour guide in a land he loved made him smile. The Air Force had stationed him at Ramstein Air Base, south of Frankfurt, in 1979, flying F-4 fighters. With his well-established love for languages and an undergraduate major in linguistics, polishing his classroom German to perfection had been a joy. He was somewhat fluent in Spanish, French, and Japanese, so it had been wonderful to immerse himself in another tongue while living in its homeland.

"Sounds wonderful, Brian," Virginia said. "Is that okay with you, Kelly?"

Kelly's voice was not so childish anymore, Brian noticed. She was growing up, and it showed in her more mature tones—if not in her use of a pet name for her grandmother.

"Are you kidding, Nana? I can be packed in ten minutes!"

"Good," Virginia said. "Then, barring a full airplane, it's settled. What time should we be at the airport, Brian? When does the flight leave?"

"At three P.M. I'll call you at nine A.M. tomorrow to coordinate things. Okay?"

"Fine, Brian, thanks. Now I'll give you back to Kelly."

"I can't wait to tell Mom!" Kelly said excitedly before hanging up.

Brian sat back for a moment, thinking about Elizabeth. She would be at her former partner's place in New York tonight, he reminded himself. She had relayed the number of the condo as well as the number of her new cellular phone through her secretary to his secretary. He had kept too busy to call, however, though he knew he was just making excuses. Brian recognized shades of a silly one-upmanship in his refusal to call.

And what difference did it make, anyway? He had nothing to say worth her listening to—nothing that would remove the wedge that had come between them.

Brian realized someone was leaning into the office. The clerical staff had been pressed into late-night service to search for the handwritten proof the FAA was demanding so that they could reconstruct and recertify the missing pilot records, and they had been busily working away for the last five hours. It was Gail, his secretary, who was clutching the doorjamb and regarding him carefully. He came forward in his chair with a smile and nodded as she spoke.

"Captain, I'll think we'll go on home now. We'll be back at it around seven in the morning, if that's okay."

"Absolutely, Gail. Thanks again for staying so late. I'll look in on you around noon, before I head for the airplane."

He heard the office doors close behind her and the others, and heard the new guard they'd hired asking if the chief pilot was still in his office.

Indeed he is, Brian thought.

Brian got to his feet and looked at the yellow legal pad on his desk. He had made some progress in trying to narrow down the field of who the thief could be. At least he had isolated the date the files were taken by backtracking through the computer training records and looking for the last date of entry, which had been done from the primary files.

It had to have been the previous Thursday.

But there were scores of people who could have wandered in and rifled through the file cabinet, and he was at a frustrating impasse without some additional clue.

Brian turned off his office light and pulled on his suit coat as he headed down the carpeted hallway. Pan Am had built a beautiful and comfortable facility for their operations staff, and he was proud of it. Everything was in its place and sparkling . . .

He came to a sudden stop and repeated the thought.

Everything in its place. Suppose everything isn't *in its place.*

He turned and headed back to the scene of the crime—the file room—with the name *Willis* running through his head.

They had two unrelated pilots named Willis, Art and David. Art was a copilot/first officer, while Dave was a captain. Dave Willis's file was one of the ones taken, but something had snagged his memory earlier when he had gone through the files himself.

He had no memory of having seen Art Willis's file either.

Brian spun in the combination on the newly installed file cabinet lock and pulled open the bottom drawer. Each file was color-coded according to crew position: red for captains, blue for first officer/copilots, and green for flight engineers.

He forced himself to slow down as he paged through the folders, stopping in the exact spot where both Willis folders should have been.

Both folders were missing.

He spun around and checked a training computer printout. With copilot Art Willis not scheduled for any recurrent training for several more months, there was no legitimate reason for the folder to be out of the file cabinet. The fact that it was meant the thief had taken both Willis folders!

Brian sat down on the rug with his back to the open file drawer, mentally picking his way through a tantalizing trail of logic that seemed to promise a solution if he could only solve the riddle.

Two files with the same name were missing, and one of them belonged to a copilot. Yet only captains had been cited by the FAA for missing training folders. Why hadn't the FAA complained about Willis the copilot, too? That had to mean that the FAA had checked only the captains' folders when they pulled their inspection, because copilot Willis's folder must have been missing at the same time.

Why? Why would the FAA team not be interested in all *the pilot folders if they had been tipped off that some pilots were illegally trained?*

The answer was quick in coming, and Brian snapped his fingers.

Of course! Because the tipster told them exactly which *captains were deficient, and those are the only ones the feds came in to check.* That's *why they wouldn't have realized that Art Willis's folder was missing too.*

But if the thief had intended to turn in only captains, why did he take Willis the copilot's folder in the first place?

Wait a minute. WAIT a minute!

Brian got to his feet suddenly and turned toward the file cabinet, holding his index finger like a gun, his voice suddenly booming his thoughts into the room.

"What if he *didn't* take the folder? What if he pulled it by mistake, discovered his error, and just stuffed it back in at random?"

He began searching through the folders again, starting with the top cabinet and working back through the alphabet, and in the third drawer— between the *U*'s and the *V*'s—the name Willis suddenly popped into focus.

Brian stood there in disbelief for a second, stunned by the chance it gave him.

"Gotcha, you son of a bitch!"

He dashed to the break room for a paper towel, then gingerly pulled the file out, using the towel to avoid smudging any fingerprints. He opened it the same way, noticing that some of the papers within were upside down.

"Okay, so you're sloppy, too! That probably means you left fingerprints on the papers inside."

There was something else this proved. What? What else?

The color-coded tab on the edge of the folder came into focus as if lighted by a sudden spotlight.

Of course! Anyone who knew this filing system would never have made the mistake of grabbing a copilot's file. The person I'm looking for is not on my office staff, and couldn't be one of the training pilots or instructors.

That was a great relief. The chance that one of his own people had turned renegade had made him sick, especially when he'd caught himself distrusting nearly everyone, Gail included.

Brian carried the folder to his desk, oblivious of the time. It took several calls to roust out the FBI agent assigned to the NTSB investigation at Whidbey Island, and several minutes of explanation to get the man to agree to a late-night meeting.

"Whoever tried to murder our passengers and crew on Flight Ten is probably the same person who took these files, and I think I've got the sumbitch's fingerprints! I need you to lift the prints and run them through your central files in Washington, as well as compare them with our fingerprint files. I know some of our prints will be there too, but the freshest ones will belong to the thief."

Fingerprinting had been required of all Pan Am employees before hiring, including the executive staff. If the culprit was a Pan Am employee, they'd catch him now for sure.

And if the thief wasn't a Pan Am employee, well, at least they'd know.

Brian slid the folder into a larger manila envelope and headed for the door. The FBI agent had agreed to meet him at corporate headquarters in two hours, and he'd already called the personnel manager to get him downtown to open the main personnel files.

Sleep would have to wait.

Tuesday, March 14, morning
New York City

Elizabeth stretched luxuriously and rolled over, fluffing the pillow and nestling her head in it, letting herself be drawn back to a dream
state as the filtered daylight played over her closed eyelids.

Daylight?

She came awake in an instant, her eyes searching the unfamiliar interior of Eric Knox's bedroom for a clock.

The lighted red numbers jumped out at her with accusatory intensity.

It didn't ring. It didn't! I would have heard it!

She rubbed her eyes and looked at the numbers again.

"Dammit!" she hissed. She had set the alarm for midnight to call
Brian. Now it was 8:35 A.M. in New York, 5:35 A.M. in Seattle, and she'd
missed the window.

The call would have to wait.

Elizabeth pulled on a bathrobe and padded to the well-stocked kitchen
to make some coffee and toast, letting her mind spin up to something
resembling normal speed.

I could call Harold Hudgins now. It's late enough.

It was going to be an immense relief to hear him confirm the eighty-
five-million-dollar loan, but she forced herself to sit and enjoy the coffee
before heading for the phone, and by the time she dialed Hudgins's number, she was energized and eager.

At first she didn't recognize the cold, distant voice on the other end.

"Harold?"

"Yes . . .who is this?"

"Elizabeth Sterling."

No reply.

"Pan Am's CFO, remember?"

"Of course. Sorry, it's been a busy morning." There was an apology in his words, but not in his tone.

"You indicated," she began "that you'd be finalizing things yesterday afternoon, so I decided to start the morning out with good news and call you."

Silence again. She could hear him muttering to someone in the background, then turn back to the phone.

"Good news?"

She tried to chuckle against rising apprehension. "I was expecting to get the good news from *you*. In regard to the note."

"Oh. I see," he said. "Well, these things normally take time, as you know, but I *was* able to get to the various lenders yesterday, and I'm afraid they simply weren't interested."

The words fell like a sack of cement at her feet.

"What about your assurances yesterday?" she blurted out in confusion.

Hudgins's voice hardened instantly.

"Now listen, I gave you virtually no assurances of any kind. I made it clear that—"

"Harold," she cut him off, her voice now firm and tinged with anger, "I am not going to have the plug pulled on me without an adequate explanation. Twenty hours ago you clearly indicated this was very close to a done deal. I want to meet at your office in an hour."

"That's not possible, I'm much too busy—"

"Ten or ten-thirty, then, take your pick," she snapped.

There was a lengthy hesitation before he replied.

"Ten o'clock, if you insist."

"I do insist."

"But there's really nothing more to say."

Elizabeth ended the call, realizing she was shaking slightly with a combination of anger and alarm.

She showered quickly and picked out a smart gray silk business suit trimmed in black, one that fit her curves perfectly without being too overtly sexy. Black patent shoes and handbag—along with the sterling silver jewelry that had become her trademark—would give just the right balance. Elizabeth was halfway into her pantyhose when the need to call the other contacts from yesterday's meetings became almost overwhelming.

After all, a voice in her head seemed to be saying, all it'll take is one "yes" and your day is made. We can forget about this strange rejection and go home.

It doesn't work that way, my dear, she sneered at herself. *It's much more complicated and you know it!*

She picked up the phone anyway.

All of the people she'd seen the previous day were in, and all of them were quite clear: Sorry, we can't do it.

Elizabeth replaced the receiver at last and sat for a moment, listening to the roar of Manhattan traffic outside and the ticking of an incredibly expensive Victorian grandfather clock in the entryway.

What in heaven's name am I going to do now? she thought as she finished dressing. An entire day had been wasted, and the deadline came in less than a week. Panic began to rise up again inside her, threatening her ability to think clearly, and she fought to contain it. She had a long list of friends and contacts on her Rolodex who had yet to be called, and she knew Eric would help as well. Silverman, Knox, and Bryson was still Pan Am's investment banking firm. All they really needed by the twentieth of March was a solid letter of intent. With that, she could buy the time from the bondholders for a slightly delayed payment without going into default.

But the first problem on the list was Hudgins. Why the sudden reversal? Why the frostiness?

With a last look in the mirror, Elizabeth grabbed her briefcase and headed out the door. She was already hailing a cab when the phone in Eric's apartment began ringing, activating the answering machine.

Tuesday, March 14, 5:40 A.M.
Seatac Airport

Who the hell is that guy?

The mechanic forgot about his freezing hands and watched the lone figure in coveralls walking with studied nonchalance across the predawn ramp, trying to pinpoint what was bothering him about the man. Everyone at Pan Am had been placed on a state of security alert, or "practiced paranoia," as his lead had dubbed it. Maybe he was overreacting, but he was sure he'd never seen this character before.

The mechanic began walking an intercept course, catching up with the man about fifty yards from Ship 610—the 747 due out on the London flight later in the morning.

"Hey! Hold up there!" He tensed for trouble, and wondered what he'd do if the man took off running.

But the man stopped and turned, looking mildly curious and unruffled.

That's a good sign, at least, the mechanic thought as he came within a few feet of him.

"Could I see your ID, please?"

The man smiled easily and unclipped the blue and white ID card from his lapel, handing it over. The mechanic studied the card and the name, Joseph F. Balkins, looking up to match the mustached face before him with the similar face on the card, though it was difficult to see in the dim lights. The bearer, it said, was with ARA Services, the fuel provider.

"Where's your truck?" the mechanic asked as he handed the ID back.

The man chuckled. "The pickup won't start, and I need the exercise, so I thought I'd just hoof it. Gotta do the morning checks on the hard-stand fuel connectors, you know. New rule."

The mechanic hadn't heard, but then handling the fuel apparatus wasn't his area of expertise. If the guy said they had a new rule, he probably knew what he was talking about. Certainly the ID seemed okay, and suddenly he felt foolish.

"Hey, I'm sorry to stop you. We're just, you know, watching our airplanes a lot closer these days."

"No problem," the man named Balkins replied, flashing a smile. "Sorry if I worried you by walking. I'll just go do my check and get out of your hair."

He thought of strolling along with Balkins and watching as he lifted the heavy cover to the hard-stand fueling connector under the Pan Am 747's wing, but decided it was unnecessary. The mechanic waved goodbye and began walking back toward the terminal. About halfway there, he turned around to check on the fueler's progress beneath Ship 610.

But Balkins had disappeared.

It was near the end of his shift when the mechanic called ARA's foreman to check on Balkins. The answer was totally unexpected.

"He's on a cruise ship in the Caribbean, overeating, chasing his wife, and taking a vacation. Be back next week. Why?"

He told him of the encounter on the ramp, and added a description.

"This guy was a white male about five foot eight, with a mustache and black hair."

"You say he had an ID with a picture that matched that description?"

"Yes," the mechanic replied.

"The ID was fake, then. We better get the police in on this."

"You sure? Maybe your man came back early."

There was a worried laugh from the other end.

"Friend, 'Big Joe' Balkins stands six foot three, weighs over two hundred pounds, is as bald as a billiard ball, and black."

Tuesday, March 14, 9:55 A.M.
New York City

Irwin Fairchild buttoned the top button of his overcoat against the cold air whistling down Manhattan's skyscraper canyons and glanced around cautiously as he pushed through the revolving door.

No one seemed to notice him, and for that he was glad. Fairchild was slight of build, just under five foot six, with deep, sunken eyes submerged in a hawkish, cadaverous face. At a casual glance, he looked merely old and tired. But to anyone who had stared into those menacing eyes over a negotiating table, Irwin Fairchild was a casting director's caricature of the grim reaper, without the robe. The thin lips and sunken cheeks gave him a look of perpetual rage, a barely contained homicidal fury just beneath the surface. There were retired corporate chairmen who swore they had sold out to Fairchild because of the implications of that inhuman stare.

"It was as if," one client had told Elizabeth, "those evil eyes were saying, 'You can either agree to the deal, or be dismembered here and now. I don't really care which.' "

Fairchild's limousine was right where he had instructed his driver to be, and the uniformed man held open the rear door as his boss slid swiftly and expertly onto the plush backseat.

It was never wise to be too visible in public, Fairchild knew. Successful financiers had enemies, and Fairchild realized his were legion.

The limo dropped into gear and began to glide away from the curb before Elizabeth Sterling could force herself to get out of the backseat of her taxi. They had pulled up just behind the limo as Fairchild came through the door, and her stomach had knotted with a range of emotions when she spotted him and watched the coal-eyed bastard move to his car.

A raspy, irritated voice lashed back at her through a small window in the divider between the cab's back and front seats.

"So is this your building or isn't it, lady? I don't got all day!"

This one was a cabby of the old school, Elizabeth realized. She paid him without comment and got out.

She walked briskly into the building and headed straight for the security desk to announce herself. While a lost tourist occupied the guard, Elizabeth let her eyes range over the building directory, assuming Fairchild's company would be listed.

It wasn't.

What was that snake doing here?

"Okay, ma'am, which office?" Having dispatched the tourist to an uncertain fate, the guard turned his attention to Elizabeth, and she found herself responding with a ploy she hadn't planned, the split-second decision made only as she turned to answer the man.

"I'm Mr. Fairchild's assistant, and I need your help. He just sent me back in here with papers that have to be delivered to one of the offices, but I guess I didn't listen well enough to what he said, because I don't see anything here that sounds like the right one."

"You don't know the name?"

"No, and I'm going to be in real trouble. I did this same thing last week, too. He talks awfully fast."

The guard nodded.

"If I can find which office he came from, will that do it for you?"

"Yes. Yes, it will. He was just up there in an important negotiation."

The guard consulted his sign-in book, pulled out another badge, and handed it to her.

"Forty-fifth floor. Just sign my book right here. Bannister Partners is the office. They have the whole floor."

Hudgins's floor. Hudgins's firm!

She decided to press her luck.

"Does it say which partner he was talking to?" she asked.

There was a momentary hesitation, but the guard looked back at his book.

"Yeah. Mr. Hudgins."

She thanked him and found the elevators, got off on the twentieth floor, and found a ladies' room. She had to sit for a minute and think.

Fairchild and Hudgins together. What did that mean? Could it be some other deal they were working on? Was it coincidence? Or could his presence here be connected with the abrupt refusal to set up an emergency loan to Pan Am?

Elizabeth settled quickly on a plan and headed for the elevators again. She got off on the forty-fifth floor and asked for Harold Hudgins.

He left her to cool her heels for twenty minutes. When he came out, there was no friendliness. He didn't show her back to his office until she insisted.

After ten minutes of noncommittal platitudes and denials that he had ever indicated it was a sure thing, Elizabeth got up to go, then turned to Hudgins.

"I saw an old acquaintance on the street when I was coming in a few minutes back. A man named Irwin Fairchild. Are you two acquainted?"

Hudgins's expression didn't change, but he paused.

"No. I mean, we've all heard of Fairchild, but I haven't talked to him."

I didn't ask you that, did I? she thought.

He extended a limp hand, and she ignored it as she left.

She was certain now. Something *was* going on between Hudgins and Fairchild, and whatever it was, it involved Pan Am!

Tuesday, March 14, 7:45 A.M.
Anacortes, Washington

Adrian Kirsch picked up the McDonald's coffee cup again before remembering he'd already emptied it. The small-town restaurant he'd parked in front of was already open for business, but he decided to wait for the NTSB man to arrive. Surely he could last a few more minutes without going into caffeine withdrawal. The local NTSB man was due to join him in fifteen minutes. The interview would be critical and clandestine. At the field-investigator level of the NTSB hierarchy, you didn't talk to the media without risking your career. But with the "go team" already safely back in Washington, Michael Rogers had agreed to take a chance.

Fishing some change out of his pocket, Kirsch walked over to a cigarette machine, stared at it, then put the coins back in his pocket. He was determined to quit without patches or lectures, because he realized the battle was really one of self-control. He unwrapped a sugar-free hard candy and popped it into his mouth instead.

An anonymous caller had rousted him from a deep sleep at 2:00 A.M. "Ask the NTSB about the FBI report on the chromium," the man had said.

"What are you telling me?" Kirsch had asked him through the mental fog.

"The chromium came from a wrench left inside the engine during the last tear-down in Pan Am's maintenance shop, okay? You got the picture?"

"How do you know this? Are you an employee?"

"Not now."

"But you were, weren't you?"

There was a long silence.

Kirsch tried again. "All right, then let me ask you this—you say someone left a wrench in the engine. Could that someone be you?"

"Hell, no! I just know how bad they are."

"Why are you calling me? Why do you want a reporter to know this?"

"Because, Mr. Kirsch, Pan Am's trying to claim they were sabotaged, when it had to be their own sloppy procedures. That's what happens when you treat people like shit. They make bad mistakes. Then the company tries to cover them up. I don't want this one covered up."

"You don't like this airline much, do you?"

"Pan Am's gotta pay for what Pan Am's done."

A sudden suspicion crossed Kirsch's mind. "The Pan Am that you worked for—was that the original version, or the new Pan Am?"

But the caller had already disconnected.

Tuesday, March 14
Off the Washington State coast

Bill Conrad gripped the metal railing of the small, tuglike vessel and tried to concentrate on something other than his stomach. He had never felt seasick on small boats and ferries, but the weird, three-axis motion of the powerful, diesel-powered work boat in heavy seas had almost pushed him over the edge of nausea.

"There they are, Mr. Conrad." The master had materialized beside him now, his index finger pointing the way to the submarine tender holding its position exactly above the remains of Clipper Ten's number-three engine, the morning sun glinting off its glistening hull. Bill Conrad had chartered the salvage submarine and tender out of Vancouver, British Columbia. They were highly recommended and very expensive.

Conrad pulled his heavy coat a bit tighter around his chest, bracing against the stiff, cold wind, and turned to the captain.

"How're they doing?"

"I got 'em by radio a few minutes ago," the captain said. "The sub's in the water and on its way down to around one hundred forty fathoms, or about eight hundred forty feet. It's shallow enough for divers, too."

"I still don't understand how the Navy found it," Bill said.

"Side-scan sonar. They can paint a reasonably good picture down to ten thousand feet with that equipment. You were incredibly lucky they were already working out there."

Bill nodded. The salvage costs were going to hit a hundred thousand dollars, he felt sure, but it would have been much worse if he had been forced to hire a commercial outfit to locate the wreckage first. Discovering a Navy-funded research vessel working for the U.S. Geological Survey within ten miles of the impact point was almost too good to be true.

"What next?" he asked the captain.

"Well, we've got the crane. Once the guys in the sub locate the engine, photograph it, and get the rigging in place, we'll position the line and haul it up. A bit more complicated than that, of course, but that's the basic procedure."

"I certainly hope it's in one big piece."

The man nodded his agreement. "Yeah, be a shame to have to get divers out here after all this expense. But unless it's in a thousand pieces and you want every last one of them, the sub should be enough."

Bill had already faced the possibility of being fired. The corporate firestorm from his foray into the media over the weekend had left him bloodied, threatened, on probation with Jennings and Lamb, and yet determined to see Pan Am's maintenance vindicated.

He thought of Chad Jennings again and quietly shook his head. The man was about as stable as nitroglycerin, and Bill had grown tired of his immature outbursts. He smiled ruefully at the thought of Jennings having to explain the bill for this salvage mission. Jennings had specifically authorized it, though, and Bill had been thinking clearly enough to get the conversation on tape.

"Anything you want to spend, Bill. Just get that engine and let's get the evidence," Jennings had said as he ricocheted down the hall at corporate headquarters, unable to sit still and listen for ten minutes.

His tiny pocket recorder had captured the words loud and clear.

The sound of a radio crackled into life from the captain's communications array as one of the submarine's crewmembers reported back to the tender's bridge.

"We've got it right in front of us now, one huge piece, at least. I can identify a part of a turbine wheel."

Bill caught the captain's attention. "Can he describe the damage?"

Before the captain could respond, the voice came back.

"The basic engine is smashed up rather badly, but the thing that holds it onto the wing—the strut—looks like it was ripped apart by some single-point force. The way the metal's splayed out, it looks like a bomb went off inside the strut."

Bill found himself nodding vigorously.

Tuesday, March 14
New York City

After leaving Hudgins's office in a combination of fury and fright, Elizabeth had gone for coffee in some tiny, nameless café on Madison Avenue.

It was an old habit, a method of regaining control and bringing the forest back into focus, and it was helping immensely now—though she had no intention of spending an hour or more, as she usually did during such mini-retreats.

She pulled her cellular phone out of her briefcase and entered Eric Knox's private office number. She was relieved when he answered, and even more relieved when she heard him shift instantly into his mature, professional mode. Eric was brilliant when it came to problem-solving, but sometimes it took a while to get him to focus.

She told him of the Hudgins debacle, the Fairchild connection, and the universal collapse of all the contacts she had made on Monday.

"Elizabeth, grab a cab and get down here. We need to talk. I know the deadline is the twentieth."

There was something in his voice, something more than a reaction. She knew that sound . . .

"I can be there in about fifteen minutes."

"Please. I've got a few calls to make in the meantime. Otherwise, Pan Am's still our client and I'm clearing the decks to support you."

Eric was just hanging up from a call when Elizabeth walked in, shutting the door behind her, and noticing the grim look on her former partner's face.

"We have a big problem here," he began.

She felt her stomach tighten around a cold void, the old feeling that someone was going to sneer and tell her she was naive, that what she thought she could do was in reality a silly illusion.

"What do you mean?"

Eric was all business.

"Elizabeth, I didn't want to say anything before when you were headed out here, but this last-minute loan for Pan Am was a tough sell from the beginning."

"You said that."

"No . . ." He had his hand up and his eyes cast downward. "No, it's more than that. I kept at this yesterday morning. I knew the people you were going to see, of course, but I've been working the phones looking for additional prospects, and what I didn't tell you over the weekend was that I was almost out of ideas and prospects on Friday. Monday I did run out. Elizabeth, there's someone out there working hard to scare everyone away from lending Pan Am a penny."

"Who?" His words had dovetailed with her earlier paranoid suspicions.

"I'll be damned if I know, but seeing Fairchild may provide a clue."

She shifted slightly on the couch, facing him squarely.

"You mean you've talked to friends of the firm who told you someone's working against Pan Am?"

"No one's said that directly, no. But I know the signs. You do too, if you'll think about it."

She nodded slowly, thinking back over each conversation as he continued.

"Elizabeth, I've seen financial interference and sabotage before, but someone, or some entity, has done an incredible job of anticipating our every move and poisoning the waters—and now I know how."

Eric got up and returned to his desk to pick up a piece of paper that he'd left facedown on the surface. He returned to the couch and sat down again, watching her closely and keeping the front of the paper away from her eyes for the moment.

"Okay, you're the First National Bank, and I walk in some fifteen minutes before Pan Am's Elizabeth Sterling has an appointment, and I say, 'Pan Am's gonna hit you up for a loan and represent everything's all right, but before you decide you'd better look at this.' Then I lay this little number in front of you."

The paper had been faxed. It was an FAA internal memo sent from the FAA general counsel to the FAA administrator, and it gave a legal opinion on the consequences of terminating the operating certificate of Pan Am. It was, the memo concluded, a drastic step, but it could be done.

Strategically missing was any discussion of what had prompted the memo, or whether the shutdown and utter ruination of Pan Am II was seriously being considered at FAA headquarters.

"*This* is what I'm fighting?"

Eric nodded. "Apparently. Our old friend at Jones and Hammersby, Lou Higginbotham, gave me a curt 'not interested' yesterday afternoon. I saved Lou's ass when Boesky was trying to seduce him. He owes me big time, and I pinned his ears back."

"And he sent you this?"

"Yeah. Said it had chattered off his fax machine Monday morning under a cover note indicating that mere possession of it could be a legal problem."

"Who sent it?"

"He honestly didn't know. The machine it came from indicated it was government property, but the number had been omitted."

"And he *believed* it? Lou believed this piece of trash?"

"Not at first. But he had one of his people in D.C. check it out with a high contact at FAA, and, Elizabeth, that memo is real."

"Still, that's little more than a poison-pen letter—a poison-pen fax in this case," she sputtered. "He's far more sophisticated than that."

Eric was nodding vigorously. "Yes, he is, and he wasn't convinced until he got an angry call from one of the FAA's lawyers demanding to know where he got that memo. *That's* what convinced him. Even Lou couldn't loan you money after that."

Elizabeth sat back and let her body sink into the soft leather, her eyes staring vacantly ahead, somewhere over the desk.

"My God, Eric, we're dead."

"Hey"—he sat up suddenly and leaned toward her—"this doesn't mean they're going to shut you down, it's merely an opinion that they *could*. They've announced a fine instead."

"But as you said, no one here will lend us money, and without the money, we're in default as of the twenty-first, and without a fleet of airplanes by the twenty-second."

"That's the key, Elizabeth."

She turned to him, her heart pounding. "What? What's the key?"

"You used the word 'here.' You said 'no one here.' Well, maybe not here, but New York isn't the only place to borrow money. We have no reason to believe that whoever did this has poisoned the London market, or Tokyo, for that matter."

"Tokyo's impossible to deal with on a tight schedule."

"Yeah, but London isn't, and that's where you should head immediately. *But*—you'll have to do it clandestinely, and that means not even your office should know."

"Why on earth?"

"Elizabeth, you've got to realize that someone's been tracking you."

That shocked her all over again, and she searched Eric's eyes for meaning without speaking. He sensed her confusion.

"Someone knew you were headed to New York, Elizabeth."

Eric got to his feet and began pacing between the couch and the desk.

"Do you really know your new secretary?" he continued. "Do you really know your assistant?"

She shook her head silently.

"Okay, then can you backtrack and figure out who could have overheard us speaking on the phone over the weekend, or who could have handled or seen or intercepted the list I left you of who to call Monday?"

He saw her head begin to move up and down in affirmation, slowly, as her mind raced through the possibilities.

"I think I can do that, but I'll have to think it through with surgical care," she told him.

Eric stopped suddenly. "You didn't fax that list anywhere, did you?"

"No. And I didn't copy it. I only have the one copy you left for me, next to the champagne bottle. And by the way, thank you. That was sweet."

Eric's head snapped up suddenly, his gaze locking onto Elizabeth, and his tone one of amazement.

"*Where* did you say?"

"On the nightstand, right beside the champagne bottle you left. Why?"

The look on his face alarmed her.

"Beside? Not *under* the bottle, but *beside* it? Are you sure?"

"Yes . . . why?" She was puzzled and slightly irritated. What did it matter where on the nightstand the papers were?

Eric stepped back slightly and balanced himself against the desk as he looked at her with alarm.

"Elizabeth, I didn't leave those papers beside that champagne bottle. I left them *under* the bottle, weighted down by it, so you couldn't miss them."

The two of them had fallen virtually silent, their eyes meeting in the frightening recognition that someone else had been in the condo.

"Eric, this scares me," she said at last.

"Me too."

"I mean, we've seen industrial espionage before, but this . . ."

"That proves it, as far as I'm concerned. Someone's been tapping your phones and possibly tailing you. Okay." He leaned against the edge of his desk then. "Here's what I recommend. You need to get to London. Do you have your passport with you?"

"Yes. Always."

"Good. First, though, there's someone I want you to see, someone I know is reliable."

"Who? Lou Higginbotham?"

"No, a fellow named Lloyd White, with Lloyds of London. He's based here in New York."

She raised one eyebrow, and he raised the palm of his hand. "I know, Lloyd takes a lot of kidding about his name, now that he's doing underwriting for his namesake. But he was in the investment banking business over there, and can be very helpful in steering you to the right people in short order."

"Suppose 'they' have poisoned him, too?"

"Unless they're taping this very conversation, no way. You don't know him, and this is the first time I've spoken his name out loud. *And*"— he held his index finger aloft—"I still have this office swept for bugs every week, an outgrowth of the Eastern Airlines thing a few years back."

"Then what? I was going to get on the phones and start calling anyone else on my lists here who hadn't already told me to take a hike."

"Useless. Whoever we're fighting is too slick. I doubt there's a bank or investment house in town that hasn't received that faxed memo."

"So now what?"

"We get you out of here without being seen, and on the way to London. I'll arrange the ticket under another name."

The meeting with Lloyd White was arranged quickly. They would meet at the Players Club, in Gramercy Park. Elizabeth let herself be driven from the basement garage of the building in the firm's limousine, the dark windows ensuring that anyone stalking her would have no chance of seeing her go by. On the way, she used the portable phone to make a reservation on United from La Guardia back to Seattle as a smokescreen, while Eric worked on getting her out in the opposite direction.

Lloyd White was waiting for her at a table near the back of the grand old club. His father, he explained, had been a well-known British actor whose American friends had insisted on bringing him to Broadway for a one-month run in the 1930s. The membership in the Players Club had been a part of that welcome. Maintaining it had become a family tradition since—though he had never been professionally involved in the arts himself.

In his early sixties with an angular face set off by a full head of white hair, White had a patrician charm about him and an easy, if tired, smile. Elizabeth found herself liking him instantly.

"Eric has explained the situation," he told her, "and I think I can help. I understand security is necessary, so I will treat this as completely confidential." He handed her a lengthy list of financial firms and houses in London, four of them circled in red, and one starred.

"You'll no doubt be somewhat startled to find that the chap I want to steer you to first is at my own Lloyds of London, on the main floor. Alastair Wood is his name, from Brighton. A common chap, really, with the heart of a shark, and very young at twenty-nine, but the best financier I've come across in the U.K. in many years."

"What's he doing in Lloyds, then?"

Lloyd White lifted his head a bit and laughed softly. "Moonlighting, I truly think. So happens he enjoys underwriting as head of a syndicate more than he likes banking and investments, and Elizabeth—if I may call you Elizabeth . . ."

"I'd be crushed if you didn't."

"That's gracious of you, thank you. Elizabeth, he's the best off-the-cuff dealmaker around. He's got the cunning of a Fagin, though he's thoroughly honest. But if he likes the depth of the challenge, he'll figure out a way to do the deal."

They talked strategy for nearly an hour before White reached into his pocket and produced a small notebook. He unscrewed a fountain pen and opened it to a blank page.

"Now . . . there's one other thing you should do, Elizabeth. There is a chap up in Scotland who used to be one of Sir Freddy Laker's executives when Laker Airlines was alive. He left and started his own airline in the Midlands, and was roundly hated by the major European carriers and everyone else who believes in monopolies. Eventually they ran him out of business—forced him to sell, really—by a campaign that bears a striking resemblance to what you're going through over here."

"You mean someone was interfering with his corporate borrowing?"

"No, I mean he and his little airline were subjected to a full-blown campaign of economic destruction. It took him eight years in the courts to win a massive lawsuit against the culprits, but win he did. He's sitting up there near Inverness now with more money than he can ever spend, but he's still bitter, and what he learned the hard way about how such campaigns operate might help your company.''

White tore the page out and handed it to her.

''Thank you very much,'' she said, examining the name.

''A bit of a warning, though.''

''Sure.''

''The old boy's as sour as a lemon drop and has a peculiar attitude toward women.''

''You mean he's gay?'' she asked with an amused smile.

Lloyd White looked for a split second as if he'd been struck. He threw his head back and roared with laughter until Elizabeth was laughing too.

''What?'' Elizabeth managed, smiling but puzzled.

''Well, you see ... ah ... I'm frightfully sorry, but ... the very thought of Craig MacRae chasing after anything but females is a hilarious image.'' He wiped an eye with his napkin and shook his head again. ''No, dear girl, watch yourself around Laird MacRae. He's a raging chauvinist heterosexual who believes a woman's place is in the kitchen and the bedroom, not the boardroom.''

''He certainly won't like me, then!'' she said, smiling.

''Depends entirely on the context. In regard to your role as a female executive, he'll be outraged and hostile. In regard to your charms as a woman, he'll be intrigued and challenged.'' He winked at her as he got to his feet. ''But by all means ring him up. The advice will be worth it to you and your company, I promise—though I'd wager you'll have to go see him. He rarely leaves his Highlands estate these days, and it's certainly not likely he'd leave it for a wee lass, if you understand my meaning.''

♦ ♦ ♦

Elizabeth found the limo waiting to take her to Eric's condo to get her things. It felt different this time, as if the realization that it had been penetrated by someone else made it feel dirty and contaminated.

She was ready to close the door behind her when the sight of a blinking message light on the answering machine registered.

It was the voice of Virginia Sterling.

''Elizabeth, I hope this is the right number, because that sounds like

Eric Knox's voice on the message. Anyway, Kelly and I are going to Europe on Brian's Pan Am flight this afternoon for two days. We'll be back late Friday night. Your secretary has the schedule. Take care, honey, and good luck. I'll call you when we get back to Bellingham.''

Eric loved logistics and planning details of trips, and he had exceeded himself this time. The driver took Elizabeth directly to La Guardia, where she bought her decoy ticket on United before being met by an airport security officer who quietly escorted her through back rooms and a maze of corridors to a waiting car, which in turn took her to Eric's helicopter in the same spot where he had met her before. In fifteen minutes they were approaching JFK, and within an hour she was sitting in the upper first-class section of a 747 just getting ready to push back for London.

"Don't fly Pan Am," Eric had warned her. "Whoever's been watching you may be on the inside in Seattle. They may have the computer programmed to look for your name in the reservations or passenger lists.''

"How about British Airways?''

"A competitor. Good. But use only the initial *L* for your first name, and have them misspell Sterling with two *r*'s or something. If their computer's looking for 'Sterling,' it won't find you.''

"I could be seen at JFK, you know," she said.

"True. You won't be invisible or undetectable, the way I'll get you out there," Eric told her, "but unless they have an army following you, or someone slipped a homing device in your bra, they'll be looking for you back in Seattle this evening instead of in London.''

She had kissed him before getting out of the Jet Ranger at JFK, a tender kiss, full on the lips. There was nothing but a thank-you involved, and he knew it, but he well understood the significance of the gesture.

In all their years of partnership, that had never happened before.

Tuesday, March 14
Mount Vernon, Washington

Adrian Kirsch had all but taken up residence in the back alcove of the Farmhouse Restaurant where the pay phones were located. The restaurant sat on the main highway to Anacortes, and in the midst of tulip country—a verdant river bottom of rich farmland that exploded each spring in a rainbow of colors when the flower fields came in bloom. With a deadline looming, there was no time to drive back to his Seattle newsroom to do the research.

The fact that their pies were incredibly good didn't enter into the decision—or so he told himself. After all, he was still on a diet.

The NTSB's field man had been some help in Anacortes, but not much. Michael Rogers claimed he didn't have a copy of the FBI lab report. Neither could he confirm their exact metallurgical findings other than to say that yes, chromium was found on the fragment taken from the underside of the right wing of Pan Am Clipper Ten, just above the area where number-three engine had fragmented—or "scattered," in his terminology.

But when it came to an on-the-record quote about where chromium could or could not be found on a 747, Rogers kept his mouth shut tight.

So had the FBI agent in charge of the investigation, whom Adrian had reached by phone. The agent had been downright hostile, and not even Adrian's threat to use a Freedom of Information Act request to break loose a copy of the lab report had impressed him.

He hadn't told Rogers about the anonymous call at first—not until he could squeeze out anything Rogers would tell him. But he had to turn over the information. He wasn't a lawyer, but he was damned nervous about sitting on such an accusation as a wrench in the engine. When he was sure Rogers had said as much as he was going to, Adrian told him the details of the call.

Amazingly, Rogers had feigned disinterest.

"We get a lot of tips," he'd said, "and that one's unique, but it was probably a crackpot."

Logic had guided him from there. The anonymous tipster who had rousted him out of bed had said that the chromium came from a wrench left in the engine. If there was virtually no other way chromium could have normally been in or around a 747 engine, then the presence of the stuff would tend to validate the possibility. At least it would indicate that something foreign to the engine—including a wrench—had been inside when it exploded.

He'd spent a solid two hours on the pay phones hunting down metallurgical experts, a former FBI agent, two jet engine mechanics, a tool and die company, and several others. At last he felt he had enough confirmation.

At 11:00 A.M., having missed two of the four daily deadlines for the afternoon paper, he called his editor—who decided to go with the story.

By midafternoon the story was gaining nationwide attention and moving on the news wires, alerting the public to the possibility that there was something more to the drama of Clipper Ten than the NTSB, the FBI, or Pan Am had yet admitted. By late afternoon the story had become the lead on the three major national networks.

Tuesday, March 14, 3:30 P.M.
Pan Am Operations, Seatac Airport

Captain Dale Silverman was beat. The flight in from New York was the last one he was scheduled to fly for a week, and he was more than ready for a rest as he put his flight bag in his assigned locker in the Seattle pilot lounge and remembered that he had one more duty to perform.

There was a mechanic in Denver who needed some talking to.

Brian Murphy's office was just down the corridor of the operations center, and he headed that way now, smiling at several people he knew along the way.

He'd thought about the situation all weekend and into Monday. He had fully expected to see an entry in the logbook Saturday morning when he and his crew had returned to their Boeing 767 at Denver's airport for the live charter flight back to Seattle. After all, he had seen the mechanic and his tool kit on the flight deck the night before, along with a couple of rack-mounted electronic boxes he assumed were to be swapped with their counterparts in the electronics bay beneath the cockpit.

But there was nothing in the aircraft's maintenance log, and the operations supervisor claimed no work had been done.

It could be nothing, but just in case something had been done and not documented, the mechanic had to be confronted.

Brian Murphy's secretary was at her desk, and recognized him immediately.

"Dale! How're you doing, Captain-san?"

"Gail!" he responded in a feigned Texas drawl, "Ah'm jes' fine, ma'am, high yew? Is the head birdman in?"

She shook her head. "Nope. The head birdman has gone off to commit an act of aviation, this time to Frankfurt. He took off about thirty minutes ago."

"Oh." He looked nonplussed.

"Something I can do?" she asked.

He could tell her the story, knowing she was quite competent to find the right people to deal with it in Brian's absence. But there was something unsettling about the whole thing that only a fellow captain would fully understand. Gail might think it trivial.

"That's okay. It'll wait. Probably nothing, anyway."

He waved goodbye and headed for the parking lot, making a mental note to drop in on Brian next week.

There was plenty of time.

16

There it was again.

Brian Murphy stared at the screen that covered the forward center instrument panel and waited. The computer-driven engine instrument displays had flickered a second time, all the information scrambling for a few seconds before returning to normal.

He leaned closer now, his eyes challenging the CRT screen to repeat the episode as he leveled an index finger at the engine readouts and addressed the copilot.

"Tyson, did you see that?"

First officer Tyson Matthews followed the captain's finger to the engine-monitoring portion of the Boeing 767's "glass" cockpit.

"What's the problem?" he asked.

"All the engine displays turned to garbage for a split second, then recovered."

Tyson shook his head. He hadn't seen it.

Brian's gaze remained on the panel, though he had to fight the urge to rub his eyes. *I'm fatigued!* he admitted to himself. It had been nearly 2:00 A.M. before his head had hit the pillow after combing through the Pan Am personnel files. He had been determined to provide the FBI agent with all the fingerprint files for those with authorized access to Pan Am pilot records. Now, any other prints the FBI lab might find on First Officer Willis's folder would have to belong to the thief. Brian had left instructions with Gail to call him anywhere, anytime, when the FBI agent reported back with results. His hopes were high that they were closing in on the bastard.

Brian refocused his attention on the center panel. There were three main displays, two of them identical flight instrument displays for the pilot and copilot respectively, and the center screen. The engine readout displays on the center screen remained mockingly normal, but he could feel himself getting edgy and apprehensive. Forty-one thousand feet below them now was land—but it was wilderness—whose barren, frigid nature had always made him uneasy. He was more comfortable flying over the middle of the ocean.

Brian thought suddenly of Kelly and her mother, back in Compartment Class, and a feeling of immense guilt rolled over him. He had enticed them into coming along—the three most important people in Elizabeth's life on the same airplane!

Without a whisper of warning, the engine display screen exploded in gibberish again, this time in a kaleidoscopic burst of symbols and lines that went rippling across the CRT's face with the intensity of a silent explosion. Again, just as abruptly, it returned to normal—leaving both pilots stunned.

"I sure as hell saw *that*!" Tyson said, snapping forward in his seat. "What on *earth*?"

"I don't know. I've seen transient warnings before, but never an in-flight psychedelic display like that."

Tyson looked down at the flight computer to double-check their position. "We're just above seventy degrees north right now, north of Hudson Bay," he told the captain.

Brian chuckled out loud. "And if we decided to pop in somewhere and have maintenance take a look at this, which way would we head, Tyson?"

"About a thousand miles in any direction but north."

"You got that right."

The sound of a warning chime resonated through his head, sending a small chill down his back.

What now?

On the forward CRT screen, a computer-generated message—

RIGHT ENGINE THRUST REVERSER NOT LOCKED

—suddenly appeared.

"Tyson, you see anything on the right side?" Brian asked.

The copilot had already whipped his head to the right window. Now he looked back at Brian.

"No, I don't. I don't feel anything, either, at least nothing that would suggest we've had a reverser come out."

"Lord! I think this is how the Lauda 767 accident sequence started," Brian said, motoring his seat forward a few inches. He rested his feet on the rudder pedals just in case, mentally running through the procedure for recovering from an unusual attitude—the sort of high-speed dive a suddenly opened thrust reverser could cause in flight in a 767.

Then, as quickly as it had illuminated, the thrust-reverser warning light went out on its own.

Brian scanned the engine panel again and looked at the flight instruments. Everything seemed to have returned to routine readouts—but both pilots were now adrenalized and on full alert.

Yet another master annunciator warning chime sounded as the screen flashed a fuel icing warning.

In several seconds that, too, was gone.

"Jesus Christ, Brian! What is this? A simulator ride?

"Look at that!" Tyson pointed to the engine gauge display when it flashed back on for a few seconds between malfunction messages. The engine instruments—displayed as small colored round dials on the computer screen—were also showing strange readings. Every thirty seconds or so the scrambled data they had seen before would return in an artful burble of colors.

"Is there a circuit breaker that could explain this?" Brian asked.

The copilot began searching the breaker panels and shaking his head. "I haven't got a clue what's going on. It almost looks like we've got some sort of weird short in the symbol generator."

"Yeah," Brian replied, "but there's nothing wrong with the other displays. The flight instruments are steady on both sides."

"I don't know, boss, but it's probably not dangerous. We'll want to get the system fixed in Frankfurt, though."

Brian started to agree, but the raucous sound of an engine fire warning bell rang through the cockpit at the same moment. Brian's full attention snapped to the annunciator panel. Number-one engine on the left side, according to the indications, was burning.

Tyson silenced the fire alarm as Brian looked to the left, pressing his nose against the side window glass in an effort to see the engine.

"I see nothing out here," he said.

"You want to run the engine-fire checklist, or wait?" Tyson asked as Brian turned back to the center panel.

"I think I'd better have you run back to the cabin and look the engine over. I don't believe it's on fire. Not with all the weird indications."

Tyson was already in motion, the seatbelt flying away from his lap as he released it and headed for the cockpit door.

The number-two-engine fire warning came on as the copilot's hand touched the cockpit door knob.

"Jesus!" Tyson jumped with alarm as he looked back up front and watched Brian cancel the audible warning. Bright red lights were now glowing in both fire handles.

"Now I know this is a false alarm!" Brian said over his shoulder. "But go ahead and check the right engine too."

The door closed behind Tyson, and Brian picked up the radio microphone in a reflexive reaction.

"Iqaluit, Clipper four-zero."

Brian looked at the microphone as if it had suddenly materialized in his hand.

Now why did I do that?

"Go ahead, four-zero," the controller answered.

So what do I say to you, Iqaluit? Things have gotten strange up here and I just wanted to hear a friendly voice?

"Ah . . . just checking to see if you were still there, Iqaluit," Brian said.

A light Canadian accent colored the controller's words as he gave a cheery reply.

"Yep, we're here all right, Clipper. You're level, then, at flight level four-one-zero, eh?"

"That's right, sir."

"Okay, then."

Tyson was back through the cockpit door and strapping into the right-hand seat again in less than two minutes.

"Nothing. No glow, no indication of any trouble on either engine."

The engine fire lights remained on, shining like giant red beacons, telling them the big lie that both engines were burning.

But the main engine instrument panel had returned to normal for the moment.

"Okay," Brian began, "what do we have here?"

At the same instant, both fire lights extinguished simultaneously—almost as if some unseen hand had flipped off two switches somewhere down in the electronics compartment, one deck below.

Two minutes passed without a flicker, then the center screen suddenly went dead, and both pilots began to feel something new and disturbing.

Brian looked at the throttles in alarm. They hadn't moved. He looked for the engine indications instinctively, but there were none. His eyes moved then, in an instant of alarm, to the instrument panel, which confirmed what they were feeling: they were slowing down.

In the background noise of the slipstream, he thought he had heard the sound of turbines winding down the scale. Tyson Matthews reached the same conclusion simultaneously.

"We've lost an engine," the copilot said.

Brian's right hand gathered the throttles and shoved them forward as far as they'd go.

There was no response.

"My God, we've lost both of them!" Brian said, his heart racing. "Emergency restart . . . airstart 'em!"

Tyson grabbed for the overhead switches to fire the ignition plugs in both engines in the hope of restarting quickly.

"I don't have any engine information . . . I don't know what we've got!" Tyson exclaimed, looking at the blank engine instrument display.

Brian was watching the airspeed decay. "I'm . . . ah . . . gonna set up a glide here. Around two hundred twenty knots, I think."

Tyson nodded as Brian fought to stay focused, disconnecting the autopilot and lowering the nose to stabilize the airspeed, as the rate-of-climb indicator began a slow descent to the fifteen-hundred-foot-per-minute indication.

Tyson was hanging on both restart switches. "Nothing, Brian. We're getting nothing!"

"Any popped breakers anywhere?"

"I looked. I don't think so."

"I'm gonna deploy the RAT." Brian reached for the lever that dropped a small propeller into the airstream. The ram air turbine would give them electrical power and even hydraulic power if everything else failed.

"I'm gonna start the APU too." Brian's hand shot to the upper panel and toggled the auxiliary power unit in the tail into the start mode, and within a minute there was a steady run indication from the diminutive jet engine. He flipped the appropriate switches to bring it on line in order to power the electrical system and the air-conditioning and pressurization systems.

"Okay, we have electrical, hydraulic, flight controls, and cabin pressure. Now we need engines," Brian said.

"Brian, we're coming through thirty-nine thousand. If anything's happening out there, I don't feel it."

"Are we in the start envelope . . . yeah, yeah, we are." Brian said, checking the airspeed. They had to keep the airplane moving in a certain speed range for an airstart of the two huge turbofan engines, but the speed checked good.

"Keep trying," Brian added. "The problem may be our altitude. It may fire off when we get a little lower."

Tyson's voice was strained and climbing slightly with alarm. "And if not? What then, Brian?"

Good point. We need help.

Brian yanked up the microphone. "Ah ... I'd better let them know what's happening. Keep working on the restart. I'll fly the airplane and talk to Iqaluit."

Brian depressed the transmit button.

"Iqaluit radio ... ah ... Clipper four-zero. We've lost both engines and are now descending, ah, through flight level three-eight-five. If there's an emergency airfield somewhere within a hundred miles, please give us an immediate vector. We're trying to restart now ..." He let up on the button, then remembered the transponder. They should be squawking the emergency code of 7700, though they would be out of radar contact. He reached over and dialed it in.

Brian glanced at Tyson, noting the flared eyebrows and the look of barely contained fright and utter frustration on his face as he met Brian's gaze.

"Nothing. *Nothing*, dammit!" the copilot snapped. "It's not happening, Brian!"

"Don't give up!"

The radio crackled in their ear with a startled operator on the other end, his voice suddenly intense and concerned, his vocal pace doubled from before.

"Clipper four-zero, roger, copy your emergency. The nearest usable airfield is over three hundred miles from your position. I recommend a heading now of zero-nine-five degrees magnetic. You're a two-engine 767, is that correct?"

"That's right, Iqaluit. And they're both flamed out and are not restarting. We may need to think about an emergency landing."

Brian thought about the first conclusion anyone below might reach, and decided to squelch it. "And, Iqaluit, for the record, we have plenty of fuel and good fuel pumps."

"Brian? We need to let the cabin ... the passengers ... know," Tyson said, inclining his head toward the rear bulkhead as he kept his eyes on the blank engine instrument screen.

Brian nodded as he scooped up the interphone handset and punched in the appropriate code. The response was nearly instantaneous from the lead flight attendant, who had been in the process of calling the cockpit.

"What's up, boys? Why are we descending?" Her feminine voice registered in Brian's ear, reminding him for a second of Elizabeth. He banished the thought and cleared his throat, which was tight with apprehension.

"We . . . ah . . . we've got a double engine flameout. We're working on a restart now, but—"

"No *engines*? Are you telling me we're *going down*?"

He realized he was nodding into the phone, and found his voice.

"We'll probably get them restarted when we get lower, but for now, get the cabin ready for an emergency landing. Immediately! Worst case, we'll have fifteen minutes."

"Oh God! Where are we? Is there an airfield?"

"Jan . . . Jan, just get busy. We'll do our best."

The line clicked dead. He picked up the PA microphone then, and looked at Tyson with a question in his eyes. If just one engine could be brought back on line, it wouldn't be necessary to scare the passengers.

Tyson shook his head angrily in the negative.

"Folks, this is the captain. I'll be very frank. We have a very serious problem, and it may be necessary to make an emergency landing. I've instructed the flight attendants to get you and the cabin ready. Please cooperate immediately. We're very busy up here."

That was enough. Brian snapped the microphone off and adjusted his descent rate to increase the speed a bit. The urge to pull back on the yoke and stop the descent was powerful, but without engine power it would be a futile gesture.

"We're through thirty-six thousand and they're not starting, Brian. We're gonna have to think of something fast. There's nothing down there." Tyson pointed down.

"Okay. Give it a rest for two minutes." He waved at the overhead airstart switches. "Let's . . . let's think options."

"We don't get one of these suckers started, we *have* no options!" Tyson said.

"Clipper four-zero, Iqaluit, say fuel and souls on board." The operator was only following the rules, but the copilot was in no mood to be interrupted. Before Brian could answer, he had pulled his own microphone to his face.

"Stand by, Iqaluit, stand by . . . we'll get you in a minute!"

Brian took a deep, if somewhat ragged, breath. It was all on the line now. "Okay, if we get restarted, we go to the nearest Canadian base and land. To that end, we need to think through what we're trying. Are we missing something?"

"And if we don't get restarted?" Tyson asked, his eyes flaring wide.

"Then let's face it. We'll have to land on whatever flat spot we can find below, with gear down, and pray we can do it."

"What's below us, Brian?" the copilot asked. Brian started to grab the map, then remembered the radio.

"Iqaluit Radio, Clipper four-zero. Still zero engines. We need your help. What's ahead of us about eighty miles? Are there any flat areas? I don't have time to read the map and fly, too."

The tense but reassuring voice of the Canadian operator came back almost immediately.

"We've been looking at that for you, sir. The terrain's pretty flat the way you're headed, but if you have to put it down somewhere, you'll want a lake, not open ocean ice."

"What's the weather below us?"

"Our remote station closest to the position is reporting winds out of the west at twenty knots, a solid overcast at one thousand meters, or around three thousand feet, and temperature in Fahrenheit is, uh, minus forty-eight."

"Can you vector us to a big lake? I assume they're all frozen?"

"Clipper four-zero, they're all frozen solid, and we have no radar here. Ah, we're looking at maps. Stand by."

Brian could hear a buzz of voices behind the operator as he let up on his transmit switch.

There was no point in looking at Tyson. The frustration—the helpless feeling—was eating the copilot alive. He was willing the engines to start, but nothing was happening.

They were below twenty-six thousand feet now, coming down at around fifteen hundred feet per minute. Brian calculated seventeen minutes and ninety miles left before they'd be out of options.

"Ah, Clipper four-zero, Iqaluit radio."

"Go ahead."

"Sir, ah, how many more miles can you stay airborne without power?"

Brian told him the calculations.

"Okay, we're doing you no good with this heading. It's taking you toward open ice pack, and you'd still be two hundred miles from the nearest runway, and that's no good. I suggest we turn you back west, to a heading of two-seven-zero degrees. We think you can find an area of many good-sized lakes, and you can pick which one you want when you break out.

Brian had already started turning back to the west as the operator spoke.

"Roger. We've got inertial navigation systems, Iqaluit. We'll give you our final position and heading just before … before we … land." The word was hard to get out. He hoped it would be a landing. He had to believe it would be a landing, and not something less controlled.

Another rush of epithets came from the right seat as Tyson gave up on the right engine and began working on restarting the left. He was holding on to the switches with one hand and banging on the darkened engine display screen with the other before reaching down to cycle the engine fuel control switches off and on one more time.

Brian rolled out of the turn and stabilized on a heading of 270 degrees as he turned to the copilot.

"We need to talk about how to handle this."

"I know it," Tyson replied rapidly. "I heard that weather. We've got nighttime and no moonlight below the overcast, and less than three thousand feet to pick a landing spot."

"Okay … okay, so we're going to need as much speed coming down through the cloud deck as we can get, and we're going to need the landing lights," Brian added.

"We've got good hydraulics," Tyson said. "We should hold off extending the landing gear and flaps until we've decided … you know … where to go in."

Brian nodded. "I know the gear's going to take about fifteen seconds, and the flaps maybe a minute. We'll be moving at three miles per minute, and our lights aren't going to show up anything on the ground until we're within a mile and probably three hundred feet."

"Goddammit, Brian, there's a full moon up here tonight. Why the hell do we have to do this with an overcast? We need that light."

The question was serious and pained, but Brian found himself almost laughing.

"Yeah, next time we do this we'll have to plan it better," he replied, but Tyson was totally focused on the restart attempts and the humor was lost.

"Okay," Brian continued, "if we're lucky enough to get a semi-flat surface, the brakes might work, but if not, I should probably aerobrake and treat it like a soft-field landing . . . you know, keep the nose up as long as possible.''

He could see Tyson nodding his head on the right.

''We're descending through twenty thousand feet, Brian. We'd better get our lights down . . . get our night vision up. We should be breathing pure oxygen, too, just before . . . you know.''

Brian nodded and began lowering the already subdued cockpit lights.

There was a knock on the door, and Brian punched the electrical unlock button on the overhead panel to admit Jan, the lead flight attendant. He looked over his shoulder at her, aware of the drained and fearful look on her face.

''What . . . what's our situation?'' she asked.

Brian shook his head from side to side. ''We aren't having any luck getting them started.''

''Are we out of fuel? Did we run out?''

''No. Something's wrong with the electronics.''

''So . . . we're going to land . . . where?''

Brian looked her in the eye. ''I won't mislead you, Jan. There's no airport out here, only frozen terrain and frozen lakes. We're going to try our best to find a lake. It could be rough. Very rough.''

She nodded stoically and took a deep breath. ''You'll remember to give us a PA warning to brace?''

''I promise,'' Brian told her.

She started to turn to go, then turned back. ''Oh, the woman and the young lady in compartment one who're friends of yours?''

''Yes?'' Brian felt his blood run cold at the reminder of whose lives were in his hands.

''The young lady says, 'Thumbs up,' and she loves you.''

''Tell . . .'' He had to clear his throat. Emotion had welled up and choked off the reply. ''Tell her . . . I love her too . . . and thumbs up.''

Jan closed the door behind her and disappeared into the cabin as the phrase rattled around Brian's head. How many times he'd used that to buck up Kelly when she thought she was facing some insurmountable hurdle. ''Thumbs up, young lady! Only 'can-do' attitudes permitted around here.''

Tyson's tired hands dropped from the overhead switches into his lap as he shook his head. The anger had disappeared, and he looked genuinely anguished. ''It's not gonna happen, Brian. We're out of options.'' He glanced at the altimeter. They were coming through fifteen thousand feet.

The moonlight glinted from the upper deck of the overcast below, and it was obvious they were only a few thousand feet from entering it.

"Okay, make a last check with Iqaluit. Give our position," Brian commanded. Tyson grabbed the microphone to comply.

Brian watched the ghostly shape of the undercast rising to gobble them, and lofted a small prayer.

Dear God, please help me do this! Please help us do this! Let Kelly get out of this okay.

"Okay. He's been told. Rescue forces are already launching, he said." Tyson replaced the microphone and reached to the engine airstart switches for one final try.

They were into the clouds now.

"I hope the weather report was right," Brian said.

Tyson checked the extremely accurate radio altimeter. It showed them now at eleven thousand feet above the surface.

"Tyson, I'm going to accelerate to three hundred knots by five thousand above the surface and hold it until at least two thousand, and probably all the way down, depending on when we can see anything. What do you think?"

"Okay," he said. "Sounds okay. You fly and I'll look. We need to get these lights down. Time for oxygen."

Tyson pulled his mask from its compartment and put it on. Oxygen increased the effectiveness of night vision, and Brian turned to do the same.

The sound of the slipstream increased now as Brian pushed the nose over and let gravity accelerate them to three hundred knots. Almost all the cockpit lights were down to absolute minimum, but there was still nothing to see except dark gray outside the windscreen.

Brian picked up the PA microphone.

"Okay, folks, everyone in the brace position."

They descended through five thousand at 310 knots, then four thousand, with no hint of a breakout.

"They said three thousand, right?" Brian asked.

"That's what they said," Tyson responded. Whether Brian had also heard Iqaluit's concern about the Arctic storm system moving into the area, he wasn't sure. They could talk about it later. He hoped.

"Okay, any time now, Canada. Show yourself. Please!" Brian muttered.

"Coming through three thousand," Tyson called out. "You're on speed."

Nothing.

"Two thousand," Tyson called.

Still nothing.

"Fifteen hundred, Brian. I don't see anything."

"Turn on all the landing lights," Brian directed. Tyson's hand reached up and snapped them on immediately. Nothing but illuminated clouds showed ahead of them, the light almost blinding as it reflected back in.

"Twelve hundred feet, Brian."

"We may have to do this on instruments all the way," Brian said.

Which would probably be suicidal! Brian thought.

"Wait a minute . . . we may be breaking out!" Tyson called out, his voice tense with hope and fear.

The reflection of the powerful landing lights suddenly ended, the beams stabbing unimpeded into the Arctic night.

"We're at nine hundred, speed two-ninety," Tyson called out.

Brian had inadvertently pulled back on the yoke, losing ten knots. He decided to hold speed until four hundred feet.

"You see anything?" Brian asked.

"Not yet . . . not yet . . . I'm looking!" Tyson's words were tense and almost breathless. They needed a target. They were losing altitude, and only from altitude could they really see far enough to plan, but without moonlight . . .

"Brian! There to the left! There's some sort of break in the overcast, and I can almost make out the surface. Turn left! Now!"

"I'm gonna stay on instruments for now. You guide me."

"Roger. Come left forty degrees at least."

"Keep descending?"

"Yeah. Bring us down to four hundred. You're coming through six hundred now and slowing."

Brian leveled at four hundred, listening to their life-giving airspeed drain away as the sounds of the slipstream faded. He looked up from the instruments then, and out in front of the aircraft as Tyson's voice cut through the tension.

"*There!* Dead ahead, I can see the outline of what looks like a lake!"

Brian couldn't make it out yet. There was filtered moonlight playing around an area up ahead of them, but it could be far beyond gliding range.

He checked the airspeed. They were under 240 knots now.

"We're close enough, Brian, we're close enough. Hold your altitude and keep coming."

"I don't see it!"

"Just ahead there. See that angled shadow cutting across in front of us? And see the slight reflection on this side? That's got to be a lake."

Two hundred twenty knots and decaying.

"I got it now!"

They were out of time, and Brian could see the shoreline—if that was what it was—moving toward them. It was at almost a forty-five-degree angle to them, the line moving away on the left into the darkness. He checked the altitude again and mentally triangulated.

"We'll have to try it," Brian said.

Dear God, let that be a lake!

At two hundred knots he pushed the nose forward and called landing gear down.

"Roger, landing gear down." Tyson snapped the lever down, and the satisfying sounds of the gear extension process reached their ears.

"Down and three green," Tyson reported.

"Flaps five," Brian ordered.

The gossamer shadow had become something more now. In the landing lights, it was becoming a real shadow of some sort. It could be a small ridge, or it could be a shoreline, but whatever it was, they were closing on it rapidly.

"You're four hundred feet, speed one-sixty."

"Flaps . . . hell, all the way."

"Roger," Tyson replied. His left hand worked the flap lever as Brian pushed the nose over slightly, the landing lights now confirming that whatever was beyond that threshold was not a frozen lake.

"Jesus Christ! We're headed for a shoreline!"

Brian banked the 767 to the left instantly. He had very little altitude but just enough airspeed. The shore angled away to his left in what seemed like a straight line. They were almost over the shore now, and coming left.

"Brian, I don't know, airspeed's one-thirty-five. We're two hundred feet."

"Come on, baby!" Brian spoke the words as his left foot mashed hard on the left rudder to skid the jetliner around. He was at forty degrees of bank now, letting the nose fall slightly to keep barely above a turning stall as the lights aligned themselves with the shoreline and then moved left onto the lake surface.

"One hundred feet, Brian, speed one-twenty. We're gonna have to land it."

He had a ten-degree angle away from the shoreline now, almost out of altitude and airspeed and praying the right wingtip would clear the embankment to their immediate right.

The thought had been haunting him that they might find only a small lake. Now they would be skimming along next to the shoreline at over a hundred miles per hour on ice, and if it suddenly curved in ahead of them . . .

"Seventy feet."

A snow-covered surface as flat as a griddle stretched ahead of them into darkness. Brian let the 767 settle into ground effect and come down slowly to ten feet, letting the speed drain away as he flared, trying to touch down at around one hundred knots, still letting it turn slightly to the left, then, at the last second, leveling the wings for touchdown.

The first indication that the wheels had kissed a solid surface was the realization that the radio altimeter was on zero. Neither of them had ever made a smoother landing.

Brian let the nose down to the surface then, and stepped on the brakes. Amazingly, they responded, the anti-skid circuits cycling on and off as the speed of the jumbo slowly decreased to under a hundred miles per hour.

The landing lights stabbed into the darkness ahead, but now there was a reflection of something linear and dark moving in from the right—the edge of the lake. Brian moved the nose-wheel steering tiller farther to the left—as far as he dared—but it was obvious they were running out of room. If the aircraft should rocket off the ice and into that embankment, the landing gear and possibly the engines could shear off, causing a fire.

He pressed harder on the left brake, feeling the anti-skid cycling on that side, but still the onrushing side of the embankment that bordered the lake filled their windscreen.

"Sixty-five knots!" Tyson called out.

Brian cranked the steering even farther left and tromped hard on both brakes, checking the airspeed as it fell under fifty knots. They were slowing, but on a collision course with the black ground ahead.

In what seemed like slow motion, the huge Boeing 767 skidded and lurched toward the end of the smooth lake surface in a high-stakes contest between remaining surface and remaining speed.

Brian and Tyson both mentally braced for impact. The nose gear would undoubtedly go first.

Over a hundred feet behind them, the chattering brakes and intermittently skidding tires had struggled in vain to find something to hold on to. Finally biting into a roughened surface closer to the embankment, the braking system of Clipper Forty began to do its job. The big Boeing shuddered and slowed, the specter of the embankment now moving under the nose, garish and menacing in the landing lights.

Finally, in almost absolute silence, the last stored kinetic energy of the aircraft played itself out, the nose wheel coming to rest within eight feet of the potentially lethal eighteen-foot embankment surrounding the nameless, sixty-foot-deep lake whose impounded water was a solid block of ice all the way to the bottom.

At first, both pilots sat in stunned silence. Tyson looked at Brian, Brian looked at Tyson. They both looked out the window at a wintry scene of light snow flurries blowing along the ice surface, and sparkling crystals of frozen water caught in the beams of the APU-powered landing lights, as they illuminated a snowy landscape of tundra beyond.

Brian closed his eyes. *Thank you, Lord.*

He took a deep breath and turned to Tyson, whose eyes were still the size of fried eggs.

"I think we did it," Tyson said.

From the rear of the cockpit, through the cockpit door, the sound of applause, spotty at first, then energetic and heartfelt, filtered through.

Brian picked up the PA microphone with a shaking hand.

They were safe.

At least for now.

17

Wednesday, March 15, 7:15 A.M.
London, England

Elizabeth was burning with impatience. The first-class sleeper seat had worked better than expected, carrying her to Heathrow Airport reasonably rested and ready to work—but she was blocked by the impenetrable wall of normal business hours. She could do nothing before her nine-o'clock meeting with Alastair Wood at Lloyds.

Instead, she decided to stay in her hotel room and work on the battle plan. Pan Am had five days left, and she was determined to work her heart out up to the deadline.

A sudden swell of sleepiness rolled over her gently. She blinked and rubbed her eyes—trying to stay focused on the screen of her laptop computer—as the thought of a warm shower became a siren song.

I guess I didn't get as much sleep as I thought.

She found herself undoing her earrings and unbuttoning her blouse, her legs propelling her toward the bath. Elizabeth left a trail of clothes and lingerie through the bedroom on her way toward the bath. She had just stepped into the luxuriance of cascading hot water when the phone rang, the bathroom extension startling her with its loud, traditional bell.

Now what?

The satellite phone call last night from the aircraft to Ron Lamb's home came to mind immediately. The connection had been so clear that before she had told him, Ron had no inkling that she was airborne, let alone headed for London. She'd related the dark frustrations of the day, but omitted any mention of Irwin Fairchild or her suspicions about his involvement in the turndown by Bannister Partners. She had to get to the bottom of Irwin Fairchild's contacts with Pan Am and Ron Lamb, but now was not the time.

The fact that she was headed for London seemed to surprise Ron, but he had seemed truly shocked when she warned him in dire terms not to tell anyone else in the company—and especially not her secretary or assistant—where she really was.

"Don't even write this down, Ron. Just memorize the hotel name. And don't call me from the office. I think there's a good chance your phones and mine are bugged."

There had been a long, skeptical silence from the other end.

The phone was on its fourth ring when she balanced herself in the shower stall and reached for it, almost losing her grip as her foot slipped momentarily on the slick tile.

She had expected Ron Lamb's voice, but there was no way to anticipate the news that Clipper Forty was down on a frozen lake in the Northern Territories of Canada. She reached back and turned off the water to hear better as he described what they knew.

"My God, Ron. How cold is it up there? That's ... you say the airplane's intact?"

"Yeah. It's minus forty degrees or more, but fortunately their auxiliary power unit is working fine and there's plenty of fuel for now, so they can keep everyone safe and warm on board for at least a couple of days— provided the APU keeps running."

"Minus *forty*? How long until rescue planes arrive? They know where the airplane is, right?"

"They know exactly. Our people still have good communication from the airplane, but less than thirty minutes after they landed, an Arctic storm front moved over them, and the Canadian Forces rescue center is not sure they'll be able to reach them until it blows over."

"How long is that, Ron?"

"Could be a day ... could be three days or more. There's a severe low over the area. The thing that's got us all scared is that APU. If anything happens to it, or they run out of fuel before rescue can get in there ... I don't know. Two hundred forty people won't make it long in those temperatures in a metal icebox, and there's nothing in any direction for several hundred miles. They've got to get them out fast."

"How could the engines just quit?"

"Our chief pilot—well, you know Brian Murphy, of course—Brian is dumbfounded, as is our chief of maintenance. Nothing like this has ever happened to a 767 before. Boeing says it *can't* happen. The computer was going haywire just before it shut down their engines, and once it went off line, it wouldn't let them restart."

The mention of Brian's name caught her full attention. She could imagine him at that moment with a phone to each ear at the operations center, managing the crisis. Brian was wonderful in a crisis.

"Ron, where *is* Brian Murphy right now? I may want to check with him."

Ron Lamb knew that Elizabeth and Brian were good friends, yet the question seemed to shake him.

"Well ... he's talking to us on the satellite phone, and there's a direct-dial number, but we need to keep that line clear."

That confused her.

"He's airborne, you mean? Or there in Seattle?"

There was a long pause.

"Elizabeth, Brian Murphy is the *captain* of Clipper Forty. He's on that frozen lake right now."

Wednesday, March 15, 3:00 A.M. EST
Clipper Forty

The winds had come up as Brian sat on an armrest in the front of the first-class cabin and talked to the passengers on the PA. The wind was only a distant roar at first, barely audible above the sounds of the air-conditioning system, but it had grown rapidly to gusts that shoved the 767 sideways at times. He could see the eyes of his passengers growing more panicky with every episode. He knew it was up to him to reassure them.

"I'm going to be completely honest and open with you," he had begun, "and I must ask the same in return, along with your complete cooperation. Rescue forces are already on the way, but as you can hear and feel, there is a storm over us—an Arctic storm. It could be a while before they can find us or get aircraft in here to evacuate us. Rescue by land would take many days because of where we are, so what we can expect is the arrival of C-130 cargo planes on skis as soon as the storm lifts."

Brian felt the eyes of every passenger following his as he met the gaze of those closest to the front, one after another. Eye contact was important, but so was a calm façade. He struggled to *look* calm as he kept a smile on his face, hoping no one would think it too thin or insincere.

The desire to flee back to the cockpit and lock the door was infantile and stupid, but it was gnawing at him. Equally compelling was the desire to get on the phone and find Elizabeth. Suppose she heard about the forced landing without the information that everyone was safe, including her mother and Kelly?

He snapped back to reality, and to the fact that an entire aircraft full of people were watching him.

He was the man with the four stripes of command on his shoulders, the repository of wisdom, and the single person to whom more than two hundred forty people were now looking for guidance and reassurance—and it was a terrifying position to be in.

I can't guarantee everything will be okay! Maybe that's what's scaring me.

"Okay, here's the bottom line, folks. We'll hope to be here only for hours, but we'll work and act as if we'll be here for days. Though I fully expect things will turn out just fine, I have to tell you that we're in a different phase now. This is no longer a passenger flight in which our principal cabin duty—after keeping you safe—is to keep you pampered and happy. This is now a survival situation in which our mutual duty is to keep ourselves alive and well. Mutual cooperation and dependency—and *teamwork*—will be essential."

There were nodding heads and smiles in return from the planeload of frightened people whom he had just empowered as a team. Brian marveled that he had found the right words, but, judging from the faces in front of him, he had.

"Okay, let me take questions for a few minutes, then I'm going to pass out some paper. I'd appreciate it if each of you would write down your occupation, whether you've had any military training, survival experience, Arctic or cold-weather experience, whether you're a physician, or anything else I might need to know. Don't assume it's not pertinent. I may even need entertainers, if we have any on board."

They laughed at that, and the response brought a smile to Brian's face.

The passengers' confusion was apparent from their many questions. How could they be in a shirtsleeve-warm environment when they were stranded in the middle of the Arctic on a forlorn frozen lake with temperatures nearly fifty below zero?

"The APU, or auxiliary power unit," Brian explained. "It's a small jet-turbine engine in the tail of the aircraft, which runs on the same fuel the engines use. It wasn't affected by the electronic problem that shut down our engines. It gives us electrical power and heat, and we have enough fuel to run it for many days."

An elderly man a few rows from Brian began to raise his hand, then decided against it. Brian saw the aborted attempt and looked him in the eye. His haunted look transmitted the question as clearly as if he'd spoken in Brian's ear: What happens if the APU fails?

That answer, Brian decided, was best left for later.

After a few more minutes of questions, Brian excused himself and walked back forward through the Compartment Class section with its nine two-person compartments, all of which had the separating glass panels switched over to the transparent mode. Brian found himself marveling at glass that could be made opaque by the mere application of an electric current, though it seemed an inappropriate thing to be thinking about. He picked up the PA microphone and asked all flight attendants to come forward for a staff meeting.

Kelly and Virginia Sterling had been assigned to Compartment 1, just behind the cockpit. He found them now and hugged them both.

"You were terrific, Brian," Kelly said, with tears glistening in her eyes. "I couldn't even feel the landing."

"I got your message, honey. It helped."

"Were you scared?" She whispered the question, glancing around so as not to embarrass him. Brian could see she wasn't teasing, and that it was important for her to know. There was no question that *she* had been scared to death.

Brian hugged her again, feeling her shake slightly, and whispered loudly enough for Virginia Sterling to hear, "Yes. Worse than I've ever been. We'll talk about it later."

"Brian, is rescue really on the way?" Virginia asked him.

He meant to glance at her with a reassuring nod, but this was Elizabeth's mother, and he found himself unable to varnish the truth. Instead he glanced at the gathering crew of flight attendants before turning back to Virginia with a worried look.

"They are, Virginia, but I doubt they'll be able to find us just yet, or land. We may be here awhile, and what's worrying me . . ." he paused, and she prompted.

"Go on."

"Okay, we're totally dependent on that APU I described." His voice was low, and he glanced over his shoulder once again to make sure he wasn't being overheard. "I've got to get us ready to live without it if the worst occurs. Do you two have heavy coats here in the cabin?"

Both Kelly and her grandmother nodded, but Virginia added a postscript, gesturing with her thumb toward the window. "Not *that* heavy."

He raised the palm of his hand. "Even if the APU died, I'd keep us huddled up inside. Two hundred humans put out one hell of a lot of body heat."

♦ ♦ ♦

The nine flight attendants were all veterans, but none of them had ever lived through such a nightmare as the previous hour. All of them were shaken, and each of them, Brian realized, were just as dependent on him for strength and reassurance as were the passengers.

With Tyson remaining in the cockpit to talk to Iqaluit and the rapidly mobilizing Canadian Rescue Forces, Brian praised his crew lavishly before getting down to organizational details.

"First, I mean it when I say we're a team, the passengers included. I need your every idea and suggestion, I need your observations, I need your strength as well. I'm still the captain. Tyson Matthews is second-in-command. Jan, your first flight attendant, is third-in-command. Anyone can communicate with me or Tyson or Jan at any time, about anything. Now, if there's a conflict, understand that the rest of you have authority over each passenger. But we will use that authority to compel *only* when absolutely necessary." He took the time to smile and make eye contact with each of the eight flight attendants then, all of whom nodded in turn. He had intended to calm them, but felt himself calmed down as well. He felt some of the apprehension and tension drain away with each set of eyes he gazed into.

Brian smiled a broader smile than before, and took a deep breath, ignoring another gust of wind that caused the 767 to shudder.

"Okay. First, communications. We have four satellite lines, as you know. We'll retain line one for cockpit use, but I want the other three used to let each passenger call home at our expense to let loved ones know they're okay. Please don't give them the inbound satcom telephone number, or our lines will be jammed solid. Ask everyone who calls to keep the call under three minutes, and tell them to be totally optimistic and not unduly worry anyone they talk to. I'm going to give you my credit card to use to charge each call. It's on Pan Am."

"Lord, Captain, that's five dollars per minute!" one of the crew said.

He grinned. "So I'll go broke when they refuse my travel voucher."

Brian let himself envision the resulting bill. If he wasn't already fired as chief pilot, that should do it.

He forced his mind back to business and cleared his throat. "Next item: food and water. Take inventory of what we have in unserved meals, standby meals, packaged food, everything, down to packages of peanuts, then report back to Jan.'' He turned to the lead flight attendant. ''Jan, let's use simple division based on three days to figure out how much we feed each person.'' He looked back at the group. ''And I'm open to any other suggestions on how to handle it. We also have some survival rations in the life rafts, but let's leave those alone for now.''

The mere mention of food reminded him that his stomach was empty, too. He'd made the mistake of turning down dinner after climb-out from Seattle.

''Captain, some people on board may have their own food. How do we handle that?'' One of the flight attendants, whom he remembered only as Beth, had raised her hand slightly.

''Ask them to please reduce their share of the group food supplies by whatever they've got for themselves, or—if it's packaged—contribute it. We also need an inventory of baby food for the infants, and any special requirements.''

They all nodded, and several were taking notes.

''Water use in the bathrooms has to be curtailed, and no showers in Compartment Class. Jan, have the faucets cut off in all but one bathroom. Toilets are recirculating, of course, so those are unaffected—but expect them to get pretty ripe after forty-eight hours of use.''

A quietly attractive flight attendant with huge dark eyes raised her hand and caught Brian's attention. ''Captain?''

''Yes. You are?''

''Brenda Wallace. Sir, we may have people with medication needs, too, such as diabetics. What if they need their luggage?''

He shook his head. ''Not possible, Brenda. None of us is tall enough to deal with the baggage compartments, and even if we could, at fifty below with a forty-knot wind, whoever tried would be risking serious frostbite—*and* we'd have to open a door and use an emergency exit slide to get him to the surface. Don't forget, our floor level is over ten feet off the ground, and it's ice out there. Getting to the luggage at this point is not an option.''

''We can't get to it from inside?'' she asked.

He shook his head. ''No, but let's see if anyone who needs medicine left it in their bags. I would think most of them have their medicine in their carry-ons. In other words, let's see if we really do have a problem before we try to solve it.''

Another heavy gust shoved the aircraft sideways, this time actually moving the wheels a few inches and pivoting the nose to the left. Brian suppressed the urge to run back to the cockpit to see what was happening. But there was nothing he could do anyway, except ride it out and hope.

Brian looked at the group. They were all looking back at him quietly.

"Okay," he said at last, "when the people have those occupation sheets filled out, please bring them up. The cockpit remains the command post. Use the interphone to call us at any time, and I'll be back in the cabin for a walk-through in a little while." Brian started to turn toward the cockpit, but another thought held him back.

"Oh, one other thing. Even though we can't serve much in order to ration what we have, let's establish a regular meal schedule and try for some semblance of normalcy."

♦ ♦ ♦

Tyson Matthews was still on satellite phone link with Pan Am headquarters when the captain returned to the cockpit, but the radio was tuned to an aeronautical radio frequency, and the sound of another pilot booming through the overhead speakers gave Brian a rush of relief.

"Clipper four-zero, Rescue Five, we've been in solid cloud cover since descending through twenty thousand. We'll continue to orbit for another two hours until bingo fuel, but until this storm lifts, there's nothing else we can do."

Tyson told whoever was on the other end of the phone that he'd call them back. He disconnected then, and picked up the radio microphone.

"Roger, Rescue, we'll be here. It's just good to know you're up there."

Tyson looked at Brian and shook his head sadly. "I think we gave them the wrong position, Brian. That C-130 made three passes right over the coordinates we gave him, and I couldn't hear a thing."

"How low was he?"

"Eight hundred feet above the surface. Low enough that we would have heard him. I had the cockpit door closed, and I opened the window just a bit. Damn near froze my ear off."

The chill in the cockpit was still pronounced.

Brian stared out the window at the diffuse landing lights, which seemed to terminate in an opaque swirl of snow and what appeared to be ice fog. Even the embankment was no longer visible. The feeling of loneliness was almost overwhelming.

"All three inertial nav units agree, don't they?" Brian asked at last, looking down at the INS control heads. "They're all within three miles of each other?"

"Yes, but we don't know what effect all those transient signals may have had on them before we lost the engines," Tyson said.

Brian was shaking his head vigorously. "No, these damn things are too independent. If they're off, it's by no more than a few miles. Maybe the 130 was off."

"No way. He's got a global positioning satellite nav system."

Brian sighed deeply. They had discussed putting GPS systems in the 767s, since the 747 fleet had them, but they hadn't had time.

"Well, there's nothing he can do anyway until this storm clears. Even if he had us pinpointed, Tyson—I mean, even if he had a perfect diagram of this lake, accurate down to a foot, and knew exactly where we were sitting—trying to land in this . . . this sort of stuff . . . would be suicidal." Brian gestured disgustedly at the windscreen, then turned back to the copilot. "We're at the mercy of this storm, that's all there is to it."

"We're getting weathervaned by the wind, too, you know."

Brian nodded. "I felt us get shoved sideways a while ago."

Tyson continued, "Our heading's changed by fifteen degrees to the left so far. If it continues, our tail's going to be overhanging the embankment."

The captain shrugged.

"Not a hell of a lot we can do about it." That was the least of their problems.

Both men remained silent for a half a minute, listening to the wind gusts roar at them through the skin of the airplane and the cockpit windows, sounds that overwhelmed the soft background humming and whirring of instrument cooling fans.

Tyson spoke first, as Brian reached up to snap off the landing lights.

"Brian, Boeing and everyone in our maintenance department are scratching their heads over all this. They keep telling me there simply isn't any way that normal failure modes in the computers could cut off the fuel switches. No way. They even asked if we could have cut off the fuel switches by mistake. I confirmed we hadn't."

"What do they suggest? Do they have any ideas on how to get them running again? I mean, if we could just get *one* of those vacuum cleaners out there fired off, I wouldn't be so worried about the APU." He swiveled around on the captain's seat to face Tyson. "You understand what we're going to be up against in survival terms, if we lose the ability to maintain heat in this aluminum tube?"

Tyson shook his head. "They have no suggestions yet, other than pulling the rack-mounted black boxes in the electronics bay below, but we don't have any tools to work on them, let alone the problem of going outside in these temperatures to get to the compartment."

Brian sat deep in thought for a few seconds, staring forward into the Arctic night, remembering the company decision to seal off the small floor hatch that normally connects the passenger compartment of a 767 with the lower electronics bay. On Pan Am, a permanent bulkhead covered the hatch.

"You're right. I'd have to go outside to get in the electronics bay. And here we sit, totally dependent on that APU."

"Brian?"

"Yeah," he answered distractedly.

"On that subject . . . I hate to bring it up, but I checked the log for past problems with the APU, and I confirmed this with maintenance control."

"And?" Brian looked around at him with an apprehensive expression.

"This APU's had a lot of maintenance troubles lately. It's not terribly reliable."

18

Wednesday, March 15, 11:35 A.M.
London, England

"Elizabeth? Are you quite all right?" Alastair Wood had cocked his head and tried to meet her gaze, which had soared off through the glass windows of Lloyds' main floor and into space.

She snapped back to London and smiled at him, anxious not to discuss Clipper Forty. For all she knew, he hadn't heard about it yet.

"Sorry. There's a lot on my mind, and I'm afraid jet lag's interfering too."

Alastair Wood had turned out to be exactly what Lloyd White had represented: a young street fighter who had acquired the manners, clothes, and linguistic capabilities required of a financier, but who still had the heart of a shark.

"Where were we?" she asked.

"Well, I have a frightful amount of phoning to do to line up our chaps, but I see no reason why we shouldn't meet again in the morning to begin drawing up the papers."

"You're . . . that sure?"

He laughed as he got to his feet and removed his glasses. "Well, the members of my syndicate and other outside investors I handle have made a lot of money listening to me over the past four years, if you'll forgive the shameless bragging. But they bloody well ought to go along with me, even though this is direct loan-making and not underwriting. Your interest rate offer is excellent, and we've got security, so why not?"

She shook his hand warmly, but her mind was on an empty office she had seen coming in. Could she use it, and the phone it contained, for a few minutes?

"Certainly," Wood replied, showing her in and closing the door to leave her in privacy.

Elizabeth fumbled through her briefcase for the satellite access number to Clipper Forty, contained in a small directory of Pan Am telephone numbers. The incredible idea that she could pick up a phone and reach a downed airliner in grave peril in the frozen Arctic—an aircraft even rescue forces couldn't physically get to—seemed surrealistic.

The number came up busy, and she tried again, hearing a ringing circuit on the third try.

The sound of a strained feminine voice rang clearly from the other end, but the words were surprisingly professional and matter-of-fact—as if the woman were calmly sitting at the desk of a cruise ship on a lazy, sunny day.

"Clipper Forty."

"Uh, this is Elizabeth Sterling, your chief, ah, financial officer . . . of Pan Am . . ."

"Yes, ma'am?"

"Could I speak with Captain Murphy, please?"

"Sure. Let me transfer you."

She had seen the so-called "switchboard" for the satellite lines in the forward galley of the 747s, but somehow she'd never thought about it working like an office or hotel phone system.

A masculine voice answered with a sharp single word.

"Cockpit." It wasn't Brian.

She identified herself and heard the receiver being handed across the cockpit.

"Hello?"

"Brian!"

"*Elizabeth?* God, it's good to hear your voice."

"And yours! I . . . I just found out about what was going on a little while ago."

"It only *happened* a little while ago. Hold on . . . hold on."

In the background, she heard Brian ask someone to go back to the cabin for a reason she couldn't decipher, and a moment later the unmistakable sound of a closing door reached her ears.

Brian's voice came on the line again, much gentler now.

"Elizabeth, I . . . I had to fight to keep you out of my head on the way down, when the engines quit. It was a spooky experience." He paused. "It's *still* a spooky experience, especially talking to you like this. You sound like you're only a few feet away."

"Where are you, exactly?"

"The coordinates wouldn't mean much unless you have a map there, but we're above seventy-one degrees north latitude, sitting on a frozen lake on a peninsula above Hudson Bay . . . and in the middle of a howling gale."

She started to reply, but his voice came back, urgent and strong.

"Elizabeth, I've been burning to talk to you since we slid to a halt here. I'm truly sorry for the other night. It scared me that I might not have the chance to tell you that. It kept eating at me all the way down . . . 'What if we don't make it? Will she know how much I love her?' "

Elizabeth had to clear her throat. There seemed to be a growing lump there. "I *do* know, Brian, and I feel the same . . . and I'm as much to blame for Saturday as you. We . . . we just have to learn to adjust to each other again. Brian, when can you get out of there?"

Several thousand miles distant, Brian hesitated, his mind racing. What should he tell her? After all, his fate was tied to her mother's and daughter's.

"Brian?" she prompted, understanding the pause only too well.

"Honey, we're in a serious situation." He filled her in without embellishment.

There was a pause on the line.

Brian continued, "It could get tough, but we'll be okay—and as for your mother and Kelly, they're doing just fine."

If he'd suddenly described palm trees and breaking surf visible from the cockpit, it wouldn't have made less sense. Mom and Kelly? Had they called Brian too? How could they get the number so fast?

Kelly and Mom are in Bellingham . . . no, that's right, they were going to Europe . . . oh God! I forgot!

Her mind finally recalled her mother's words on Eric's answering machine in New York: "Kelly and I are going to Europe on Brian's Pan Am flight."

"I . . . ah . . . knew they were flying to Europe, but I forgot they were with you."

"I'm sorry to shock you."

They talked for five more minutes before Brian called Virginia and Kelly to the cockpit for a short conversation with Elizabeth.

When the call was over, Elizabeth sat in the vacant office, still holding the receiver and staring at the wall, a tide of conflicting emotions welling up inside her.

I've got to get up there . . . be there when they're rescued. I can fly on one of the planes, I can . . .

Elizabeth looked around suddenly, reminding herself where she was and what she was doing. There were five days left for Pan Am, and no one but Elizabeth could possibly carry the financial ball. In the Arctic wilds of Canada, there was nothing she could accomplish but to get in the way.

But in London—by staying to finish her mission—she might be able to save an entire airline.

She had no choice.

Wednesday, March 15, 3:55 A.M.
Seattle

"You look like hell warmed over, Conrad!"

Chad Jennings stood in front of the nose gear with his hands on his hips, shaking his head in mock disgust. Bill Conrad turned a poker face toward the younger man.

"I *feel* like hell warmed over too, Chad." The words held not a hint of humor. "But I figured getting our people some power before they freeze to death up there is a little more important than getting eight hours of sleep."

Jennings ignored the remark and focused on the open hatch to the electronics bay of Ship 103, their other Boeing 767. He had breezed into the Pan Am hangar at Seatac in his Porsche, driving through the security gate and right up to the aircraft, smelling lightly of bourbon. Bill noted the same business suit and tie he'd seen Jennings wearing earlier in the day.

A collection of men stood beneath the nose of the aircraft, including FAA, NTSB, and Boeing engineers, and Conrad began introducing Jennings to those the operations vice-president wouldn't know—reminding Chad with a discreet whisper that the man with the FAA badge on his coat lapel was Pan Am's PMI, the FAA's principal maintenance inspector. Twice before, Jennings had forgotten the inspector's face and name, and effectively snubbed him.

"Okay, fill me in, Bill. What are we doing here at three A.M.?" Jennings asked.

Michael Rogers of the NTSB and the FAA man listened carefully as the maintenance chief explained to the operations vice-president what he already should have known about Clipper Forty's engine failure.

"So, Chad, we're up in the electronics bay trying to find what could possibly introduce a stray signal to the fuel switch logic circuits that could cut off the engines.'' He gestured to several stands of testing equipment under each open engine cowling. ''Those switches aren't hard-wired, they feed a computer logic circuit, but none of us—and especially not Boeing's folks—can find a way a normal failure mode could do this.''

Bill Conrad let that sink in a minute, satisfied that Jennings was at last concentrating. Jennings had been truly shocked at the pictures of the recovered number-three engine that they'd hauled out of the water around noon the day before. Risking censure for the cost, Bill had hired a helicopter to bring an NTSB team out—and all of them back—along with the pictures. There was no doubt now that Clipper Ten had been sabotaged with a bomb in the engine, and the NTSB was going to announce that to the world later on Wednesday.

But was Clipper Forty a victim of sabotage too?

Captain Dale Silverman had reached him around midnight in a panic. Silverman now stood quietly to one side, watching the proceedings with an ashen expression. A quick check had revealed that the man he had seen on Ship 102 in Denver on Friday night did not match the description of anyone working for the contract company Pan Am had used, and there had been no maintenance scheduled that night.

''There was no way,'' Bill Conrad explained to Jennings, ''that anyone should have been changing out electronic units like the black boxes Captain Silverman here saw on the floor of that cockpit.''

Jennings nodded solemnly. ''And . . . Ship 102 . . .''

''Is the very one sitting on the ice slab above the Arctic Circle as we speak,'' Bill finished.

''Bill, look at this.'' One of the Boeing team leaned down through the hatch and motioned the maintenance chief over to the ladder beneath the electronics bay. Bill climbed in carefully.

''Okay, this is the main box controlling the center display. The way it feeds data into the adjacent systems, it could conceivably be *programmed* to cause havoc, but any normal circuit failure will simply drop that function out of the loop. We built it to fail to null, or fail-safe.''

Bill Conrad fingered the ends of the cannon plug. ''If you wanted to bring down this airplane—cut off the fuel—and you had this box and all the time you needed to monkey with it, could you engineer that result?''

The man shook his head. ''I can't for the life of me see how, unless you screwed this thing up so badly you were putting wild currents and signals in where they shouldn't be. I guess you could overpower and confuse the other computers that actually relay the engine on and off switch signals . . . I guess you could, but I don't know.''

"If so, once you removed the problem, the unwanted system . . .''

The man smiled and nodded."Yeah, then it should work again.''

Bill started to climb out.

"One problem.''

"What?''

"You remove this box, you have virtually no engine indications.''

Bill looked the Boeing man in the eye. "They didn't anyway. Thanks, Phil, this may be our edge.''

He climbed out and spoke to one of the Pan Am maintenance team.

"Go run a telephone line over here and up into the electronics bay. We're gonna get Brian on the satellite connection and talk him through this—if he can find a way to get outside and up into the compartment.''

A large hand landed gently on Bill's shoulder, its owner a stranger who extended his other hand in greeting and introduced himself as Loren Miller of the FBI. His hand was huge, and Bill had the impression his grip could crush. With the NTSB's Rogers, the FAA's man, and Chad Jennings in tow, they compared notes—Agent Miller finally raising his hand with an inevitable conclusion.

"We have to assume,'' he told them, "that there is someone willing to commit mass murder by bringing down a Pan Am airplane any way he can. Whoever it is, he isn't finished. There is no way you people''—he gestured to Jennings and Conrad—"should allow a single additional departure without a massive security effort, including complete examination of each and every aircraft and locked-down access to all aircraft.''

Chad Jennings swallowed hard and sighed. "I'd better get Ron Lamb on the phone. This sounds like an emergency board meeting.''

The FBI agent checked his watch. "My records will read, gentlemen, that you were warned about this as of four-twenty-three A.M., Pacific Standard Time. Liability being what it is, I suggest you heed the lesson of the original Pan Am's disaster at Lockerbie and act immediately.''

"All of us are witnesses,'' the PMI added gratuitously.

Bill Conrad's middle contracted with a combination of apprehension and anger.

As if I'm not taking this seriously! He must think we need a two-by-four across the head to get the point!

He glanced at Jennings then, and understood.

Wednesday, March 15, 1:00 P.M.
London, England

The message was waiting for her the moment Elizabeth opened the door to her suite. Call Ron Lamb at the office, whatever the hour.

He answered his private line on the first ring, anxious to notify her of what she already knew about her mother and daughter's presence on Clipper Forty. In turn, she filled him in on the optimism of the first meeting, and the next appointment, set for 2:00 P.M.

"Unless someone's figured out I'm here and moved in to interfere, as I'm convinced they did in New York, I may get this done. Can you have our general counsel sworn to secrecy and on standby late tonight, Seattle time? I'm meeting with Alastair Wood again in the morning at nine, one A.M. there, and I don't want to waste a split second. Have the fax machines ready."

Ron sounded grateful, hopeful, and agonizingly tired.

"You okay, Ron?"

There was a long delay in his answer. "My head's killing me, Elizabeth. I used to have migraines. I think they're back."

He told her of the security precautions, the massive schedule disruptions, and the pending NTSB confirmation that Clipper Ten had been bombed—and Clipper Forty more than likely sabotaged as well.

"Ron, could this all be connected? The financial interference and these emergencies?"

"We have a saboteur, yes. You may have uncovered one on that end. Are they connected? God, I don't know, Elizabeth, but if so, what force are we facing here? The Mafia can bomb airplanes, so can the PLO, but who can also turn everyone on Wall Street against us and be sophisticated enough to mess up our reservations computers?"

There were no answers, and they ended the conversation with mutual fears growing exponentially.

Elizabeth spent less than a minute in thought. There was no time to waste, and keeping busy was probably as good a remedy as any to the bow wave of anxiety that Clipper Forty's dilemma had created.

She pulled the list of contacts and phone numbers out, but called the concierge first, to order a U.K.-compatible cellular phone. Her U.S.-based cellular was useless in England, and she was not going to be out of touch again.

That done, she began phoning down the list, making additional appointments, explaining Pan Am's attractiveness as a loan customer, and explaining as well what was happening in the Arctic.

In the background the television stayed tuned to CNN's world service, the constant updates on the rescue attempts in northern Canada catching her attention from time to time. She would call Brian and Kelly again in late afternoon.

The two-o'clock appointment with a major bank went well, but it was obvious they needed more time than Pan Am had. Her three-o'clock with a major investment house held similar hope, with the prospect of greater speed than the bank, and her four-fifteen also showed refreshing promise. She returned to the hotel, anxious to get back on the phone.

The lines to Clipper Forty were continuously busy, even after an hour of continuous dialing. She turned the television on at last to check CNN for any late news, hoping to hear they'd been rescued.

The sound of a live telephone interview with Brian from the aircraft dashed those hopes—and explained the blocked lines. Most of the media would be trying to dial in, she figured. It was going to be difficult to reach him again.

There was nothing they could do but wait out the storm, Brian told the news anchor in Atlanta. Yes, it was dangerously cold outside. Yes, it was true that only a small jet engine in the tail was keeping them warm, and no, there had been no damage to the aircraft and no injuries.

She was proud of Brian's steadiness. He handled the questions with authority and confidence, and it was a strange feeling to know that there was uncertainty and worry behind that strong voice.

"Captain Murphy," the CNN anchor asked, "forgive the question, but what happens if that power unit you're relying on fails?"

The quiet buzzing of the satellite line could be heard for a few seconds as Brian thought it over.

"Well, it would be a problem . . . but one way or another we'd keep ourselves warm. We would be out of contact, though."

Elizabeth ordered dinner from room service and decided to hold off trying to get through to Brian for a little while. There was another call she should make in the meantime, one Lloyd White had insisted on, though she couldn't really see the use.

Then again, I've got to leave no stone unturned.

White had briefed her that his friend in Scotland had been the victim of a sabotage campaign, and if there was any chance he could help, it was worth a try—though there was only one trip she was yearning to make: to northern Canada.

She searched her notepad for the name, Creighton MacRae—Craig, Lloyd had called him—and punched in the number.

The phone rang nine times before someone picked it up. Even then, whoever was on the other end took his own sweet time in bringing the receiver to his mouth. Elizabeth began to wonder if she'd called an invalid, when at last a gruff voice with a distinct Highland accent rang through the line.

"Yes?"

She introduced herself and mentioned Lloyd White's name.

"And?"

She related in capsule form what was happening to her company, and why she had been told he might help.

There was no response.

Finally, in frustration, realizing she was talking faster and faster to fill the void, Elizabeth hit the breaking point.

"Would you be kind enough, Mr. MacRae, to at least say something in return?"

"What would you like me to say?" he asked. His voice was smooth and cultured, but there was a hint that he might be laughing at her.

"Well ... I was told by Mr. White that you were once head of your own airline company, and that you're an excellent financier who can appreciate another professional's need for advice or assistance."

"White exaggerates. Did he also tell you I'm retired?"

"Yes, he did."

"Yet you call me at suppertime in need of advice. Very well, my advice, Miss ... Sterling, was it?"

"Yes. Elizabeth Sterling."

"And your position, again?"

"Senior vice-president, finance, and chief financial officer of the new Pan Am."

"Ah, the bloody carrier that tried to wipe out Lockerbie—or its ghost, at least."

This is useless! Elizabeth thought to herself.

"My advice, Miss Sterling, is to go ring up someone in the business of providing corporate financial advice. I'm finished swimming with sharks. Good night."

The line went dead suddenly.

The jerk hung up on me! Elizabeth held the receiver out and looked at it in disbelief, then slammed it back in its cradle.

That was that. She had tried.

She turned the volume up on CNN again and began dialing the satellite number for Clipper Forty's telephone once more, but still it was busy. She tried turning her attention to other things then, but Lloyd White's voice kept working its way back through her subconscious, reminding her again of the similarities of the fight that MacRae had fought and the one Pan Am was facing.

MacRae might be as hard as a stone, but if so, he was a stone unturned—and that was intolerable.

She dialed his number again.

"*Yes,* Miss Sterling?" he said instantly on picking up the phone.

"Are you always this insufferably rude, Mr. MacRae? Or is that a Scottish tradition?"

"Rude? You interrupted *my* supper. I didn't interrupt *yours.*"

"A gentleman doesn't hang up on a lady."

"Ah, but I was interrupted by a self-proclaimed chief financial officer. Now I am to understand you're a lady? Which is it?"

"This may come as a shock, Mr. MacRae, but in my country it's possible to be both."

There was a snort from Scotland. "I tend to forget that America always trends to the bizarre."

"Perhaps you've also forgotten that your head of state, the Queen, is a woman—and a lady? Not to mention your former prime minister, also a woman—and a lady. So what's your problem?"

There was no answer.

"Look, Mr. MacRae, hear me out just a second, and if you refuse what I'm going to ask, I'll leave you alone."

"If that's what it takes to dine in peace, by all means proceed!"

"Okay," Elizabeth continued. "I know you won a large judgment after a long and torturous lawsuit against a plethora of organizations and individuals who forced you to sell the airline it took you so much agony to build. The tactics that you proved in court they had used against you included financial sabotage, operational and financial interference, and even physical sabotage of your company's property. In addition, in the process of investigating what happened, you singlehandedly uncovered a network of foreign companies that had joined in a collusive effort, through offshore banks, to provide the eight-point-six million pounds they spent to wage the war against you—a war that cost you personally every penny you had, and that forced you into personal bankruptcy—until after collection of the thirteen-point-two-million-pound judgment you received in 1990. Does that about sum it up, Mr. MacRae?"

"Well done, Miss Sterling. You obviously know how to absorb a briefing paper." His voice was still somewhere between gruff and flippant, but there was a change—a grudging acceptance that she wasn't a complete twit.

"Mr. MacRae, someone is now doing the same thing to us. If that in any way makes you angry—because we're underdogs like you were—then please have the decency to let me come to Scotland and discuss this further."

More silence.

This man is impossible, Elizabeth concluded. *I shouldn't be wasting my time.*

"When would you be coming, then?" he asked.

The question caught her off guard.

"Ah ... in a day or two. I'm trying to work out a loan for our company here in London. It's very critical. But as soon as I'm finished—"

"Call me, then. I can only promise you a meeting in Inverness, you understand, but I will do that."

She felt herself soften a bit.

"That would be helpful. *Thank* you, Mr. MacRae, I really—"

"No need for thanks. I doubt I'm doing you a favor. Frankly, I'm just curious to see a hybrid lady vice-president."

Elizabeth couldn't decide whether she was hearing a chuckle or a sneer in his words.

"May I get back to my supper now, Miss Sterling? My chips have gone stone cold." The tone was as abrupt as before.

"By all means. I'll call you," she said.

"And I can hang up now without offending you further?" he asked with affected concern.

"You may, Laird MacRae."

She disconnected before he could think of another reply, hoping the use of the Scottish equivalent of "Lord" had been an appropriate parry to his sarcastic thrust.

Lloyd White warned me! she recalled.

Wednesday, March 15, 8:00 P.M. EST
Clipper Forty

The interior of Clipper Forty had been plunged into darkness, the cabin illuminated now only by the ghostly glow of the emergency exit lights. The howling of the wind outside rose to demonic levels as the frigid Arctic void began sucking the heat from the winged aluminum tube known as a Boeing 767.

Brian could hear the sound of the APU's turbine winding down as he cleared the doorway and headed for the cockpit, a few steps away. It was Tyson's watch. Why wasn't he restarting it?

How long have I been asleep? Could we be out of fuel?

Brian heard the turbine wind back up as he burst onto the flight deck and saw the copilot holding a flashlight beam on the start switch with one hand while he tried to coax it back into operation with the other.

They waited through tense moments, wondering if the 767's battery was up to the challenge of spinning the small jet turbine engine fast enough to let it restart.

Brian slid into the left seat, watching intently.

"I think we're going to get her back!" Tyson said, the concern in his voice deep and obvious. In the reflection of the flashlight, Brian could see the enlarged diameter of his bloodshot eyes as clearly as he could feel the cold void at his back through the cockpit windows.

There was the unmistakable sound of a lightoff then—the ragged, almost pained acceleration characteristic of small jet engines as the sudden presence of hot expanding gases rudely forced the turbine wheels to spin up to operating speed.

"There!" The APU stabilized, and Tyson's hand moved toward the electrical panel to reconnect its generator. He toggled the appropriate switch to reconnect the APU electrical power. Instantly they were awash in light and the sound of heated air coursing through the vents.

They sat in tense silence for nearly a minute, watching the gauges and listening, Brian expecting the APU to die again at any second.

But for the moment it remained stable.

"What do you think?" Brian asked at last.

The copilot shook his head, lips compressed.

"I don't trust it. I . . ." He gestured toward the overhead speaker. "I talked to the rescue forces about ten minutes ago. They relayed the latest forecast. Brian, they don't expect any change in this storm for at least another thirty-six hours! This low is deep and stable, and it's killing us."

Brian winced.

"Sorry," Tyson added. "Poor choice of words."

Brian swiveled around and put his face close to the frigid glass of the side window as he reached up to flip on the left landing light. Columns of dry snow were streaming horizontally past them in the teeth of forty-knot subzero winds. The gusts had continued to shake and shudder the aircraft all day and all night, slowly causing it to weathervane into the gale. As a result, the tail and rear fuselage of the Boeing 767 now hung over the embankment of the lake.

Brian gestured out beyond the window.

"That amazes me, that we're not getting any snow buildup on the wings."

"Wind's too high," the copilot replied.

"I'm going to have to go out there, Tyson."

The sudden statement caught Tyson off guard.

"Brian, you can't—" Tyson began.

"No," Brian continued, "I'm going to have to go out there and try to get us fixed. You heard Seattle. If we can pull that box and find out whether someone's screwed around with it, we might be able to get the engines restarted. Then we can live without the APU."

"We've been through this before, Brian. It would be a crazy risk. The wind-chill factor's close to a hundred below. We don't have a ladder to get up to the electronics bay, and you don't have the cold-weather gear—*plus,* we haven't got the slightest idea whether Seattle knows what they're talking about. You . . ." He let his voice trail off.

Brian had been incredulous at first when the suggestion had come over the satellite phone.

"I don't think you understand what you're asking," Brian had said to maintenance. "One of us would have to go down an emergency exit slide into this deep-freeze and somehow not only manipulate the forty-below-zero metal hatch release on the electronics compartment, but then pull himself straight up through that hole—and then reverse the process to get back.'' ''Captain,'' the voice on the other end had said, ''if it's what we think, someone sabotaged that black box, and with our help you could repair it.''

At the time maintenance was talking to him, all the cabin doors of Clipper Forty hung more than ten feet above the surface. Since then, the wind had pivoted the aircraft nearly 90 degrees. The tail and rear fuselage now hung only a few feet over the embankment. Suddenly, getting out and in without a jetway or stairs could be fairly easy.

Brian took a long, deep breath. ''I'll bundle up and cover every inch of skin. We'll toss out an empty galley food container to stand on. I'll just have to pull myself up into the compartment.''

Tyson had opened his mouth to protest again when the APU died once more.

This time it took several attempts to get it restarted. Whatever opposition Tyson had felt to Brian's plan was overwhelmed by the very real fear of facing the Arctic cold without a source of heat.

♦ ♦ ♦

Within a half hour, Pan Am's maintenance team in Seattle had reassembled in the Seatac hangar, the company's top avionics man sitting once again in the electronics bay of the company's other 767, wearing a telephone headset, while Bill Conrad and several others waited below on extensions.

Anchoring the other end of the satellite phone was Tyson Matthews in the cockpit of Clipper Forty, ready to relay instructions to Brian Murphy—provided Brian could get into the electronics compartment.

Brian zipped his coat over several layers of sweaters and opened the right rear door, pulling the handle on the emergency slide and letting it flop out and inflate. The slide filled with air and lay at a shallow angle on the frozen tundra that formed the perimeter of the lake. With help from two bundled-up flight attendants, he positioned himself and slid down the plastic slide into a pain-filled void of wind and cold deeper and more frightening than anything he'd ever experienced. He looked up, then, as the flight attendants closed the cabin door behind their captain, leaving him alone in the alien world that had only been an image outside their windscreen until now.

The electronics compartment lay a hundred and fifty feet ahead of him in the frozen gloom. With the cabin access hatch closed off, a small hatch in the belly of the 767, just behind the nose gear, was the only way in. If he could get inside, he could plug the headset he had stuffed in his pocket into an interphone panel and communicate with the copilot, one floor above in the cockpit.

The wind was an incredible torrent of icy fury sucking his body heat away at a furious rate. The lake ice beneath his feet seemed impossibly slick, and the need to keep his face covered was disorienting. The distance from the tail to the nose gear seemed to stretch into miles—every step an agony of fighting for balance and traction against a wall of painfully frigid wind.

Brian stole a glance to one side, expecting to see the wing's leading edge now behind him.

It wasn't. It still lay ahead. He looked forward slightly, startled at how little distance he had covered.

Slowly he taught himself how to move forward without falling, passing the main landing gear step by step, and moving with greater urgency now toward the nose strut.

All the warmth he had felt in the cabin was long gone, and the cold had penetrated his inner core. His toes felt slightly numb, as did his fingers in the inadequate leather gloves he had borrowed from a passenger. The need to get into the warmth of the electronics bay was becoming urgent.

The food carrier box he had dumped out the forward galley door had been blown backward. He retrieved it and positioned it under the compartment.

He could touch the hatch, but the aircraft was sitting with its nose strut fully extended and a slight depression in the ice right under the electronics bay, leaving the hatch painfully high. He had begun to shiver now. A bad sign. There wasn't much time left.

Brian stepped gingerly up on the box, feeling it slip slightly on the ice, his numb fingers feeling along the surface of the smooth, frigid aluminum underbelly of the 767 as he searched by feel for the recessed door lever.

There!

He pushed his fingers in around the arms of the recessed T-handle and pulled on it with both hands, clumsily, his trunk beginning to shake energetically now as his core body temperature began an alarming drop.

He pulled with wide-eyed determination, but nothing was happening. The handle stayed recessed, apparently frozen in place.

He put his entire weight on it then, lifting himself in the air, finally feeling the handle snap down and out of the recess—at the same moment the howling wind whipped the metal food carrier from beneath his feet, leaving him dangling by the handle.

He bent his knees and let go, letting himself roll when he hit the ice as his feet slipped out from under him.

The wind was too loud past his bundled head to hear the APU, but he had the landing lights and the windows to help him see as he got to his feet—a steady source of light that felt comforting as he struggled to retrieve the box.

Suddenly the lights went out.

The APU again!

In near-total darkness he fumbled for the metal carrier and repositioned it, praying that Tyson could bring the APU back to life once more. He was proceeding on faith now. He could hear only the wind and the sound of his heart, which was pounding.

By feel alone—shaking and shivering violently—Brian pulled himself back on top of the box and stood up, reaching for the frigid metal belly above him. Without the APU, they couldn't start the engines even if he was successful in fixing the problem. Without the APU, he wouldn't have enough light to work. All he had was a tiny flashlight. Maybe it was a mission impossible, and Tyson had been right. Maybe he should move back to the rear door and get back on board and forget the electronics bay before he literally froze to death.

But there was residual warmth in that electronics bay, and none outside. He *had* to get in!

He grabbed the handle again, and pulled. This time it came out without a fight. Slowly, gingerly, he applied a twisting movement, feeling nothing move in response. He had to turn it a full 180 degrees. His arms ached. It wouldn't be long before he wouldn't have the strength to support himself.

The sound of something distant distracted him. As he tried to decide if it could be the sound of an APU, the lights came back on with a glorious—if painful—glare.

Brian jerked at the handle then with renewed confidence. Over and over, as the shaking of his body became distractingly violent, Brian hung on and jerked at the hatch handle, praying for some indication that it was going to move.

He had made the decision to give up and scramble for the rear entry door when he realized with a start that the handle *had* moved!

Not much, but a little.

He renewed his efforts now, putting everything he had into it. His teeth gritted, Brian was rewarded at last by the sudden surrender of the mechanism as the hatch moved inward and the handle twirled around to the full open position.

He slid the hatch out of the way. Then, feeling the slight warmth spill from the compartment above as he gripped the edge of the compartment to haul himself inside, Brian tried to ignore the burning pain of using nearly frozen arms and protesting muscles for the task. His body was clearly in emergency override.

Brian reclosed the hatch from the inside and braced his back against an electronics rack with his eyes closed, letting the heat radiate back into his clothes and body. The shaking was severe now, but slowly it subsided. In the glow of several red and yellow indicator lights on various rack-mounted boxes, he managed to find the light switch.

Tyson would know by the Door Open light that Brian had succeeded in opening the compartment, and now in closing it. Brian had thumped the ceiling—the floor of the cockpit—to let him know he was inside.

But now they needed communication.

Brian pulled the lightweight headset from his pocket and found the interphone panel, plugging it in and making the appropriate switch selection.

"Tyson, you there?" He was panting.

"Thank God! You okay?"

"A little worse for wear, but warming up."

"I've got them on the line, Brian, and I'll relay when you're ready."

"Just keep the heat coming down here."

"I will. Brian, uh, did you open . . . ah . . . any other compartment?"

Brian's head was still muddled. He decided he had misunderstood the question. Tyson must have meant the electronics bay.

"You mean the electronics bay?"

"You didn't open anything else?"

Brian shook his head. "No. Why?"

There was momentary silence from the cockpit.

"And no one else came out with you, right?" Tyson asked. "There's no one else out there?"

"Tyson, what're you asking?" Brian's tone was short.

"Uh, Brian . . . the rear cargo compartment Door Open light?"

"Yes?"

"It suddenly came on a few minutes ago, and I felt something up here too, at the same moment—a sideways nudge."

Brian found himself staring at the closed hatch at his feet with a renewed cold chill down his back. That was an alien world out there. Alien and frightening. But there was no one else out there, and nothing that could physically open a 767 cargo door—as far as he knew.

He thought about polar bears. He thought about wandering Eskimos looking for a shelter. He thought about Bigfoot and monsters and anything else that could explain what they were hearing and feeling, and he realized it didn't matter.

But he fought down the feelings of fright—fear of the unknown—and latched onto an explanation.

"Probably just the Door Open microswitch. It's too cold or out of rig or something," Brian told him.

The electronics compartment suddenly moved sideways with the rest of the airplane, as if it had been thumped by something. Tyson's voice came through again.

"There it is again, Brian. It came on steady, now it's off, and one of the girls in the back called up here, asking if you're in the rear cargo compartment. She says she hears someone moving around down there!"

"Tyson, forget it. We've got more important duties. Whatever's causing that, there's a logical explanation."

If he couldn't convince himself, at least he could put Tyson's mind at ease.

The thought of polar bears, however, reimposed itself. What if there was one out there now, waiting for a midnight snack to emerge from the electronics bay?

Thursday, March 16, 1:00 A.M.
London, England

Elizabeth stared at the ceiling of her London hotel suite and wondered what was *really* going on. The copilot of Clipper Forty had said that Brian wasn't available just now, but he wouldn't elaborate, and he wouldn't let her hold.

The fact that she could still reach them was comforting, but there was no hope of sleeping.

Elizabeth threw off the covers at last and dialed Ron Lamb's private office number, which rang only on his desk. He should be home, but she suspected he'd still be at the office, yet the phone rang with no answer.

For some reason she let it ring twenty times, which was ridiculous.

If he was there, he would have answered. Yet she kept on—physically startled when the receiver was suddenly raised, six thousand miles away.

At least *someone* had picked up Ron's private line. Elizabeth heard the sound of the receiver being hit by something, as if bumping against a hard surface.

"Ron? Ron, are you there?" she asked.

No answer. Just the bumping and scraping from the other end.

"... hee ... heeah ..." The sounds were human, but words weren't forming.

"Ron? Is that you, Ron?"

The banging and scraping had stopped, but she could hear the sound of a hand moving on the plastic receiver.

"... whaa ... ?" The voice was nothing more than a strained whisper that didn't sound anything like Ron Lamb, and yet ...

"Ron, this is Elizabeth. Ron, are you okay?"

Elizabeth had her finger a millimeter from the disconnect button before she stopped herself. Instead, she grabbed the cellular phone.

Within three minutes she had reached the emergency center in Seattle, giving them instructions on where to find the owner of the small voice on the other end of the phone connection to Ron Lamb's office.

For nearly fifteen tense minutes she listened to what sounded like the distant sound of labored breathing before a new noise—that of hurried footsteps and voices approaching—rose to a crescendo as the paramedics burst into the office and began working.

She half expected someone to replace the receiver and cut her off. Instead, a worried guard picked it up.

"Hello? Anyone here?"

"Yes!" She explained who she was and asked what he was seeing.

"It's Mr. Lamb. He was on the floor behind his desk." She heard the guard ask a question, then return to the line. "The paramedics say it looks like he's had a stroke."

Wednesday, March 15, 9:00 P.M. EST
Clipper 40

Brian Murphy sat with the opened electronics box in his lap, feeling helpless.

Working by intercom with Tyson, who in turn was relaying instructions coming over the satellite phone from the team in Pan Am's Seatac hangar, he had located the "black box" that controlled the engine instrument displays and opened it—but found nothing out of place.

"Tyson, tell them I see nothing unusual in here."

With the difficult lighting and only a pocket flashlight, it had taken Brian some time to analyze the myriad circuit boards in the black box. It took even longer to relay the questions and answers back and forth to Seattle about strange wires, odd clips or connectors, or other obvious signs that someone had tampered with it. He could see nothing out of place.

"Did they check out the overall serial number on the case?" Brian asked.

Tyson had relayed the serial number a half hour earlier. Now he was back on the intercom.

"That box, Brian, was stolen from United's bench stock in San Francisco. They want you to read the serial numbers of each circuit card."

One by one, Brian pulled the electronics-laden cards and relayed the numbers.

The sixth one held the key.

"Tyson! Tell them this one looks funny. There are marks all over it, as if things have been resoldered sloppily. There's also a tiny device that doesn't look like anything else wired to the card. I couldn't see it before."

He read the serial number. It didn't match United's records.

They were discussing it when the lights went out for the seventh time.

Brian waited for the APU to start again and the lights to come on. Instead, Tyson's voice rang in his headset, battery power alone keeping their connection alive.

"It's not starting, Brian! I've tried it three times. If I keep on, I'll be out of battery."

"Okay . . . okay, let's think this one through. I'm going to plug this box back in without the bad component."

"Yeah, but we still can't even try an engine start without an APU."

"I know. But hold off any more start attempts. If we can get it running just once more, I want to be ready to fire off an engine."

Working by failing flashlight, he pushed the box back into place, carefully checking the connections—and then stopped. They might have only one chance to start. As long as the APU was down, the satellite phone was dead and there would be no way to check the theory with Seattle. But *if* they could restart the APU and keep it running for just a few minutes with the box out, they might get an engine started even without readings for oil pressure and engine speed.

It would be a gamble.

"Tyson, why don't I stay here? You try to fire off the APU again. If you get it going, immediately try to start engine number two. If she doesn't start in forty-five seconds, I'll yank this box out of here. You'll keep your finger on the switch in the meantime. That should give us the best of both possibilities."

The tiny beam of the pocket flashlight was dying. Brian would be in utter blackness in a few seconds. He positioned his hand on the end of the box and waited as Tyson answered.

"Let's try it."

On the third attempt, the APU caught. Both pilots held their breaths as Tyson began the start sequence, talking Brian through every step.

"Okay, I'm showing 15 percent N-2. Moving the start switch. Nothing . . . nothing. Nothing, Brian."

"Hold on to it. Don't worry about starter limits."

"I've got nothing, Brian." Tyson's voice was rising in volume and tone as Brian watched the digits of his watch and waited for forty-five seconds to elapse.

"Brian, this isn't cutting it!"

"The engine's cold-soaked, Tyson. The fuel may be frozen. Boost pumps on?"

"Yeah! They're on. Nothing! We've got nothing!"

Brian yanked the box back toward him, feeling the electronic connectors separate from those on the end of the electronics rack. Almost immediately, Tyson was back in his ear.

"All my engine instruments dropped to zero!"

"Don't stop the start!" Brian yelled, angry with himself that he hadn't warned Tyson what he was doing.

"You pull the box down there?"

"Yeah. I should've told you. Keep going!"

From the right side of the aircraft—or perhaps through the skin—Brian heard another noise now, the sound of vibrations starting up a long scale, from a very low frequency and climbing, accompanied by the sound of . . .

"We got it! Brian, it's starting! Number two . . . we've got it!"

♦ ♦ ♦

The controlled fall from the electronics bay to the ice, the struggle to reposition the metal box and close the hatch, the trip back to the rear door, and even the painful hand-over-hand climb up the inflated emergency slide, all seemed minor inconveniences now that the comfortable whine of number-two engine running played with the sweetness of a concerto in Brian's ears.

When he had returned to the cockpit, they decided to start number one as well. It took over a minute to start, but it ran. Brian explained the victory to the passengers, then reinitialized the satellite phone and reported the good news to Seattle, getting Bill Conrad on the other end.

"So it *was* a monkeyed-with card in the box?" Conrad asked.

"Looks like it to me, Bill. I'm no avionics expert, but this is an amateurish job." Brian turned the circuit card over in his hand, holding it with a handkerchief. "Whoever put this in didn't care what it looked like, which tells me he didn't expect there to be anything left of us but wreckage."

Conrad was silent for a few seconds. "Maybe, but I'm not convinced that whoever did this intended to kill the engines. You said the first effect was to scramble your display screen, right?"

"Correct."

"Could be he screwed up the wiring, and maybe even the timing. But you're undoubtedly right on one point."

"What's that?"

"Whatever he was trying to do to our aircraft, it was supposed to happen within days, so that no routine maintenance check of that box would find his modified card. Otherwise he would have taken care to make it look right—y'know, like every other circuit card in the box."

"I suppose," Brian said.

Conrad told Brian of the confirmation that Clipper Ten's engine had been bombed, and of the FBI's response.

"The FBI is fully with us now, Brian, and we're having to check every component, compartment, and corner of every aircraft on every departure. Now we're going to have to check all the rack-mounted electronics as well. This keeps up very long, the delays alone will put us out of business."

Brian was still cold, and still bundled in the parka, but he sat up suddenly in the captain's seat. "Bill, get with the FBI agent and find out if he's finished running the fingerprint checks on my files. There's got to be a tie-in between whoever screwed around with our pilot files and what's happening to our airplanes." Brian laid out the details of his midnight search of the files. Bill Conrad promised to get on it immediately.

"Brian, how's your fuel holding out?" Bill asked.

"Thirty-two thousand pounds. At present rate of consumption, with two engines running, we'd run out in fifteen hours, but we're going to shut one down and alternate engines to keep them from cold-soaking. That'll give us thirty hours."

Brian ended the call with Bill Conrad's question ringing in his ears. He snapped on the landing lights and stared into the void ahead. The 767 was now pointing toward the middle of the frozen lake, its far shoreline virtually invisible in the darkness.

"Tyson," he said at last, his eyes flaring with surprise at the obvious conclusion.

"Yeah?"

"We've been going at this with tunnel vision."

"What do you mean?"

"That wind's pretty steady, isn't it?"

Tyson nodded. "Yeah, I've been reading thirty to forty knots of airspeed with us just sitting here."

"Okay, and it's possible that this lake is two or three miles long, right in the direction from which this wind is blowing, okay so far?"

"What are you getting at, Brian?"

"What are we sitting in, Tyson?"

The copilot gave him a worried look, as if suddenly concerned that Captain Murphy was losing it. Just as suddenly, a small gleam of understanding flashed in Tyson's eyes, a gleam that worked its way into a broad grin.

"An airplane with both engines running, and enough fuel to—"

"To get to Gander, or Goose Bay, or Thule, or maybe even Montreal!" Brian finished the sentence.

Tyson was engaged now, but a cloud obscured the sudden smile. "But we can't just accelerate into the night. We've got to know what's out there."

"So we taxi out and look. This lake's frozen solid. We taxi ahead and calculate the distance and direction and confines of the lake with our inertial nav readout, and make sure we've got enough room. Then we taxi back to this starting point and get the flock out of here!"

"That would solve the other problem."

"What problem?"

"Did you consider the effect of thirty hours of jet exhaust on an icy lake surface? We could sink."

Brian looked startled. The thought hadn't crossed his mind. Now the idea that the main landing gear could be mired in melting and refreezing water, locking them in for good, seemed to scream for action.

"Tyson, call the aft galley. Get Linda back there to jettison the emergency slide and lock the door. Let's start some checklists, secure the cabin, tell the folks, and get moving!" Tyson reached for the interphone as Brian adjusted his seat forward and ran through routine control checks, feeling for the first time in two days that he was in control again.

20

Wednesday, March 15, 11:00 P.M. EST
Clipper Forty

The satellite phone call from Elizabeth came through as Brian taxied Clipper Forty back to the northeast end of the lake. The lead flight attendant had balked at disturbing the captain, but Elizabeth pulled rank—her sleeplessness and apprehension overruling other cautions.

"Brian! I've been trying for hours to reach you. What's happening? How are you holding out?" She envisioned him still sitting in a land-locked cockpit.

"We're not holding out. We're *getting* out!" Brian filled her in on what they were preparing to do.

Elizabeth's head was swimming with a combination of elation and alarm. What did a blind takeoff from an Arctic lake in darkness involve? How dangerous was it?

She spoke her worries aloud.

"Not as dangerous," Brian explained, "as waiting to run out of fuel. We can't stay here, honey. We're out of options."

A severe gust of wind shoved Clipper Forty sideways a few inches as Brian called Kelly and Virginia to the cockpit, letting them speak with Elizabeth for a few minutes while he and Tyson ran through the checklists and tried to make sure nothing had been forgotten.

The lake, which was at least four miles long, seemed to trend from the northeast to the southwest, perhaps a half-mile wide, with the entire surface frozen solid and relatively smooth. With the ferocious headwind, the 767 would probably need less than a mile of runway, and they had far more than they would need for an aborted takeoff. The so-called airfield, as Brian had explained by phone to Seattle operations, was adequate.

They had taxied around and explored for thirty minutes before Brian brought them back to the same northeast corner where they had sat helpless for so many hours. As they approached, the landing lights illuminated the same embankment and the ruffled area of tundra where the bottom of the aft fuselage had bumped and wiggled against the surface with every major wind gust.

Brian pointed to the spot before pivoting the 767 back toward the southwest.

"See that depression, Tyson?"

"Yeah."

"That's my polar bear. I forgot to tell you when I came back in. The aft baggage compartment door was hitting the dirt and wiggling the microswitch."

Tyson chuckled. "Ah, so that was it. I figured you hadn't run into any bears out there, since you came back in one piece."

Brian turned the 767 into the wind and set the parking brake. The airspeed indicator on his display screen was showing a steady thirty-five knots, with gusts to forty-five. The only thing they were missing was the center display, and all the engine instruments.

Kelly handed the phone back to Brian, hugging his neck from the jumpseat behind.

"Elizabeth? You still there?" he asked.

"Yes. And scared to death!"

"Don't be. We're in good shape, and this takeoff'll be a piece of cake." Another howling gust thundered around the aircraft, stopping Brian for a second as he read forty-eight knots on the airspeed indicator. The storm was getting worse without question, and his anxiety to get moving was growing with each shudder.

"Sorry. A small distraction. I've got to get Kelly and your mother back to the cabin and strapped down now, so I'd better go. I'll call you back as soon as we're airborne."

He turned around and motioned to Kelly, who leaned forward and gave him a hug before retreating to the cabin with her grandmother.

"Ready?" Brian studied Tyson's face.

"Ready," the copilot confirmed.

"Okay. Since we have zero engine indicators, we'll have to guess at everything. I'll push up the throttles to where the engines sound about right, hold the brakes until we start sliding, then I'll try to keep her steady on two-zero-zero degrees true heading down the lake until you call 'rotate.' You added ten knots to the rotate speed?"

"Yeah. It's a hundred thirty-eight knots."

"Okay. If we lose power in either engine for any reason prior to your calling rotate, I'll pull off the remaining power and we'll abort. If we're anywhere close to rotate, I'll make the decision then and there, but as long as we're not on fire, and since we know we've got enough runway, I'd say let's get out of here."

"Amen," Tyson said.

Brian's right hand began advancing the throttles, the engine speed following, the whine of the two high-bypass turbofans becoming a loud roar as the 767 began to buck against the restraint of the brakes, and then to skid forward, the nose pivoting to the right suddenly in the teeth of another gust.

Brian released the brakes and used the nose-wheel tiller to straighten them out quickly, his left hand on the tiller, his right hand on the throttles as Tyson kept both his hands on the control yoke, holding it almost full forward to keep the nose wheel firmly on the surface of the frozen lake.

The airspeed leaped within seconds to eighty knots, then ninety, then a hundred. The frozen surface had seemed perfectly smooth while they were taxiing around at low speed, but now it became a washboard, bucking, bouncing, and vibrating the instruments as well as the occupants of the cockpit and cabin as Tyson called out 110, then 120 knots.

There was nothing in front of the windscreen now but swirling snow and ice fog streaming past. No more than three hundred feet of lake surface ahead could be seen. The landing lights stabbed into an indeterminate wall of frozen particles and disappeared impotently, but Brian kept his eyes down and on the HSI, the horizontal situation indicator, a compass projected in color on the screen in front of him. With his feet working the rudders left and right, he struggled to keep them rolling on the 200-degree heading as seconds ticked by in slow motion.

They were accelerating blindly into a storm on the ground at over 120 miles per hour, with no hope of avoiding anything that might loom out of the ice fog ahead, and he longed to hear Tyson say the magic word.

"ROTATE!" Tyson's voice finally filled the cockpit. Brian responded instantly and gratefully, pulling the yoke and feeling the nose of the 767 rise smartly as the wings increased their angle of attack on the 140-knot wind stream, finally producing more lift than the aircraft had weight.

The big Boeing bounded free of the surface then, the welcome sound of the main gear struts clunking into full extension reaching Brian's ears as his eyes confirmed a positive rate of climb on the instruments. He pulled them smartly to fifteen degrees nose up, and at five hundred feet above the surface ordered gear up.

"Roger, gear up," Tyson responded, his hand snapping the gear lever to the retract position.

As they climbed through six thousand feet, Brian reached down and retrieved the PA microphone.

"Okay, folks, we're safely airborne and headed back to civilization. I'll talk with you more in a few minutes, as soon as we get to cruise altitude."

Cheering and applause broke out throughout the cabin, the happy sound filtering up through the cockpit door.

As soon as Brian had called Seattle he dialed Elizabeth.

Some three thousand miles away, sitting on the edge of her bed in London, Elizabeth Sterling let her breath out as the phone rang. Her voice cracked and failed her on the first attempt to speak.

"Elizabeth?"

"Yes ... I ... um ... I'm here, darling."

Thank you, God! Thank you, thank you, thank you, thank you! Elizabeth ran the words like a mantra in her mind as Brian's voice filled her ear again.

"We're going to Goose Bay, Labrador, and I'll call you again from there. We're all fine, Elizabeth. It's going to be okay now."

Thursday, March 16, 9:00 A.M.
Pan Am Headquarters, Seattle

Chad Jennings stood in the door of Pan Am's boardroom. One by one he shook the hands of the departing board members, each of them grim-faced and shocked at the necessity of appointing an acting president while Ron Lamb struggled against partial paralysis in a nearby hospital. Jennings kept a tight rein on his facial expression, cloaking the excitement he felt at his new position.

Joseph Taylor, Pan Am's rotund chairman, was last out the door, grasping Chad's hand in his meaty grip.

"Okay, you've got the ball. Keep me informed, daily if possible. And if Ron can regain speech, you keep him in the loop. He's still the titular head of this thing."

"I will, Joe. Don't worry."

"Damn shame. I've known Ron a long time. Margaret and I will be praying for him."

Chad Jennings nodded with great solemnity.

"Another thing," Taylor added. "Ron thinks very highly of Elizabeth Sterling. I'll admit she did a hell of a good job on setting us up, but so far all she's done here for us is to go chasing around New York looking for money. But we're running out of time. Now I think . . ." Taylor noticed Fred Kinnen, the staff vice-president of finance and Elizabeth's assistant, standing close by, trying to look disinterested. He was straining to hear the words that followed his new boss's name. Taylor could see the young man leaning in their direction.

"C'mere a minute," Taylor said quietly to Jennings as he put his arm around the operations vice-president and walked him toward Ron Lamb's office. They stepped inside and Taylor closed the door behind them.

"Okay, here's the deal, Chad. Elizabeth Sterling's a smart financier, but she's still a broad, and I don't think she's gonna cut the mustard in forcing good ol' boys to loan us money, especially with Wall Street convinced we're in trouble. Women's lib aside, there are men out there who simply won't trust a female in corporate finance, and who won't trust us 'cause we've got a female representing us in a crisis."

"What's the point, Joe?" Jennings asked.

"Point is, that's your most important assignment. You start looking for a loan, too. Right now. We need eighty-five million by Friday, or we're all out of a job! Call our local bankers or whatever, but do it."

"And if they ask me why our finance chief isn't the one calling?"

"Hell, say you're calling *for* her. You're the acting president. You're her boss in that position."

"Joe, what if we sold a plane? One that's not mortgaged, I mean."

Taylor scowled, wondering if they'd made a mistake in trusting Jennings.

"Chad, get with that scarecrow Kinnen over there and learn the ropes—fast. We don't own any airplanes anymore. They were all sold and leased back. You'd forgotten that?"

"Sorry." Jennings rolled his eyes and smiled. "I was thinking of the good old days last year, when we still did own our hardware."

Joe Taylor's eyes bored into Jennings, suspicious of the answer. But that made sense. They had been stupid beyond reason to let the former finance man sell the fleet.

"Yeah, well, make sure you understand all the details. But as far as I can see, bailing us out is on your shoulders."

Chad thought over the loan officers he knew. Probably none of them had ever made a loan for more than a million dollars. He had no network to contact, but there was no way on earth he was about to admit that to Joe Taylor. "So you think *I* ought to arrange the loan?"

Taylor nodded. "To hedge our bet. I think Miss Elizabeth's scheme to get that money is already tits-up. You, however, are male, and the bankers will listen to a male."

Thursday, March 16, 5:00 P.M.
Inverness, Scotland

Elizabeth Sterling tightened the collar of her black cashmere coat against the stiff north wind and pushed through the door into an ornate interior of dark woods laced with the aroma of beer against a background din of conversation and clinking glasses. Creighton MacRae had been curt and specific: "The Phoenix at five sharp."

"Phoenix? Is that a restaurant?"

"It's a pub, Miss Sterling. Ask anyone. Bottom of Academy Street."

"How will I know you, Mr. MacRae?"

"Don't worry, I'll find *you*," he had said before hanging up abruptly.

Elizabeth hesitated, letting her eyes take in the small circles of men sitting and standing in various places from the bar to the far corners of the room. The clientele was an eclectic mixture ranging from mackintosh-clad locals to three-piece suits with briefcases.

There were three women in the room besides the barmaids. Two of them were obviously wives or girlfriends, but the third was out of place: a colorless lump of a woman in her early thirties, clad in a tweed business suit and sitting primly by herself at a table across the room, her briefcase lying open before her. Elizabeth found herself staring at the woman's owlish glasses and the tightly woven bun at the back of her head.

But where was MacRae? Elizabeth peered around the corner self-consciously, scanning the faces of the men in the pub, looking for one that might belong to Craig MacRae. A young, foppish-looking male at the bar looked up toward the doorway suddenly, spotted the striking American blonde in the black coat, and returned her gaze with an expectant smile. She looked away, her eyes landing instead on a half-scowling, rough-hewn Scot in his sixties who sat at a table to her left, busily engaged in running his eyes up and down Elizabeth's body with leering interest.

No one, however, came forward to greet her.

She felt uncomfortable and out of place, but she forced herself to move into the room, selecting a small table a few feet from the woman in tweed—a good vantage point from which she could watch the entrance.

She was exhausted emotionally, but with the immense relief of Clipper Forty's safe landing in Gander, and the hopeful word from Alastair Wood that the loan had been tentatively approved and papers were being drawn, she had suddenly been left with no reason to stay in London. A meeting with MacRae would probably be a waste of time, but it would be at least a day before Wood was ready to finalize the deal, and she just might learn something in the meantime from the prickly Scot.

The Danair flight from Heathrow had not been unpleasant—though she'd slept most of the way after formulating her plan: Meet with MacRae, learn what she could, hire him as a consultant if possible, and then spend the night at an Inverness hotel before returning to London in time to finish the paperwork.

A smiling barmaid materialized before her, and Elizabeth tried to decide what to order. The woman in tweed next to her was nursing a glass of wine.

"A glass of Watney's Light, please."

The barmaid nodded and left.

The sudden presence of a neatly groomed man filling the doorway caught her attention. She guessed him to be six feet tall. His dark hair was neatly combed, and his prominent eyebrows seemed to connect across his brow, framing a set of smoldering eyes that captivated her even across the room. Elizabeth could see a glint of deep blue in those eyes, set wide apart over a mouth that seemed to be frozen in a slightly amused expression—one end turning up, the other slightly down. He stood there with confidence, holding a folded umbrella and wearing a tan sports jacket beneath a matching topcoat as he surveyed the room, then moved into it.

Elizabeth watched him, his eyes scanning in her direction but never quite landing on her as he moved with forceful agility across the room. She felt slightly confused, like a little girl calculating the power and authority of her father walking resolutely toward her.

Yet this man had to be only in his late forties or early fifties, if she read the lines in his face correctly. So why was his approach stirring visceral feelings deep within her that were anything but daughterly or businesslike? Elizabeth forced the startled look from her face and reminded herself who she was and why both of them were there. He was ten feet from her table now, and Elizabeth squared her shoulders and lifted her head in anticipation just as he stopped at the table to her left, his eyes focusing on the dowdy woman in tweed.

His sonorous voice carried merely a hint of the growling male she'd dealt with by phone from London, but his words confirmed his identity.

"Miss Elizabeth Sterling, I presume?"

The woman in tweed looked up in confusion as Elizabeth realized what was happening and held her tongue.

"I beg your pardon?" the woman replied, startled.

"If you expect me to call you Madame Vice-President, you'll have a bloody long wait, lass," the man said, shifting the umbrella to his left arm and abruptly extending his right hand like a perfunctory peace offering.

The woman looked down at his hand, and back to his face. "*Whatever* are you talking about?"

Elizabeth struggled to keep from grinning as the man withdrew his hand and cocked his head.

The woman folded her hands on the edge of the table before her and cleared her throat before looking back up at him. "You've obviously mistaken me for someone else," she said.

MacRae stepped back a half-step and prepared to apologize as his eyes noted Elizabeth at the same time slowly rising to her feet, keeping a neutral expression, and bobbing her head in his direction.

"Mr. MacRae . . . I presume?"

The various expressions moving across his face were a mural of confusion as his eyes locked onto the attractive blonde to the left of the woman in tweed, his mind suddenly registering the fact that she'd spoken his name, and therefore must be . . .

"Miss *Sterling*?" he managed.

Instantly he turned his back to the other woman and muttered an apology as he moved toward Elizabeth, his eyes never leaving hers.

Elizabeth extended her hand, feeling amused and slightly overwhelmed. He was nothing like she'd expected, and it was obvious he was equally startled. There was almost friendliness in his voice before he resumed his authoritative, slightly irritated air.

But for a second she had glimpsed someone else beneath that frosty façade, and she was intrigued.

Elizabeth spent half an hour explaining the perils of Pan Am, drawing a detailed picture from memory of the changed loan agreements, the fleet sale, the strange appearance of Irwin Fairchild in the equation, and the apparent sabotage campaign that had even imperiled her own daughter and mother.

She made no mention of Brian. Somehow it didn't seem necessary.

MacRae seemed to be listening carefully to every word with his eyes probing hers, but occasionally she saw his eyes flicker over the rest of her body, and in those fleeting moments it was obvious he found her more acceptable physically than she had intended.

Lloyd White had warned her of this very thing, but she hadn't expected MacRae's instincts to lock onto her so obviously and so soon—and she *certainly* hadn't expected herself to respond to his interest, as she felt herself doing.

His frosty manner on the phone had been a sneer—as if he regarded the term *businesswoman* as an oxymoron—and Elizabeth had been determined to rise to the challenge by choosing her clothes with calculated care: a very feminine, deep-cut ruffled blouse, a suede jacket, and a matching skirt.

But now, without her coat, she found herself wishing she'd worn something more severe—something more like the lifeless clothes of the sexless woman in tweed who had departed soon after MacRae sat down. The Elizabeth Sterling who sat before him was in total contrast to what Creighton MacRae would have expected from a woman who could discuss bonds and loans and other serious things that men had traditionally arranged with each other in the parlor—while their women hovered at a respectable distance.

And it was dividing his attention. Though he appeared to be listening, his obvious enjoyment of her femininity made her wonder how much he was absorbing of what she was saying.

The mention of sabotage, however, changed all that.

MacRae began talking in urgent and angry terms about the battle to destroy his airline. He described the detective work that had drained his resources as he traveled the world for two years trying to find out who his enemies were, trying to document who had participated in bringing him down financially, and preparing the monumental lawsuit he had eventually won, and which had left him wealthy if bitter.

"I knew, you see, that no one person or firm could have done the coordination necessary to deny me credit worldwide. I knew there were banks and companies that were innocent, influenced by others who wanted me out, but finding them was quite a trick. I came to know computerized banking and communications systems very well. It's amazing what you can find out when you know where to look.''

''Do you still have that network?''

MacRae smiled and nodded. ''Aye, I do.''

''Would you help us? As a paid consultant, of course?''

He sat back and looked at her as if seeing the executive under the exterior for the first time, his eyes studying hers, making it hard for her to concentrate. At last he leaned forward.

''I had no intention of doing this, but you were right to think this would arouse my anger. It has. I don't know what I can do for you, but I'll try.''

''Your fee?'' she asked.

He smiled. ''Ever the financier, eh? Very well, I'll charge you what the best of the bunch I dealt with charged me. Two thousand pounds per day, plus expenses, and no nitpicking on the expenses.''

He smiled at her, eyes half closed, studying her reaction.

She suddenly extended her hand and gave his a firm shake.

''Done. Ten days in advance, whenever you want it.''

He raised those magnificent eyebrows in surprise and nodded with grudging respect at her decisiveness. ''I'll bill you later.''

Elizabeth had made it clear she wasn't planning to return immediately to her hotel, but MacRae excused himself and left her to dine alone. She had a sandwich before beginning the fifteen-minute walk back through the heart of Inverness to the Craigmonie Hotel, chilled by the cold wind but enchanted by the aromas and atmosphere of the Highlands of northern Scotland.

A taxi slowed at one point, the polite driver inquiring if she needed his services, but she declined. Walking and thinking were synonymous for her, and she needed the time to sort out what had just happened. It was a lifelong habit she'd learned from her father. Beaches were the best place for long walks, but Inverness would do as a chilly substitute.

Craig MacRae had seemed confident that whoever might be orchestrating a financial sabotage campaign against Pan Am could be discovered and neutralized. That was the most important task, he had told her. Until the poisoning of the airline's financial prospects was halted at the source, there would be very few institutions willing to risk their money. ''It doesn't take much,'' he had told her, ''to destroy the financial prospects of a small company. There were only six people ever directly involved in killing my company, but they were bankrolled by larger entities. In your case, we've got to find out who's doing it as well as who's bankrolling the effort.''

"How about why?'' she'd asked.

"If I find the *who*, you'll know the *why* automatically.''

The memory of his deep, resonant voice triggered another small twinge, and her mind strayed from business to their mutual attraction, surprised more by her feelings than by his.

The thought of Brian interjected itself at that moment, and she found herself bewildered. She had always assumed that being in love would insulate her from being attracted to another.

Am I really in love with Brian?

This is silly. I don't even know MacRae. I was just intrigued by the challenge, that's all. The challenge and those eyes!

She resolved to shake off all thoughts of Creighton MacRae except those concerned with business—and instantly broke her resolution.

His abrupt, almost rude, departure still puzzled her. She felt perversely cheated that he hadn't at least asked her to dinner, or invited her to visit his farm near Forres, to the east. He had mentioned it briefly, and it sounded warm and inviting. She could imagine him back there now, sitting before a coal fire with a glass of Scotch, or whatever he drank.

There was no wife in his life, according to Lloyd White. But was there a girlfriend? Elizabeth's mind searched the ethereal image of his castle for evidence of another female, and could find none. He was the closest thing to a Henry Higgins she had ever met. Single, crusty, and . . .

Maybe he's afraid of me! The thought came unexpectedly, and with it, Elizabeth's composure began to return. She'd let herself get so wrapped up in the surprising effect of MacRae's overpowering masculinity, she hadn't focused on what *he* might have been thinking.

Straighten up, girl. You're not over here to be bowled over by a gruff, sexist Scot! You're trying to save an airline!

Head clear for the first time that evening, Elizabeth was almost whistling as she approached the entrance to her hotel. She had every right to be happy. After all, Brian and her mother and Kelly were safe, it looked as though the loan she had sought in London would come through, and she had succeeded in enlisting Creighton MacRae to their cause.

Only the remembrance of Ron Lamb's stroke broke the spell. She'd been thinking of calling him, forgetting for a moment the lonely personal battle he was fighting back in Seattle.

Elizabeth returned to her room and picked up the phone. When she'd left London, Joe Taylor was in charge and mulling over whom to appoint as interim president. It was time to find out whom she should be reporting to—and to do just that.

Friday, March 17, 7:45 A.M.
Inverness, Scotland

The flight back to London departed at ten, but the phone by Elizabeth's bed rang at 7:45 A.M. She found an agitated Alastair Wood on the other end.

"It's bloody well coming apart, Elizabeth. Someone's got hold of a list of my people, and the bugger's been faxing a devastating little packet of information to each of them, implying that you and Pan Am are lying about your performance and prospects. My phone was ringing off the hook late last night at home."

There was no time for cobwebs, and she forced her head to clear in an instant. Whoever had pursued her down the concrete canyons of New York had obviously discovered her mission to London. Craig MacRae had warned her it would happen. It had happened to him.

"What's being said? And by whom?"

"I don't know who's responsible, but I have copies of what he's sending, and I've already faxed copies to your hotel. They should already have shoved them under your door."

"Hold on," she told him, fumbling for the switch on the lamp by the bed and finding it. She looked at the rug beneath the door, spotted the papers, and leaped out of the bed to get them.

"Hold it, Alastair, I'm looking."

There were four pages to the fax, two of them appearing to be purloined Pan Am interoffice memos, and two purporting to be financial summary sheets for the previous four days. One memo was supposedly a note from chairman Joe Taylor recommending to Ron Lamb a rapid Chapter Eleven bankruptcy filing as the "only way out"; the other was supposedly from Elizabeth's assistant, Fred Kinnen, pleading with Ron Lamb against any corporate admission that the load factors were less than forty-eight percent. "If the financial community discovers this," the memo said, "they'll never lend us a cent. We've got to let them believe everything's all right."

Of the two financial summaries, one was the current weekly cash flow through Thursday, a litany of declining prospects that, if representative of the average week, showed an airline in deep and potentially fatal trouble. It was accompanied by a list of available cash in various bank accounts and available credit, which seemed to show a company on the verge of insolvency.

For a split second even Elizabeth was taken in, her stomach knotting at the possibility that she had been lied to and these papers told the truth. She couldn't help but remind herself that she'd never had a moment to get familiar with the current financial state of affairs, and Ron Lamb had conveniently omitted several key problems before she came aboard. She had trusted Ron's summaries, though, as well as a quick summary prepared by her staff vice-president—the same Fred Kinnen whose name appeared on one of the memos.

But she had seen nothing to indicate that the company's situation was anywhere near this bad.

"These are all fraudulent, Alastair! I'll have my office provide the true ones in an hour. They'll show a totally different picture."

"I'm sure they will, but the problem is, they've already poisoned the waters. I've got two of my key participants ready to bolt."

"Are they in London?"

"Yes, they are."

"Can you get them to come in for a meeting this afternoon? Can I talk to them? Can you keep them from reneging before I talk to them?"

There was silence from the other end.

"Maybe. I can certainly give it a go. Who's doing this, Elizabeth?"

"I don't know. That's why I came to Inverness, to get some help finding out."

"Strange place for such a mission. Edinburgh or Glasgow I could understand," he said, fishing. For some reason she had been reluctant to tell him about MacRae.

"Alastair, we can't let this fail. My back's against a wall. I can make the investors you've lined up feel better if you'll get them in a conference room by, say, one-thirty P.M."

"It shall be done, dear lady. Have a good, quick flight back."

On her first day in Seattle she had insisted that her new secretary reduce all the company telephone numbers to a floppy disk so she could load them on her computer. She snapped her notebook computer on now, pulling out Fred Kinnen's home number. Letting him know where she was seemed inevitable, but there was no longer any need to pretend anyway. "They" already knew where she was.

"Hello?" The voice was sullen and sleepy.

"Fred? This is Elizabeth Sterling. I need some emergency help."

"Eliz ... oh. Are you still in London?"

The question froze her in her tracks.

He wasn't supposed to know where I am!

Ron Lamb was supposed to have kept her whereabouts secret.

"What did you ask?" she said.

"In London. Weren't you in London?" he repeated.

"Fred, who told you where I was?"

"You did. I got a fax from you, remember? You asked me to send a packet of financial data to a number over there immediately."

She sank back on the bed.

"Fred, I sent no such fax."

"But—"

"I'm telling you, I did not send you any such instructions."

"It had your *signature* on it!" He sounded panicked.

"What *exactly* did you send out of the office, Fred? And to whom?"

"Well, it didn't seem very smart, since this has been our worst week ever, but I prepared a special weekly cash flow printout through today's close of business, along with a weekly traffic analysis, and several others. This week our load factor's been at forty-eight percent, because of all the bad press, you know, and we're down in current cash to less than twenty-three million."

She felt her head swimming, but pressed on. He had the name of the company and the fax number he had sent the materials to, and a copy of "her" fax with a forged signature.

"Okay, Fred, did you send a memo of any sort at any time to Ron Lamb discussing the load factors and asking him not to let the financial community know?"

"A memo?"

"Yes, a memo. Did you write one or send one?"

There was a telling hesitation, as if he needed time to formulate an acceptable answer.

"You mean an interoffice memo?"

"Dammit, Fred, you speak English. Did you send a memo to Ron Lamb about the load factor, or didn't you?"

"Uh . . . no. No, I . . . I didn't write any memos about the load factor."

She could read the hesitation. "Okay, Fred, what did you send to London in the way of a memo?"

"You asked me to write one to Ron Lamb and send a copy to that number, and I did. I had no way of knowing it wasn't you. The memo just said you were making progress, and as long as nothing leaked out, you'd have things put together in a few days. That's all."

Someone used it as a template and inserted their own language, Elizabeth thought.

"Get a pen, Fred. Here's what I need, and I need it in the next three hours, faxed to Mr. Alastair Wood at the following number."

She gave him a list of financial summaries for the previous five months.

"Those will show a prettier picture, I trust?"

"Yes. Of course. We were doing well, until the past week."

He promised to dress and head for the office instantly.

"And, Fred, call Joe Taylor at home."

"The chairman?"

"Yes. Ask him if he ever wrote a memo to Ron recommending Chapter Eleven. And fax me a copy of his signature off a letter or anything else. I want to compare it to something over here he supposedly signed. Also send me a copy of that damn memo you wrote."

"I'll have to call him at home—"

"You sure will! And while you're at it, call our entire corporate finance staff and get them into the office. My secretary, too. Have everybody stand by to provide figures, summary sheets, facts, and whatever else I need to convince a roomful of doubting financiers that we're not really in trouble. This is an all-nighter, and everyone's job is at stake. Understood?"

"I guess so." There was, at last, the sound of real fear in his voice. "One thing, though."

"Go."

"That forty-eight-percent load factor?"

"Yes?"

"Our director of reservations believes that's essentially false. She told everyone yesterday that she thinks someone's worked a computer scam on us to show our flights as overbooked. It started last week."

"Call her at home. Tell her to be prepared to tell that story to me by phone at five-thirty A.M., your time. Have her give you the appropriate number and stand by the phone.''

"Elizabeth, she's not in our department. I can't order all these people around like that.''

"Fred, order whoever needs to be ordered, and do it on my authority. I don't have time to argue. If I don't succeed, kiddo, we're out of business.''

"Yes, ma'am.''

"Oh, and one other thing. Unless you actually hear my voice, don't follow any orders that supposedly come from me. If you get any more faxed orders to do something or provide something over my signature, get me on the phone immediately. In the meantime, don't do it.''

She checked her watch then and called Brian at his office, feeling a warm rush when his voice came over the line.

With their passengers placed on other airline flights to Frankfurt, and replacement electronic components installed, Brian and his crew had ferried their 767 back to Seattle from Gander, with Kelly and Virginia Sterling aboard. While they headed for Bellingham, Brian had headed for the office, eager to get back on the trail of whoever had monkeyed with his files.

"I'm gonna find that bastard, Elizabeth. I'm convinced all of this is the same person or the same team, well financed and organized, and determined to kill us.''

"What do you mean?''

"The files, the blown 747 engine, the attempt to bring us down on Clipper Forty, and probably even the stuff you're fighting with the loans. It's all the same campaign.''

She told him briefly of the latest agony, including the upcoming briefing.

"I don't know whether I can pull it off, Brian. I've asked to speak to these men, and they're not going to be eager to believe me. It turns out some of the devastatingly bad financial data they received is correct, and was in effect stolen from my assistant, but it isn't representative of what the company's been doing.''

"Tell them the truth. Tell them we're being attacked, and we're about to gain the upper hand.''

"Brian, would *you* want to lend large amounts of money to a company under such an assault, on the gamble that the smear tactics won't be successful? That's what I'm going to be asking them to do.''

"Tell them," he said, "that they've had smoke blown in their faces by people who know we're going to succeed. Tell them that Pan Am has the opportunity for faster growth and greater monetary success than any other airline on earth. And tell them that eventually whoever is behind this will end up paying Pan Am hundreds of millions in damages."

That puzzled her. "You've got an idea, don't you? Who?"

"Not on the phone, Elizabeth."

"No, I need to know now. If you've got a theory, let me have it."

There was a long silence before he answered.

"You can't tell anyone this. They'd think you were paranoid. Hell, *I* sound paranoid, but ask yourself this question: Whose profits do we threaten?"

"Well . . ."

"We threaten the big three in North America, don't we? Which carriers own the biggest reservations systems and have the biggest bucks to sabotage a growing airline like ours?"

"Brian, that's crazy."

"Is it? Think about it."

"You're saying the three major air carriers of North America are engaging in criminal *sabotage*?"

"Not directly. But who'd have to refurbish their fleets if our interiors and service—Compartment Class, for instance—became the standard? Suppose we get too big? You're talking about literally hundreds of millions, if not billions, of dollars at stake."

"Brian, that's nuts. And there are foreign carriers with as much at stake, too. It could be any one of them."

"Elizabeth, I'm not saying that the leaders of those airlines or their boards would ever do anything like this, but *somebody* with money and some degree of sophistication *is* tearing us apart. The only reason I can see that happening would be to protect the dominance of the big three. Nothing else makes sense to me. There's no way a single nut case could plant a bomb in our 747, slip a reworked black box in my 767, sabotage the reservations computer, and block you at every turn in the financial world. No lone wolf could be that clever or powerful or sophisticated."

"Brian, you're scaring me."

"I know it. I'm scaring myself," he said.

"Have you told Ron Lamb? I'm sorry, I mean—"

"You mean Chad Jennings?"

"Yes." The thought of Jennings running the company still seemed very strange. He seemed competent enough, but Brian had already hinted at a darker side to the man's abilities.

"Not yet," he replied, "but I may. We've got to act fast before they finally succeed and bring one of our airplanes down in flames."

"What can *Jennings* do about it, Brian?" Elizabeth asked.

"I don't know, but something has to be done. I feel like the kid pointing out the naked emperor. No one wants to believe me."

They ended the call with Elizabeth feeling hunted again.

She was opening the door to leave when the phone rang. This time Craig MacRae's voice filled her ear.

"Miss Sterling?"

"Elizabeth, please."

There was an uncomfortable hesitation. "Very well. Elizabeth, then. Lloyd White insists on calling me Craig, but I prefer Creighton."

"Thank you, Creighton. I'm in a rush for the airport . . ."

"I'll be brief. I spent last evening in research, and I've some promising leads. I'm leaving this morning as well, but I shan't tell you where just yet. Be careful not to mention my involvement to anyone. Do not even inform your office of our arrangement. I have your numbers. I'll be in touch within a few days. But . . . Elizabeth . . ."

"Yes?"

"I must warn you of something. If your company is up against the level of adversary I believe you are, understand that they have enough money to corrupt anyone. Trust no one with any information, however hackneyed that advice may sound."

"Don't *trust* . . . what exactly does that mean?" She knew she sounded skeptical.

"Dammit, woman, it means don't confide in anyone you aren't absolutely certain of, and give no substantive information over the phone at any time! I'm going to try to find you a new credit line, as well as a path to the enemy camp. But you'd be well advised to assume they're watching and listening to you at all times. Considering what they've already done, I feel certain they'll bend all efforts to deny you the money you need."

She sat deep in thought and said nothing as he slowly took offense.

"Look here. *You* searched *me* out because I'd been through the same. Kindly give me the benefit of experience and take the ruddy advice.''

She should have been irritated all over again at his outburst.

Instead, she was overwhelmingly glad he was on her side.

♦ ♦ ♦

The flight to London was a blur of conflicting thoughts and rapid notetaking as she tried to organize what to say. She had tried to call Ron Lamb in his Seattle hospital room before getting on the plane. But his speech was still massively impeded, and his wife recommended she wait a few days before trying again.

"Tell him I'm pulling for him, and I'm doing my best over here," Elizabeth told her.

"I will, dear, and he'll be appreciative. he's mentally sharp, he just . . . has trouble speaking." She had ended the call with an audible sob.

The taxi ride from Heathrow to East Central London was uncharacteristically quick. Alastair Wood greeted her at his office door with a stack of faxed financial reports from Fred Kinnen and a detailed briefing on the men who would be in the meeting—as well as detailed background information on those who had yet to sign. Elizabeth took thirty minutes to prepare herself before Alastair showed her into the modern, diminutive screening room and introduced her to the two dozen tight-lipped men who limply shook her hand and sat quietly, staring at her with cold skepticism.

All but five of them had already signed the loan agreement. She'd memorized the names of the five holdouts and emblazoned their faces in her memory as Alastair introduced them. As he closed the door to the small theater, she walked to the front with a relaxed air and smiled at them—willing the shaking inside to go away.

"Gentlemen, I appreciate your coming on short notice. In a nutshell, someone is trying to sabotage our deal by misrepresenting our performance, our stability, and our potential for profit. Even our own Federal Bureau of Investigation is working on this. In the meantime, I have verified data faxed in from my office in Seattle to prove to you that we are an excellent risk. The new Pan Am is *not* unprofitable. We are *not* failing as a going business. We are hiding nothing. And we are perhaps the brightest star in the airline constellation, which is why we have frantic enemies who become more desperate as we succeed.''

She moved to one side and examined the rug for a second. "You probably already know that I have only been CFO of Pan Am for the past two weeks. So how could I possibly know this airline's potential and its performance?" She let the question sink in as she moved to the edge of the stage and leaned against it. "Because I'm the very investment banker who spent two years constructing the financial package that put this airline in the air to begin with. You're all aware of Pan Am's marvelous start-up package, and I expect that most of you saw the cover article in *The Economist* two years ago about it. Well, the architect *and* the engineer of what they called a 'stunning success in orchestration of financial interests' is the person you're listening to right now. Me. That's what I do for a living, bring investors and investments together for mutual profit, and Pan Am's smooth start-up and subsequent success was no accident. It was carefully engineered."

Alastair had converted the new information sheets from Seattle to overhead transparencies, and Elizabeth began showing them now, tracing the rising curve of business and load factors through the previous months down to the previous week, when all of a sudden the sabotage of the reservations system had begun chasing away passengers by the thousands. She ticked off the elements of sabotage, including the FAA violations, the physical tampering with two airplanes, the files, and the reservations systems, and outlined how the first CFO had stupidly dismantled her carefully constructed start-up package, which she was now in the process of repairing.

"Not only is this week's downturn unusual and temporary, but I have on a speakerphone our director of reservations, to tell you just how artificial it really is."

The men in the room were slightly startled by the phone connection, but the voice of Laura Perkins in Seattle could be heard clearly as she explained that the legitimate load factor would have been above eighty-eight percent for the same week if the reservations computer hadn't been penetrated.

"Our projected load factor next week," Perkins told them, "despite all the bad publicity, is currently showing eighty-two percent."

"That's twenty-one percent above break-even," Elizabeth added.

Alastair Wood was smiling quietly from the far corner of the room as he watched her deft performance. He had seen her hands shaking before they walked in, and had harbored his own doubts about her abilities—doubts that were now gone.

There was a smile in the first row, the first break in the icy façade of professional caution that had greeted her.

Then another investor caught her eye and nodded. Many of them had been attacked before in business, and they could identify with what Pan Am was experiencing, as she went through the litany now of the frantic efforts of their enemies to scare away investors and interdict Pan Am operations.

She opened the floor to questions and they came hot and heavy, Elizabeth fielding each one with ease and a few with a promise for more information accompanied by a nod to Alastair's assistant, who instantly relayed the request to Fred Kinnen back in Seattle. By the time the questions had subsided, all the additional answers had been faxed in from Pan Am's offices in an impressive show of coordination.

After an hour and twenty minutes, Elizabeth permitted herself to survey the room once more. She had hardly dared to poll the expressions on those twenty-three faces, but now she was overwhelmed to see that the vast majority of the men were smiling and relaxed—and all but one of the critical five seemed satisfied.

That last one, however, raised his hand at last with a deep scowl.

"Yes, sir?"

The man was portly and distinguished, and he readjusted his position in his seat now, crossing his legs as if to underscore what appeared to be contempt. His voice rasped into the room with thundering authority, the Oxfordian accent carrying a laconic string of words designed to put this bit of American fluff in her place.

"Young lady, nary a bit of this blizzard of paper with which you are attempting to inundate us has had the benefit of notarization, nor, for that matter, has any of the glib and pretty promises you're purveying had the underscoring security of being sworn to by some responsible party, *nor*, I might add, have any of your polished polemics regarding the nay-sayers of Pan Am's future been counterchecked or endorsed officially by any independent auditor we've yet heard about. Put another way, dear girl, I've heard nothing I can well and truly trust. You may indeed be correct. And then again you may be selling worthless paper. Now"—he shifted position again, recrossing his legs as he propped his meaty right hand under his chin and waved some papers in his left—"perhaps the bloke who sent me these damning pages last night was lying, and perhaps he was an angel of mercy determined to prevent me from mucking up my portfolio with a dangerous loan. I can't tell which. And when I can't resolve an issue like this, I stay bloody well clear of the thing!''

The poisonous comment settled over the audience like a shroud. His eyes were hard and hateful and boring into her. How she answered this would be the ball game.

Elizabeth reached for a reserve of strength and confidence and found it. Her smile never wavered as she glanced at the ceiling for a second, smiling even more broadly, like a tenured professor achingly familiar with questions he'd answered a thousand times, yet determined to indulge the student as an intellectual equal.

"Lord Richards," she began, noting the subtle facial response that confirmed his surprise that she knew his name, "you were the driving force behind the successful growth of St. James Publishing through the acquisition of two old-line hardcover houses in New York and the acquisition of a major Japanese publishing house." She was reaching to the bottom of her memory, marshaling a dozen half-read magazine articles and praying she wasn't overstepping her ability to recall the details, but the facts came cascading in from distant corners of her mind.

"You, sir, in 1989, if I recall correctly, faced a massive difficulty on Wall Street when a major junk-bond issue was imperiled by the Boesky scandal, and what at that time was your highly leveraged empire seemed to be virtually teetering on the brink. You needed that financing badly to complete the plan you'd already set in motion, but you told the financial community in a series of meetings that your basic enterprises—the components of this empire—were very sound and well run and profitable. They almost didn't listen to you, because they didn't know you in America, and in fact a number of your backers bolted. You had to refinance the entire package and issue new common stock as well as bonds, a process that cost you millions of pounds and months of time. Do I have my facts straight, Sir Edward?"

She held her breath as she watched his face, which remained impassive for a few seconds. Finally a slow, sly smile began to spread across his craggy features as he answered. "Indeed you do, Miss Sterling."

"Good. Because my point is that those who believed you and stuck with you in what was an artificial crisis profited handsomely, and I have long admired you for not giving up in the face of rancid opposition. In regard to the sound and profitable nature of your company, the world discovered that you *were* telling the truth . . .''

She looked directly in his eyes, relieved to see him soften a bit and nod, a gesture observed by everyone else in the room.

"... and, sir, so am I."

♦ ♦ ♦

The papers were faxed to Seattle to a surprised Chad Jennings, who signed them as acting president and faxed them back by 3:30 P.M. By 4:00 P.M., Barclay's Bank had transferred via wire eighty-five million dollars in loan proceeds to Pan Am's main receiving account at Seafirst Bank in Seattle.

Friday, March 17, 10:00 A.M.
Pan Am Headquarters, Seattle

As Elizabeth Sterling settled back in a first-class seat aboard a British Airways flight direct from London to Seattle, an exhausted Brian Murphy was sounding an alarm to a roomful of shocked executives eight time zones away at Pan Am headquarters—and fielding questions laced with contempt.

Acting President Chad Jennings and most of the company senior executives had listened quietly to the idea that the three largest airlines in the country would ever engage in a criminal conspiracy to put Pan Am out of business, and had rejected it totally.

One by one, however, Brian had poked holes in any alternate theory. Ninety minutes after he started, the leaders of the new Pan Am filed out of the boardroom in a dazed consensus: apparently *someone* was out to ruin the new Pan Am.

Chad Jennings was still in the boardroom, questioning Brian, when Ralph Basanji, Pan Am's public affairs vice-president, arrived late for the meeting and caught corporate general counsel Jack Rawly on his way out the door.

"Can you fill me in what happened in there, Jack? I couldn't get away in time."

Rawly nodded and wordlessly motioned Basanji toward the elevators.

"I heard," Basanji continued, "that our chief pilot has a theory on what happened to his flight. What'd he say in there?"

Rawly silently put his finger to his lips as they rode down to the Fifth Avenue level.

"Care for a latte, Ralph?" Rawly asked at last, pointing to a Starbuck's coffee shop in the corner of the main floor.

"Sure." Basanji lowered his voice as he scanned around, looking for eavesdroppers. "Why the secrecy?"

Once again Rawly's finger came up to his lips as they ordered the espresso coffee drinks, and then retreated to a tiny table in the far corner by a plate-glass window that separated them from the street.

The corporate lawyer leaned over toward Basanji then, and cupped his hand, speaking in an urgent, low voice.

"Basically, Captain Murphy thinks we're under some sort of a coordinated assault designed to assist the big three in dominating the North American market. The theory is ridiculous and dangerous."

Basanji looked as if he'd been punched in the nose without warning, and Rawly raised his eyebrows to echo the surprise before continuing. "Murphy's had a hell of a couple of days, and his actions are heroic, but I think he's been without sleep too long." Rawly took a sip of his caffe latte and continued, "I'll admit he gave us a compelling argument that all the things that have been happening to us could be a coordinated assault by *someone*, but the overall question of exactly *who* could be responsible is a ticking bomb if we go off half-cocked and accuse someone powerful."

"What do you mean, 'coordinated'? What's coordinated? The Clipper Ten bomb and Clipper Forty's problem? I expected that."

"No. There's more," Rawly said. "Murphy's convinced that the files taken from his office were taken by the same people he says are creating deficiencies in our maintenance and training sections and then turning us in to the FAA for those same artificially created deficiencies. We're being framed, in other words. In addition, he thinks they're the same ones who've been giving our new CFO so much trouble trying to borrow more money, *and* the same people who've criminally sabotaged our aircraft. This is like listening to the John Birch Society's views on the American political process. Everything's riddled with sinister conspiracies, and 'they' are out to get us—whoever 'they' are."

"What if he's right?" Basanji asked.

"He may be!" Rawly shot back. "But to my way of thinking, the idea that the big three airlines would ever have anything to do with such a campaign is crazy!"

Basanji shook his head silently and stared at the street. Rawly let the silence sit for a few seconds before speaking again.

"Ralph, we may have a problem here. Jennings is buying this theory, and a few minutes ago up there he was talking about going public with his suspicions. Even Brian Murphy seemed horrified and warned him not to. But I saw a look in Chad Jennings's eye that has me spooked."

Ralph Basanji's mouth dropped open. "Going public?"

"You know, to the media. Your bailiwick. Your turf."

"He . . . he wouldn't!"

"He might. And he could trigger a massive lawsuit if he did. We certainly don't need that right now, any more than we need to make enemies of the big boys." Rawly paused, studying Basanji.

"Surely he knows better than to accuse other airlines of . . . of . . ."

"Does he? I don't know Chad all that well, Ralph. How prudent is he?"

Basanji shook his head. "He's not, really. You're right about that. He's a loose cannon—very smart, but temperamental and brash and sometimes embarrassingly immature. He's—" A Pan Am middle-level manager Basanji recognized passed outside the window at street level, and the public affairs chief glanced at him self-consciously. The man was looking down the street, however, and Basanji felt momentarily silly for hesitating. He turned back to the company attorney. "He's like an actor who occasionally steps out of character. As long as he's *in* character, he's great. But let something not go his way—get him upset, in other words—and Chad can become a petulant child."

"Wonderful," Rawly said, dripping sarcasm. "Does Joe Taylor have any idea of this?"

Ralph Basanji shook his head. "Taylor doesn't really know half of us very well. Ron Lamb assembled this management team."

"How much stock does Jennings hold?" Rawly asked out of the blue.

"*Our* stock?"

"Yes. I can look it up, of course, but I wondered if you might know."

Ralph Basanji studied Jack Rawly's face. The veteran corporate lawyer was difficult to read, but there was something worrisome behind that question.

♦ ♦ ♦

Brian Murphy's rapid departure from the Columbia Center past the same coffee bar went unnoticed by Basanji and Rawly. His appointment with the FBI was set for 11:00 A.M. at the Federal Building, several blocks away. He was already late.

Agent Miller and NTSB field investigator Michael Rogers were waiting for him in a small, utilitarian conference room.

"Okay, Brian," Miller began, "on the file folder we found only one print not attributable to your staff, and it was someone's single index finger. That print, however, is a bit strange. It's as if the guy took off a glove at one point and purposefully left a single print on the folder. It was clear, crisp, and pressed right into the fibers. For everything else he did, I'll bet your burglar wore latex gloves, but I'm beginning to believe the man replaced the folder on purpose—like he wanted to be discovered.''

Brian was confused by the presence of the NTSB man, but put the matter aside for the moment.

"Have you matched the print to anyone?" Brian asked.

Miller shook his head and raised a finger. "Wait. There's more." He smiled a knowing smile and pulled some papers from a transmittal folder. "We *have* found a better set of fingerprints on one of the circuit boards in that black box of yours."

"That's one of the reasons *I'm* here," Mike Rogers added.

Miller plopped the papers down in front of Brian.

"The index fingerprint from your black box, *and* the index fingerprint on your file folder?"

"Yeah?"

"They match! They belong to the same individual! The guy who rifled your files, and most likely tipped the FAA, also had contact with the circuit board that forced you down in the Arctic."

Miller let that sink in before continuing. "If the owner of these prints is in the national files—criminal, military, government service, or anything else—we'll find him. I've made it a high-priority search in Washington."

Brian mulled that over for a few seconds before looking up. "Would you let the FAA know this too?"

Miller nodded. "Already have. But we've got still more to tell you."

Brian found himself sitting on the edge of the chair.

"Go ahead. Please."

Mike Rogers took over.

"Okay, you'll recall we found some pieces of chromium on the underside of the wing of Clipper Ten, the 747?"

Brian nodded, and Rogers continued, "You also know about the newspaper reporter who got a tip that a mechanic's wrench had been left in the engine?"

"I saw the article. The little jerk tried to imply we were feigning sabotage to cover up our so-called negligence."

Rogers nodded. "Adrian Kirsch was the reporter you're talking about, but give the man credit. He came to me and reported the phoned-in tip before he printed it. I tried to make light of it to throw him off, but he saw through that. I, in turn, reported it instantly to Loren here. Though we weren't sure at first, we all now believe that the man who called Kirsch was the same one who planted the bomb on Clipper Ten. He knew damn well there was no wrench in that engine, but he'd set it up to look that way."

"How?" Brian asked.

"We think the plastic explosive was wrapped around a real chrome-plated wrench and placed inside the cowling near the top of the engine, where it connects to the pylon. We also believe he intended to just blow the engine off the wing at the strut and leave some residue of the wrench. He had to realize that if we found the engine, we'd know instantly it hadn't come apart from anything maintenance had done, so he tried to time it so the engine would drop offshore."

"Didn't he know you'd find explosive residue too?" Brian asked.

"Probably figured we'd seize on the wrench first. It was a sloppy plan. Whoever designed it was not a professional saboteur. He used far too much plastic explosive. We confirmed the presence of plastique residue on the underside of the wing at about the same time your man Conrad dredged up the engine."

"Wait a minute!" Brian said. "You mean this guy had no intention of crashing the aircraft?"

"I don't think he did," Miller said. "If your intention is to blow an airplane out of the sky over the ocean, you'd figure the wreckage might never be brought to the surface, or if it was, that it would take a long, long time to find it. Therefore, planting any misleading pieces of metal, like pieces of a wrench, on an airplane you expected to blow away would be a wasted effort. They'd never be found and you'd never get your red herring across."

Brian nodded, his eyes widening. "In other words, if you want to make Pan Am look incompetent, you do just enough damage to destroy the engine in a way that makes it look like mechanical failure, but you want the airplane to limp back so all this can be found out."

"Exactly," Rogers replied.

"By the same logic, then," Brian said, "provided it's the same guy, he didn't expect *I'd* lose both engines in flight with what he did to the circuit board, which means that in the case of my flight he may have been trying to cause an in-flight abort and merely cost us money and public humiliation."

"We're still looking at the circuit board," Miller said. "One of our technical people has flown it out to the manufacturer, and we're supposed to get word today on what the saboteur was trying to get the board to do."

Miller was studying Brian's face. "You see any logic in all this, Brian?"

Brian Murphy sat impassively for a second, staring at the wall as his mind turned over the possibilities. Slowly his head began to move up and down before he turned to the FBI agent and the NTSB investigator and snapped his fingers.

"It fits. It dovetails."

Loren Miller and Mike Rogers glanced at each other in puzzlement.

Brian jumped to his feet, his eyes aflame, and began pacing.

"I decided yesterday that all this garbage we've been going through was part of a single, coordinated campaign to run us out of business, but I had no proof, and I had no unifying motive. I needed a unified field theory, so to speak. Something that would explain why someone was not only creating trouble for us with the FAA, stealing files, and blocking us economically in the marketplace, but why such a person or persons would also try to commit mass murder. Everything made sense *except* the sabotage of our airplanes." He turned to Miller with the palms of his hands held to the ceiling. "You know, why in God's name would anyone who was just trying to run an airline out of business for economic reasons resort to wholesale slaughter? But that's just it! He didn't, and you've hit on the answer! Whoever did this was an amateur at sabotage, someone who was just trying to cause trouble for us, not kill people. In both cases, though, he went too far and screwed it up."

Loren Miller sat with his head cupped in one hand, his fingers tapping the side of his face thoughtfully as he watched Brian and listened to his words.

"Any idea who the perpetrator might be?" Miller asked.

Brian nodded. "Not a name, but a type. The sort of person or persons you're looking for would not normally know how to buy plastic explosives or how to get their hands on the right black box, let alone mess around with the circuit boards. A person like that would have had help for the technical aspects. Since he or she wouldn't know where to find it, there should be a trail a mile long for the FBI to follow. These have to be trial-and-error saboteurs, and I'd guess at least one principal and a confederate or two. There should be a bunch of people who'd remember dealing with someone purchasing parts and asking strange technical questions about the avionics of a Boeing 767."

Loren Miller made a note on a steno pad in front of him and looked up with a smile.

Brian studied the FBI agent's face before continuing. "One other thing, and this is just a guess, too, but I'll bet that when you find this individual, you'll find he was working for one or more of our competitors." He outlined his suspicions of the big three carriers.

Loren Miller listened carefully, as did Mike Rogers, but neither man seemed eager to accept the theory.

Miller cleared his throat at last. "There's one more item you and your company need to be aware of. The Bureau is of the opinion that someone on the inside is making this sabotage campaign much easier for whoever's carrying out the specific acts."

"A *Pan Am* employee, you mean?" Brian knew he sounded alarmed. Hadn't they eliminated that possibility when none of the employee fingerprints matched the one Miller had found on the file?

Brian let his mind flash quickly back over the assumption. All Pan Am employees were supposed to have their fingerprints on file. Even company officers. He remembered Ron Lamb complaining good-naturedly about the ink on his fingers when they took *his* prints, so that had to mean everyone. Unless . . .

Loren Miller's voice snapped the line of thought prematurely.

"Or a former employee, which is equally possible. We've already been working with your personnel department on that possibility."

"You've checked all our file prints against the one you found?" Brian asked.

Miller nodded. "Every index fingerprint in your personnel files has already been checked. There's no match."

♦ ♦ ♦

As Brian Murphy left the Federal Building, Pan Am public affairs chief Ralph Basanji was slamming the door of his car and fumbling with the key, trying to calm down so he could get it in the ignition. After leaving Jack Rawly, he'd searched quietly through the corporate offices for Chad Jennings for half an hour before discovering that Pan Am's acting president had just done a telephone interview with a newspaper reporter and was now headed to the local CBS affiliate for a network TV interview.

That Jennings would dare go on national television without at least having the courtesy to inform his PR chief was insulting, but what he was probably about to say to the world would be impossible to take back. Basanji reminded himself of the newspaper interview. It was probably already too late, but he had to try.

Basanji punched the number of the *Seattle Chronicle* from memory into his car phone and asked for Adrian Kirsch, the reporter he assumed Chad Jennings had been talking to. There was no way Kirsch would suppress the story if Jennings had launched an attack on the other airlines, but perhaps he could lessen the damage.

Kirsch's extension rang fruitlessly. Basanji left an urgent message on Kirsch's voice mail.

♦ ♦ ♦

The cameraman was dismantling his equipment and Chad Jennings was just getting to his feet when Ralph Basanji located him in a back room at KIRO television.

"Ralph!" Chad said with a saccharine smile when he spotted Basanji.

"Uh, could we talk, please?" Basanji began.

"Sure. I'm finished here." The reporter and crew thanked him, and he walked out to the parking lot with Basanji.

When they were out of earshot, Basanji whirled on Jennings.

"Chad, did you say anything in there about blaming other airlines? Did you say anything to a newspaper reporter before?"

Chad Jennings met Basanji's gaze and didn't blink.

"Yeah, I did. Is that why you're down here?"

"What did you say?"

"The truth. That United, Delta, and American are trying to run us out of business with a dirty-tricks campaign."

"Oh, jeez!" Basanji's shoulders slumped as he folded his arms and looked down at the sidewalk. "What else did you say?" Basanji asked quietly.

"Well, I said that because we refuse to fly cattle-car interiors like our competitors, and because our special interiors and our service are truly first-class, even in coach, the big three in North America are facing the terrifying prospect of having to reconfigure their aircraft to meet our challenge. That's why they've panicked and started hurting us."

Basanji looked back up at Jennings with a hard stare. "What did you accuse them of *doing*, Chad? What, specifically?"

"Sabotaging our reservations computer. But I also said we're actively investigating whether they've had a hand in anything else adverse to our interests, and that the FBI is also involved in the investigation."

Basanji closed his eyes momentarily and groaned.

"Hey," Jennings said harshly, "I'm in charge now, and that's my decision! We know they're behind this stuff."

"You also have a board of directors, Chad, and an executive committee, and they should have been in on this, as should I. We don't have any proof, Chad! This is grossly premature! What did you say about the accidents? What did you say about the 747 and the 767 incidents?"

Jennings snorted and smiled. "Nothing, of course. I'm not crazy."

They returned to the office separately and walked in on a frantic beehive of activity. Every telephone line seemed to be in use, and executives and secretaries alike were ebbing and flowing in fluid confusion back and forth through the various offices and hallways of the fifty-sixth floor, awash on the crest of some new crisis.

Basanji caught the eye of an administrative assistant and motioned her over to ask what was happening, already expecting the worst. Obviously, he thought, Jennings's hell-bent drive toward self-destruction had already blown into the media, and this was the opening round of the response.

"The baggage computer!" she said. "It's gone nuts."

"The . . . what?"

"Our baggage-routing computer. You know, the one that puts the bar-code tags on each bag and then tracks each one wherever it goes? Sometime this morning it decided to start sending every passenger's bag to the wrong location on different airlines, all over our system. Our first flights of the morning just began arriving in New York and in Washington, D.C., and not a single passenger's bag was on board, and it's the same for every flight worldwide that departed this morning our time."

"None?"

"None. The planes are carrying bags, but they're all the wrong ones. Our passengers' bags have been interlined all over creation!"

"By the computer?"

"Yeah. You wouldn't believe it! We've got"—she checked a long computer printout—"fourteen bags headed for Bangkok on Thai Air, several dozen routed on United to all sorts of destinations, about fifty into Delta's system, headed for Frankfurt, and several were even routed to Aeroflot."

"Aeroflot?"

"Right. To Kamchatka. We've got other bags headed for Buenos Aires, Cairo, Kotzebue in Alaska, Beijing, Cape Town, and"—she looked up at him over the top of her reading glasses—"and one lonely little cosmetic case bound for Katmandu, Nepal."

A harried-looking secretary hurried up to the woman with more printouts and Ralph excused himself and slipped into his office, closing the door on the baggage disaster. There was a worse disaster in the making. The CBS evening news would air on the East Coast in less than an hour, and the newspaper story would probably hit the wires later in the evening. Adrian Kirsch had not returned his call, which probably meant he had filed his story and gone home. With the media following what had already been dubbed "The Perils of Pan Am" in the previous week, Jennings's accusations would undoubtedly be a lead story. He decided to warn Joe Taylor, but first the legal department needed to gird for warfare.

He picked up the phone with a weary sigh and dialed Jack Rawly's extension.

Friday afternoon, March 17
Over northern Canada

Elizabeth came awake slowly, aware of the glare in her eyes as the British Air 747-400 chased the sun westward toward Seattle. She had been asleep since takeoff, some five hours ago.

She checked her watch and calculated their position. Somewhere below the solid cloud cover was the frozen lake that for many long hours had been both savior and captor to Brian, Kelly, and her mother.

At 41,000 feet there was only the soothing sound of the slipstream outside and the gentle rush of heated cabin air through the sidewall vents. Whatever might be going on in Seattle without her, she would be back in the thick of things soon enough. Another few hours of blissful ignorance seemed a reasonable indulgence.

She thought of Brian then. He would be there at Seatac Airport when her plane arrived, waiting to take her home. Maybe they could clear away the hurt of the previous weekend.

She glanced out at the clouds and let the full terror of almost losing her beautiful daughter wash over her, examining the fears that had been triggered and suppressed when she found they were all three on the ice. She had been panicked for Kelly's safety, and scared for her mother's.

But she had been *terrified* of losing Brian, and in that realization lay a decision. She wondered if he felt the same.

Elizabeth slowly closed her eyes, feeling herself relax, and let Brian's image smile at her as she drifted off into a dream state.

23

Friday, March 17, 4:45 P.M.
Denver, Colorado

*T*hrough the huge western window of the penthouse, the Front Range of the Rocky Mountains hung like a frosted living tapestry of rock and snow, a craggy backdrop spread from south to north beneath a cold azure sky dusted with the lacy beauty of cirrus clouds.

In the center of the industrialized frontier city, the skyscrapers of modern Denver stood like sentinels around the one glass-and-metal spire that supported the two-story penthouse—a five-million-dollar aerie reachable by private elevator or the helipad on its roof.

The owner—a lone figure clad in a silk bathrobe—paced now in silhouette before the mountain panorama, cordless telephone in hand. His footsteps echoed softly from the surface of the oak floor as he navigated around his expensive leather furniture and past a massive floor-to-ceiling collection of signed, first-edition works on the American West.

A lone servant, an elderly Filipino man, quietly cleared breakfast dishes and checked the progress of the brewing coffee as he practiced a long-standing and deliberate ignorance of his boss's business—while tracking his every move.

"By the way, where the hell have you been?" The man growled the question into the phone. "I've been waiting for you to call back for the past three days."

The man fell silent for thirty seconds as the person on the other end talked.

"You bet your ass I'm concerned! I sit here in Denver watching the news and hear that a 747 almost crashed because someone blew up an engine, and then a 767 loses both of its engines, and I can't help wondering if these little inconveniences might just be connected to you somehow, in which case I'd want to ask . . ." He stopped pacing and leaned over

229

as if bowing deeply, shouting into the phone, "HAVE YOU LOST YOUR ALLEGED MIND?"

With the window still vibrating from the words, he reversed direction and began pacing again, his right hand and arm flailing toward the window for emphasis.

"HEY! Don't forget this for a second. I didn't authorize—I haven't even SUGGESTED—screwing around with their planes! Yeah. Yeah. You damn well better NOT have had anything to do with—"

The man paused to listen.

"The woman's smarter than you thought she was. We lost her in New York, and it took days to find her again. She turned up in the U.K., and we tried to neutralize her efforts there, but we were too late. So now she's sucked the money in to pay off the bonds and that's that. We just go on to the next phase, that's all."

Silence.

"Yeah, well, it's time to finish this. It's been rather entertaining, shadow-boxing with that bimbo the last few days, but enough's enough. Her ability to interfere is coming to an end. I've got a timetable, and I'm under more pressure than you'd ever understand."

The servant quietly slipped a coffee service tray on the ledge in front of him and departed as silently as he'd come. The man in the bathrobe picked up the coffee cup and took a sip as he watched an airliner climbing out to the west over the mountains.

"Let's just put it this way: we're on schedule, and the clients are happy. It should be all over by the first. Now get back to work before somebody sees you hanging around a pay phone."

Friday March 17, 5:00 P.M.
Maple Valley, west of Seattle

Marvin Grade replaced the telephone receiver with a shaking hand and sat back in a rickety kitchen chair, his mind in confusion. His dark, fulminating hatred for the airline that had ruined his life had suddenly been emasculated by the reality that they were offering him a job. It made no sense, but it was an answered prayer.

After the collapse of the original Pan Am, he had spent the following years in a mist of deep depression, alcohol, odd jobs, and overdue bills. But when the new version of Pan Am started up, suddenly there had been hope again.

He remembered all too well having been turned down by the new Pan Am in the days that followed. The shock had left him broke and devastated, and nursing a dark and fetid hatred that grew like a cancer.

Grade's thoughts returned to the present, and he checked his watch. The Pan Am recruiter had said to be at the Seatac Operations Hangar at 9:00 P.M. He needed a shower, and looked down at his torn undershirt with embarrassment. He decided to wear his one remaining business suit and look sharp.

It was just after 5:00 P.M. The urge to get cleaned up and ready was overwhelming. He knew just how long it would take to get to the Pan Am Operations Center, and the last thing he wanted to be was late.

Friday, March 17, 8:05 P.M.
Seatac Airport

Elizabeth rubbed her eyes briefly before reaching down to close her briefcase and her carry-on bag, pointedly ignoring the irritated look on the face of the customs officer as she waited for Elizabeth to clear her table.

She'd slept for hours on the flight from London, but not well. Now she felt disoriented and tired—and disgusted with the dishwater blonde in the customs uniform and her obnoxious, officious attitude.

Elizabeth lifted the bags and walked the short distance across the bland linoleum floor to the exit and pushed through the doors—right into Brian's arms. They stood there holding each other tight as passengers navigated around them.

She sighed deeply at last and rested her head on his chest.

"I missed you so much!"

"I missed you, too," he said, gently pushing her away to look in her eyes. "You won't believe what's been happening!"

Brian took her bags and pointed toward the underground shuttle to the main terminal. Elizabeth reached up with her free hand and brushed Brian's cheek as the car began to move. "I want to go straight to Bellingham. Will you come with me? After what happened up there in Canada, I want all three of you with me."

He thought it over quickly and agreed. It was Friday night, and he'd done about as much as he could do before Monday.

"Thank you!" she said, relieved, not taking her eyes off his.

Brian smiled and nodded.

"Okay," Elizabeth said. "So tell me what's going on."

Brian leaned toward her and lowered his voice.

"In a nutshell, the FBI has evidence that whoever rifled my files also caused my engines to fail over the Arctic. Chad Jennings has gone public and accused United, American, and Delta by name of trying to run us out of business."

Elizabeth drew back, shocked, and looked at Brian's half-scared, half-incredulous expression. She had noticed his pent-up excitement, but she had assumed she was the cause.

"Gone *public*?"

He bobbed his head in a rapid, staccato motion.

"Lead story on two of the three networks this evening, and sure to be all over the newspapers in the morning."

Elizabeth realized her mouth was hanging open, but she was too preoccupied to care. She felt destabilized, her mind racing to calculate the effect on the financial community, none of whom would believe for an instant that the big three could be behind any of Pan Am's problems.

"Did you . . . ask him to do that?"

"Hell, no!" Brian looked slightly offended, then defensive, his right hand rotating palm-up in an apologetic gesture as a nearby passenger turned to scrutinize the source of the outburst.

His voice lowered, Brian continued.

"I . . . all I did was what I told you I was thinking of doing. I called a meeting this morning and told him my suspicions. I never recommended or even thought for a second he'd go public, but the next thing I know he's on the tube and flatly saying they're out to get us."

"This is what I warned you about. We're going to sound paranoid, Brian!"

"We already do," he agreed. "The FBI *is* on the trail of these people, and I *am* still convinced I'm right, but—"

"We have no evidence yet," she finished the sentence for him, watching him grimace and nod.

The doors opened and they moved out of the security area and up the escalator into baggage claim, Brian guiding Elizabeth to one side and away from other ears.

He filled her in on the FBI's theories and what he had told them of his suspicions, talking with animated gestures punctuated by flaring eyebrows. Elizabeth followed every syllable, interrupting occasionally with questions, until they both noticed that the bags had arrived on the carousel.

"I need to get my briefcase and overnight bag from the office," Brian said. "You need to stop by the condo?"

She shook her head. "No, but I'd like to stop at the Safeway up the street first.'' She raised the palm of her left hand and shrugged slightly, looking for an explanation. ''There are some things I need to pick up. There was no time in London.''

Friday, March 17, 8:05 P.M.
Maple Valley, east of Seattle

Marvin Grade ignored the fact that he'd already retied his tie three times, and did it again. He wanted to look professional.

He slid behind the wheel and fired up the throaty engine, checking his watch as he put the old Chevy in gear.

Eight-fifteen. I've got forty-five minutes. Good!

He accelerated slowly down the rural street—mindful of the noise his decaying muffler would make if he gunned the engine—and turned the corner, oblivious to a dark, late-model sedan that had been sitting in the shadows a half-block away.

As Grade's taillights disappeared around the corner, the sedan's engine came to life, and it began to move forward slowly, without headlights at first, following at a discreet distance the same path Marvin Grade had taken.

Friday, March 17, 8:45 P.M.
Seattle

Brian slowed as he rolled his BMW across the double speed bumps at the entrance to the Operations Center parking lot.

''No gate guard *yet?*'' Elizabeth asked, surprised.

Brian shook his head. ''The guard box will be installed next week. Meanwhile, we've got a guard twenty-four hours a day just inside the entrance to the complex, and a second one roving around with a radio.''

Brian nosed the car into his marked parking space adjacent to the office building's main door.

''Why don't you run in, and I'll stay out here,'' Elizabeth said.

Elizabeth locked the doors before reclining the seat and adjusting her head against the door post. It would feel good to catch a few minutes' sleep.

♦ ♦ ♦

Marvin Grade saw the double speed bumps too late to avoid being propelled into the ceiling of his car as he rolled into the Pan Am

Operations parking lot. He braked to a halt on the other side of the bumps and took inventory of his frazzled nerves. Then, he headed for the parking spaces in front of the main building adjacent to the hangar, as he had been instructed, and quietly selected a space to the left of an expensive-looking BMW.

Grade checked his watch. He had ten minutes.

I'll get out of the car in five minutes and walk in exactly on schedule, he decided.

He felt a chill shudder through him, and reached over to turn up the heater, leaving the engine idling as he watched the time and waited for the appropriate moment.

♦ ♦ ♦

Elizabeth had slipped almost instantly into a deep sleep. But now the dream she was in was being rattled by the sound of a loud car with a bad muffler. Slowly she swam back to the surface of consciousness. Without moving her head, she noticed the driver next to her, and the odd fact that in the dark—in an almost empty parking lot—he would choose a spot right next to Brian's car.

The engine was running. Why?

A creepy feeling began to grip her. She found herself taking mental inventory of possible defenses.

She glanced at the glass door that was the entrance to the building. She could see partway down the hall in the direction Brian had gone. There was no one in sight. She wondered if he'd locked the door behind him.

He's just sitting there! The way the man sat hunched over the wheel and staring straight ahead was unnerving. That and the fact that the engine was still running.

She caught a glimmer of light reflecting from the building door and slowly moved her head to see what had caused it. A dark car was entering the far side of the lot, triggering feelings of relief that she wasn't all alone. But the car stopped just inside the gate and sat there with the engine running. In the dim glow of the few overhead lights in the parking lot, she could see the car's exhaust fumes curling up into the night. She watched with increasing apprehension as the driver killed his headlights.

That's weird. Why did he stop there?

Elizabeth forced herself to calm down. She was locked in, and Brian would be back in a minute. Besides, she told herself, the sort of people they'd been fighting wouldn't be driving a beater like the car to her left.

Her mind ran through a summary of the malicious attacks on Pan Am: the airborne sabotage, the computer problems, the financial troubles . . . *and the presence of someone in Eric's apartment just before she'd arrived!*

A small voice began to whisper urgently in her mind: *Get out! Now! Get out of here!*

That made no sense, but she found herself leaning over the driver's seat and searching for the trunk release. She opened the gas tank and the hood before she found the right one, the satisfying *thunk* confirming that the trunk lid had opened. In one swift motion she opened her door and closed it behind her as she swept to the trunk and grabbed her briefcase— the instinctive need to protect the papers and the computer inside as great as the need to protect herself. She slammed the lid closed then, noticing that the car in the distance hadn't moved—and neither had the driver next to her.

Elizabeth moved toward the door that had swallowed Brian, feeling time dilate. Panic clawed at her stomach as she reached for the door handle.

It wouldn't open!

There was a sound from behind her now, the sound of a gearshift being moved. She began pushing at the door, harder and harder, until her hand hurt. She glanced over her shoulder and saw the shadowy figure behind the wheel look at his watch, and then glance in her direction.

She rattled the door as hard as she could, finally pushing against it with her shoulders.

The sound of a car door being opened reached her like a thunderclap. The man was getting out!

This is stupid! Calm down! Logic sought to regain control of the wild emotions propelling her—but logic was no match for panic.

''Damn!'' she said out loud, giving the door a mighty shove.

It wouldn't budge.

Panicked, Elizabeth began alternately pushing and pulling on the door, nearly falling backward when it flew open in her hands.

She rushed inside then, closing the door behind her and turning the lock as she saw the man in the old car begin to turn his body to get out of the driver's seat. She headed down the hallway as fast as she could without running, her heart pounding, half expecting to hear the sound of smashing glass behind her.

She found Brian closing a file cabinet in his office. He looked up, startled at her wide-eyed appearance.

"Elizabeth? You okay?"

As she opened her mouth to reply, the soul-jarring impact of a massive explosion shuddered through the office complex, accompanied by the sounds of breaking glass and crashing metal.

"What the hell was *that*?" Brian's voice was loud and panicked, his eyes—like hers—huge with adrenaline and shock.

They reentered the hall together, tentatively, and began moving carefully toward the front of the building.

The glass door had been shattered and thrown inward, completely off its frame, as had an adjacent window. Glass and flying metal had wrecked the outer reception area. They had to step gingerly over various unidentified debris as they walked through the opening where the door had been and out onto the parking lot.

Wreckage was everywhere. The shadowy form of the flaming hulk of a car lay on its side some fifty feet to Brian's left. He recognized it as the remains of his BMW.

Where the Chevrolet had been sitting, there was only the twisted skeleton of a car, its interior on fire. People were beginning to converge from various directions. Elizabeth recognized at least one guard in the group. In the distance, she thought she saw the occupant of the dark-colored car get out and run toward the scene as well. She and Brian began circling the wreckage warily, her mind numb as Brian's amazed voice rang in her ears.

"My God, Elizabeth, there was a bomb in my car!"

She realized she was shaking her head. His BMW was shattered, but the basic structure was still intact. The old car, however, had been literally blown apart.

"No. It was the car next to us. He came in . . . sat there . . . was running his engine."

"There was someone *in it*?"

She nodded as her mind filled in the implications. There was no one—no *body*—visible in what was left of the old beater. That meant that . . .

Elizabeth looked down, confirming the grisly fact that more than metal debris was strewn at their feet. She backed up slowly, checking every footfall, as other would-be rescuers converged on the scene, realizing as they drew close that the remains of at least one person had been scattered in small bits.

Brian's arms suddenly enfolded Elizabeth, and he swung her around to face him. He was ashen. Even in the soft sodium-vapor light of the parking lot, he looked as if he'd seen a ghost.

"I . . . what made you . . . I mean, thank God you came in!"

"He scared me," she said simply, knowing there had been more to it. Her voice sounded small and distant. "It was creepy."

Brian hugged her, aware that she was dazed, and kept her face in the direction of the building as his eyes surveyed what was left of his car.

He could make out the remains of the steering wheel of the BMW. In the light of the flames, he could see clearly the twisted framework of the passenger seat Elizabeth had occupied.

It had been shredded instantly.

"Dear God, I guess I was wrong," he said quietly, stroking her hair and holding her tight. "They *are* homicidal."

Monday Morning, March 20
Seattle

The mood in Pan Am's corporate headquarters was dark and angry. Elizabeth's attitude matched. They were under attack, and the weekend had been a joyless search for answers as she and Brian had huddled at her mother's house in Bellingham, the seriousness of the situation suppressing even Kelly's ebullient personality. There was, Elizabeth had explained to her daughter, a very real possibility that Pan Am could fail if much more happened.

"Leaving you both unemployed," Kelly had observed quietly.

No one yet knew precisely why the car had exploded in the Operations parking lot at Seatac. But the campaign against Pan Am seemed to have taken a very personal turn—something Elizabeth had never expected.

She wasn't sure who the target had been, but the car bomb had been an epiphany—the straw that broke the back of her fears—and her attitude had steadily evolved through the weekend from shock to pure anger.

By Sunday afternoon, Pan Am's frantic Executive Committee had called a Monday-morning board meeting to deal with the burgeoning public-relations crisis Jennings had unleashed. Over the weekend, the articles and television reports about Pan Am's accusations against the big three had ballooned into a major story. The mood of the board was vindictive, the possibility of firing Chad Jennings being openly discussed.

Thanks to Jennings, the airline industry was in an uproar of collective indignation, all aimed at Pan Am. The big three carriers had each returned fire with a fusillade of bitter denials and furious denunciations, all laced with counter-threats of legal actions for defamation. Jennings had been snarled at personally by all three chairmen, and lawyers on all sides were reportedly drawing up lawsuits—while the media continued to press Jennings for evidence he didn't have.

The board ordered Jennings to apologize or be fired. At first he refused, but just as quickly relented, retreating to his office to call the media for yet another round. Grumbling and furious, the outside directors milled toward the door, an embarrassed and angry Joseph Taylor among them. Elizabeth was heading quietly for the same door when Taylor snagged the sleeve of her dress.

"That was good work, getting the loan from London. I'll be frank with you. I didn't think you could do it."

She smiled at him. "I'll be frank with you, Joe. With the constant harassment and interference I was getting, I wasn't sure I could, either. But I've found some new allies for us."

"Oh? Who?"

She shook her head. "I don't trust even this room to be free of bugs. Let me keep that to myself for a while." She watched his bulging eyes, wondering if he was going to take offense, but a smile spread across his face and he chuckled out loud.

"Always been my method to hire good people and get the hell out of the way, so you tell me only when you think I oughta know."

"Thanks."

"Just keep on plugging. I have faith in you." He patted her arm with an overly solicitous grin and turned away, leaving Elizabeth in no doubt that he would jettison her the instant she seemed no longer useful.

The board meeting had been over less than ten minutes when Brian phoned from Operations with the news that the Seattle police and the FBI had discovered the identity of the man killed in their parking lot.

"Marvin Grade is the name. Get this. He was a former mechanic for the old Pan Am. Personnel says he applied to us for a job during the start-up a year ago, but wasn't hired."

Elizabeth sat back in her desk chair and cocked her head.

"So this was just a . . . he was just holding a *grudge*?" she asked. The possibility seemed crazy. After all, other than the obvious mess, what would be the point of committing suicide in the parking lot of a company he didn't work for? Elizabeth hadn't expected that possibility. She and Brian had both assumed the bombing was related to all their other troubles.

"Who knows? They're thinking suicide, but the police are searching his house in Maple Valley right now."

Over the years in New York, Elizabeth had lost two co-workers to suicide. In the case of one, there had been months of warnings that everyone—including Elizabeth—had ignored. In the other, a quiet middle-level account manager she had just upbraided for a small mistake had apologized and then retired to his office to retrieve a special tool he'd lifted from building maintenance months before. Without leaving a note, the man had quietly opened a window and stepped out to oblivion. His gruesome death and his grieving family had left Elizabeth profoundly shaken and racked with unfocused feelings of guilt.

She closed her eyes and tried to shrug away the memory.

"Brian, a suicide like that seems . . . pointless."

They had tried out theories most of Saturday night in front of the fireplace in Bellingham, Elizabeth trying to recapture a vague memory—a nagging feeling that there was something she had seen or heard or felt just before the explosion that might be material.

But the memory—if there was one—wouldn't come.

"You reminded them about the black car?" she asked at last.

"Yes."

"Was it the FBI?"

"Nope. The FBI says they weren't aware of this poor fellow. And they don't believe the black car you saw was connected, either. You said you saw the driver run toward us after the explosion?"

"I thought so, yes."

"They say that shows that whoever was in the black car wasn't involved. So it was probably a spectacular suicide—or an accident."

"What do you mean, an accident?" she asked.

"Remember our alternate possibility? The guy brings a bomb into our complex planning to install it in an airplane, but it blows up prematurely and kills him."

"Which would make him the saboteur," she said softly.

"Could be. It makes sense. A former mechanic who probably knew the 767 and 747. Whoever's been fooling with our aircraft has done a pretty amateurish job in some respects, but he also knew our planes and how to get to them."

Elizabeth heard Brian sigh on the other end before he continued. "Anyway, we might know something after they search his house. I'll call you as soon as I hear anything."

Elizabeth hung up the receiver at the same moment she noticed an ashen-faced Fred Kinnen in the doorway, holding some papers. She motioned him to the chair across the desk. Kinnen closed the door before sitting down.

"Fred? You look like you're in shock."

He glanced nervously at the papers in his hand, then looked up at his boss before speaking.

"I am," he said, sliding the two-page fax across the desk to her. "I think we're screwed."

She recognized the letterhead. It belonged to the lead bank of the consortium that provided Pan Am's revolving credit line.

She read the terse paragraph over twice in disbelief.

> You are hereby notified that in accordance with Section Five, Page 42, Paragraph 13, subparagraph (a.) and (b.), the Lenders do hereby declare that they have, for good cause, lost confidence in the credit worthiness of the Debtor, and in accordance with Section Seven, Page 53, Paragraph 8, do hereby declare the entire balance of the loan proceeds advanced under this agreement to be due and payable in accordance with the schedule set forth thereby.

Elizabeth looked up at Kinnen with an equally shell-shocked expression. "Did you look up that . . . that section?"

He nodded. "We've got seven days to repay one hundred forty million dollars, and half of the remaining balance at thirty days and sixty days respectively from the date of this notice. Otherwise they formally declare us in default."

"My God!"

"I know," he said.

"They"—she placed the fax on her desk and gestured at it as if someone's pet rattlesnake had been dumped on her blotter—"can *do* this?"

Kinnen shrugged.

"*Why* are they doing this, Fred? What do they mean, 'lost confidence'?"

She saw his eyes fall to the papers on her desk and realized there was something else he was holding back.

"Fred? *Fred?* What do you know about this?" Her words came through clenched teeth, her voice shaking with anger. "What happened?"

His head bobbed up and down once, then again several times, and his eyes finally rose to meet hers as he took a ragged breath.

"Jennings happened. After you called from London, or wherever you were. Just after the board appointed Jennings acting president, the chairman took him aside. I couldn't overhear all of the conversation, but a few minutes later Jennings told me that Taylor said he had no confidence you could get the money in time. Joe Taylor directed *him* to try to get the eighty-five million through other channels, including local—or so he claimed.''

"Local? You mean, Seafirst Bank, U.S. Bank, that sort of local?''

"Yes.''

"That's idiotic!''

Kinnen nodded. "I tried to explain that. I tried to tell him he'd be touching a lit cigarette to the tail of a tiger if he approached them without the proper buildup, but he set up an appointment and raced right over.''

Elizabeth sat back, thoroughly stunned. "And, of course, the first thing they did with our financial reports was call up and ask questions of our current debt holders, tipping them off that we were desperate, and giving them all the excuse they needed to trigger this provision.''

"Yes.''

She looked down at the desk and drummed her fingers for a second, formulating a battle plan.

"First, go get the general counsel—what's his name?''

"Jack Rawly.''

"Right. Ask him to come in here immediately. Then locate Joe Taylor. Don't tell him anything yet, just don't let him leave town.''

"How about Mr. Jennings?''

"We'll deal with him later.''

By noon, Elizabeth had cleared the small crowd of officers and co-workers from her office, closed the door, and relayed the depressing news to Brian. She was probably violating officer confidentiality, but it didn't seem to matter anymore. Brian was the only one she could really trust.

"If we don't repay one hundred forty million in seven days,'' she explained, "they declare us in default, the lessors reclaim the airplanes, wherever they are, and we're no longer an airline.''

"Can we do it?'' Brian asked, his voice as cold sober as she had ever heard.

"No. Not conventionally. I mean, I'll try my best, but . . .''

"What *can* you do?''

She rubbed her eyes and thought. "I've tried to talk to the lead banker, but he's as cold as ice and about as responsive. I'll keep trying to negotiate, but, Brian, I don't think they *want* to negotiate. This is part of the campaign, don't you see? I surprised them by getting the eighty-five million.

They didn't think that would happen. When it did, they had to find another way to shut us down, and this is it."

"Then it's all but over," he said.

"Not necessarily. I could save us if I could replace the entire credit line, which was what I was getting ready to do anyway and eventually can . . .''

"You need more time, then?" Brian asked.

"Yes. If we could get that deadline extended somehow, I think I could do it." She winced inside at floating such a pretty lie to Brian. There was no outside source of money to go to. She had already been to the one trough not contaminated by whoever their enemy was, but now the entire financial community of Planet Earth would be alerted.

There was another line holding for Elizabeth. She ended the call with Brian and punched the appropriate button, unprepared for Creighton MacRae's baritone voice to fill her ear. She had all but forgotten about MacRae.

"I want you to call me back in thirty minutes from a public phone somewhere else in the city. The reason should be obvious," MacRae said, and relayed the number.

"Creighton, we've got a major crisis in progress, and I shouldn't leave the office."

"You want to solve that crisis?"

"Of course. Yes."

"Then do as I ask. Please." There was a long pause before he continued. "Do you remember I warned that you might be dealing with a very powerful adversary?"

"I remember."

"Turns out I was right. Call me in thirty minutes, and don't be followed to whatever phone you use. With modern surveillance equipment, people can read lips from a thousand yards, or pick up the vibrations of your voice from the same distance."

She left the office almost immediately, and took the elevator to street level, walking north at a brisk pace as the cellular phone rang in her purse with Brian on the other end.

"Elizabeth. Marvin Grade was our saboteur!"

"What?"

"They found plastic explosive, timing devices, false ID badges, the whole works in his house, *and* electronic parts stolen from United in San Francisco. They got him, honey. The son of a bitch was just too ham-handed to do things right, and he blew himself up accidentally. He wasn't after either of us.''

''Thank God for that,'' she said, wishing she could sound more convinced. ''But what *was* he doing there?''

Brian was breathing hard with excitement. Even against the background noise of the traffic, she could hear him almost gasping for breath.

''Probably getting ready to sneak into the hangar and wire up another airplane to explode in mid-flight. I feel sure this is the same character who rifled my files and got us in trouble with the FAA. This should clear away all that talk about the FAA considering a Pan Am shutdown.''

''It doesn't explain all the other things, though,'' she said.

''What? You mean the financial stuff?''

''*And* the computer interference with reservations, *and* our baggage computer, *and* the creepy thing in New York at Eric's apartment.''

''Yeah, well, Grade monkeying with our airplanes at the same time someone else out there is hurting us through financial dirty tricks is probably just a spooky coincidence. We're still obviously on somebody's target list, but at least we know now that that somebody isn't an assassin or an attempted mass murderer.''

I wish I could be sure, Elizabeth thought.

''Where are you?'' he asked. ''I can hear traffic.''

''Heading up the street to a meeting,'' she lied.

''With whom?'' he asked.

It seemed an idle question, but when she decided not to mention Creighton MacRae, a small shiver of apprehension ran down her back, as if she were about to do something wrong and might be caught.

''Just a small matter with one of the banks,'' she told him, unhappy with herself that the little lies were flowing so easily from her lips.

Elizabeth dodged a young man on a delivery-service bicycle and stepped off the curb momentarily before regaining the sidewalk.

''I'd better go before I run into a wall talking on this thing,'' she told him, promising to check in later.

Seattle was radiant beneath clear blue skies, but in her mind the city had already begun to fade at the same rate as Pan Am's prospects. The thought of a happy and stable life in Seattle with Brian and Pan Am had seemed like a distant dream back on Cape Cod as she had stared westward and wondered whether to accept Ron Lamb's offer. Her relationship with Brian had seemed ethereal and uncertain, but the closer she got to Seattle, the more real it had promised to be.

Now she caught herself thinking about Eric in New York, wondering whether she should tell him to cancel the sale of her partnership. She remembered all too clearly the disastrous night in the new condo with Brian. A sudden suffocating pall of sadness draped itself over her determination, as if defeat were inevitable. Returning to Manhattan would be a loser's retreat, but where else could she go?

Elizabeth realized she had come to a halt in the middle of the block, and several people were trying not to stare. She folded the phone and put it away as she resumed walking, making certain no one was tailing her.

She found the perfect pay phone in a back alcove in the Four Seasons Hotel—out of sight, out of earshot, and out of the mainstream.

MacRae answered immediately.

"Can you meet me this afternoon in Vancouver?" he asked.

"I . . . suppose so. Why not Seattle?"

"You're being watched in Seattle. Even if you got away, you could be spotted again."

"Watched? You're sure?"

"Yes," he said. "Elizabeth, I'm in Houston, Texas, at the airport. I've got an old friend here who's interested in helping. We're flying up there in his jet in a few minutes. I've arranged for a financier from Hong Kong to meet us in Vancouver as well. Incidentally, I'm aware of what your president did last Friday. While he's correct that the interests of the three major airlines are involved, they're not responsible."

"I don't understand. You mean United and—"

"All three airlines stand to benefit greatly if Pan Am fails, but it isn't the airlines themselves who've been working against your interests. Their hands are clean. Someone else is doing all this to protect their investment in the big three, someone who obviously feels you're going to impact the comfortable cornering of the market the big three have managed under deregulation. You've made the mistake of becoming too successful and upsetting their neat little plan for raping the U.S. airline consumer."

"My God, Creighton, how do you know all this? Do you have hard proof? Do you have anything we could take to court?"

"Not yet, but I'm certain of what I'm saying. I can't tell you why just yet, and I can't tell you who's doing it. I'll tell you more in Vancouver."

"Our enemy is a stockholder of all three airlines?"

"My guess is a huge, very rich company."

"You don't have a . . . a suspect, for want of a better word?" she asked.

"I know what to look for, but I've got to find the needle-in-the-haystack financial trail through the electronic banking networks first. That's going to take a bit of bother. In the meantime, you need money."

"More than you know." She filled him in on the cancellation of the revolving credit line. Creighton MacRae was silent on the other end for so long, Elizabeth began to suspect the line had gone dead.

"Very well," he said at last, "then we're going to have to dance to their deadline. March twenty-seventh, you say?"

"Yes," she said. "Next Monday. The same day our new round-the-world service is supposed to start from New York. I suspect they timed this for maximum public-relations impact so they could seize the airplanes in front of network camera crews."

"Indeed."

"Creighton, if we had anything we could take to court about this linking the revolving debt holders with any of these dirty tricks, we could get an injunction and stop the clock."

"I understand that. I just don't have the proof yet. It should be easier and quicker to get you the money to pay them off than to find enough evidence to make a court case this rapidly. As I warned you last week, people at that level are very good about covering their tracks."

"If it's a stockholder common to each airline, shouldn't the name show up pretty easily by examining their stockholder lists?"

"We've already looked," Creighton responded. "No one company or name shows up substantially on all three, and that wouldn't be a very smart way for them to do it, in any event. What I suspect they've done is to purchase a large amount of common voting stock of each airline. Then they scatter it in the hands of many small dummy holding companies that are all, in turn, owned by the single large company. It could take weeks of digging to ferret out such a clandestine ownership chain, and it might be impossible to uncover—unless we get a lucky break."

"You feel lucky, I hope?" she asked without a tinge of humor.

His reply was almost sarcastic.

"I always hope for luck, dear lady, but I never depend on it. The bottom line is this: I don't know who the ultimately responsible company is, but it's very powerful. If you expect to refinance that revolving line, you're going to have to do so in complete secrecy. That's what I'm trying to arrange."

"When do you want me to be in Vancouver?"

"First let's deal with the method of getting you there without uninvited guests tagging along. Hire a car and drive. Don't fly. If you talk to an airline, they'll pick your name up in the reservations computer in a second. Use some disorganized, computer-poor, second-level hire-car company. Just walk up. Don't make a reservation, and for heaven's sake, don't tell anyone at your office.''

He gave her the rendezvous address in Vancouver and rang off. They would meet in the Tai Pan Suite of the Delta Court Hotel at 6:00 P.M.

Monday, March 20
Seatac Airport

Captain Dale Silverman had been the only Pan Am employee to get a good look at the man who'd apparently sabotaged Clipper Forty's electronics in Denver on March 10. The description he'd later given the FBI fit the late Marvin Grade like a glove. Silverman had been on a layover in Tokyo when he heard the news of Grade's death from an inbound Pan Am pilot. Back home at last, the Pan Am captain stood at the bulletin board in the pilot's lounge at Seatac Operations, intensely scanning a clipping about Marvin Grade's demise—a story containing a picture the local newspaper had obtained from Grade's ex-wife in New Jersey. Grade, it reported, was a disappointed job-seeker who'd stalked the new Pan Am with murderous intent, and sabotaged two Pan Am aircraft.

There was only one thing wrong.

Silverman removed the clipping and walked straight to Brian Murphy's office, finding the chief pilot behind his desk.

"Brian, you got a minute?"

"Of course, Dale. What's up?"

"You've seen this picture?" Dale Silverman carefully placed the clipping on the desk in front of Brian and pointed to the face in the photograph.

"Yes. Why?"

"Brian, this is not the man I saw in Denver!"

Monday, March 20, evening
Vancouver, British Columbia

Elizabeth accelerated across the Cambie Bridge and into the heart of Vancouver, her attention momentarily lost in the sheer magnificence of the scene before her.

Beyond the frieze of downtown structures, a carpet of twinkling lights climbed the north shore of Vancouver's harbor beneath an indigo sky as the last vestiges of orange and red disappeared to her left over the craggy outline of Vancouver Island. At sundown, the premier metropolis of western Canada transformed itself with magical synergy into a rare and exquisite blend of manmade and natural beauty, and to Elizabeth—having grown up just to the south, in Bellingham—it was always like coming home.

There was a single parking spot left on the street near the hotel. Elizabeth took it gratefully, locking the car and pulling her briefcase from the trunk—surprised when the routine act suddenly brought back the horror of Friday night.

With three hours on the road from Seattle to think, the elusive memory she'd searched for over the weekend returned. The doomed man in the old Chevy had been in the process of getting out when she last saw him. Somehow that seemed significant. She would call Brian later and relay the information—though it probably meant nothing.

A gaunt young man with pronounced Asian features and a distinct Chinese accent answered the door of the Tai Pan Suite and introduced himself as Jason Ing from Hong Kong. Creighton MacRae had already arrived with Jack Bastrop, the owner of the three-engine Falcon 50 business jet that had carried them up from Texas in a four-hour flight. Both men got to their feet to greet her.

She wasn't prepared for Jack Bastrop. He stood well over six feet tall, but the physically intimidating effect of his barrel chest and heavily jowled round face became even more pronounced when he extended a huge, beefy hand to Elizabeth, shaking hers with shocking gentleness. His voice, too, was subdued. He spoke in deep, rumbling tones.

"Delighted to meet you, Miss Sterling," he said, relaxing her with a friendly smile.

Creighton's handshake in turn was proper. But it was not businesslike, and she realized he had lingered a few seconds with her hand in his. She refused to let herself acknowledge the warmth his touch aroused—the same feeling that had shocked her in Scotland.

"It's good to see you, Creighton," she said, managing her voice.

Creighton motioned them all to the large couch. Elizabeth sat next to Jack Bastrop as Creighton took a flanking chair closest to her and leaned forward earnestly.

"In brief, Jack is the man who helped me when no one else on the planet would consider it. In the end, we didn't succeed in keeping the airline alive, but—''

Bastrop raised his hand to silence Creighton, and finished the sentence for him. "We didn't succeed, Miss Sterling, because the consortium against Creighton was far too well organized. I, too, have a score to settle, whether your attacker is the same group or not. This is not altruism, of course. I expect to make a profit on anything I do for you. But I'm equally incensed, and equally eager to block international bullying.''

"Please, call me Elizabeth," she told him. "You . . . think there's a chance I'm fighting *the same company?*''

Jack Bastrop looked at Creighton MacRae as if to ask how much he should tell her. MacRae nodded.

"Elizabeth," Bastrop began, "does the name Irwin Fairchild ring a bell?''

She knew she looked shocked, but there seemed no reason to hide it. "I should have known that worm was involved!" Elizabeth said through clenched teeth. "I saw him in New York last week, and yes, I know the felonious little snake all too well.''

Jack Bastrop explained that Fairchild had been the operative who spent more than a year engineering the financial isolation of Creighton MacRae's start-up airline in Britain.

"He was working," Bastrop continued, "for want of a better description, under contract to a group of corporations in the U.K., France, and Germany. When Creighton finally won his lawsuit, it was against that consortium, but Fairchild escaped liability. Yet, he was the dirty-tricks facilitator—the financial trigger man, so to speak.''

"So he's doing the same thing to us, and for the same people?'' she asked.

"No," Creighton interjected. "We're sure it's not the same group. But we were equally sure walking in here that Fairchild is involved. You've just confirmed it.''

She filled in the details of the New York encounter, and Fairchild's obvious interference with the loan she had been trying to arrange.

"By the way, Jason knows Fairchild from an even closer perspective. Fairchild does a lot of his money laundering through a bank in Hong Kong, a competitor of Jason's called the International Trading Bank, or ITB.''

Jason Ing had disappeared before they sat down. He returned now, and sat opposite Creighton on Elizabeth's left. A bartender appeared quietly to take drink orders, and just as quietly departed to fill them. The background was filled with the sounds of a Vivaldi concerto.

Creighton spread a hand-drawn chart on the table. "Elizabeth, I want to get to the subject of securing Pan Am enough money to replace your five-hundred-million credit line, but first let me give you a clear picture of what I believe you're facing, and why."

"In our opinion," Jack Bastrop added.

"Right," Creighton agreed, turning to Jason Ing. "Jason, this is for your benefit, too." He looked back at Elizabeth. "Jason represents a substantial investment house in Hong Kong that has never held any airline interests." He pointed to the names of United, American, and Delta along the bottom of the chart. "Okay. U.S. deregulation was an unmitigated disaster, of course. The idiot idea of zero government control of what is essentially a public utility destroyed the U.S. airline industry. It also created opportunities for fast-buck artists like Irwin Fairchild and Nick Costas and others to steal billions and leave old-line airlines like Columbia Air in ruins. What's left are the big three and a few successful niche carriers, like Southwest and Alaska. Now, Elizabeth, when your Congress finally awoke and decided to block foreign takeovers of U.S. airlines, that frustrated a powerful group of investors in Europe and Asia who had been planning to cash in on the lucrative U.S. airline market. That's the major part of this story, because those chaps didn't go away. They've now secretly secured a huge interest in each of the big three airlines—or so we believe—and you've become a threat to their plans."

The waiter returned with a silver tray of drinks. Elizabeth took her glass of wine before continuing.

"How," Elizabeth asked, "can anyone expect to make a killing just by owning shares in all three? Especially if the ownership is secret and they can't exercise any voting control or hold board positions?"

"Because their plans are global. The consortium I ran afoul of had a master plan to hold monopolies in various world markets. If there were three carriers in a particular market or country, they would quietly buy up all three, and then slowly eliminate competition among them as they divided up the pie. The idea didn't work in Britain, and it hasn't happened fully in Europe. But if you trace the corporate ownership of many of these international airlines, you'll begin to find the same interests in the background. It's happening."

Elizabeth's eyes must have flared in surprise, since Creighton moved back a few inches in reaction to her expression. "You're telling me this is a worldwide *plot?*"

"No. Not a plot, as in 'conspiracy.' This is a business plan, and a brilliant one, designed to create huge multinational transportation giants with monopolies all over the world and unlimited power."

"I had no idea!" Elizabeth said.

"Just think of the potential, if you could own and control major airports, and all sides of the transportation equation coming in and out of them—airlines, taxicabs, trains, hire cars, buses, and all cargo shipments. Certainly you'd divide it up into a multitude of different companies and names so the unwashed masses and their politicians wouldn't catch on they were being fleeced. But if you were the ultimate owner and the ultimate authority who eventually collected the dividends from a controlled market, you'd have an endless money machine and more power than many governments. Anyone who wanted to go anywhere or ship anything would, ultimately, have to deal with you."

"Could they really put such a thing together?" Elizabeth asked.

Creighton nodded. "Unlike American corporations, which seem to plan only for the next thirty minutes, the men running this type of organization think very clearly ten to twenty years ahead. They're like a geological force, Elizabeth. They operate on the same principle that permits tectonic forces to warp the earth's landscape so slowly and steadily that we aren't aware it's happening. Slow, determined, steady, and backed by immense financial force."

"That's quite an analogy. I know a few things about plate tectonics," Elizabeth said.

"It's an apt analogy, though. These people have the wisdom to know that if they move slowly, they can change almost anything to their liking. The problem comes when you block them cold, as my airline did, or conceptually threaten their master plan, as I believe Pan Am has done. Then giant companies like that can move with frightening speed to protect their interests. You remember that I warned you that organizations with this much money and power at stake are capable of anything?"

"I do," she said, her mind flashing back to Friday night.

"I'll tell you one more thing of great significance. If governments all over the planet don't get off their arses and learn to exercise at least some control over their domestic transportation markets to protect them from multinational lockup, such plans will succeed. This is the new colonialism, don't you see—the new building of empire—and this time consumers everywhere become the manipulated colonials."

Jack Bastrop raised a finger. "After all, Elizabeth, it's the extreme of a free market when the market forces a fight to the finish and the victor ends up with all the spoils, in a monopoly or oligopoly.''

A telephone had rung in the background as Bastrop was speaking. The waiter was back to tap Ing on the shoulder.

"Excuse me, please," Ing said, getting up.

Creighton spread out his hands in an explanatory gesture. "Look at your situation in America, Elizabeth. Jack and I have talked about this extensively. The big three are no longer in real competition with each other. They don't have to be. They essentially own the North American market, and they've been able to divide it up without ever breaking anti-trust laws just as a natural consequence of deregulation. They're stable, now they're profitable, they've raised fares through the roof, they fly in and out of fortress hubs, and they're keeping their costs down and packing passengers into what could charitably be called cattle-car interiors. Since foreign airlines can't fly point-to-point in the U.S., and foreign companies can't *legally* control a U.S. carrier, the big three have become independent money machines poised to grow fat and rich in the next decade. Anyone who holds their stock will benefit greatly.''

"And Pan Am is the skunk at that tea party?" Elizabeth interjected.

"Quite right!" Creighton agreed. "If you succeed in redefining what a quality airline is, they'll have to redo their interiors, change their fare structure, upgrade their service and their salaries, and drop the density of their seating to compete with you. This is akin to the idea of democracy afoot in a totalitarian regime. It's dangerous and heretical and threatens their control and their profits. If one of the three retrofits their fleet and the others don't, you've set up internecine competition again. Competition results in shrinking profits for those quiet stockholders who sit in the wings and pull strings on the board.''

Jason Ing returned quietly, sat down, and resumed sipping the soft drink he had ordered.

Elizabeth smiled an acknowledgment at him and turned back to Creighton. "But you said the big three themselves aren't behind this anti–Pan Am campaign.''

"I'm sure they aren't. Oh, don't be fooled. The three majors would be very appreciative if you'd just go away quietly. But they're far too ethical and concerned about being prosecuted themselves to ever engage in sabotage. I'm convinced they have no inkling of what some of their stockholders are doing on their behalf, and also that their leaders don't even realize their boards have been infiltrated, so to speak.''

"This unidentified company in Europe? Can we unmask them?"

Creighton hesitated, then nodded slowly. "Eventually. You asked about going to court. We've got to uncover three connections first. You've got four entities here." He began counting the fingers of his right hand. "Your revolving-loan bankers, your dirty-tricks group, the big three stockholders, and the mastermind organization in Europe. First we've got to prove direct links between your revolving-loan bankers and your dirty-tricks group. If, for instance, we found that Irwin Fairchild held some of your revolving debt, we've got the beginnings of a case, since you already have circumstantial evidence that he's part of the dirty-tricks group. At that point you would probably have enough to go get a court injunction against the revolving-loan bankers shutting you down by, ah . . ."

"By pulling our credit line," Elizabeth added. "They're demanding repayments we can't meet so they can declare us in default, which will let the owners of the fleet cancel the leases and repossess our airplanes."

"Right." Creighton nodded. "Okay, second, we've got to find a provable connection between your revolving-loan bankers and the mastermind organization, which I suspect is European. They're pulling the strings and financing the dirty-tricks group. But we have to find that connection to explain the actions of the revolving-loan bankers. Third, we've got to find the connection between the mastermind organization in Europe and companies that are stockholders in the big three. We have to prove that thesis in order to find a motive for the mastermind organization to want to hurt Pan Am. You know, why would financiers want to shut you down and lose money in a bankruptcy unless they had another agenda?"

Elizabeth was shaking her head sadly. "That sounds like years of investigatory work."

"Maybe. Maybe not," Creighton replied. "That's why the first order of business is to get Jack and Jason here busy finding you five hundred million dollars by next Monday."

There was a chance, Jason Ing told her, that the money could be made available that fast. They would all have to move rapidly. Jack Bastrop, an independent oilman on the Forbes 500s list who'd made the right investments at the right time and left the Texas oil market before it collapsed, was willing to put up seventy-five million as part of a package. He owned real estate in Hong Kong, and had come to know Ing during previous negotiations.

They all fell silent for a moment, and Elizabeth searched each of their faces before looking at Creighton. "On the phone, you said I should keep an open mind about the source of investment. What did you mean?"

She thought she saw Jack Bastrop catch himself short of a smile, but Creighton's expression didn't waiver.

"What I mean," Creighton said, "is that Jason's bank is a neophyte at airline investments. They have money in ships and shipping, real estate all over the world and especially here in Vancouver, and several factories in the electronics world. But they draw money in from various sources. Whatever Jason here puts together may be completely unconventional."

She looked at Jason Ing, who was nodding. "We will meet all your legal requirements," Ing said, "but Mr. MacRae is correct. It could look rather strange when the final list is assembled, the different names of participating investors, I mean."

Elizabeth was in a compromising position, and the cautions from both Ing and Creighton MacRae held some worrisome overtones. Who would these strange investors be?

She took a deep breath. "As long as it's legal," Elizabeth said carefully, "I can't see why unconventionality would be a problem."

"Can you follow me to Hong Kong tomorrow?" Ing asked. The question took Elizabeth by surprise. Her inclination was to say no. The airline was unraveling around her. Brian had put himself in the middle of an FBI investigation. Ron Lamb was still hospitalized. The big three were firing at Pan Am. Chad Jennings was running around creating more problems by the day.

The future of Pan Am once again came down to one person: Elizabeth Sterling. Without a new credit line or a hundred forty million in cash by next Monday, the new Pan Am would be yet another footnote in the corporate history books.

I have no choice, she told herself.

"Would you like to drive back to Seattle with me and fly from there?" she asked Ing, noting his immediate discomfort.

"I . . . ah . . ." he said hesitantly, ". . . cannot enter the United States just now."

"Oh, a visa matter? You didn't get a visa?" Elizabeth asked. It seemed a simple enough question, but shades of distress were crossing Ing's face like the shadows of clouds on a breezy day.

Creighton came to his rescue. "Jason is not permitted in the United States. It's an old matter, and really unfair, but diplomatic in nature."

Ing nodded gratefully at Creighton.

"Okay, then. I'll book myself on the first flight out of Seattle."

"No!" Creighton's voice was a little too forceful, and he raised his hand in apology. "I ... think it would be far safer if you let me book you under another name. You mustn't be traced to Hong Kong, or followed anywhere."

She looked at him, searching his eyes, wondering if she was imagining a slight edge of personal concern in his tone. She smiled and nodded. "Okay. We can work that out." Elizabeth checked her watch as casually as she could.

"Well. You've given me much to think about." She looked at all three in turn. "I'm afraid I'm getting a bit hungry. Would you gentlemen consider joining me for dinner?"

"Jack's got another engagement, and Jason has a party to attend, but I'd be delighted to take you to dinner," Creighton said instantly, before either of the other two could respond.

I asked you, *fella! And not alone, either.* She smiled as wryly as she could at Creighton. "On Pan Am's expense account?"

He looked momentarily off balance, then recovered as he extended his hand to help her up, and smiled back at her in shared understanding.

"Eventually, of course."

26

Monday, March 20, evening
Vancouver, British Columbia

Elizabeth was in her element in Vancouver, and the discovery that Creighton MacRae had never visited the city before gave her a delightful advantage that she found herself using with untoward delight.

The night was clear and mild, and despite the traumas of the previous days, she felt electric and alive.

"There is only one appropriate restaurant for an evening like this," she told Creighton when they had stepped out on the lanai of the Tai Pan Suite for a few minutes while Jason finished another phone call.

"Oh?"

"The Teahouse, in Stanley Park. Are you familiar with Stanley Park?"

She knew the answer, and waited with some amusement while he calculated how to respond.

"I believe I've heard of it, but I can't recall any details," Creighton said at last, his eyes focused on the distant north shore of the bay and the area known as North Vancouver.

"The most magnificent park in North America, in my opinion. One thousand acres of largely undeveloped virgin timber, an aquarium, cricket fields, totem poles, beaches, and all of it within walking distance."

"The Teahouse, you said?"

"Yes."

He placed his glass on the ledge and excused himself to make a reservation.

He'll ask directions, too, she told herself with a smile.

She turned down his idea of a taxi and insisted on driving her rental car, enjoying the opportunity to play tour guide as they navigated the short distance to the park and drove around the perimeter road counterclockwise.

"You're very accomplished at this," he told her. "All the facts and figures, and the part about Captain George Vancouver. I must say I'm impressed."

"I worked as a city tour guide one summer, getting on and off buses endlessly. You never forget the basics after that. It's a great tourist town."

She paused on the overpass crossing the Lion's Gate suspension bridge, watching the traffic whiz by beneath them.

"Creighton, is Jason Ing a millionaire in his own right?"

There was silence for a minute, as if he hadn't heard the question. She studied the back of his head as he tracked the path of the bridge to the north shore, then turned slowly to her with a serious expression and what seemed like a guarded answer.

"He's very wealthy, and from a wealthy family in Hong Kong. He was planning on moving to Vancouver when Hong Kong reverts to China, and that's why he owns the hotel—but he's changed his mind."

"He owns the hotel?"

"Yes, didn't I mention that? He's made the Tai Pan Suite his home. Supposedly the book by that name was written there, and when he bought the hotel last year, he made it his North American headquarters. By the way, there's a suite reserved for you at no cost."

Elizabeth turned into the restaurant parking lot, aware that Creighton was examining the restaurant with obvious pleasure.

"Rather like something out of the Victorian period in Covent Garden. Almost a greenhouse, with all that glass."

"I've always loved it here. The establishment and the view," she inclined her head toward the west and he followed her gaze into the light-studded blackness.

Their table by the western windows was perfect, the candlelight a warm complement to the twinkling lights of freighters at anchor in English Bay—ships waiting their turn to enter the harbor. The meal, too, was world-class, as she had expected. She let him order the wine, impressed with his knowledge of California whites, and the talk finally drifted from business to personal matters as she watched the candlelight play off his weathered features, basking in his occasional smile.

With the dessert gone and coffee before them, Creighton replaced his cup and looked down a moment before letting his eyes rise to engage hers.

"I must say, Elizabeth, you are without a doubt the most unique combination I believe I've ever encountered."

He paused, leaving her an opening and obviously hoping for a response.

There was none, as she smiled and waited for him to continue.

"What I mean is, I've never encountered a woman in business who could be both, if you understand. A woman and a businessman—or business*woman*, that is . . ." He smiled and wiped his mouth with the napkin before trying again, his eyes returning to hers.

"Permit me to rephrase that. You're feminine and businesslike at the same time—smart and hardened, yet soft and beautiful. That's quite an elegant contradiction, Elizabeth Sterling, CFO."

"I'm glad you approve," she said.

"I was prepared to dislike you back home."

She felt her way through a smile that had several layers of meaning. She imagined the wine was influencing her, but she felt wonderful, and she was quite sure he was the cause.

She excused herself for a trip to the ladies' room, to let him pay without embarrassment.

A grassy park, high above the bay, replete with benches and low bushes, separated the Teahouse from the sparkling night scene beyond. They walked together toward the water, hands pushed deep in the pockets of their respective coats, letting the conversation drift to more personal matters.

He was ten years older than she, and their childhood memories of the world were slightly out of sync, but it startled her that he, too, had grown up in love with the seashore and the wind, and the gentle bite of cold sea breezes in early spring. The climates of Bellingham, Washington, and his childhood hometown of Wick, on the wind-whipped northeastern coast of Scotland, were not too dissimilar.

They sat on a wooden bench and he fell silent. Elizabeth saw again the reflective look she'd noticed several times earlier—another glimpse of the complex man she had seen for a second in Inverness, beneath the irascible exterior. The expression was seldom more than a shadow passing across his face, but it was the look of someone used to facing life alone.

The real Creighton MacRae was a mystery she couldn't ignore. He could help save Pan Am, and that was all she really needed to know, yet there was an internal curiosity about him stirring around inside her like a persistent craving she had to satisfy.

Yet at dinner he had avoided talking about his early years, deflecting her gentle questioning until she'd given up the effort.

"There's a bit of the Heathcliff in you, Creighton MacRae," she said at last, staring westward toward the freighters riding at anchor in English Bay. "Though I hope that doesn't insult you as a Scot."

He glanced at her, surprised, and smiled. "Not at all. I'm very familiar with Emily Bronte's *Wuthering Heights*, though I'm neither a gypsy nor a foundling like Heathcliff."

"But you do plead guilty, I take it, to a brooding nature?"

She expected a defensive response, and regretted asking the question, but instead he turned to her, this time with a puzzled expression.

"I was raised to be a vicar," he said, "and vicars are by nature brooding. At least my father was."

"What happened?"

His gaze returned to the bay. "Rebellious sons determined to embrace the world, and all the ladies within it, are hardly suited to a life of stern, unyielding drabness—or to the role of spiritual Gestapo. I was, you see, as much a disappointment to my father as he was to me."

"You were a rebel?"

"Indeed. A well and truly defined hell-raiser. The more my father beat me toward conformity—and beat me he did—the more I was determined to break loose and scandalize the countryside. There's an American phrase—'so many girls, so little time.' " He glanced at her as if slightly embarrassed at the reference, then looked away. "I decided I couldn't escape my father unless I escaped Scotland, too. Going to college in America seemed the perfect answer. Of course, in one respect I had little choice if I wanted a degree. Neither Oxford nor Cambridge was particularly interested in a poor-as-a-churchmouse Scot with spotty school marks. If you want respect in the U.K., you must arrange to be born properly, and I had already failed that test."

"Which university over here?"

He snorted softly and smiled, still looking seaward as she studied his face from the side. "The University of Texas, on a scholarship. An American tourist left an alumni letter from UT in our church pew one Sunday, and I was fascinated. Texas became a metaphor for freedom. Cowboys, wide open spaces, limitless opportunities. I wrote for information on scholarships, and began a letter campaign they couldn't ignore." Creighton shifted his position slightly and looked at her. "It was a wonderful school, and I shot through a bachelor's and MBA program in five years, shed most of my accent, and headed back for London to enter the airline business as an executive—only to find that my American business degree impressed no one."

One of the freighters had suddenly turned on all its deck lights, and the throbbing sound of a massive engine rumbled across the water.

Elizabeth looked over at him again. "Your MBA didn't open doors?"

Creighton shook his head. "Without the appropriate background and family, British Airways wasn't interested, nor was British European, and at the time they were the only games in town. Three years later a gentleman named Freddy Laker took me in and taught me the practical side of business in Britain. Mind you, this was before Mrs. Thatcher democratized the process somewhat, and yet I've never really been accepted in that club."

"Would it surprise you if I said I understood?"

He looked at her a long time before answering. "Indeed it would. You've never lived in Britain."

She shook her head in the negative. "No, I haven't, but on the subject of not being accepted in the good old boys' club of *American* business, a female with an MBA understands that problem all too well."

Their eyes met again, and she sensed momentary confusion as he followed her logic to the inevitable conclusion.

"We do have something profoundly in common, it seems," he said softly. "I'd never thought of that."

Nor understood it, she thought, remembering his arrogant responses to her first calls.

There was an electricity in his gaze, and she felt herself responding with an insatiable desire to touch him, as if he needed comforting.

This is silly! she told herself. *He's the same chauvinist he was last week, and I hardly know this man.*

She looked away, unable to ignore the resonant response she was feeling, and the warmth rising within her. It made no sense. He was a pleasant enough fellow, but she wasn't *attracted* to him ... was she? No! She refused to be!

Her feelings, however, weren't cooperating with that judgment.

There was only one way to regain logical control of the situation, and that was to end it.

"I'm getting cold out here," she lied.

"Permit me to remedy that, Elizabeth."

His arm moved expertly behind her, his right hand gently gathering her in toward him as he looked out to the bay again with chaste disinterest.

A thunderstorm of conflicting emotions erupted in her head as she fought the desire to snuggle against him and respond, lightning flashes of desire crackling around the core of her resistance like Saint Elmo's fire.

She jumped to her feet suddenly, leaving him awkwardly fighting for balance on the bench as she turned to face him.

"I'm ... sorry, Creighton. I ... it's getting late, and if I'm going to get an early start back to Seattle in the morning, I'd better ..."

Dammit! I sound like a confused school girl, she chided herself.

He stood slowly, smiling, as if to say he understood.

"I didn't mean to startle you."

She laughed, but it came out a nervous giggle. "You didn't. I'm ... not sure what I was thinking."

With him standing before her, Elizabeth reached down and took his right hand, wrapping it around her waist as she moved in to his side and inclined her head toward the car, feeling back in control and embarrassed.

"There. It wasn't you! But we *should* go."

♦ ♦ ♦

It would be better, he pointed out, if she left on a Canadian airline for Hong Kong from Vancouver. She could be tracked in Seattle, and if she'd been successful in coming north without detection, the dirty-tricks group—as they'd begun referring to Pan Am's enemies—were probably frantic trying to locate her. They would have the airport staked out, as well as her condo.

"You said from Houston I was being tracked. How do you know?"

Creighton nodded his head and watched the street as she drove them back toward the hotel. "Let's just say Jack has some friends in low places, too. One of them reported back this morning that a West Coast security firm has been making a lot of money in the past few weeks, following a particular airline executive all over the map. The executive is female and lives in Seattle. That's all they could say, but it was enough."

The same chill she had felt before worked its way up her back. She couldn't shake the feeling that someone had been in Eric's New York apartment with her, watching her, close enough to attack her.

"Okay, Vancouver it is."

He smiled. "I took the liberty of arranging the ticket. Can you leave with Jason tomorrow at ten A.M.?"

"I really didn't bring enough clothes, and I lost my other bags in that explosion Friday, but I can make do. Ten is okay. Are you coming too?" She asked the question in matter of fact terms, but she found herself hoping the answer was yes.

"No. I'm going to fly back to the East Coast with Jack and his crew.

We've got a mountain of wire-transfer records to probe. I'll track you through Jason, however. You'll need to conclude an agreement by Wednesday, but don't tell your office where you're calling from before then.''

"Will we meet later in the week, then?''

There was a long pause before he replied. "I don't know where this will take us. It's all very unexpected.''

She felt herself blush. It certainly was.

Creighton secured the entry cards to their two rooms from the front desk while she parked the car. They met at the elevator. He punched the button for the top floor as he handed her the electronic card key.

"Our rooms are next to each other,'' he said with a casual air.

Elizabeth felt her heart jump with a rush of adrenaline. Since leaving the park she had been concentrating on business, determined to shut out the confusing thoughts that had been battering down the door of her resistance—and she had almost succeeded.

But now the barbarian named desire was at the gate again, and making progress.

She thanked him with a chaste and proper handshake for the dinner, and he responded appropriately, carefully masking the disappointment she knew was there. Almost in unison they approached their respective doors. She heard his latch click open, but she found herself fumbling with the key card, and without warning he had come to her aid, moving behind her, his right hand moving over hers as he tried to help her move the card in the slot correctly. The electricity of his touch made her knees feel wobbly. She could feel his warm breath on the back of her neck, and his hard, conditioned body gently brushing her back.

"These bloody things can be a bit tricky,'' he said, his voice resonating through her with sensual results.

The latch clicked and the door swung open, but she turned to him instead, wondering why it felt so good to get lost in his eyes, startled at how close his face was to hers. She started to speak, but there was nothing to say, and he came to her with great gentleness, his right hand caressing her face like a feather as his lips brushed hers, then engulfed her as his arms pulled her to him. She rose on the balls of her feet to meet him, and the kiss intensified, warm and deep and long. His body felt incredibly good against hers, but there was a voice screaming at her in the back of her mind to back off. There were no reasons given, just the urgency that she was approaching a threshold—a point of no return.

She felt herself pull back ever so slightly and their lips disengaged.

She could feel his heart beating at a furious rate, or was that only hers? They stood, startled, looking at each other.

"Elizabeth . . . I . . ."

She came to him again, eyes closed, letting herself be pulled even closer to the fire, like a sleeper returning to the warm pleasure of her bed despite the time, wanting just a little bit more.

She felt herself slipping toward complete surrender, and the realization caused her to pull back suddenly.

He instantly relaxed his grip, as she put her hands on his chest, her eyes fearing to meet his.

"We . . . better get some sleep."

She felt him swallow hard and nod.

"Why don't I want to let you go?" he said quietly, his voice a warm train of vibrations that coursed through her, challenging her shaky resolve.

"I don't . . . don't know . . . but we must," she said.

He let her pull back, his hands gently holding only her shoulders as he lowered his head and forced her to meet his eyes—which were pulsing with desire.

"We share a common door, Elizabeth. If you want anything, just tap on it."

She nodded and mouthed an "Okay," picked up her bag, and moved into the room, gently shutting the door without looking back.

♦ ♦ ♦

Elizabeth tried to ignore the sound of him moving around next door—sounds that came from the other side of the connecting doorway. She thought of Brian. She thought of Ron Lamb. She thought of anything she could to get her mind off the fact that she was aching to rip that door off the hinges and engulf him.

Logic had won over emotion, and emotion was not happy.

She undressed then, and looked at her naked body in the mirror, patting her flat stomach with some pride before turning out the lights and moving resolutely toward the bed.

She was anything but sleepy, however.

♦ ♦ ♦

She turned her head on the pillow and looked at the lights of Vancouver through the sliding glass door. Finally, giving up thoughts of sleeping right away, she got up and wandered toward the lights of nighttime Vancouver twinkling through the sliding door, and parted the sheer curtains with one finger, startled to see Creighton standing in a white bathrobe on his lanai, his hands gripping the railing, his head turned toward the harbor, the wind ruffling his hair.

She stayed in the shadows, watching, as he turned away and walked back inside.

She turned as well then, slipping between the sheets of the king-sized bed and forcing her eyes closed.

But sleep wouldn't come.

For more than an hour she tossed and turned, getting to her feet at last to peek out once again at the harbor lights, half expecting to see Creighton in the same place.

The lanai next to hers was empty, but the connecting door was pulling at her like a magnet.

She left the window as if in a dream state, and moved to the door without a sound, her mind in turmoil.

What am I doing? The question was clear, but logic had lost control.

She stood before it then, and gently—slowly—she pressed the palm of her left hand against its surface.

There were no sounds, no vibrations beyond, yet it felt alive. She was tingling with anticipation, and lurched slightly as she brushed the door with her left cheek, putting her ear on it, pulsing a tiny noise into the wooden surface as she stood there.

So close! It would be so easy to just . . .

She looked at the doorknob, wondering if his side was really open. If so, only the doorknob stood between them now.

Her right hand moved toward it, hesitating, as if she were teasing herself. Then suddenly, she gripped it, causing a tiny metallic noise as the mechanism adjusted to her touch.

The feel of it, and the knowledge of what lay beyond, aroused her even more, and she felt an urgent aching in her breasts as she imagined what his body was like.

If she did decide to turn it, should she put on a robe, or perhaps a blouse? Or should she just walk through in naked surrender?

All it would take is a tiny flick of the wrist! she told herself. He would be startled, but pleased. He would rise from his bed and come to her in an instant, his gentle hands running like coarse velvet over every inch of her skin as his mouth sought hers, and they began the sensual pleasure of merging in every other way.

And just for tonight, what would it matter? They were consenting adults.

Her breathing had become rapid and shallow, her eyes fixated on the doorknob, but Brian's image reimposed itself, propelled by conscience and memory and loyalty into confusion that paralyzed her hand.

Quietly, sadly, she released the doorknob and stood there for the longest time before returning to bed—alone and confused.

27

Wednesday, March 22, 2:05 A.M.
Bellevue, Washington

Brian Murphy sat at the kitchen table of his new house and poured the last of the orange juice as he stared at a blank steno pad. Three hours of sleepless tossing and turning was enough. Something about the riddle of Marvin Grade's death was just out of reach and tying his mind in knots.

He picked up a pen and drew the pad closer, writing the names of those Pan Am employees who had seen an intruder they couldn't identify as Marvin Grade.

The list was short, but important.

Dale Silverman, Jake Wallace, and a Seatac mechanic whose name he couldn't recall.

He drummed a brief percussion solo on the top of the polished glass table before adding the word "definite" to Captain Silverman's name, and "unsure" to Wallace's.

Whoever it was that Captain Dale Silverman found in the cockpit of his 767 in Denver on March 10, Silverman was certain it hadn't been the late Marvin Grade.

But the mechanic who had seen an intruder in the Moses Lake hangar was *not* certain—nor was the Seatac mechanic who had encountered a bogus fuel man on the Seattle ramp. It could have been Grade in both cases, they said, but it could also have been someone else with a mustache and a similar build. Maintenance chief Bill Conrad had been equally worried as he helped Brian locate his men and question them. Conrad was the only other Pan Am manager who seemed to think that the danger to Pan Am's fleet hadn't necessarily died with Marvin Grade.

Brian had called a worried meeting Monday afternoon with the FBI's Loren Miller. Miller had listened carefully before opening a folder and tapping a five-page investigative report.

"Fingerprints don't lie, Brian. Our Mr. Grade physically touched your file folder, touched the bogus electronics in your 767, and had explosives in his house of the exact type used to blow the engine off your 747."

But the feeling that Grade *wasn't* the man—or at least wasn't working alone—haunted Brian all Monday. Now the idea was robbing him of sleep for a second night.

He picked up the pen again and wrote, "No computer equipment in house."

Brian had gone to Grade's house himself Monday evening with a flashlight and a screwdriver, half expecting to be arrested for breaking and entering as he forced his way in the back door. Miller had let him examine in detail the seizure list of incriminating items removed from the home, but the urge to see the house itself was irresistible.

Grade had supposedly rewired a sophisticated computer board from a stolen 767 black box. Yet Brian saw no home computers, no books on computer technology, and no collection of wires and switches of the kind amateur electronic buffs always have near their workbench as mute relics from a thousand little jobs. Nor had there been any listing of such items on the FBI seizure report.

Little incongruities were everywhere. The house was neat and clean, though threadbare. Newly paid bills lay on the corner of his desk, along with pay stubs from his job as a light aircraft mechanic at a local airport. There were no lunatic-fringe magazines, no defaced posters of Pan Am, and no copies of angry letters or threats. Brian could find nothing that would indicate that anyone but a quiet divorced man with a low-level job, a run of bad luck, and a distant family had lived there.

Nothing, he reminded himself, but enough evidence to convict Grade of attempted mass murder—all of that evidence now in the hands of the FBI.

The sound of a passing jet broke his concentration, bringing him back to the present in his own kitchen. Brian yawned long and uncontrollably before looking at the kitchen clock. It was 2:21 A.M. He wished he could call Elizabeth, but there was no telling where she was. She had called from an unknown location on Tuesday morning, saying she'd be out of town for several days and couldn't risk telling him where over the phone.

He imagined her blond hair now gracing the pillow of a reclining first-class seat in some 747 headed somewhere, and hoped she was okay.

He looked back at the steno pad, the word "fingerprints" catching his eye. That was the most difficult problem to explain. If Grade had been innocent, how could his fingerprints have ended up on the file folder and circuit board?

Not prints, plural, but print, singular, he reminded himself.

There was also the matter of the dark car that one of Grade's neighbors had seen lurking near Grade's house Friday night just before they heard him leave—the same type of car Elizabeth had sighted just before the explosion.

But why was Grade dead? Had he detonated the explosion accidentally as he was getting ready to slip into Pan Am's hangar to sabotage another airplane, as everyone was assuming? Or . . .

Wait a minute! Wait just a minute!

Brian stopped pacing, his eyes staring far beyond the walls of his kitchen.

What if Grade *hadn't* come to sabotage another airplane? What if he'd had an attack of conscience and decided to come tell Pan Am what was happening, and what he'd done?

And what if his co-conspirator had found out?

Brian thought back to the meeting with the FBI's Loren Miller, and their shared conclusion that whoever had bombed Clipper Ten and tampered with Clipper Forty's electronics had probably not intended to destroy either aircraft, but merely disrupt the airline's operations. The two near disasters that resulted, however, could have panicked a man like Grade and driven him toward confession—something a more sophisticated co-conspirator couldn't allow.

Brian returned to the table and began scribbling rapidly on the steno pad, drawing lines connecting various elements of the equation. He put the pen down and sat back again, his mind racing even further down the dark road of logic he had entered.

The dark car fits, too!

Elizabeth saw it enter the Pan Am parking lot and just sit there with the motor running, a perfect position from which to detonate a radio-controlled bomb.

The dark car, the soft side of Grade he'd seen in the house, Grade's obvious distress as Elizabeth had observed him in his parked car, hunched over with his hands gripping the steering wheel—and the fact that the car had exploded as Grade was getting out—all of it made sense.

And killing Grade would have been a double benefit for his co-conspirator; for with the sabotage supposedly a thing of the past, Pan Am would relax its security, which would leave the airline vulnerable to another attack.

And if that *was* the explanation, the plan sure seemed to be working. Nothing Brian could say, no arguments he'd been able to raise, had succeeded in convincing Chad Jennings to clamp back down on security.

He turned suddenly, his eyes landing for a fleeting instant on his own wall calendar.

Whatever the bastard is planning, he'll have to be quick about it. If Elizabeth doesn't succeed in getting the money, it's all over on the twenty-seventh anyway—five days from now.

Brian stopped in his tracks and replayed the previous thought, looking at his own words from a different angle, assigning them a different meaning—and realizing suddenly where they pointed.

My God, that's it!

He lunged for the phone and dialed Bill Conrad's home number.

A sleepy voice finally answered.

"Bill? Brian Murphy. Sorry to wake you up. You remember our conversation this afternoon?"

There was a brief pause. "Yeah. We were trying to figure out what the bad guys will sabotage next, if they're still there."

"Bill, I'd like you to meet me at seven A.M. at Seatac. I know exactly when and where they're planning to hit us again!"

Wednesday, March 22, 7:05 P.M.
Hong Kong

Jason Ing's limousine pulled up at the front door of the new Conrad Hotel in Hong Kong as Elizabeth closed her briefcase.

"I'll see you in the morning, Jason."

"The car will be here at eight."

She patted his arm and nodded as she climbed out of the stretch Mercedes and headed to the room that Jason's staff had rented for her.

Once in the room, Elizabeth double-latched the door behind her and began stripping her way to the shower, leaving a trail of clothes. The water felt wonderful, but hours of uninterrupted sleep would feel even better.

She had developed a deep appreciation of Jason Ing's capacity for work in the previous eighteen hours as they had negotiated and discussed their way across the Pacific, forging the basic agreement at last on their respective computers. Two hours out of Hong Kong, he had smiled at long last and snapped the lid of his laptop closed, happy with the basic outline. The terms of the loan were a bit lopsided in favor of the lenders, but it would be Pan Am's salvation if they could fund it.

Elizabeth dried herself and randomly flung away the towel as she stumbled to the bed, pausing only long enough to leave a wake-up call.

♦ ♦ ♦

She was awake and alert and optimistic when she climbed into the limo at 8:00 A.M.—though a little embarrassed to be wearing the same outfit. She promised herself a quick shopping trip in late afternoon.

The offices of Cathay Alliance, Ltd., were an elegant blend of modern architecture and traditional Mandarin decor. Elizabeth complimented them profusely as she and Jason entered the executive suite and a smiling secretary waved them into the large corner office that belonged to the board chairman. The office was empty.

Elizabeth paused in the doorway, taking in the library along one wall, and the magnificent view.

Jason crossed the room and sat down behind the desk, delighted when Elizabeth's expression cycled from surprise to an acknowledging nod of her head and a broad smile.

"I must apologize, Jason," she told him. "I didn't realize you were the chairman of this firm!"

"You were polite not to inquire," he said. "I could have been merely a functionary, but you treated me like a chairman all day yesterday—even if you did raise an eyebrow at my tender age."

She had finally looked him over closely the day before and given up trying to guess. At times he seemed eighteen in face and stature, at others in his late thirties, but he had noticed her scrutiny and guessed her question.

"I'm thirty," he had told her. "I could tell you were wondering."

After extensive introductions among the other officers of the company and a quick briefing on their widespread interests, Elizabeth spent several hours with Cathay's legal staff, finalizing the form of the agreement. A copy would be faxed to Pan Am's general counsel within the hour, she was told.

At noon, Jason Ing thanked the last of his departing staff and quietly closed the door of his office before turning to Elizabeth.

"I wanted a few minutes alone with you to discuss the source of these funds," he said.

Elizabeth watched him circle the expansive office with his hands in his pockets as he tracked her reaction carefully. The floor-to-ceiling windows behind him revealed a breathtaking view of the city and the hills beyond. Elizabeth found herself watching a jumbo jet on approach to the airport as she replied with a sudden caution.

"I'm not sure I understand, Jason. You were going to pool various sources for the money, were you not?"

Her heartbeat had accelerated as a sinking feeling began to grip her stomach. Maybe she didn't want to know whether the money might be from nefarious sources.

He sat down in a leather wingback chair next to hers and gestured to the city, as Elizabeth sought to concentrate on what he was about to tell her.

Jason's voice was calm and smooth. "We talked briefly yesterday, Elizabeth, about the coming reversion to Chinese ownership in 1997 of Hong Kong."

She nodded, only half hearing the reference to China. She was well aware of the havoc and panic the end of the British rule was bringing.

"The Chinese government," he continued, "has no desire to dismantle what the residents and businesses of Hong Kong have achieved. We are, in fact, world traders, world bankers, and manufacturers. While all this decadent capitalism threatens communist ideology, Beijing's leaders are well aware that there is more to learn and gain financially from leaving us alone and nurturing us as an autonomous island of free commerce than from trying to convert us to something else."

"I'm aware of the changes in general terms," she hedged, puzzled by where this was going.

"A few years ago we were planning to flee by 1997, to move to Vancouver. But something none of us had foreseen changed our minds. The minute we put this company in play for sale, we found that certain . . . shall we say *interests* . . . could make it very expensive for us to leave. Those same interests were determined that Cathay would stay in Hong Kong with the same people running it, or it would probably be torn apart financially trying to leave. These interests are in a position to have ruined us if we hadn't complied, because of real-estate investments and so forth. Essentially, they presented us with an offer that, well . . ."

"*Who* was it, Jason?"

"Beijing."

"Beijing? The Chinese government?"

He nodded, watching her make the connections.

"Are you telling me you're in business with, or owned by, the government of the People's Republic of China?"

"Yes. We look for good investments worldwide for them now. Very quietly. They do not wish to be known as investors in the capitalist system, even though they're going about it in a big way. There's even a school now in Beijing for training Chinese businessmen on how to prosper in the capitalist system. Sort of a home-grown MBA."

"Jason, are you saying . . . that at least one of the principal investors in this loan, if we conclude it, will be the government of *China*?"

He nodded again. "As represented by another intermediate corporation here in Hong Kong, for purposes of discretion. Does that shock you?"

She sat perfectly still for a second, letting her mind absorb the small bombshell. They had two working days to conclude the loan, but if the Chinese government was in any way involved . . .

Elizabeth picked up the glass of Diet Coke she had been nursing and sipped it as she stared past him. They had been so close . . .

"Does this present a problem?" Jason asked. "I know you Americans are very upset over Tiananmen Square."

She looked at him at last. "Tiananmen Square has nothing to do with it, Jason." She sighed deeply and replaced her glass on the small table between them. "U.S.-certificated airlines are required by law to clear certain transactions with the Department of Justice and other government agencies in advance. Under the new laws passed last year, I can bring in foreign loan money without going through that approval process as long as, first, I formally report it within ten days; second, we're not selling or obligating common or voting stock or equity; and, third, we're not dealing with an arm, an agency, or a business subsidiary of a foreign government."

"But I barely mentioned—"

She shook her head again, crushed. "I can't lie about it, Jason. I can't misrepresent it. Not even to save our airline."

"Can't you get an expedited approval from your government?"

She rolled her eyes. "I can try, but we're looking at a month at the minimum, and by next Monday, without the first payment, we're out of business."

Elizabeth wanted to leave. The urge to get up and go find a hole somewhere to crawl into was almost overwhelming, but she had to persist. She had to think. At long last she took a deep breath and dropped her hands from her temples, trying to smile at him as she shook her head. "I guess you didn't know about that law."

"I'm sorry, no. Everything was so fast, and we have never dealt with a U.S. airline before."

Elizabeth got to her feet slowly and picked up her briefcase. "I need to make a lot of telephone calls. And I'd really appreciate it if you would please keep trying from this end in the meantime."

♦ ♦ ♦

Back at the hotel, she walked the short distance from the elevator to her room, knowing she had hours of phone calls ahead.

It was 8:00 P.M. in Seattle and 1:00 P.M. in Hong Kong when she reached the airline's general counsel at home. Jack Rawly had received the faxed agreement and had been upbeat and hopeful. The news that the government of China was involved changed everything.

"Your instinct was right, Elizabeth, I'm sorry to say."

"Is there any way to accelerate the approval process?"

"Don't hold your breath," he told her.

"Then I have no idea what we're going to do, Jack. We're out of ideas and time, and I suppose there's nothing we can do to stop a default declaration on Monday if we don't pay the revolving-credit group?"

There was a long sigh from Seattle. "Elizabeth, I've read that damned contract six ways from Sunday, and had our outside law firm do the same. We've been had, it's as simple as that. At best, I could buy us a day or two with a friendly federal judge. In the meantime, if you get anything I can use—any evidence whatsoever that our lenders have tried to hurt us illegally—let me have it."

"I will, Jack. Thanks."

"We hardly know each other, Elizabeth, but I appreciate what you've been doing. You're a tough fighter. I'm glad you're on our side."

For some reason she felt tears rolling down her cheeks as she kept her voice steady and answered, "Thank you, Jack. I needed that."

She replaced the telephone receiver gently, feeling very alone.

So it's going to end, after all.

Brian's face popped into her mind, and another wave of sorrow washed over her at the thought that the possible renaissance of their love in Seattle could now be destroyed before it really began.

The phone rang and she picked it up almost instantly, praying for a familiar voice on the other end.

"Elizabeth?" It was Fred Kinnen with news of an unsolicited offer of a new revolving credit line received from a bank in Hong Kong called ITB. "I think they were fishing," he said. "They wanted an incredible amount of financial information sent by computer transmission, but the man who called Chad Jennings said they would consider a new six-hundred-million credit line."

Creighton MacRae's casual comment about ITB popped into her memory instantly. It was the bank used frequently by Irwin Fairchild!

"Give them nothing, Fred, but fax me anything they've sent us in writing. I'll check it out here."

"Does it sound hopeful?" he asked.

She realized she was shaking her head, an unseen gesture half a world away from her assistant.

"It sounds sinister."

Thursday, March 23, afternoon
Amsterdam, Holland

Jacob Voorster stood for a moment in the outer office of the managing director, his thoughts immersed in the damning evidence he had just given the leader of Van Zanten and Vetter, Ltd.

The receptionist gave him a brief glance and an even more abbreviated smile. He acknowledged her with a correct nod, but held his position, his eyes returning to scan the rooftops of Amsterdam beyond.

Out of habit, he let his right hand smooth the few hairs left on the top of his head. He didn't feel fifty-eight years old, but apparently he looked his age. Young women were always kind, but he missed the spark of interest he had once been able to inspire in their eyes.

He smoothed his neatly trimmed mustache and checked his appearance with a sideways glance in the full-length mirror to his left, pleased that he had looked thoroughly professional in the presence of the company's leader.

Voorster loved Van Zanten and Vetter. After thirty-three years of service, it hurt terribly to have to turn in one of the officers—a senior director—and, by doing so, expose the firm to the possibility of international scandal.

He let his eyes wander to the polished, lovingly displayed artifacts from the two-hundred-year history of the old-line Dutch shipping company: paintings of ships launched in 1798 with the first version of the famous VZV logo; a brass engine telegraph from the company's first steamer in the 1880s; and a fifteen-foot model of the company's first supertanker, encased in glass on a mahogany pedestal.

The managing director, Herr Frederick Ooest, had treated him with deference and respect and had called him one of the most capable financial analysts VZV had ever employed. Ooest had listened intently and even taken notes as Jacob described his initial suspicions over his discovery of a sudden, unexplained transfer of millions of dollars to an American corporation from an obscure account—transfers for which he could find no authorization. The managing director had also complimented him highly for working nights and evenings to track down the name of the VZV employee who had triggered those payments—and why.

And Ooest had promised swift action as he showed Voorster to the door.

"I will need, Jacob, all copies and computer disks or anything else that contains working material you used to compile your analysis of this. Everything. Immediately. You are to retain not the slightest trace of this work in your possession. That includes all notes, memos, scratch pads, or other working papers."

"Yes, sir," Jacob had replied.

"And you will speak of this with no one, Jacob, inside or outside the company. That is a very solemn order."

Jacob Voorster nodded to himself and moved energetically toward the big double doors leading to the elevator lobby. He had done his duty. Now it was time to follow through.

The managing director would see to everything else.

Friday, March 24, 9:50 A.M.
Hong Kong

As far as Elizabeth could tell from outward appearances, there was nothing unusual about the International Trading Bank of Hong Kong. It was simply a small commercial bank mostly focused on international finance. But a bank, she reminded herself, somehow associated with Irwin Fairchild.

The assistant manager of international banking greeted her warmly when she walked into his office unannounced and asked to see the operation.

The need to see the place in person was strong, even though she knew it would tell her little about the motives behind the sudden offer. Elizabeth had pulled her hair back, worn dark glasses, and presented herself as Ann Murphy, a wealthy widow from Atlanta with money to invest and the need for a correspondent bank in Hong Kong.

As she expected, a low-level administrative assistant was assigned to show her around. It took only a few dozen technical questions about the bank's computer banking system to bore the man beyond tolerance, causing him to pair her off with one of the bank's computer programmers as he fled to "other duties."

Elizabeth found herself enjoying the company of the programmer—a young Hong Kong woman who seldom got to meet the bank's customers in person. They sat side by side before a computer terminal in the woman's small office as she explained how the system could be used by a customer with a home computer as easily as a bank officer could access all the files from halfway around the world.

"So," Elizabeth asked, "I could call from Atlanta using my computer, and move my money around, right?"

"Yes," the woman agreed with a broad smile, "from anywhere in the world. It's a simple menu-driven program, even for our internal usage. With the proper passwords, our officers can get to anything they could access here in the building."

The technician's fingers flew over the keyboard, and instantly a page of entry codes and passwords appeared next to a list of employee names.

She pointed to the screen and turned to Elizabeth. "My department is the only one that can open these security files, of course. But everything else is safely available on line because we use a three-tiered entry-code sequence that's impossible to break."

She deleted the security-code display as she reached for a ringing telephone, and then excused herself for a minute, leaving Elizabeth alone with the computer terminal.

Elizabeth had quickly memorized the keystrokes the programmer had used to open the security file. She reached up now to the keyboard. The possibility of searching ITB's files from a distance with her laptop computer and a telephone hookup was too enticing an opportunity to pass up.

She scanned the doorway, listening for footsteps. There were none.

Elizabeth repeated the keystrokes, delighted that after a brief pause the entire list of internal security access codes and passwords reappeared.

She looked at the empty doorway again across the desk, listening to the small noises from the hallway with the care of a cat calculating the moment to pounce—her left index finger positioned above the Delete key in case she had to go back to a blank screen and look innocent.

But for the moment the hallway was empty of all but the distant sound of rock music.

With her right hand, Elizabeth took a pad of yellow Post-it notes from the woman's desk and rested it on her knee, using a pen to scribble down the code and password sequences for two of the names listed. She was on the third group when the sound of footsteps reached her ear.

Suddenly the technician was back in the doorway, smiling at her guest as she moved back into the office, unaware that the internal security codes were showing on her screen.

Elizabeth froze, afraid to push the Delete key for fear the noise would reach the woman's experienced ears. Her right hand held the pen and notepad on her knee, all in plain view if the woman came back around to her chair—which was where she was headed!

Elizabeth stood up abruptly, keeping the pad and pen out of sight behind the desk as she gestured down the hallway.

"A young man came in here just a minute ago looking for you," she fibbed.

The programmer looked confused and came to a halt.

"A tall man? Balding and tall?" she asked Elizabeth.

"Yes."

"Oh! Excuse me a minute." She was beaming from ear to ear, her face turning beet red as she gestured shyly behind her. "That's my, ah . . ."

"Boyfriend?" Elizabeth offered with a sly grin.

The woman nodded and laughed self-consciously as she stepped from the room.

The second the footsteps had faded down the hall, Elizabeth finished copying the last few digits and hit the Delete key as she slipped the pad and pen in her purse. She had adopted a slightly bored expression by the time the woman returned.

"So, was he the guy looking for you?" Elizabeth asked her, smiling.

"I know he was, but he wouldn't admit it. He's shy."

♦ ♦ ♦

Elizabeth excused herself politely after another half hour with the programmer, and returned to the hotel room at last to connect her laptop computer to the phone line.

Her entry to ITB's main computer was almost instantaneous. As the programmer had said, everything was done with easily understood menus.

For a half hour she navigated around the different files, slowly figuring out the organization plan—thankful that the English language was the bank's official tongue. She downloaded several telephone lists to her hard disk before finding the one listing that promised to hold the names and stock-ownership interests of the officers. With two short commands on her keyboard, the file poured through the phone line and into her computer's memory. She paused to open it and take a peek.

The short list of names of the principal stockholders was arranged alphabetically. Elizabeth stared at it in disbelief.

Irwin Fairchild's name was not there, but another name was: Nicolas Costas.

Elizabeth felt a bit lightheaded. Nick Costas, the American-born son of a wealthy Greek shipping magnate, was the most hated man in American aviation—a two-legged scourge whose mere name could incite a riot among the employees of any U.S.-based carrier. She knew his face from newspaper and magazine photos. Short and stocky with silver hair and the incongruous look of a loving grandfather, Costas was hated and reviled in airline circles. For years he had been a respected legend on Wall Street for his devastatingly successful attacks on organized airline labor. Brilliant, heartless, and determined, even she had once defended him during a heated dinner-party discussion, describing his amazing ability to pull massive amounts of financing from thin air to build an empire.

That empire had crumbled by 1990. The memory of her defense was now an embarrassment.

Nick Costas owned over eighty-five percent of ITB! Which meant that Nick Costas had to be behind any loan offer from the bank.

The image of Irwin Fairchild popped into her head.

"Where Nick Costas slithers, Irwin can't be far behind," Elizabeth muttered to herself, sending another fusillade of keystrokes into the telephone line as she probed deeper into the stockholder lists.

But Fairchild was not listed, nor was the name of his company.

Elizabeth sat back for a second, trying to figure out what Costas's ownership meant. Could ITB's sudden interest in offering money to Pan Am be an innocent commercial transaction? Or was Costas himself trying something? There was a resonance to the idea that Nick Costas could be trying to manipulate them, but how and why?

Her curiosity surged to new heights, propelled by the feeling that there was information in the bank's computer that could be invaluable to Pan Am. It was an unfocused gut feeling, almost a premonition, but it drove her as she hunched her shoulders over the small laptop and began typing.

She reentered the main account listings, using the bank's internal search routines to look for any occurrence of the last name Costas.

There were dozens of Costas accounts: checking accounts, investment accounts, savings accounts, transfer accounts, and more. As rapidly as she found them, she copied the files to her hard disk without examining them, then went back in search of more until the Costas name was exhausted.

The menu prompt returned again.

ENTER SEARCH NAME: ■

On a hunch, she typed the name FAIRCHILD and hit Enter.

That'll be a waste of time, she chided herself.

The word WORKING appeared again.

Suddenly, listings for two checking accounts under the name of ''Fairchild, Irwin B., New York, New York, USA'' appeared on the screen.

A cold feeling began creeping up her back as she stared at the listings. She gave the command to copy the files to her disk.

But if she *had* uncovered a rat's nest, what other parts of it should she document?

Creighton MacRae believed some huge European company was behind the sabotage effort—a company big enough to try to corner the North American market. She tried searches for various corporate customers of the bank then, looking for companies headquartered in various European cities, and pulling in long lists of corporate clients in London, Paris, Frankfurt, Brussels, Rome, Madrid, Copenhagen, and Amsterdam.

She had finished the latest file transfer when the screen to her computer suddenly changed, and a new message generated from the ITB computer took over:

YOU HAVE EXCEEDED ENTRY TIME OR DOWNLOAD ALLOWANCE—ENTER APPROPRIATE EXTEND CODE.

Elizabeth stared at the message for less than a heartbeat before recognizing what was about to happen. The bank's computer had probably been programmed to embed a security destruct program whenever data was downloaded to a distant computer. It had been triggered now. If she broke the phone connection without the host computer sending the right sequence of machine language to disarm the program, it would work like a virus and destroy her data.

But if she couldn't figure out the right code sequence to cancel the program, the only hope was to locate that particular security program on her disk and kill it before it activated.

Heart pounding, she triggered a pop-up window and guided her computer to display a directory listing which she searched as fast as possible, looking for the one file with a name she didn't recognize.

There was nothing she could identify.

She returned to the main screen as the message changed:
ENTER EXTEND CODE WITHIN THIRTY SECONDS.

She could snap off her computer and the data would be saved, but when she started it up again, the program would be triggered and every scrap of data would be lost. It could take a computer technician weeks to decipher everything on the hard disk manually.

The codes!

She had placed the piece of paper with the purloined entry codes next to the computer. Now she pulled it to her, remembering a strange reference on the bottom of the security screen that had said something about inverting the codes.

She had entered 3376 for the last of the three required code sequences. She had less than fifteen seconds now. Would it be the first string or the second or third that she should invert? What had it said?

Ten seconds left, she calculated.

Go with instinct! she told herself. The third sequence felt right.

Elizabeth typed in 6733 and hit Enter, expecting the worst.

The screen went blank and her heart sank. Then her own hard disk revved up again, indicating that something was happening.

Suddenly the normal prompt was back!

She paged carefully through the files and the data, finding it all there. She quickly ended the session, commanding a disconnect—relieved to be finished.

ITB's computer shot back a parting message:
THANK YOU MR. LEE. YOU WERE CONNECTED FOR 58:04 MINUTES, AND YOU WERE CALLING FROM 521-3838.

Elizabeth stared at the screen for a few seconds before understanding its meaning. She grabbed a book of matches and checked the hotel telephone number against the number on the computer screen.

They were the same!

Elizabeth felt her stomach tighten and her throat go dry.

The computer thought it had been dealing with Mr. Chong Lee, an ITB loan officer. But it had the number of the hotel she was in. The computer programmer would surely remember her visit, though she'd used the name Ann Murphy to cover her tracks.

But even if someone found out immediately that Chong Lee wasn't calling from the Conrad Hotel, she told herself, they wouldn't be able to pinpoint her.

Elizabeth removed the phone cord from the computer and began looking through the downloaded files—relieved that she was dealing with only her computer now.

The Fairchild accounts appeared on screen with all the details of deposits and checks over the past year. She paged through the listings, quickly learning where to look for the dates and amounts of checks, and noticed that a flurry of activity had occurred in early March. There was one very large deposit for two hundred thousand dollars on March 10. Interestingly, a check for the same amount had cleared on March 13.

The computer listed the payee of the check as Fairchild himself.

Where was I on March thirteenth?

She had arrived in New York looking for an eighty-five-million-dollar loan the day before, on March 12! The coincidence was titillating.

Each check and each deposit had a corresponding tracking number. On a whim, she switched to the long list of Costas's checking accounts and tried a universal search for the tracking number of the two-hundred-thousand-dollar deposit to Fairchild's account, fully expecting nothing to match.

The computer chattered away quietly to itself for nearly a half minute as it compared the number she had entered against every other string of numbers in the subdirectory, then stopped.

The listing for a particular check appeared on the screen, a debit on one of Nick Costas's checking accounts at ITB for exactly two hundred thousand-dollars. It had been deposited directly into Irwin Fairchild's checking account!

There was no doubt. The tracking numbers were identical.

Elizabeth got up and paced around the plush hotel room for a few minutes. Beyond the plate-glass windows, Hong Kong harbor bustled in the distance. Junks and smaller watercraft skittered like waterbugs among the ocean liners and freighters against the background of blue skies and distant hills, but Elizabeth was focused instead on the realization that Nick Costas himself had made at least one large payment to a man she had caught interfering with a pending Pan Am loan.

She fairly lunged for the telephone. It was 2:00 P.M. in Hong Kong and midnight back in New York where Creighton MacRae was staying.

He answered on the first ring, and she let the story of ITB's loan offer and Nick Costas's ownership of the bank tumble out. MacRae said nothing until she was through.

"Elizabeth, Jack and I were successful in tracking computer transfers from your debtholders and the lessors of your fleet." She could hear his hand rubbing his head and eyes and brushing the phone in the process. "We spent two days risking prison to run computer searches on perhaps millions of transactions, but we distilled a major provable pattern of off-shore monetary transfers. We also tracked telex records and telephone and computer hookup pathways to the same place. None of it would make any sense if you weren't being buggered."

"I didn't follow all of that, Creighton. You found offshore money transfers to our lenders?"

"Hear me out. During the last year, each time the debtholders made large advances to Pan Am under the revolving credit agreement, those very same sums of money were imported from a single offshore bank."

"What?"

"That's right. Your debtholders aren't really your debtholders. They're nothing but a conduit for someone else who's providing the money, but without any security. Sound a bit fishy, that?"

"Good Lord!"

"You are sitting, aren't you?"

"Why?"

"It's a bank right there in Hong Kong."

He let her make the connection.

"ITB?" she asked at last.

"The same."

She told him then of her raid on ITB's computer, impressed that he remained silent until she was through.

Creighton's voice was in her ear again, carrying a new and urgent tone. "Elizabeth, get the hell out of there. Now! Come back to New York, and I'll help you take this to a judge."

"I need to check with Jason Ing first, because—"

He cut her off.

"I've been talking to Jason this morning because I didn't know what the hell you were up to, and of course he didn't know either. He's sup-posed to contact you. He thinks he can get the money in time, and get you past the U.S. government restrictions. But you can't wait. You've got to get out of there *now!*"

"I don't understand." Elizabeth felt the chill hit her spine again.

"These people are powerful and ruthless, Elizabeth. They can have you arrested for breaking into their system. You've stumbled into the middle of a snake pit, so get out of there! Right now! Call me from an airplane headed back to the States. I know *I'll* feel better when you're airborne!"

He said goodbye and they disconnected. The phone had been back on the cradle less than thirty seconds when it rang again. She picked it up, fully expecting to hear Creighton's voice once more. Instead, a high-pitched computer tone warbled in her ear, probing for a silicon-based mate to warble back.

She hung up, slightly annoyed, and dismissed it as a wrong number.

But the phone rang again within thirty seconds. Once more the computer tone warbled in her ear—triggering a chilling recognition: the ITB computer had found her room number and was trying to reestablish the link!

Elizabeth dropped the receiver back on the cradle and backed away, as if it had suddenly become a poisonous snake.

It rang again and she jumped, her heart racing. She then let it ring continuously as she turned to the closet and began flinging her things into a bag.

Wait! Leave something in the closet and on the bed, she cautioned herself. *Don't let them think you're checking out!*

She zipped the overnight case with shaking hands, closed her briefcase with the computer inside, and yanked open the door to the hallway, gasping at the sight of Jason Ing standing just outside her door.

He muttered something and grabbed her shoulders as she tried to twist away in fright and run for the elevator, ignoring his voice.

"Elizabeth! *Elizabeth*!"

She stopped and looked back at his face.

"Where are you going?" he asked in an amazed voice.

"Is your car here, Jason?"

"Yes, but—"

"Take me to the airport. Now. Please!" She realized her voice sounded panicky, but there wasn't time to care. The urge to get out of the hotel and out of the city was becoming overwhelming.

"If you want to go, of course, but—"

"I mean *now*!" Her voice was almost a shout and it startled Ing, who nodded immediately and joined her in a dash to the elevators and the lobby. She shot out the door and into the backseat of his limo before the driver could emerge from the car. Jason followed, shutting the door behind him. As they pulled away, two police cars rushed past them and turned into the entrance of the hotel.

She already knew what they were looking for.

Jason Ing seemed stunned. He turned to Elizabeth, full of questions—which she deferred.

They rode in silence for several minutes before Elizabeth spoke again. "How close are we to concluding this loan, Jason?"

He looked confused. "Close, if you can solve your regulatory problem, and I think I may have the key to that. Cathay Alliance will loan you the one hundred forty million in an unsecured note by Monday, which will make your deadline. But we'll wait for your government's approval before bringing in the other funds, which originate from Chinese sources. We'll take the chance ourselves for the first payment."

"But the corporation is owned in part by the Chinese government, right?"

She had swiveled around to look out the small rectangular rear window, expecting to see flashing lights chasing them down.

"Technically, no. My family holds almost all the stock, but we're a captive instrument of the Chinese government if we want to stay in business beyond 1997, like I explained to you."

Elizabeth's eyes widened as she searched his. "That may solve the problem, Jason! I'll have to talk to our lawyers again, especially since the next installment is due in fifteen more days, and that's probably too quick for government approval."

"We can't advance any more than the first payment until the whole package is approved, Elizabeth."

"I've got one other straw to grasp at. I think we can go to court and block the creditors from calling a default now. That will give us some additional time."

"How?"

She shook her head. "Not right now, Jason. I'll explain later, but Creighton was right about Irwin Fairchild. I think we've found a connection between Fairchild and the lenders."

◆ ◆ ◆

A British Airways 747-400 was scheduled to leave nonstop for London in thirty minutes when they reached the airport. Elizabeth bought a one-way ticket, worried about using her own credit card, but having no choice. She said goodbye to Jason Ing at the curb and thanked him profusely, promising to call within the next twenty-four hours. Jason waved as they pulled away, deep puzzlement still showing in his face.

The security and passport checks loomed ahead of her like the shadow of a noose on a distant wall. If the police had already been notified, they would certainly call the airport and make sure that neither Ann Murphy nor Elizabeth Sterling slipped through the net. She analyzed the motions of the immigrations officer as she stood in line, tensing for the mere flicker of an eye in her direction.

But nothing seemed abnormal.

The young man stamped another piece of paper and called up the passenger in front of her, and then it was her turn.

She walked to the podium and smiled in his direction, but there was no smile in return. He opened her passport and looked from the picture to her face and back twice, then paused.

Elizabeth could hear her heart pounding in her ears loudly enough to be heard throughout the airport. Her mouth was dry and her mind out of options. With each passing second she was sure she was going to be spending the next few hours in a Hong Kong police station rather than the first-class cabin of a British Airways jet.

She realized he was looking at her with some irritation, and holding out her passport.

"Please move along, miss."

"What?"

The security officer rolled his eyes and motioned toward the gate. He was through with her. She could go. He *wanted* her to go!

She heard herself exhale as her fingers closed around the passport.

♦ ♦ ♦

Not until the 747 had reached cruising altitude could Elizabeth relax fully. She checked carefully to make sure no one was watching, and opened her computer, using several spare diskettes from her briefcase to make copies of the most incendiary information she had purloined from ITB's computer. The plan had been forming in her mind since leaving the hotel. If something happened to her computer—or to her—the information had to survive.

Brian had once told her about an alcoholic steward who had for years hidden a flask of vodka behind the mirror in the restroom of a Boeing 727 before every flight sequence. The man would nip at it on numerous trips to the facility. There were removable panels in each restroom, Brian told her.

She locked herself in one of the first-class restrooms and began searching the wall, finding a small latch that gave access to an inside compartment that would work perfectly. She wrapped the three diskettes in an airsickness bag and carefully placed them behind the insulation in a remote section of the compartment before closing everything up and returning to her seat.

She picked up the satellite phone at her seat and called Creighton in New York. She was shocked at how surprised he seemed that she'd called.

"Elizabeth! Thank God. Where *are* you?"

"In flight. On a British Airways jumbo headed for London. Why?"

There was a momentary silence from the other end.

"I just got off the phone with Cathay Alliance. Jason Ing was kidnapped at gunpoint just outside the airport, and his driver was killed. I was afraid you might have been with him. I've been frantic—"

"What do you mean, kidnapped?" she interrupted, trying to keep her voice low and out of the ears of the adjacent passengers, but she'd wanted to scream the question into the phone.

"Hundreds of people saw it happen, I'm told, but the police couldn't get there in time. They blew his driver away and pulled Jason into another car and sped off. So far, there's no ransom call."

"I know what they want, Creighton. They want me, and what I've got in this computer!"

The memory of the police cars driving into the hotel as they left replayed in her mind. But the police wouldn't have shot a driver, which meant that Costas's people were on the trail as well, and were probably the ones who had Jason Ing.

"Can I trust this satellite phone to be secure?" she asked Creighton.

"No, you can't. Anyone could listen in."

"Okay. Creighton, listen closely. There's a story about an airline crewmember and a flask of vodka our chief pilot tells. If anything happens to me or my computer, that story will lead you to copies of what's on my hard drive."

"I don't understand that, but I'm writing it down. When are you scheduled into London?"

"Ten P.M. tonight," she told him. "I'll need to come on to New York immediately."

"Someone will meet you at the gate in London with the tickets on the next flight out."

She scribbled a note to herself. She needed to call Jack Rawly, the general counsel, Chad Jennings, her mother and Kelly, and Brian.

But she hated to let Creighton go.

"You still there, Elizabeth?" he asked.

"I'm here. Will you wait for me in New York?"

"I will," he said instantly. "I've got some of the evidence you'll need, you know."

The call ended, but Elizabeth sat for many minutes staring out the window and holding the receiver on her lap as the sounds of the high-speed slipstream passing the metallic skin of the 747 washed a roar of white noise into her consciousness. She found herself wondering what Scotland was like the rest of the year.

Friday, March 24, noon
Amsterdam, Holland

The police inspector made one last note to himself before looking at Jacob Voorster with a disgusted sigh and a shake of his head.

"For the moment, you are free to go, Mr. Voorster. I thank you for
coming straight here."

Jacob's right hand fluttered above the scarred surface of the wooden
conference table. "And what is to happen now?"

"Mr. Voorster, we will continue to gather the evidence, and then we
will present it to a magistrate who will decide whether or not you are to
be arrested and tried for embezzlement. Until then, you remain free."

"I . . . did nothing. I have told you that. I know nothing of any private
accounts. I've never taken a penny of my company's money."

The inspector got to his feet and gestured toward the door. "You will
have a chance to present your arguments to a magistrate, not to me."

Jacob retrieved his overcoat and hat with shaking hands and walked
through the door of the police station, certain that dozens of eyes were
following his departure with the utter disdain reserved for the newly unmasked criminal.

He sat behind the wheel of his car for fifteen minutes, seeing nothing,
his head in a fog, as he tried to relive the previous hour.

The police had been waiting for him when he arrived at his office, as
had his immediate supervisor, who slammed a computer printout down in
front of him listing the transactions of a bank account at Barclay's in
London that now contained over three hundred thousand guilders, all of
it coming from VZV payments of bogus invoices for stock investments
that didn't exist.

The account—which he had never seen before in his life—had been
traced back to him, they said. A passbook for the same account had

been found in his desk. It had been planted there, of course, but the passbook was damning. As soon as it surfaced, no one at VZV was willing to listen.

He was fired instantly, his pension canceled and his office sealed. The police had given him a choice: voluntarily follow the officers in for questioning, or be handcuffed and arrested and transported to the same place for the same purpose.

His blood pressure soared and his head pounded, his mind filled with hurtful thoughts of disbelief and betrayal.

It hadn't taken him long to realize that recent events were no coincidence. It was the morning after he had turned in a senior director to the managing director. The connection—though he longed to believe otherwise—was obvious.

For a few optimistic minutes he wondered if the false accusation had been launched without the managing director's knowledge. But the sickening sight of Frederick Ooest's signature on the formal VZV complaint snatched the last vestige of hope from his fingers.

Not since his wife had died of breast cancer five years before had life looked so bleak.

Jacob started his car and drove slowly home, his mind roaming in a daze of pain back over the evidence he had found—a trail of computer records of strange payments that he had spent the past two months following and unraveling. At the end of the long, tortuous trail of deception and international intrigue, he had unmasked the identity of the perpetrator: the VZV director he had reported.

Jacob parked his car in front of his small suburban house and approached the front door, looking for signs of forced entry. He had been told to turn over all his office files and disks to Ooest, and he had. But had they guessed he had copies at home?

Now the second set was the only hope for proving himself innocent.

The house was pristine, and the damning collection of evidence was where he had left it, including the strangest evidence of all—the trail of VZV's purchase of a Hong Kong bank that had been subsequently all but given to Costas. For what reason he didn't know.

He reached into a file cabinet and rummaged around for the folder marked "Costas, Nicolas." There had been an article several years back in *The Economist* about Costas and the collapse of Columbia Air Systems. As he reviewed it now, his determination built by the minute.

It would be useless to fight VZV's trumped-up charges directly. VZV was too strong and clever, and could create a hundred such fake accounts with correspondent banks if it liked. It came down to a tradeoff and a matter of survival: to prove himself innocent, he would have to prove his beloved company guilty, and of a much greater crime.

The enemy of my enemy is now my friend. The paraphrased quotation rolled around in his head as he began stuffing the papers and disks into his briefcase along with his passport. He had but one possible ally on the planet now, and that was the new Pan American Airways. He would approach them in London. He had already made a reservation on a seven-o'clock flight to Heathrow.

If he could save *them*, perhaps they might be persuaded to return the favor.

Friday, March 24, 9:00 A.M.
Seattle

Brian Murphy found Bill Conrad in the upper first-class lounge of Ship 609 as it sat behind the closed doors of the Seatac hangar.

"We've been over all four engines, Brian, every inspection plate and door on the outside, and the electronics and baggage compartments. They're starting the interior in about an hour. I told my people we think someone's likely to try to blow this bird out of the sky on Monday between Seatac and Kennedy. They're determined as hell not to let that happen. If anything's been messed with or planted on this ship, we'll find it. You still going to captain it on Monday?"

"Damn right. Since I'm the one who predicted the attempt, either we cancel the flight or I'm honor-bound to fly it."

Conrad got up and walked over to one of the windows. "Jennings thinks all this is nonsense, but I could care less. I've hired all the security teams we need. No one's going to get close to this bird, or any of our other airplanes, for that matter."

"Bill, did you ever order a rubber stamp?"

Conrad turned suddenly from the window and stared at Brian.

"A rubber stamp," Brian continued. "You know, like one with your signature on it, or something that says "Received" or "This End Up"?

Bill sat down again, his eyes searching Brian's face for clues to what was behind the question. "I suppose I have, at one time or other. Why?"

"I found out today how easy it is to get creative with rubber stamps. You can take a Xerox copy of a fingerprint, for instance, and one of these companies can make a rubber stamp that, when you ink it, will print that same impression line for line on a piece of paper or anywhere else.''

Bill shot an even more quizzical look at Brian. ''Then you could go around and stamp your fingerprint on things. Why would you want to do that?''

''Indulge me a second. I get your fingerprint, have a stamp made, and instead of ink, I just rub my hand on the stamp to get it full of natural oils, and then I press it down on a piece of paper, say a manila folder. Someone comes along with dusting powder and finds the print. Could they tell it wasn't you in person?''

Bill was staring hard at Brian, but now he nodded slowly. ''I've never been in law enforcement, but no, I don't see how they could. Why? What're you driving at?''

''Suppose someone did exactly that with Marvin Grade's index finger—made a stamp, that is?''

Bill Conrad sat down, his right hand stroking his chin. ''Jesus, Brian. You did say they only found the print for Grade's index finger, right? And that's the sole reason they maintain Grade was the saboteur?''

Brian was nodding energetically. ''On my pilot file folder and on the circuit board, that's right. 'Fingerprints don't lie, Brian,' was what Agent Miller said.''

''Have you talked to Miller about this new idea?''

''That's where I'm headed now.'' Brian pulled a small, red-handled stamp from his coat pocket, rubbed it with his hand, and pressed it onto a glass inlay on one of the teakwood tables. The clear image of a fingerprint was left behind.

''That's my fingerprint, by the way. I had it made yesterday to prove the point.''

♦ ♦ ♦

Ten miles to the north, at Swedish Hospital, Pan Am President Ron Lamb looked up from a stack of papers and focused on Public Affairs Vice-President Ralph Basanji's worried expression. The right side of Lamb's face still drooped a bit, but he had been struggling night and day to recover his ability to speak, and the effort was working—though not as fast as he would have liked.

''Ra . . . Ralph . . . get me . . . th . . . the computer.''

Basanji picked up the small laptop from an adjacent table and placed it on Lamb's lap.

''Reee . . . read . . . what I . . . write here.''

Basanji watched the screen as the fingers of Ron's left hand flew over the keys, typing his side of the conversation.

> Jennings is ruining us! Why didnk . . . didn't Taylor fer . . .
> fire him after the newspaper/tv attack on the big guys?

Ralph Basanji had been standing by the bed and leaning over to watch the screen. He stepped back a bit to face Ron and reply.

"I don't know, Ron, but he's so busy playing games with this issue of who's after us, he's doing nothing about the real problem. Elizabeth Sterling is . . . I don't know, somewhere . . . trying to get us the money, but as far as I can tell from her assistant, Monday morning we're going to be shut down."

Ron Lamb resumed typing, motioning Ralph over to sit on the bed for a better view of the screen.

> eliz . . . Elizabeth's good person . . . capable and smart. if
> anyone can do it she can, but need . . . we need to know
> what's going on with her. who is she talking to daily?

Basanji shook his head, palms up.

> ok ralp . . . sorry, Ralph . . .

"Forget about the capital letters, Ron, I can figure it out."

> ok fine. its easier without trying to hit upr case. get joe
> taylor in here to see me as quick as you can. tell the old
> fart im not a vegitable, and that i can run this thing from
> this bed better than jennings is doing on his feet. basically
> i want jennings out of my office. i intend to resume my duties
> as pres. find elizabeth for me too please. tell her to call me
> here. my wife will standby and interpret whad . . . what i
> write. were not going to let all these years of hard work go
> to hell without a fight to the last minte . . . minute. hows the
> faa actions?

"All fines are suspended until they finish investigating who did what to us and when. I think we'll end up in the clear on everything, and that's Murphy's and Conrad's opinion too.''

wunnerful!!! now the sobs need to tell the rest of the world.
ralph . . . tell murphy and conrad to redoubel security . . .
i dont belive . . . believe its over. the sabotage i mean.

Friday, March 24, 10:25 P.M.
Heathrow Airport, London

Elizabeth had just cleared customs at Heathrow when Creighton MacRae appeared at her side, scooping up her bag and smiling at her as she tried to hide the depth of the pleasure she felt.

He was supposed to be in New York!

''I've brought a legal team along, Elizabeth. Jack Rawly, your general counsel, and another attorney he's retained in New York. They're waiting for us across the field on board Jack's Falcon 50, which will be ready to go back to New York in about thirty minutes.''

''Good grief! What's that going to cost us?'' she asked.

''Cheaper than four tickets on the Concorde at, what, three thousand a pop?''

He took her arm gently and guided her through the throng of passengers, brushing past a portly, balding man in a business suit who suddenly turned and called out to Elizabeth.

''Excuse me! ma'am? Excuse me!''

Creighton stopped as Elizabeth turned.

''I'm Jim Cleghorn, Ms. Sterling, *right*? You're our new chief financial officer?''

''Our?''

''I'm Pan Am's London station manager, Ms. Sterling. We met last week when I got you the pass back home on British Air?''

She relaxed then, and smiled at him as she took his hand. ''Of course, Jim. I'm sorry I didn't recognize you.''

''Ah . . . Ms. Sterling, would you have a moment to come to my office and help me out with a slightly odd situation?''

Creighton moved closer to her side now, speaking out of the corner of his mouth.

''We really do need to get cracking.''

She nodded ever so slightly at Creighton while keeping her eyes on Cleghorn. "What about, Jim?"

"I've got a fellow in my office, a well-spoken gent who wants to relay some information to us that he says is urgent, but he'll only speak with a corporate officer."

"A complaint, you mean?"

Cleghorn shrugged. "He won't tell me. I had him wait while I took care of another matter, and then I was going to try again to get someone on the phone from Seattle, but since you're here . . ."

Creighton shook his head openly and looked at Elizabeth. "We really don't have time, Ms. Sterling."

She smiled and raised the palm of her right hand. "I'm sorry, Jim. We have a private plane waiting for a transatlantic flight. This fellow sounds like someone Ralph Basanji in Seattle would want to talk to."

He reached out and shook her hand again, smiling. "Not to worry. I'll take care of it. Let me know if I can ever help when you're in town."

Creighton led the way to the driveway, where a black Bentley was waiting to take them to the aircraft.

"I know you're probably exhausted."

"Not really. I'm okay."

"Good. I thought we could work and plot strategy across the pond. We've got three extra computers aboard, and if we each copy and search through the data you've brought back, maybe the legal types can get their case together."

"Have they scheduled a hearing?"

He shook his head. "Rawly says he wants to find his favorite federal judge in his rose garden. Gives us a better shot."

Elizabeth stole a sideways look at Creighton, noting the glitter of combativeness in his eyes and the way he was sitting forward on the edge of the seat, fists clenched, watching the driver's actions like a pensive hawk. She had wondered if his legal victory over the companies that killed his airline had given him the freedom he sought, or made him a captive to his ultimate success. With the money came no need to fight further, and she could imagine his irascibility growing in direct proportion to his boredom as he sat, season after season, like a brooding lion atop the personal hill of his Scottish farm.

Creighton noticed her silence and turned his head toward her, delighted to find her eyes on him.

"What exactly am I doing that you find so amusing?" he asked, half amused himself. "Come on now, be brutally frank."

She cleared her throat and diverted her gaze forward.

"I was merely thinking that you seem to be up for this fight." She looked back at him, locking her eyes on his. "And it makes me feel very encouraged."

He smiled and looked away. "Don't buy any Dom Pérignon yet. We've a long way to go."

"Any word on Jason Ing?" she asked.

Creighton shook his head as they pulled up to the airplane.

Maybe he's forgotten about Vancouver.

He helped her out of the car, and Elizabeth could see the other two men through the open door of the jet, but her mind was occupied with a disturbing debate.

I hope he doesn't remember, and yet I hope he does.

As Elizabeth was fastening her seatbelt in the cabin of Jack Bastrop's Falcon 50, less than a mile across the airport in the main Heathrow Terminal Jim Cleghorn replaced the handset of his office phone and shook his head at the distinguished-looking man seated on the other side of his desk.

"I'm sorry, sir, but as you heard, I'm getting nowhere. It would really be helpful if you told me what this was about."

"I cannot. Only to an officer."

"Well, that's what I mean. I ran into our chief financial officer just a few minutes ago in the terminal, and if I could have told her what you wanted—"

The man lurched forward in his chair, his eyes flaring. "Your chief financial officer is here?"

"*Was* here. She's headed for New York, I think, on a private jet."

Not smart, Jim! he told himself. *Don't give out details to strangers!*

"I must stop . . . her?"

"Yes. Our CFO is a woman."

"I must stop her!" The man was on his feet and threatening to dash out the door.

"Not possible, sir. I don't know which airplane, or which airport they're leaving from. If you want to catch her, you'll have to do it in New York."

Jacob Voorster whirled back to Jim Cleghorn. "Will you send a message to your people in New York that I must speak with her? This is vital for your company!"

Jim Cleghorn leaned forward and concentrated on his visitor's eyes.

"This . . . doesn't concern any threat to our airplanes, does it?"

Voorster shook his head firmly. "But it is so important that I will fly to New York at my own expense to speak with her."

Cleghorn sat back and sighed. *You're sure not flying at our expense, fellow,* he thought to himself. He looked up at the man. "Okay. I'll let them know, and they'll let her know."

He pulled a pad of paper across the desk. "Your name, sir?"

"Jacob Voorster, formerly of Van Zanten and Vetter of Amsterdam."

Saturday, March 25, 7:00 A.M.
Hong Kong

Nicolas Costas gripped the balcony railing of his multimillion-dollar apartment on the mid-level slopes of Victoria Peak, staring at the harbor as he ground his teeth.

Two very alarmed men stood in the shadows of his living room expecting the worst, one of them the British expatriate chief operating officer of ITB, the other the head of ITB security. Neither of them had ever met the third man in the room, whose name was Choi, but from what they knew of his reputation, they would just as soon not have been on the same island with such a dangerous sort. Choi, for his part, was ignoring what he considered Costas's lackeys. The leading member of a powerful Kowloon underworld family stood to one side looking quietly comfortable, and waiting for Nick Costas to come back in.

Costas muttered a four-letter epithet toward the bay and returned to the room, eyes ablaze with fury as he looked at his two employees, then softened his expression as he turned to face Choi Hee.

"How bad is your guest feeling?"

Choi smiled an evil smile. "He'll live. He has all his parts. But he'll be sore for some time."

"And he doesn't know who snatched him?"

Choi shook his head. "He will be unable to identify anyone."

Costas nodded. "It would be appreciated if he were to remain your guest until Monday evening. It would also be appreciated if he were to find himself dumped somewhere near the border, where he'll have to walk home. He comes from a powerful family, Choi Hee. They will want him back."

"I believe those wishes can be accommodated by our family, which is also a family of some substance." Costas saw Choi's eyes flash in anger at the perceived insult.

No matter, Costas figured. Choi owed him.

"And on the subject of what he knew," Choi continued, "we don't believe the woman told him anything of substance. All he seemed to know was that she was flying back to San Francisco, as we told you."

"He fooled you, I'm afraid. I had one of my people meet that flight in San Francisco. She wasn't there. This is the second time she's slipped out of the net."

Choi bowed and left. Costas waited before turning to the two bank officers, fury painting his features again, and his voice at high volume. "You two idiots better be telling me the truth about the files."

The COO, a ruddy-faced native of Cornwall, England, with a lantern jaw and sunken eyes, nodded furiously. "We know she looked at the files, and which ones she tried to download. But the security system would have erased them when she couldn't come up with the right code."

"But the bitch saw them!" Costas shot back.

"She came in the building under a false name and spent time with one of the programmers, as I told you, Nick. The girl, the programmer, can't recall whether Sterling saw one of the security-code lists or not. They were talking about the technical capabilities of the system."

"Fire her."

"I already have, Nick. I wouldn't really worry about those files—"

"Oh you wouldn't?" Costas walked up to the COO face to face. "I've got records in those files that could be misinterpreted and used against me in a hundred lawsuits. Hell, she probably knows, now, that I own the bank."

"Nick, if you can grab her computer—"

Costas grabbed the man's tie with the quickness of a striking snake, and jerked the man viciously within inches of his face.

"Where the fuck *is* her computer, wiseass? Where is *she*?"

The phone rang, and Costas released him as he moved to answer it. After a brief exchange he replaced the receiver with a disgusted look.

"Well, the bitch showed up in London and got on a private jet bound for New York a while ago."

"What are you going to do?" the COO asked.

Nick Costas turned back to the balcony, his voice low and guttural and almost inaudible. "What I should have done to begin with. But it's probably too late."

30

Cathay Alliance
Friday, March 24, midnight
Seattle

When his panicked client had finished talking, the man replaced the telephone handset and returned to his makeshift workbench.

He shook his head and chuckled to himself, contemptuous of his client's worries. So the airline was bending heaven and earth to keep anything from happening on the round-the-world inaugural aircraft as it flew from Seattle to New York. So what? A small change in plans he could easily handle.

The man slowly inserted a battery, and carefully soldered the positive wire to the positive terminal.

With the wires in place, he checked to see that the enabling switch was in the off position and began to pack it in a video camera battery case.

Once finished, he placed the package in the bottom of his camcorder case before peeling off his latex gloves. There was still the mustache. He'd grown attached to it. But it was time to shave it off, change his hair color, and pop in a set of blue-tinted contact lenses.

Pan Am's head of maintenance and their chief pilot were trying to play detective and find him, he knew. So far, neither was getting close. But both men were wild cards in a game it was deadly not to control.

And wild cards had to be neutralized.

Saturday, March 25, 9:30 A.M.
New York

Elizabeth awoke before ten and showered quickly, amazed that she felt rested and awake. She had made several calls and finished putting on her last serviceable dress from her small suitcase just as Creighton knocked on her door, holding a pot of coffee and two cups.

"How are you holding up?"

"Through sheer determination. Come on in, and bring that transfusion with you!"

He sat on a chair while she perched on the end of the bed, forcing herself to focus on nothing but business as they drained the coffee and reviewed the bleak situation. Jason Ing was still missing, and Cathay Alliance had confirmed by phone minutes before that they couldn't complete the loan without him. The only route to salvation lay through the federal courts.

"That's why I won't be with you this afternoon, Elizabeth."

She looked up, surprised.

"I can't promise anything," he continued, "but I have a hunch I can find one of the last links. I'm certainly of no use to you in a legal strategy meeting."

"But you have direct evidence—" she started to protest.

He finished the thought, "Which can be presented in affidavit form for these purposes. No, I'm not needed this afternoon. I'll rejoin you before you go see the judge."

She put the cup down and studied him, sensing uncertainty in him for the first time. "Creighton, what are you planning to do?"

He shook his head side to side. "Nothing foolish, I assure you. But there are people in this yet to be heard from, and remember, you got me into this because I'd been here before. Trust me."

She smiled, slow and warm, her eyes looking directly into his. "I do."

Saturday, March 25, 10:30 A.M.
JFK Airport, New York

Jacob Voorster was astounded and angry.

"You are telling me I was misled in London?"

The Pan Am passenger service agent smiled a rueful little smile and shrugged her shoulders. "I don't know what to tell you, sir. Ms. Sterling is our chief financial officer and vice-president, and she's based in Seattle. I just called back there to operations, and they said that as far as they know, that's where she is."

"You must help me reach her, or your president, or someone in authority by phone!" he asked.

"Not on a weekend, sir, unless this is an emergency—and even then we can't give out home numbers."

"This *is* an emergency. Your airline is under financial attack. I have worked for the company that is trying to put you out of business. I have vital information to give your leaders. If I do not reach the right person in your company, you will have no company. Can you not understand that?" He stopped suddenly, having said more than he'd intended to say to anyone other than a Pan Am corporate officer.

The station manager drummed her fingers on her desk for what seemed like forever, her eyes boring into Jacob's. He didn't flinch, and finally she spoke.

"Okay. We get to use our own good judgment around here. If you'll wait in the outer office, I'll find someone back there of corporate rank, and we'll see what can be done."

"Thank you," Jacob said.

Thirty minutes later, Judy Schimmel emerged from her office with a notepad and a smile. "Okay, Mr. Voorster. Will the vice-president of operations do?"

He nodded.

"Very well. That's a Mr. Chad Jennings. Until this morning he was acting president while our corporate president recovered from an illness." She handed him a Pan Am ticket envelope and another slip of paper. "Our flight to Seattle leaves tomorrow at eight A.M. I've got a round-trip pass for you in this envelope. I'm going to put you up tonight at a hotel right off the airport at our expense, and have one of our people take you over there and pick you up again in the morning. Mr. Jennings will be at the airport on your arrival in Seattle. Okay? When I told him what you told me, he was very eager to meet you. He also asked me to ask you to discuss this with no one else. He says you've found the right officer."

Saturday, March 25, 6:15 P.M.
New York City

Jack Rawly had lost count of the cups of coffee he had guzzled since late morning. The Pan Am general counsel drained his latest now and looked at the paper-strewn table of the ornate conference room, the battle-field of nearly eight hours' work. In reality it was the living room of a suite, connected to a bedroom in either direction, and it occupied the southeast corner of the tenth floor of the hotel. But it had served as the Pan Am war room since he had assembled with three additional New York–based attorneys just before noon.

Elizabeth had stayed for the first few hours, departing in midafternoon to make a series of calls back to Seattle and continue her last-minute efforts to secure a loan.

Now she was back, relaying word that Chad Jennings had been relieved of his temporary post as acting president by Ron Lamb, who was running things from his hospital room. Elizabeth saw the relieved smile on Jack Rawly's face.

"Any word from Hong Kong?" Rawly asked, trying to change the subject.

"Jason Ing is still missing, and his company is unwilling to transfer any funds without him, even if we resolve our problems with U.S. approval."

"So it's the courts or nothing," Rawly said, more to himself than to Elizabeth.

She nodded, feeling somber, as if the gathering were something between a wake and a hopeless gesture.

Jack Rawly got to his feet suddenly and slapped the table. "Right. Okay, I was about ready to summarize everything, Elizabeth."

"Good. I'm not sure what I missed." He walked to a large white posterboard propped on an easel and examined the different boxes representing such players as Nick Costas, ITB, the lenders, and Irwin Fairchild.

"We have the connection and money transfers from Costas to Fairchild down cold." Rawly looked at one of the other lawyers. "Bill, you've got the copies of those computer printouts?"

"Right here, along with the formal petition for the restraining order."

"Okay, good." Rawly looked back at the board. "Now, thanks to Creighton MacRae's work, we also have a clear trail of the huge sums of money sent to our revolving-loan lenders from Costas's bank in Hong Kong, and pretty good circumstantial evidence that those sums were always to be passed on to Pan Am as a loan. That tentatively connects Costas with our lenders, since Costas is the owner of that bank, ITB. But what's missing is this." He tapped the empty box at the top of the chart. "Whatever name fits in this box, we must assume they own or control, through intermediaries, large amounts of stock in United, Delta, and American. We presume they've commissioned someone—probably Nick Costas—to kill off Pan Am because Pan Am's threatening the big three's lock on the North American market." He turned back to the others. "I think we're all in agreement that we don't need to prove this part of it to get a temporary restraining order, but we will need proof to get a permanent injunction.''

Rawly looked at the other attorneys. ''By the way, guys, I think we should haul this chart along to show the judge. You agree?''

They both nodded.

''Okay,'' Jack Rawly continued. ''Now here's the weak point. Elizabeth, we have your testimony that Fairchild met with Mr. Hudgins of Bannister Partners after you secured the deal in principle on the eighty-five-million-dollar loan, and after you saw Fairchild walk out of Hudgins's building, the deal collapsed. Does that state it correctly?''

She nodded.

''The problem is, that's purely circumstantial. In the first place, we can't prove Fairchild went in there with the intent of interfering with Pan Am's interests. In the second place, even if we *could* prove he meant to interfere, we can't absolutely prove that the two hundred thousand dollars Costas paid him had anything to do with such activities.''

''So what do we do?'' Elizabeth asked.

Rawly shook his head and sighed. ''We desperately need more evidence. We need *someone* who'll have the guts to come forward and testify that Fairchild tried to convince them not to deal with Pan Am. In the meantime, what we're going to say to the judge in a little while is that our lenders, by actively trying to destroy our ability to repay their loans, have breached the loan contract. We are therefore entitled to mitigate the damages by withholding any further payments while we sue. Since they breached the contract, they can't declare *us* in default, and we would appreciate a temporary restraining order to prevent them from doing so.''

''Have you called the judge?'' one of the other attorneys asked, looking at his watch.

Rawly nodded. ''He'll see us at eight P.M. sharp, at his home south of White Plains, which means we'd better get going.''

31

Saturday, March 25, 6:45 P.M.
White Plains, New York

The chief federal judge for the Northern District of New York had made the short list of candidates for the United States Supreme Court twice, but both times Walter Hoover Hayes had taken himself out of the running—just as he had refused many opportunities to leave the trial court behind to sit on a more sedate appeals court.

"The damn peace and quiet would kill me," he had explained to *The New York Times* on the occasion of spurning the last promotion offer.

At age sixty-two, slightly overweight, bald, and fond of wearing a handlebar mustache, Hayes was an original. With a gravelly voice that could scare the hell out of the most hardened attorney across a crowded courtroom, he had become a bit of a legend for his intolerance of elliptical arguments and time-wasting questions. He would come springing out of his chair with eyebrows flaring as he launched the rolling thunder of his voice at the offending lawyer.

He was also known for being one of the bravest judges on the federal bench when it came to trying to right wrongs as he saw them, yet his decisions were seldom reversed by his younger brethren on the appeals court.

In the opinion of Jack Rawly—who had begun his law practice as a clerk for Walter Hayes—the judge was the perfect choice in the matter of Pan American Airways, Inc., versus Intertrust Bank et al.

Judge Hayes threw open the door of his French Provincial mansion with a broad grin and grabbed Jack Rawly's hand.

"Young Counselor Rawly, I presume? How the hell are you?"

"Not so good, Judge."

The judge motioned to the other four people on his porch and Rawly introduced them, noticing Hayes's eyebrows rising a notch as he squeezed Elizabeth's hand.

They settled in the dining room around an ornate polished pecan table. The judge reached out and snapped on a small tape recorder, then uncapped a fountain pen and laid it on a legal pad before him.

"This informal session of the Federal District Court for the Northern District of the State of New York is in session. Counselor, I take it this is an ex parte application?"

"It is, Your Honor."

"Proceed."

After nearly forty minutes of presenting the case, Jack Rawly sat down, watching carefully as Judge Hayes pulled at his mustache and thought.

The silence became excruciating, and at last the judge dropped his hand and sighed.

"Under Rule 65 of the Federal Rules of Civil Procedure, a temporary restraining order can be granted without notice to the adverse party only if the specific facts show that immediate and irreparable injury, loss, or damage will result before the adverse party can be heard, *and* if the applicant's attorney certifies, in writing, good reason why notice of the other party should not be required. I am satisfied that irreparable harm will be done if a default is declared on Monday. I'm also satisfied that there is sufficient justification not to require notice to the adverse party before granting a TRO this weekend, provided some reasonable attempt is made at giving notice."

The judge stopped and surveyed the faces around the table as they all held their breaths. He moved forward slightly in his chair and continued.

"What I'm *not* satisfied with is the level of proof I'm being presented in regard to the central allegation of your complaint. In other words, you allege breach of contract by Intertrust Bank et al., in that they hired certain parties to interfere materially with the ability of Pan Am to perform in accordance with the terms of the contract, and therefore they cannot issue a notice of default under that same contract. This is actually in the nature of estoppel. There's the terrible old example of a boy who kills his parents and then asks the court for leniency because he's now an orphan. He would be estopped from using that defense because he brought about his own handicap. So, too, would Intertrust Bank et al. be estopped from presenting you with a notice of default if they in effect created that default."

Judge Hayes paused and sipped his coffee.

"Okay, I'm persuaded that this Mr. Costas paid a Mr. Fairchild a lot of money. I'm persuaded that Mr. Costas owns a bank in Hong Kong that has some extremely suspicious transfers of funds to Intertrust Bank et al., your creditor. We have almost a complete loop except for one thing. All you have is circumstantial supposition that this Mr. Fairchild actually accepted Mr. Costas's money for the purpose of interfering with Pan Am's ability to raise funds and stay solvent.''

Judge Hayes sat back and slapped the table lightly.

"So I'm going to deny the petition for tonight, but I'm going to be in my courtroom at five P.M. tomorrow in Manhattan. I want you, Counselor''—he inclined his head toward Jack Rawly, who nodded in return—''to be there with additional proof, in whatever form you can find it, to persuade me that there is, in fact, reason to believe that Mr. Costas hired Mr. Fairchild specifically to interfere with Pan Am's ability to get a loan. I also require you to notify opposing counsel by tomorrow, or report your best efforts to do so. If they show up, I will hear them. I also require you to be prepared to post a surety bond in the amount of two days' interest on the balance of one hundred forty million dollars at the interest rate set in your contract with the defendant. This matter is continued until then.''

♦ ♦ ♦

At the same moment, Creighton MacRae was sitting on a packing crate in the dank and filthy basement of a large, expensive apartment building near East End Avenue, worrying about rats.

He had seen nothing so far, but the occasional sound of scurrying in the darkness chilled him, and resurrected a lifelong phobia.

Unchallenged entrance to the basement had taken a thousand-dollar bribe. The doorman had been ready to call the police, but the cash erased his memory of the man he'd admitted to the basement stairway in early evening.

It had taken most of Saturday to locate the right person, a professional friend of Harold Hudgins—someone who would report to Hudgins instantly any rumor connected to Hudgins's name. By 4:00 P.M., however, Creighton had done it.

Something else scurried across the stale room in the darkness. Creighton turned on a tiny flashlight and stabbed the blackness with its puny beam. Then he turned it back on the job at hand, checking the connection between his lineman's handset, a caller ID box, and the two specific terminals on the building's master telephone distribution panel from Apartment 14F.

He picked up his rented cellular phone and dialed the number across town that belonged to a twenty-eight-year-old investment banker to whom Hudgins had been a mentor.

The man answered, flabbergasted to find himself talking to someone who identified himself as an investigator from the Securities and Exchange Commission. Creighton could hear fright tighten the young man's voice.

"What I need, Mr. Chadwick," Creighton told him, "are a few answers regarding an associate of yours, a Mr. Harold Hudgins. Right now this is just a background, off-the-record, no-attribution inquiry. But you are a licensed broker, and your license gives you certain responsibilities. And, of course, we could always subpoena you on the record if you don't want to help us this way."

"That's . . . okay. What do you want to know?"

Creighton's questions were crafted to startle and scare: Did he know a man named Fairchild? Had there ever been any rumor that Harold Hudgins had off-the-books accounts, or offshore banking accounts he used personally? Was Hudgins living beyond his means? And would Hudgins's brokerage house react badly if presented with evidence that Hudgins had accepted a payment under the table from Irwin Fairchild in exchange for canceling a pending loan deal?

The increasingly nervous Chadwick wanted no part of being a stool pigeon or an SEC target. His answers were careful and very vague, not that his answers mattered. Creighton thanked him at last and disconnected, shifting his eyes then to the telephone connection between apartment 14F and his lineman's handset.

Something dark and furry shot out of the blackness and ricocheted off Creighton's left shoe, then disappeared as rapidly in another direction. Creighton forced himself to concentrate on the mission.

The phone rang within seconds, the small caller ID device in Creighton's lap showing the inbound number as the same one he had just talked to across town on the cellular phone. It was Chadwick, and he was losing no time in reporting to Hudgins that the SEC was hot on his trail.

♦ ♦ ♦

The two men hung up after less than five minutes. Creighton braced for the main event, checking the small recorder and the tiny pickup attached to the cellular phone's earpiece. He snapped the recorder on now and waited, worrying about whether or not Hudgins had seen the fax.

Apartment 14F's phone line remained silent. Creighton spent the long moments reviewing everything, looking for any missing links, or any tasks left undone.

There were none.

Creighton had sent a message to Hudgins earlier in the day, a single-page fax that appeared to have come from Irwin Fairchild.

> *Harold H.—Very important you call my associate Craig Mac-Rae around 9 tonight. He'll be at my private number, which has changed and is unlisted: 582-7873. Something's come up. Tnx/I. Fairchild*

Someone in apartment 14F lifted the phone and began dialing.

There was a pause as the various relays mated through the city, routing the call to Creighton MacRae's cellular phone, which rang now.

"Yes?"

"Irwin?" Hudgins's voice was shaking.

"This is Mr. Fairchild's line, but he's not in at the moment."

"Oh ... then this is ... is Craig MacRae, right?"

"Who's calling?"

"This is Harold Hudgins."

"Oh yeah, Mr. Hudgins. Irwin said to expect your call tonight."

"I've got to talk to Irwin immediately. Now! Tonight!"

"He's not here, but you can talk to me. Is something wrong?"

"Damn right, something's wrong!" Hudgins said. "I just got a call from a friend of mine. The SEC's asking questions about me regarding—"

"Ah, not on the phone, okay?"

"What do you mean, not on the phone? Are they tapping my phone? I had a message to call you anyway."

"I know, but not about this. What I need to discuss with you at Irwin's request is routine. Look, where can we meet in an hour or so?"

Hudgins fell silent for a few seconds, apparently brainstorming amid a sea of fear.

"I ... I don't know. My office, I guess." He gave Creighton the address. They disconnected with an agreement to meet at 11:45 P.M.

Creighton stuffed his equipment back into a small jump bag and took the back exit from the building as the doorman had begged him to do, removing his latex gloves just before stepping out to the street.

His car was two blocks away. He walked briskly in that direction now, checking to make sure no one was following.

◆ ◆ ◆

Elizabeth had known all along she'd probably end up in front of her apartment building in the Village again, but now it was more than wistfulness that had propelled her there. She would have to decide whether to move back to New York. Tonight seemed an appropriate time to face the question.

The building looked older and more decrepit than she remembered from just eleven days before. The entire neighborhood, in fact, seemed seedy and slightly threatening compared to the sparkling cleanliness, charm, and modernity of Seattle.

But Manhattan itself was shimmering through a veil of drizzling rain, a surreal vision of quiet, glistening streets and sporadic surges of traffic.

Elizabeth drove aimlessly, her mind rehashing the critical puzzle of how to satisfy the judge. She wasn't aware of having returned to the office tower housing Bannister Partners and Harold Hudgins's office until she found herself across the street from it.

She braked to a halt, remembering the angry morning less than two weeks back when Hudgins had reneged on their deal, and she had caught Irwin Fairchild oozing his way from the lobby to his limo right in front of her.

She kept her foot on the brake as she casually watched a tall man in a tan overcoat walk up the street and turn into the entrance of the building, which appeared to be open.

Something about the man looked familiar. As she watched, he stopped to talk with the guard and sign in before walking to the elevators out of her range of view.

Elizabeth suddenly let off on the brake and steered diagonally across the street until she was at the curb in front of the building with the elevator lobby clearly in view.

"Creighton!" Her voice echoed around the interior of the car as she slammed the gear lever into Park and stopped the engine.

But she hadn't seen Creighton all afternoon. What could he be doing *here*?

She reminded herself that there were other offices in the building, as well as a restaurant on the top floor. She locked the car door behind her and rushed into the lobby of the building as the man disappeared into one of the elevators.

The guard was a large black man with penetrating eyes. An ex-cop, she decided. He had a knowing look, as if nothing escaped him.

She glanced at the sign-in book, startled to see Creighton's name clearly inscribed.

"I'm . . . sorry, but I did it again! I let my husband get in here with our house keys. Can I chase him down?"

"This fellow?" The guard launched a fat finger at the register and Creighton's name. She nodded.

He hesitated less than a second.

"Sure can. Don't have to sign in. He's going up to the forty-fifth floor."

"I know," she told him with a thank-you wave as she moved to the elevators and waited an eternity for one to arrive. The clock in the lobby showed 11:35 P.M. as the sound of the main glass doors opening from the street reached her ears. Another man was entering now, and she glanced in his direction, her blood running cold at the instant recognition that Harold Hudgins was headed at flank speed toward the sign-in book.

He hadn't looked in her direction, and her name wasn't on the book. Those thoughts ricocheted around her head as she stepped into the elevator and punched the forty-fifth-floor button repeatedly, praying the doors would close before Hudgins reached her.

Her elevator door wasn't closing, and Hudgins would reach her elevator in a matter of seconds!

She could hear his voice around the corner, and then the sound of his shoes on the terrazzo floors as he began walking rapidly toward the elevator lobby.

She punched all the buttons above the forty-fifth floor, repeatedly, hitting the Close Door button as she melded into the front corner.

Hudgins was in the elevator lobby now, pausing, probably scanning the elevator "up" lights. She heard him take two more steps. He stopped mere feet away. She realized he was punching the call button angrily.

"Come on, dammit!" His voice echoed from the stone walls.

Please close, please! Her thoughts seemed loud enough to be heard. Somehow he hadn't seen the open elevator. He was just standing there impatiently facing the other bank of elevator doors.

Silence seemed to stretch for minutes, but in a matter of seconds the doors began closing.

She heard his shoes scrape on terrazzo as he heard the door and turned, surprised that an open elevator had been waiting just behind him. She heard him move toward the closing door, knowing he would calculate the possibility of stopping it without hurting his hand.

As she feared, Harold Hudgins lunged for the closing door with his hand outstretched. Elizabeth saw his fingers enter the airspace of the elevator for a split second, then just as quickly pull back as the doors came together and the elevator cab began moving upward with only her on board.

She slumped against the wall, adrenaline filling her bloodstream, knowing he hadn't spotted her.

She reached up and punched the button marked 44, and the elevator seemed to get there instantly, the doors sliding open on a deserted hallway.

She got off and searched for the nearest fire exit. She saw one in clear view of the elevator lobby. She slipped her high heels off and carried them as she tested the door, verifying that she could get back in from the stairwell.

Quickly she scampered one flight up to the forty-fifth floor, knowing the door would have a clear view of the elevator lobby. She heard the sounds of elevators moving in the distance, and ever so slowly turned the knob and pulled just enough to let her peer out.

The glassed-in entrance to the Bannister offices was on the opposite end of the hallway, within view. Creighton was standing there, hands deep in his pockets, watching the elevator as the doors opened and an agitated Harold Hudgins stepped out.

She opened the door a bit more to hear.

"You're Fairchild's man, right? MacRae?" Hudgins's voice.

"That's right." Hudgins opened the door to the offices of Bannister Partners and they moved inside, leaving Elizabeth to monitor a quiet hallway.

The glass doors swung closed, but Hudgins had not stopped to lock them. The fact was not lost on Elizabeth.

Creighton had mentioned Fairchild! Hudgins had called Creighton Fairchild's man! The phrase sent chills up her spine, testing her faith in him.

What on earth was Creighton doing? And how had he suddenly become Fairchild's agent in Hudgins's estimation? She couldn't be sure, and she couldn't stay hidden in a stairway, nor could she fail to walk out of the building before or at least at the same time as they did. The guard would spot that in a second, and say something in Hudgins's presence.

She wedged the heel of one of her shoes in the door so that she could monitor any sounds in the hall, and turned to sit on the top step of the stairway to think. She should go down one flight, take the elevator back down, and leave.

She should, but she couldn't.

Elizabeth stuffed her shoes in her purse and checked the hallway again. It was clear, and the unlocked door to the Bannister offices beckoned.

♦ ♦ ♦

Creighton had turned on the tape recorder in the hallway as he heard the elevator approach. Hudgins was agitated and upset, but he wasn't suspicious. He motioned Creighton through the labyrinth of desks and into his corner office, gesturing to the couch as he paced around like a caged tiger.

"Why don't you tell me what's happened?" Creighton began with casual concern.

"The goddamned SEC, that's what's happened! An investigator called tonight—*tonight*, for God's sake—and questioned a friend of mine."

"What do you mean, questioned?"

Hudgins related with admirable accuracy the conversation with his friend and the questions the friend had been asked by the SEC inspector.

Creighton feigned alarm and sat forward on the couch.

"Oh jeez, they're apparently trying to build a case against you."

"Why? Why me?" Hudgins was anguished *and* panicked. "You know this business!" he told Creighton. "You know what happens when someone develops an odor in this community. You don't have to be indicted and convicted, or even charged. All you have to be is accused in the rumor mill! The fucking SEC could ruin me, just making a call like that!" He paced back and forth two more times before continuing. "Who *else* have they talked to? Who *else* have they poisoned against me?"

Creighton shrugged. "The important question is, how protected are you?"

Hudgins whirled on him as he'd hoped. "Me? The question is, how protected are *we*! I'm not in this alone, I guaran-damn-tee you! I go down, Irwin goes down!"

Creighton raised the palms of both hands. "Okay, okay. *Our* deal. I didn't mean to imply you were being abandoned. Now, I need some details. Irwin didn't fully explain his deal with you, and I've come in a bit late as the troubleshooter. I've been working on some of the European aspects of the Pan Am thing for him, so I'm trying to spin up here on what's what. Let me ask some questions, some of which are going to sound naive, but they all have a purpose.''

"Okay."

"This SEC snoop asked about an under-the-table payment, you said. But I didn't think there was anything traceable in the way of a payment that Irwin gave you for dropping the Pan Am loan, was there? Is there something I don't know about?''

"There wasn't! I mean, you guys didn't pay me anything. You just bought my bonds. That was the deal. I told Pan Am we weren't interested, and in return, Irwin buys twenty-five million of the bond issue I was having trouble moving. I save your bacon, you save mine. He was frantic to block Pan Am from getting that loan!''

"Okay, so, just as I figured, there were no payments under the table that could be uncovered at a later date, right?''

"Of course not! I mean, there was my commission, but that's normal. What scares me are the dates.''

"Tell me,'' Creighton prompted.

Hudgins had his right hand out, palm up; his face looked as though he had a migraine. "I didn't listen. Irwin warned me that we should wait a week or so after I sent Pan Am packing before he bought my bonds, but I was under the gun and the bond issue was dying. But now, don't you see, the dates coincide, if the SEC really looks closely. The same day I toss that blonde out the door—''

"Blonde? What blonde?''

"Oh, Elizabeth . . . ah . . . Sterling, I think. Pan Am's CFO. She was the one trying to get the loan. She's blond and sexy, you know, so I remember the hair.''

"Okay. I know who you mean.''

"The *same day* I toss her out and say no, Irwin transfers twenty-five million to us for the bond issue.''

Creighton smiled and waved his hand in dismissal. "I don't think we've got a problem.''

"You don't? If they're asking about bribes—''

"It's not a bribe, okay? I mean, the basics are these. You dropped the Pan Am loan *in return* for that twenty-five-million bond subscription, right?''

"That's exactly right, and that's another thing. They asked about my firm's reaction. I'd be instant history around here if Bannister found that out.''

Hudgins looked at the door suddenly. "Did you hear something? Did anyone come with you?"

"No," Creighton replied with a genuinely concerned expression as he watched Hudgins dart through the office and around the corner to check the entryway.

Hudgins had barely disappeared when a small movement to one side of the office caught Creighton's eye. He turned in horror to see Elizabeth's head pop up from behind a desk. She smiled a nervous smile, mouthed the word "Hi," and submerged again, leaving him completely off balance.

Had he really seen Elizabeth? What in heaven's name was she doing here? Hudgins was coming back!

Hudgins was agitated that he couldn't locate the source of the noise. Creighton jumped to his feet and came out of the office door to meet him. Elizabeth was safely out of view, but how the hell could he give her an escape route without Hudgins spotting her? And if he did, would she take it?

"Anything?" Creighton asked as they stood outside his glassed-in office.

"No."

"I think you've let that phone call get you spooked, my friend. Now look, Irwin asked me to look into this and advise you, and I'm advising you to relax."

Hudgins was not happy. "Goddammit! I want to know what to do!"

Creighton flared his eyebrows and grabbed Hudgins's shoulder. "Hey! Get a grip on yourself! I'm the specialist in these matters, that's why he wanted me to come. You've got no worries. We'll work on the SEC, but if you panic, you'll blow it. Right now, there was nothing but a legitimate business deal. It's Irwin who's exposed because of what we're trying to accomplish for another client."

"Yeah," Hudgins said. "I asked him. He told me Nick Costas was behind the project to scrap the new Pan Am."

"I know, but forget you heard that, okay?"

Hudgins nodded.

"By the way, may I use your copier for a second?"

Creighton had seen nothing resembling a Xerox machine on the way in. With any luck, it was around a distant corner. Elizabeth needed a clear path of escape.

"Sure. This way."

Hudgins led him in the right direction and Creighton followed, certain he had seen a flash of blond hair move toward the exit as they rounded the far corner.

Downstairs, Elizabeth tried to sound nonchalant as she breezed past the guard and out the front door.

"Thanks for the help!"

"Long time to get keys, lady."

With a wife like that, the guard thought, perhaps they'd taken time for something else. She looked a bit ruffled.

Elizabeth climbed behind the wheel of the rental car and ignored the ticket on the windshield. She started the engine and pulled away from the curb, circling the block as fast as she could and coming in view of the building again. From a safe distance she watched as Creighton and Hudgins emerged and shook hands, then blessedly went in opposite directions. She tracked Creighton as he approached on the far side of the street and spotted her. She saw him check to make sure Hudgins was out of sight, then cross the street. He got in the car, a furious scowl on his face.

"Drive, damn you!" he said, ducking down below the dashboard until they were at least a mile away.

"Creighton, I—" she began, trying not to flare up in anger over his greeting.

He exploded at her, sitting sideways, speaking in a low growl, the restrained power making her cringe inside.

"What in heaven's name did you think you were doing in there? How long have you been following me?"

He continued sputtering until she slammed on the brakes and maneuvered the car to a curb in an open spot between a line of other parked cars along an unlighted and deserted street. She put the car in Park and looked at him with equal anger, both their voices rising in a full-volume exchange, neither fully hearing the other, their faces inches apart and barely illuminated by the glow of the dashboard lights.

"Who the hell do you think you are? James Bond? You accepted this assignment to work for us, not play secret agent!"

"You want your bloody company alive?"

"I've got a federal judge to satisfy, I—"

"The sonofabitch will be satisfied, I guaran—"

"Ever heard of inadmissible evidence? It's a little quirk we have in the colonies, and—"

"—have the evidence right here in case you weren't close enough to—"

"—good mind to . . ."

They both stopped cold as Elizabeth stared at him, and saw the anger change to a small smirk.

"You . . . what did you say about evidence?"

Creighton pulled the tape recorder from his shirt and rewound it.

"Under your laws, the rules of admissibility of evidence in a federal court for the purposes of issuing an injunction are much more lenient than for a full hearing or a trial. In any event, the federal courts adhere to the laws of the state they find themselves in. We're in New York. A recording of a conversation, when at least one party knows about it and agrees to it, when that person is recording to gather evidence of a crime, is admissible."

"I couldn't hear what you two were saying to each other in there," Elizabeth told him. "I couldn't get close enough."

He punched the button, and his recorded voice filled the car, followed by Hudgins's response.

". . . That was the deal. I told Pan Am we weren't interested, and in return, Irwin buys twenty-five million of the bond issue I was having trouble moving. I save your bacon, you save mine. He was frantic to block Pan Am from getting that loan!"

Creighton fast-forwarded the tape a few feet, and started it again.

". . . I mean, the basics are these. You dropped the Pan Am loan *in return* for that twenty-five-million bond subscription, right?"

"That's exactly right, and that's another thing. They asked about my firm's reaction. I'd be instant history around here if Bannister found that out."

Creighton turned the recorder off and looked at Elizabeth, whose large eyes had grown enormous.

"That's *admissible*?"

"That's admissible!"

"My God, that's the proof we need!"

She threw her arms around his neck on impulse and hugged him. "Creighton, I love you, and I'm sorry I yelled!"

She had caught him by surprise. She could feel it in his physical response, and she pulled away now to look at him just as the thunderstorm overhead unleashed a massive downpour. A series of lightning flashes spotlighted his face clearly, and she was startled to see his eyes boring into hers with a disturbing intimacy that caused her spontaneous smile to begin to fade. Slowly, his eyes never wavering from hers, he put his arms around her and drew her to him, kissing her gently as his arms enfolded her hesitantly. She felt herself melting against him, willing him to go on. The rain was a wall of water now sealing them off from the city, the urgent drumbeat of the downpour sealing the privacy of the little world the front seat had become, but she felt him move away.

"Not here, Elizabeth."

32

Sunday, March 26, 5:00 P.M.
Federal Courthouse, Manhattan

When the tape recording of Harold Hudgins's conversation with Creighton MacRae from the night before had ended, Judge Walter Hayes leaned forward in his chair and fixed MacRae with an inquisitive stare. Jack Rawly, Elizabeth, and the two local Pan Am attorneys held their breaths.

"Mr. MacRae, you have told me that Mr. Hudgins, whose voice we just listened to, mistook you for an associate of Irwin Fairchild. I am still unclear, though, as to how, exactly, Mr. Hudgins agreed to this meeting and this conversation."

"Your Honor, I purposefully misled him. I sent him a fax earlier in the day that, although it was unsigned, he would have believed to have come from Irwin Fairchild. The fax asked that he, Hudgins, call Fairchild's associate—me—at nine in the evening, and gave as the phone number the number of my cellular phone. When he called, I did nothing to dissuade Hudgins from the mistaken belief that he was talking to Irwin Fairchild's associate. He agreed to the meeting and suggested his office. He was very concerned that the Securities and Exchange Commission was investigating his involvement with Fairchild. As you've heard, it was due to this misperception that Hudgins revealed the truth about what he'd done. I knew Fairchild had somehow compensated Hudgins for dropping the Pan Am loan, but I didn't have the details. Pan Am needed those details to convince this court that they've been the victims of a sabotage campaign by their own lenders."

Judge Hayes sat back, pulling his mustache again. "If this were a criminal matter, such revelations of how you manipulated this man to make these statements could jeopardize the case. It would raise the question of whether this constituted a confession or self-incrimination, extracted by fraud or deception. Of course, there *is* information here that can be independently verified—that is, the dates of when the Pan Am loan application was rejected and when Mr. Fairchild suddenly purchased the twenty-five-million-dollar bond issue Mr. Hudgins was selling.''

The judge hesitated a full minute before continuing.

''Very well.'' He turned toward Jack Rawly. ''Mr. Rawly, the unsuccessful efforts made to serve notice on the lenders I find to be sufficient under Rule 65. I'm going to rule that your evidence and representations establish a prima facie case that Mr. Fairchild, acting on behalf of, and perhaps by direction of, the lenders, compensated Mr. Hudgins for maliciously interfering with Pan Am's ability to raise funds. Therefore, given the previous affidavit and statements of counsel, under the doctrine of estoppel, Pan Am is entitled to a temporary restraining order blocking any attempt by its lenders to declare Pan Am in default until a full hearing for a temporary injunction can be held. I assume you have the order, Mr. Rawly?''

''Yes, sir.''

''Slide it over here and I'll sign it!''

♦ ♦ ♦

Elizabeth relayed the news to Ron Lamb and Brian before going to an instantly called victory dinner. They were all profoundly relieved. But Jack Rawly sternly cautioned them all that the battle would be joined within twenty-four hours when the lenders, under the name of Intertrust Bank et al., would be formally served with the restraining order.

''At eight A.M. sharp, I'll slap it in the hand of their general counsel in person, with copies to the aircraft lessors. We'll also fax a copy to each of our station managers around the world, just in case someone tries to seize an airplane by local court order.''

Elizabeth paused over a second glass of wine and searched his eyes. ''How will they respond, Jack? They won't just roll over, will they?''

Jack Rawly looked down at his Scotch for a moment, in a gesture Elizabeth could easily read. It was a milestone they were toasting, not their arrival at a destination.

Rawly looked back up with a strained smile. ''They'll immediately try to get a hearing to vacate this TRO. They'll send in a battery of people to swear they've had nothing to do with Irwin Fairchild or Nick Costas or anyone else. They want to shut us down tomorrow, when the media is set to watch us anyway on the round-the-world inaugural.''

"But can they succeed?" The question hung there, and she hated asking it. She noticed Creighton, deep in his own conversation with the other two lawyers.

"Let's put it this way, Elizabeth. If there's any way you can still make that payment, make it. If we hand the bastards the one hundred forty million as demanded, they can't do a thing until the next repayment is due. That's the only guarantee I can give you."

"I called Hong Kong on the way over here," Elizabeth told him. "Jason Ing is still missing, and his house won't invest a penny without him. I've also been on the phone for hours with my assistant in Seattle. We can raise about half of it internally, but we wouldn't have a penny left in our corporate bank accounts."

Rawly was nodding. "Please keep trying, Elizabeth. We've won this inning and we're leading by one run in the top of the ninth. But they've still got one turn at bat, and their pitcher is showing no signs of fatigue."

She smiled at Rawly. "I hate baseball analogies!"

Creighton was seated diagonally across the table and had been half-listening to their conversation. He leaned in her direction now with a mischievous look. "I take it you feel the same way about golf analogies?"

Elizabeth met his eyes, smiling slowly as she recalled his love of the game.

"On the other hand, I've always found golf to be a deeply exciting game." Her eyes stayed locked on his.

Jack Rawly heard the crackle and spark and resumed looking at his drink. It was, he figured, to be expected. He had seen the handsome Scot's eyes linger on their CFO more than once in the past few hours.

♦ ♦ ♦

When Creighton entered his room at 10:30 P.M., an envelope lay under the door with a message to call Jack Bastrop in Houston.

"Jason's been found," Bastrop told him. "He's alive, but he's been beaten pretty badly, and one of his brothers wants to talk to you."

It was 11:00 P.M. Sunday night in New York and noon on Monday in Hong Kong when Jeremy Ing, Jason's brother—a key executive of Cathay Alliance—came to the phone. Jason had been dumped in a wooded area near the Chinese border, he said, and had staggered to a highway several hours later, asking for help.

"In his conscious moments he's frantic to know whether Elizabeth Sterling is okay, but he's unconscious right now," Jeremy told Creighton. "I'm with him here in the hospital. The doctors expect a full recovery.

When he's awake, which is only a few minutes at a time, he keeps saying he has something important to tell you, Mr. MacRae.''

"Elizabeth is fine. Tell him that when he wakes up next time. She got away safely, thanks to him. She's with me in New York. But please tell him Pan Am still needs that loan most desperately.'' He gave Jeremy his hotel and room number in New York. Jeremy Ing agreed to call him back as soon as Jason came around again.

"I'll stay here by the phone,'' Creighton promised.

Sunday, March 26, 11:45 P.M.
Near Kennedy Airport

Jacob Voorster turned off the TV and the bedside light in another room of the same hotel he had occupied the night before. Sunday morning he had gone to the Pan Am terminal only to find that his flight had been cancelled. He had agreed to stay over another day at Pan Am's expense and meet with Chad Jennings in Seattle on Monday instead.

As Voorster drifted into sleep, a few miles away at the international arrivals terminal used by Lufthansa, two neatly dressed men stepped off a flight from Frankfurt and entered customs. Once they had cleared through, they stepped over to a bank of hotel phones and quietly began going down the list of airport area hotels, hoping for an easy break.

The call to the desk clerk of the Airport Ramada Inn was the thirteenth one they made.

"Excuse me, I am looking for a Mr. Jacob Voorster. Is he registered in your facility?''

The clerk was doing the nightly billings, which were a mess. Papers and registration lists lay everywhere on the counter, and instead of clearing a path to the computer, he grabbed the printout he assumed was current.

"Yes, here he is. Oh, wait a minute.'' The printout was for the night before, but the registration had been for one night only, direct-billed to Pan Am. There was no need to look for the current registration printout. "I'm sorry, sir. He checked out this morning.''

Monday, March 27, 8:00 A.M.
New York City

Creighton MacRae awoke to a ringing phone, confused that daylight was streaming in the window. He was still in a shirt and tie, lying on top of his bed.

It was Jeremy Ing, calling from Hong Kong. Jason was stable and had been conscious long enough to tell his brother to go ahead with the hundred-forty-million-dollar loan to Pan Am.

"It is nine at night here. We cannot finish the deal until tomorrow, but I will work on it."

"Should I have Elizabeth Sterling call you back?" Creighton stood and shook his head to clear the cobwebs.

"Yes, but in the morning. In the meantime, tell her that Jason is afraid for her life."

"What do you mean?"

"The people who kidnapped him? They were looking for her. They were trying to find out where she was, because they believed she had something, some information they wanted."

He had barely replaced the phone in its cradle when Jack Rawly called with the news that Intertrust Bank, as expected, had scheduled an emergency hearing to attack the temporary restraining order.

"When, Jack?"

"Ten A.M., and not before Judge Hayes, either. They went to Judge Hayes last night and he refused to vacate the TRO. You know, as I explained to you, TROs are usually not appealable. But these clowns are claiming they're about to be greatly damaged, and they've filed a writ of mandamus—"

"A what?" Creighton asked.

"Oh, sorry. It's basically a request for the higher court to order the lower court to do something it doesn't want to do on the grounds that the judge of the lower court has screwed up badly. In this case, they want the appeals court to force Judge Hayes to throw out our TRO. So we go to the seventeenth floor of the Foley Square courthouse and fight it out before three circuit judges."

"Circuit judges? There's another bloody term I don't know, Jack."

"Well, a circuit judge is a judge of the United States Court of Appeals. They're one level above Judge Hayes."

"They can tell him what to do, then."

"They can indeed. And we should leave the hotel here by nine-fifteen this morning at the latest."

"Have you talked to Elizabeth?"

"Yes, I woke her up. One more thing, Creighton. The media are onto this. The other side probably tipped them to make us look bad. We can keep cameras out of the courtroom, but there will undoubtedly be bad publicity and all our faces on the news today."

"Thanks for the warning."

Monday, March 27, 9:55 A.M.
Manhattan

Two television camera crews and a handful of print reporters were waiting for them in front of the courthouse. One of the TV cameras was broadcasting live to the New York area, the reporter reminding his viewers that the successful resurrection of Pan Am was suddenly in trouble, the company facing disaster on the very day it was supposed to launch its new round-the-world service.

"A-control, as CNN's nerve center in Atlanta was called, elected on the spur of the moment to pick up the broadcast from Manhattan and take it live on the main CNN line around the world. Creighton MacRae was shown walking just behind Elizabeth up the courthouse steps, both of them identified—mistakenly in Creighton's case—as officers of Pan Am arriving to make a last-ditch attempt to rescue the airline from an immediate shutdown.

A battery of three attorneys and the chief operating officer of Intertrust Bank were waiting inside with the grimmest of faces when the Pan Am contingent walked in. Neither introductions nor words were exchanged before the three appeals court circuit judges entered and took their places in the marble and granite courtroom.

Monday, March 27, 9:57 A.M.
Near JFK Airport

Jacob Voorster had repeated almost exactly the routine of twenty-four hours before. He found himself seated in the identical compartment of the same 747, now getting ready for departure for Seattle. He had noticed the personal entertainment system the previous morning, but this time he turned it on, amazed at the quality of the liquid-crystal color TV screen as he tuned across several stations and settled on one in New York that was covering some sort of trial.

Suddenly Pan Am's name caught his ear, along with the chilling explanation that Pan Am's lenders were preparing to find the airline in default and seize all their aircraft.

My God! There is no time for a flight to Seattle!

The face of an attractive blond woman moved past the camera, and the newsman identified her as Elizabeth Sterling, the corporate officer he had been told was in Seattle, and the one he had barely missed in London.

But it was the face of the man with Sterling that propelled Jacob into action. Jacob Voorster had seen that face in the financial press years before. He knew of his accomplishments, his failures, and his successful suit against a group of European companies—which included VZV.

That was, without a doubt, Creighton MacRae!

Jacob grabbed his briefcase and rushed to the door, which was closing.

"No! Stop! I must get off!"

With some puzzlement, the flight attendant pushed the door open again far enough to let Jacob escape up the jetway at a dead run. He raced for the driveway at the entrance to the terminal, passing a host of curious passengers, and startling the two men who had arrived from Frankfurt the night before in search of the person they now saw submerging in the backseat of a New York taxi.

One of the men grabbed the other and swung him around by the collar, speaking excitedly in his own language.

"*Da! Er ist da! Das ist Voorster!*" Together they raced for the curb, shoving their way past a line of people and into another waiting yellow cab whose driver immediately got out and refused to move.

The taxi dispatcher heard and saw what was happening. *Two foreign jerks,* he concluded, *who don't give a damn about local rules.*

"Hey, mister! Both of you! This is America, *capisce?* You gotta stand in line like everyone else."

The cabby had been standing by the left rear window of his cab when he suddenly felt something shoved in his stomach from within the vehicle. Looking down, he saw the barrel of a gun. The man holding it was warning him through clenched teeth to get back in the cab instantly and drive, or take a bullet in the gut, and probably through the spinal column.

"Awright! Awright!" The cabby swung into the driver's seat and jammed the car into gear as the dispatcher realized his instructions weren't being followed.

"Hey, jerk! Get outta that seat! You go two inches, I got your medallion!"

Tires squealed as the cabby accelerated away from the curb and pulled into traffic, trying desperately to carry out the demands of the two men in the rear who wanted to follow the previous hack, which was now out of sight.

The dispatcher cursed and threw his hat on the ground, angry and embarrassed at being ignored. "Number 46657, the bastard! Where's my pen? Hey, Harry! You see that? Where's my goddam pen!"

On the other side of the terminal, at Gate 14, Voorster's suitcase had been removed from the forward baggage bin while a mechanic quickly checked over the compartment he had occupied in the cabin, looking for anything suspicious.

He found nothing out of the ordinary. The plane departed on schedule.

Monday, March 27, 10:10 A.M.
Manhattan

The lead attorney for Intertrust, Sol Moscowitz, a senior partner of the heavy-hitting firm of Shearson, Moscowitz, and Katz, went through the background of the arguments used by Pan Am for the TRO before tearing into each allegation. No one in their bank or their lenders' consortium, he claimed, had any knowledge of any actions taken against Pan Am by Nick Costas or anyone else.

Moscowitz, a stubby, angry, but well-dressed man, adjusted the lightweight podium set five feet in front of the bench and waved his glasses as he warmed to his argument with restrained outrage.

"Your Honors, virtually *all* these allegations, even if proved, amount to absolutely no proof at all! They have shown virtually nothing but a series of perfectly legal commercial transactions between ITB, which they allege is owned by Mr. Costas in Hong Kong, and our bank, which deals extensively in the international banking arena. Without even addressing the highly questionable methods by which some of the evidence presented before Judge Hayes was obtained, and without attacking specifically the late-hour sessions Saturday and Sunday before Judge Hayes, which were conducted without adequate attempts to notify us, what these plaintiffs have shown here is nothing but a frantic determination to save themselves through misuse of the court. They allege that the mere fact that we and ITB have transferred funds in like amounts justifies a temporary restraining order. I submit that it does no such thing."

Moscowitz looked down at the podium before him and consulted his notes before looking up at the judges and continuing.

"Legally borrowing funds from an institution does not make you automatically liable for the misdeeds of that institution. Yet that's what's being alleged here. Even assuming ITB in Hong Kong set out, for God knows what reason, to ruin Pan Am, proving only that we have borrowed money from them does not make us a party to such actions, nor does it justify using the doctrine of estoppel to stay our hand in recovering our money."

Moscowitz moved back to a counsel table and took a drink of water.

"The facts are, Intertrust and the consortium lenders in the Pan Am revolving loan have legally notified Pan Am that they have lost confidence in the airline's ability to repay its obligations. We have demanded our money back in accordance with the repayment schedule. One hundred forty million dollars is due today, this morning—now. They say they can't pay it. That means they are now in default. We request that you overrule Judge Hayes and vacate this ridiculous temporary restraining order so that we may hand them here and now their notice of default, which I have in my briefcase."

The man took a deep breath and sat down.

Jack Rawly took the three judges through the evidence again, reminding him that Pan Am stood on the brink of imminent destruction.

"We need the time to bring forth the evidence to establish this nefarious relationship and justify an injunction. The purpose of a TRO is to stop irreparable harm, and that's what we're facing if you permit him to hand us that notice of default. The lessors of our aircraft will follow within the hour with a notice of seizure. By this afternoon, Pan Am will have no airplanes and be forced into bankruptcy, which we believe to have been the plan all along."

Rawly fell silent as one of the judges glared down at him.

"Are you through, Mr. Rawly?"

"I'd like to reserve the right to comment or move further if necessary, Your Honor."

"Granted."

The three judges conferred among themselves for a minute before the chief judge turned back to the attorneys and continued.

"If that's your case, Mr. Rawly, we can't see that you've set out sufficient reason to grant an injunction. Yes, you will be irreparably harmed, and I can accept your attempts at notifying your lenders as sufficient, but Mr. Moscowitz is correct in saying that you've presented no credible evidence or claim that Intertrust and their lending consortium had a hand in whatever Mr. Costas or Mr. Fairchild or Mr. Hudgins did or did not do to Pan Am."

Jack Rawly moved back to the podium.

"Judge, this is an action for a temporary restraining order, but the court appears to be holding us to the level of proof required for an *injunction*. For a TRO, all I have to do is honestly swear to the court that we truly believe the evidence is there and that, given some small amount of time, we *can* find it. But, in essence, you're saying that we can't *have* the time to develop the proof you want to see until we've already developed the proof you want to see, by which time we will need neither a TRO nor an injunction, because there will be no Pan Am left to prosecute the case. This becomes, then, a legal tautology, or a Catch-22, and that's *not* what Rule 65 is all about.''

Judge Kenton, the chief judge, began to speak, but Rawly held up his hand.

''Your Honor, I swear to you that I am completely confident, in accordance with the spirit and intent and the statutory requirements of Rule 65, that given the time requested, we *can* provide the proof that the connection between ITB and Intertrust was something other than benign. At least don't interfere with Judge Hayes's decision until nine A.M. tomorrow.''

Moscowitz was on his feet instantly. ''Your Honor, that's a transparent ploy. They've got no hope of producing anything new out of thin air. There's nothing there to begin with, of course, but what he's attempting to do is let this TRO run past the departure time for their new round-the-world service. They want to launch the flight as a last futile gesture, and put us off until the next banking day. Don't be a party to such manipulation, Your Honor.''

Jack Rawly glared at Moscowitz. ''That's a slanderous accusation! We do indeed have reasonable grounds for saying that by tomorrow morning, or before, we may well be able to provide proof that would satisfy this or any other court. This is not a ploy to get our aircraft off the ground. Consider, though, Your Honor, that even in the absence of proof, a few additional hours might also give us the time to make the payment they appear to be so desperate to receive, thus forestalling a default. Since they will undoubtedly lose tens of millions of dollars if they push us into a bankruptcy by the mere act of handing us that notice of default now burning a hole in Mr. Moscowitz's briefcase, delaying that move through this TRO prevents, in effect, a form of irreparable harm to Mr. Moscowitz's client as well. The alternative is the wanton and possibly unnecessary destruction of a successful new airline that employs thousands of honest Americans who deserve to have the chance to prove that they are the victim here.''

Judge Richard Kenton sat back for a moment with an acid scowl on his face while the other two judges listened. He moved forward again, suddenly.

''Very well. Mr. Moscowitz, you're correct that the facts are insufficient. But Mr. Rawly is correct as well that under the rule, Judge Hayes had the authority to take reasonable actions to protect against catastrophic and irreparable result. He can do that by merely accepting Mr. Rawly's representations. Mr. Rawly has not yet proved a collusive connection between the admittedly onerous actions of Mr. Fairchild and Mr. Hudgins on one hand, and your client on the other. But I cannot say categorically that Mr. Rawly will be unable to prove such a connection. He swears that he can, given time."

Kenton looked hard at Jack Rawly. "Mr. Rawly, I'll give your client some gasping room, but not for the purpose of launching any last-minute flights. I'll give you until five P.M. this afternoon to come back here and demonstrate why I should believe that there really is a connection between this lender and the things done to your client. I will reverse Judge Hayes and vacate his TRO at five P.M. if you fail to present the required additional evidence before that date and hour. I'll be available to you all afternoon through my clerk."

Moscowitz was on his feet again with a whining tone. "Your Honor, I'd like to implore you to reconsid—"

Judge Kenton shook his head. "Overruled, Sol. You've got a half-full glass here. Wait until five-oh-one P.M., and you can hand them your papers if they can't find a rabbit in their hat."

Kenton rose and disappeared into his chambers as the small contingent got to their feet.

Monday, March 27, 7:30 A.M.
Seatac Airport

As Elizabeth and the Pan Am team were leaving the courthouse in Manhattan in a state of mild shock, Brian Murphy taxied from the gate at Seatac to the end of Runway 16 Left for takeoff. The passenger load was light for a 747—only 142 people—but the aircraft was booked full out of New York for the first leg to London on what would become Pan Am Flight One—their first round-the-world flight.

Brian glanced up at the stream of cirrus shooting by in the teeth of the jetstream high overhead, the only cloud formations in an otherwise crystal-clear sky. With light winds from the south and mild temperatures, it was a perfect day for flying—despite the gnawing worry about possible sabotage.

Ship 609 had been all but disassembled and reassembled, and kept under twenty-four hour guard in the hangar. Brian was confident no saboteur could have slipped through the net. But there was a rumbling nervousness in the pit of his stomach when he thought about the tempting target they made, because of the publicity surrounding the inaugural flight. Maybe they should have canceled the flight, just to be completely safe. But how could they do that with no evidence or warning of sabotage? The damage in the eyes of the public, coming on the heels of the other near disasters, would most certainly be an irreparable death blow to Pan Am—even if they were, by some miracle, able to get the $140-million payment today. It was too late to cancel now, of course, but his feeling of something dangerous left undone was visceral, like that of a worried vacationer who can't remember turning off the oven.

He'd be relieved when they blocked in at JFK and he could safely turn the ship over to the crew flying to London.

His thoughts turned to Elizabeth for a second as the first officer called for takeoff clearance. After the sendoff ceremony, he planned to monopolize her time for the rest of the evening. They needed time together. They needed to talk.

And he needed to buy a ring.

"Clipper Fifteen, cleared to go, one-six left."

"Clipper Fifteen's rolling."

33

Monday, March 27, 10:25 A.M.
Near Kennedy Airport

Singhman Nahjib passed the exit for Interstate 278 just seconds before he caught sight of the taxi he'd been ordered to follow.

He's headed south!

Pure fear gripped him as he realized there was no way he could correct the error and get off the Grand Central Parkway in time to catch them, but his two passengers hadn't yet noticed.

If they see what has happened, he concluded, *they will kill me!*

He pressed the accelerator harder, weaving in and out of traffic as a desperate distraction until one of the men in the back yelled at him.

"I was trying to catch up," Singhman explained.

"You sure they went this way?"

He nodded vigorously.

By the time he had changed course and reached the interchange leading to the Queens-Midtown tunnel, it was obvious the other cab had eluded them.

"He had too much head start!" one of the men in the back muttered.

Nahjib confirmed that the cab they were following was equipped with a two-way radio to communicate with several other cabs in a special group. They ordered him now to stop at a phone booth. The shorter of the two phoned the company whose name had been on the side of Voorster's cab. After he'd spent five minutes claiming to be an FBI agent and making threats, the manager relented.

"Okay! He's goin' to the federal courthouse in Brooklyn."

"Good. Tell him to wait there with his meter running. I will pay the wait time. We must talk with him, but do not tell him the FBI is involved."

The man hung up and jumped back in with his partner as he gave new directions to Nahjib. Nahjib turned south and sped up, blending back into the moderate parkway traffic as he glanced in the rearview mirror, horrified to see one of the men quietly screwing a silencer on a chrome-plated nine-millimeter pistol.

Monday, March 27, 10:45 A.M.
New York City

The Pan Am team left the grand Federal Courthouse Building in Foley Square in a daze. the victory of the night before now reduced to nothing more than a temporary reprieve.

Elizabeth, Creighton, Jack Rawly, and the two New York Pan Am attorneys stood on the sidewalk in some confusion, talking in low, urgent tones, while a cold breeze tugged at their overcoats and a fast-moving carpet of cumulus clouds sailed by overhead.

"We've got six hours," Elizabeth said at last. "The question is, how can we use them to maximum advantage?"

Jack Rawly shook his head sadly, looking at his shoes, his hands shoved deep in the pockets of his coat. "I don't know." He looked up at Creighton suddenly. "Can you think of any other possibilities? Anything to show that Intertrust is colluding with Costas?"

Creighton sighed and shook his head as well.

Bill Phillips, one of the two New York Pan Am attorneys, hailed two cabs to move all of them to his nearby office, where Elizabeth immediately commandeered a phone. Twenty minutes later she hung up and sat down on an office couch with Jack Rawly, as Creighton MacRae continued an animated conversation with someone in an adjacent office.

"Jack, if we virtually empty the corporate accounts, we've got seventy-three million dollars. We need sixty-seven million more. Ron says there are representatives from the lessors already calling and asking the location of each aircraft, and it's obvious they're going to try to repossess the entire fleet instantly, wherever they are at five-oh-one P.M. So what I need to know is this: if I'm able to find enough cash, how do we handle the situation? Will these vultures take a cashier's check, and if so, how far in advance of five P.M. do we have to place it in their hands?"

Jack Rawly nodded. "I'll get my entire staff on it back in Seattle."

"Ron authorized me to use all the cash we've got, since, if we don't succeed, we're instantly out of business anyway."

"How'd he sound?" Jack asked.

"Actually, it was his wife, Louise, reading what he was typing out on his computer screen. But she says he's doing better every day."

Jack grimaced and smiled. "Thank God. Ron's a good friend, and a fighter too, as you can tell."

Creighton materialized beside them suddenly and settled onto the corner of the desk across from the couch. "Well, I just talked to Jason Ing. He's recovering slowly, he's been conscious for the last few hours, and he said to tell you the loan *is* definitely authorized for the first one hundred forty million, Elizabeth."

"Yes!" She slapped the table and smiled.

Creighton looked mildly alarmed and shook his head as he raised the palm of his right hand.

"*But* . . . the bad news is that there's no way they can transfer it in time. The earliest is noon tomorrow, Hong Kong time, which is eleven P.M. tonight here in New York." He turned to Rawly. "Jack, can we go back to the judge and ask for six more hours?"

Jack Rawly shook his head. "Not without more evidence. A scrap of paper, a smidgen of testimony, *anything* new, and I could beg for more time. Without it, we could try, but we won't succeed, because it's obvious these people don't care about the money. They just want us out of business. They'll fight any extension request to a standstill."

Elizabeth had been chewing on a fingernail in deep thought. She looked up at Creighton suddenly. "You know Jack Bastrop well. Would he have enough money, and enough gambling instinct, to loan us sixty-seven million dollars for twenty-four hours?"

Creighton was silent for a few seconds as he toyed with his fountain pen, then looked up and into Elizabeth's eyes.

"If *I* ask him, he'll do it, provided he's got that much in cash." He stood up.

"I'll give him a call right now."

Monday, March 27, 11:00 A.M.
New York City

Dieter Hoffman, the cabby driving Jacob Voorster, had heard the words "federal courthouse" and driven straight to Brooklyn. The surprise at finding another Dutchman in his cab was pleasant but short-lived; the fellow seemed preoccupied and only marginally responsive—even when he spoke to him in Dutch.

"Are you in trouble?" Dieter asked him in Dutch after a long silence.

"*Ja*," he said, "I have lost my freedom and my job. Other than that, there is nothing wrong."

Dieter stayed silent and pulled up in front of the courthouse feeling sorry for the man in the back, but suddenly anxious to be rid of him. He wished him well as he accepted his fare and pointed the way to the courthouse entrance.

Dieter looked at his watch as he set his meter to the waiting position. He would probably have to wave off a half-dozen prospective fares while he waited for the incoming fare his partner had assigned him, but it was so rare to be asked to wait that he was curious and couldn't refuse.

♦ ♦ ♦

Once inside the courthouse, Jacob stuck his head in several offices, asking for the court where the Pan Am matter was going on. Each bored or harassed employee whose eyes he caught motioned him wearily to yet another office. Eventually he reached the office of the chief clerk.

"Oh, the Pan Am matter on TV a while ago? I was watching that. You're in the wrong place. That was the *Southern* Federal District Court of Appeals, on the sixteenth floor of the Foley Square courthouse. This is the *Eastern* District. You want to take the subway or a taxi and go into Manhattan." The clerk saw confusion in Jacob Voorster's eyes.

"Hold on, I'll write it down. Take a cab, 'cause the cabby can find it for you."

♦ ♦ ♦

The squeal of brakes caused Dieter Hoffman to look up from his newspaper. Another cab had stopped inches from his rear bumper. It was being driven by a man with swarthy features whose two fares were spilling out of the backseat and moving in his direction.

Both of the men appeared at his driver's window as he rolled it down.

"Did you just drop off a man named Jacob Voorster?"

Dieter nodded before thinking.

"Which entrance did he take?" the taller man asked with obvious menace. The man had cold eyes, Dieter noticed, cold and hateful.

"You owe me waiting time, you know," Dieter replied weakly.

A twenty-dollar bill was tossed unceremoniously through the window and fluttered into Dieter's lap like a snide insult.

But it was money, nevertheless.

"The main entrance—there." He pointed in the distance at the building.

"That's all. You can go," the shorter man said.

Dieter made a show of changing his meter to "off duty" as the two men stepped back by the rear bumper of his car and lapsed into German, in which Dieter was completely fluent. Their words chilled him.

"We can't kill him in a federal courthouse. There are guards with guns there. I'm not even sure we can get our guns *in* there. They use security screening," the tall man said.

"You take my gun, then. I'll go through any security they have and find Voorster, and get him to come out the same entrance. We'll get him back here and find another place to dispose of him."

Dieter tried to look engrossed in his paper as the gun changed hands, the transaction visible in his rearview mirror.

Jacob got out of the elevator on the ground floor, just as another elevator door closed next to him. He reread the directions. It would be easier, the clerk had told him, to cross the main avenue to the east to catch a cab into Manhattan. He headed for the other exit now, pulling his overcoat around himself more tightly against the cold wind as he reached the curb and looked back.

He saw two taxis waiting on the opposite side of the building where he had arrived, and noticed one of them suddenly race away. There were also taxis streaming by on Adams, the main street he was facing, all of them headed toward Manhattan as the clerk had said.

He turned and walked briskly toward the crosswalk.

♦ ♦ ♦

Dieter negotiated the next intersection and then turned north on Adams toward the bridge, driven by the urgent need to put distance between himself and the killers at the courthouse. He had the number of the other cab, and had relayed that as well.

The image of a tall man in an overcoat with a briefcase shot by on his left as Dieter passed the crosswalk.

It was Jacob Voorster!

Dieter pulled across two lanes of traffic toward the curb. The maneuver was met by the sound of squealing brakes, honking horns, and a few shouted obscenities.

Voorster looked up, but didn't understand. Dieter opened the door and yelled at him, relieved when Voorster broke into a trot and finally reached his cab.

"Get in! Don't ask why, just do it!" He'd said it in Dutch, not realizing he had lapsed out of English.

They were halfway across the bridge to Manhattan before Dieter finished blurting out the story, noticing the haunted look on Jacob Voorster's face as he sat forward in the backseat and faced the fact that someone had been hired to kill him.

"You want me to take you to the police? I think that's best."

"No. I must go to this address."

Dieter looked down at the slip of paper.

"*Another* courthouse?"

"You took me to the wrong one," Jacob told him evenly. "I should be angry with you, but perhaps you have saved my life."

"I'll save it again, Mr. Voorster. Don't go to the courthouse. Go to the police!"

Jacob Voorster shook his head. In his mind, there was a short-range problem and a long-range problem. Pan Am's assistance was the key to getting his job and his reputation and freedom back. Without them, the short-range problem of being stalked by hired killers seemed immaterial.

He checked his watch, which had been reset to New York time.

It was 11:40 A.M. With any luck, the Pan Am officers would still be there.

Monday, March 27, noon
Manhattan

The midtown law offices of Jamison, Reed, Owen, and Phillips had become Pan Am's de facto war room. Elizabeth called another impromptu conference after finishing a call from Jeremy Ing in Hong Kong. Creighton, too, had just finished a round of calls to Jack Bastrop. Both of them were looking grim as Jack Rawly joined them with the news that an attempt to talk Intertrust Bank into postponing the deadline six more hours had been rudely rejected.

"I even used the argument," Jack began, "that since the minute we shut down they lose perhaps a hundred million, so their unwillingness to wait a few hours is conclusive evidence that they don't care about getting their money back. What they're determined to do is ruin us, which validates the allegations we've already made."

"What was the reaction?" Elizabeth asked.

"I was talking with Moscowitz. He's convinced his client is blameless, and that they just want to cut their losses. He says I'd be laughed out of court with that argument, and he may be right.''

Jack sat heavily in an office chair and looked at them sadly. ''I know it's there. I know that somewhere, almost within our reach, there is some piece of paper, some testimony, some *evidence* we could thrust in the faces of those three judges that would save the day, and it's driving me crazy that I don't know where to look, or whom to call.''

Creighton raised a finger. ''I am right, am I not, that all you need is evidence that the money transfers to Intertrust from Hong Kong were not arm's-length transactions?''

Jack nodded. ''I need to show that those payments, and the revolving loan to Pan Am, were all part of a plot to get Pan Am dependent, like a drug addict, on money that could be yanked away at the appropriate moment. They could call the loan any time they wanted, because of that stupid loan agreement we signed, but what they had to be sure of was that we couldn't repay it when they called it. I'm convinced this whole thing has been a masterful plot to eliminate us as a competitor, and there is some company out there other than ITB or Intertrust or Fairchild or Costas orchestrating all of it.'' He sighed deeply. ''But without evidence, they're going to win. I think we'd better face it.''

Elizabeth looked at Creighton, hoping for another lifebuoy, but he shook his head. ''Jack Bastrop is worth ten times what we need, Elizabeth, but the most he could put together in the next few hours would be thirty-five million, and the penalties and interest it would cost to break that free is steep. He'll do it if you need it, but it still leaves us short by thirty-two million.''

''What time is it?'' she asked, her voice edged with despair.

''Twelve-fifteen,'' Jack Rawly replied. ''We've got four and a half hours.''

Monday, March 27, 10:30 A.M. Mountain/12:30 P.M. Eastern
In flight, Clipper Fifteen

Brian left control of the aircraft with the first and second officers and returned to the cabin for a private telephone call to Elizabeth's cellular phone in New York. He was hoping for good news.

He didn't get it. The sound of her soft voice carrying tones of inevitable defeat broke his heart. He longed to hold her. With less than three hours' flight time left before landing at Kennedy, they tried to arrange a logical time and place to meet.

"I was going to be there for the sendoff ceremony, but it looks like I'll be in court, hoping Jack Rawly can produce a miracle," Elizabeth said. "Call me at about five-thirty on the cellular, okay?"

"Okay, babe. Keep your chin up."

There was a small, rueful snort from the other end.

He didn't want to return to the cockpit just yet. He had already decided not to tell the others how grim things were looking. One terrified crewmember was dangerous enough.

Brian strolled toward the back of the half-empty main cabin. He wore an artificial smile and uttered a few pleasant words to a passenger here and there, and stopped to chat with a passenger who had a sizeable video camcorder case on the seat next to him. Brian had wanted to bring his camcorder on many trips, but had been afraid of the jostling and rough treatment it might receive. Something about the fellow seemed familiar. *The way I feel right now,* Brian cautioned himself, *my memory is not reliable.*

He said a few falsely encouraging words to the worried flight attendants before retreating back to the flight deck, feeling like a damned liar.

Monday, March 27, 12:35 P.M.
Foley Square, Manhattan

Jacob Voorster had gone straight to the sixteenth floor after thanking Dieter Hoffman, the driver who had rescued him and rushed him to the courthouse. He had to wait his turn in the clerk's office in the appellate division, but at last the young man behind the counter turned his attention to Jacob.

"Excuse me, please. It is urgent that I speak with the corporate officers of Pan Am who are here for a hearing."

The man cocked his head and thought. That was a curious request.

"I'm sorry, sir, but that matter was heard this morning in a special session at ten. They've all gone. Hours ago."

Jacob Voorster looked staggered. He had just assumed . . .

"How do I find the Pan Am people, then? The officers from Pan Am?"

The clerk thought for a second and sighed, shaking his head. "You know, Pan Am in the old days was headquartered here in New York at the Pan Am Building, but I've heard they're now somewhere else. Anyway, you could call the law firm representing them in New York, the attorneys of record on the case this morning."

He looked around, trying to decide where to find the papers, but another clerk nearby had overheard the conversation and turned toward him.

"That was Sol Moscowitz's case. I know him."

"Was it?" the first clerk asked.

"Yes. His office is right where you indicated, in the Met Life Building—the old Pan Am Building—by Grand Central."

"Would you be so kind as to write it down for me?" Jacob asked. "Where to find this lawyer's office, and his name?"

"Sure. And I'll give you the location of the nearest subway entrance. That's the way to get right into Grand Central." The clerk grabbed a preprinted memo pad embossed with the court of appeals name and justice department logo, and began writing.

♦ ♦ ♦

On the western perimeter of Foley Square, Dieter Hoffman sat parked on a side street facing the courthouse, watching with mixed emotions as Jacob Voorster left his cab and headed toward the courthouse on foot. He should burn rubber and get the hell out of there, he thought, but he just couldn't force himself to drive away.

Instead he circled the block and parked up the street, partially screened from the main entrance, but within view of it. Within ten minutes another taxi screeched to a halt in front of the courthouse—the same one, Dieter saw, that had brought the two gunmen to Brooklyn. This time he didn't hesitate. The two Germans scampered up the steps and into the building. *Seconds later, Jacob Voorster emerged from the same entrance!*

Jacob had just placed his hand on the door to the street when he spotted two men who fit Dieter Hoffman's earlier description running toward the same entrance. He'd dropped back instantly, out of sight, and spotted a maintenance man coming out of a door a few feet away. Jacob slipped through the door before it swung closed. He'd then turned around to peer back toward the entryway through the crack, watching with rising apprehension as the two men rushed inside and moved directly into an open elevator.

♦ ♦ ♦

When Dieter saw Voorster, he nearly sideswiped a delivery van as he accelerated back into the street and through a green light, screeching to a halt in front of the Dutchman as he reached the curb.

"Get in!"

Voorster, surprised and relieved, complied instantly.

"This time to the police?" Dieter asked.

"No. I need to go to the lawyers' office. They will take care of me. Thank you for waiting." He showed Hoffman the memo with the address of the lawyers' office. Dieter wheeled the cab back into traffic and made a left at the next intersection.

They had driven for two blocks before the pieces fell into place in Jacob's mind.

Oh my Lord! They'll get the same information I obtained!

"Stop! Here, please! I must make a call!" Jacob's voice was a barked order, and Dieter complied instantly, slamming on his brakes and maneuvering to the curb in front of a small restaurant.

Jacob leaped out and dashed through the door of the restaurant. Finding a pay phone on the wall, he fed it a quarter and dialed the number on the memo, relieved that the court clerk answered so quickly.

"This is very important," he said. "I came to your office a few minutes ago, looking for the Pan Am lawyers. I was carrying a briefcase. Do you remember me?"

"Sir, everyone who comes in here carries a briefcase. But I remember your voice," the clerk answered. "Why?"

"My name is Jacob Voorster. There may be one or two men coming in there shortly looking for me by name, and asking you where you sent me."

"You're right. One of them is already here. Do you want to talk to him?"

"No! Listen carefully. If he can hear you, please do not give away the fact that you are talking to me. Your life may depend on following my instructions."

There was a hesitation, and he heard her say to someone in the background, "No, not you."

"Listen very closely," Dieter continued, "and answer yes or no only. Have you already told him where I am headed?"

"No."

"Then for God's sake, don't. The man in front of you has a partner, and both of them are hired gunmen from Europe, probably Germany. You have probably already heard an accent in his voice. They intend to kill me. They have no connection with any law enforcement agency."

"You're kidding!"

"This is not a joke. Please pay attention. You cannot take the chance that what I'm saying isn't true. When the man leaves, if you can alert your security police to catch this man downstairs with his partner, you'll find that at least one of them has a pistol with a silencer. The partner may be waiting just outside the security checkpoint. There's a cabdriver waiting for them at the curb who's probably had his life threatened, too.''

The voice on the other end had tightened with nervousness, but she was following his instructions.

"Okay, I . . . ah . . . thank . . . thank you, we'll . . . handle it.''

"Please understand. If you tell them where I'm headed, a murder will occur. Mine.''

"Okay.''

Jacob hung up and returned to his taxi, relieved to find Dieter still where he'd left him. Within ten minutes they had pulled up to Grand Central Station.

"Okay. Go through the doors into the main terminal lobby. The steps on the other side lead directly into the Pan Am elevator lobby.''

♦ ♦ ♦

The shorter of the two Germans had acted innocent and puzzled when a team of federal security guards surrounded him in the lobby of the federal courthouse. He was carrying no weapon, and his passport seemed in order. But security held him for ten minutes while running a computer check by hand-held radio—a check that came up with no "wants or warrants.''

"Must've been a hoax,'' the supervisor told his dispatcher by radio. "This one's German, okay, but he's clean.''

It would have ended there except for the last-second decision of the lead guard to walk the man to the exit by holding his upper arm lightly in his big fist.

The German's accomplice, trying to remain casual on the outside of the security checkpoint, saw movement and looked up to see his partner apparently in custody.

There was no time to waste.

The accomplice pushed his hand in his coat and fingered his 9mm, calculating the right moment to move. They were coming straight toward him. When the guard and the short German closed to ten feet away, the waiting accomplice dropped to a shooter's stance and pulled his gun free, taking careful, rapid aim at the guard's head. He squeezed off two perfectly placed rounds.

The shorter man saw his accomplice crouch and take aim, but there was no time to warn him off. He heard the two soft thumps and felt the guard's hand slip from his arm as the uniformed body crumpled to the floor.

There was no time for regret. He abandoned the dying guard and sprinted toward the security checkpoint, broad-jumping the table as his accomplice dropped a second guard. As a score of lawyers and litigants dove for cover, the two men fled to the waiting taxi.

"Drive!" The taller gunman shoved the barrel of his gun in the back of Singhman Nahjib's neck before turning to his partner.

"Where do we go?" he asked in a tense voice, his eyes flaring. New York City would be alive with cops looking for them now. They should abandon the hunt for Voorster and flee. But the price on Voorster's head was too good to pass up, and they were professionals.

"The woman in the court office mentioned the Pan Am Building when I walked in. We go there. Driver? Go to the Pan Am Building."

Singhman knew that the name Pan Am was no longer on the building, but he wasn't about to argue. He made a left on Third Avenue and accelerated northbound. The shorter gunman turned a dark expression on his companion, his voice an evil hiss as it reached Singhman's ears.

"Why did you start shooting, you fool? I wasn't arrested. The guard was walking me to the door!"

♦ ♦ ♦

Jacob Voorster felt strangely at home in the elaborate reception room of Sol Moscowitz's office because the dark woods and elegant decor reminded him of VZV's executive suite. He suddenly felt sad and apprehensive at the same time.

Moscowitz was in.

Voorster had cooled his heels for ten minutes before his patience ran out and he approached the receptionist again.

"Tell Mr. Moscowitz, please, that I have come from Amsterdam with vital information about what is happening to Pan Am, and with evidence involving the Pan Am case."

The receptionist looked slightly startled and searched Jacob's face before nodding and relaying the message to an unseen secretary.

Within five minutes he was shown in to an even more sumptuous office, where a short, fierce-looking man stood in front of his desk. The lawyer had his arms folded, and did not offer his hand. He gestured to a large leather armchair instead.

"Your name is Voorster?"

"That is right."

"I'm very busy, Mr. Voorster. What is this evidence you mentioned to my secretary? Kindly give it to me in summary form."

Jacob briefly described his years with VZV first. "In short, Mr. Moscowitz, I have proof that VZV hired Mr. Nicolas Costas and his company to put Pan Am out of business, and VZV also supplied the money to do that, nearly five hundred million of which was loaned to Pan Am as their revolving credit line after we laundered it through several financial institutions, including one in Hong Kong and several banks right here in New York."

Sol Moscowitz leaned against his desk and looked hard at the ramrod-straight way Jacob Voorster sat in his chair, his eyes meeting his head-on.

"What," Moscowitz began, "is the name of the lead New York bank in that revolving loan you mentioned, and were they innocent bystanders?"

Voorster shook his head in the negative. "Intertrust Bank, here in New York, and no, Intertrust is one of our indirectly owned institutions. VZV's, I mean. VZV pulls the strings."

Sol Moscowitz stood up, his eyebrows flaring. "Mr. Voorster, those are potentially slanderous allegations. Do you have any proof at all?"

Voorster reached down and snapped open his briefcase, handing over a thirty-page report that Moscowitz scanned quickly, his face becoming more ashen with each page. He handed it back then, and turned, walking to his window and standing there with his hands clasping and unclasping behind his back in full view of Jacob Voorster, who was very puzzled.

This man should be happy, Jacob thought, yet he seems agonized.

For several minutes, Moscowitz stood in silence before turning back to fix Jacob Voorster with an unyielding stare.

"You've made an unfortunate mistake, Mr. Voorster. You're the Yankee pilot who's mistakenly landed his fighter on a Japanese carrier."

Voorster looked lost. "I beg your pardon?"

"Mr. Voorster, I am the lawyer for Intertrust Bank. From what you've told me, I think you were trying to find the lawyer representing Pan Am, and I'm going to give you his name, address, and phone number. I should not hear any more of this, and I want you to make sure you have left none of your papers here. I'm sorry I didn't catch the error when you first came in."

Jacob was in shock. He had told everything to the attorney for the wrong side?

Jacob nodded and retreated in confusion after Sol Moscowitz handed him a piece of gold-edged notepaper with the address of Jamison, Reed, Owen, and Phillips, and Bill Phillips's name and number.

"Call them, Mr. Voorster. And tell them I told you to do so immediately when I discovered your mistake."

Jacob turned toward the door as Moscowitz addressed him one last time.

"Tell them, Mr. Voorster, that I play by the rules."

34

Monday, March 27, 1:40 P.M.
New York City

Dieter Hoffman heard the news flash on his AM radio just as he finished dropping off a fare on the East Side. The words "federal" and "courthouse" riveted his attention. The on-the-scene report that the gunmen had last been seen rounding the corner in a taxi caused him to race back to Grand Central Station.

♦ ♦ ♦

It was 1:45 P.M. by the time Jacob boarded the elevator and started down to the lobby of Moscowitz's building. For the first time, he felt truly frightened. He submerged into the main Grand Central terminal and into one of the passageways as fast as possible, looking for a public phone with some privacy.

He found one at last, in a back passageway. He had to struggle through Dutch coins for several more American quarters, but found them at last and dialed Bill Phillips's number. It took the attorney several minutes to come on the line, but the news that a semihysterical man was demanding an immediate audience with him and claiming that the life or death of Pan Am hung in the balance was too much to ignore.

When Phillips answered, Jacob Voorster took no chances. He grilled Phillips to make sure he really represented the airline, then finally told him the story in capsule form.

"Good Lord!"

Jacob asked to speak to Elizabeth Sterling.

"I'll do better than that," Bill Phillips said. "I'll connect all of us on the same line." He had already been waving at the others to gather around him as he activated the speakerphone.

Phillips introduced Jack Rawly, Creighton MacRae, and Elizabeth, and asked Voorster to repeat who he was and the information he had.

Jacob Voorster took a deep breath and went through it again, mentioning the report that summarized it all, with attachments that provided proof of VZV's intent and involvement.

"Where are you?" Elizabeth asked.

"Somewhere in Grand Central Station," Jacob replied.

"Okay, we'll be there in fifteen minutes." She told him which street to find and where to wait at the curb before Jacob interrupted to tell them about the two men who had been chasing him with guns, and about his close encounter at the federal courthouse.

They had heard the news report of the shootings at Foley Square just before Voorster's call. Undoubtedly the murders at the courthouse were related to Voorster.

"Okay, find the bookstore," Elizabeth told him. "It's on the eastern side, off the main atrium. Go in the bookstore and stay tucked away in the far corner, in the science fiction section. I'll find you there in twenty minutes."

Jacob hung up, feeling better. He had told them of his mistake with Moscowitz. Bill Phillips had been incredulous, but had taken careful note of the fact that Moscowitz had not attempted to mislead or divert Voorster.

Jacob left the phone booth and rounded the corner, deciding to head back toward the line of shops he had seen, and ask someone where the bookstore was. But no one seemed to want to answer, and the entrance eluded him. He stopped at last near a stairway up to the main terminal, wondering where to go for information. He thought about Dieter Hoffman and what Dieter had done for him. He was grateful for the man's help. He owed the cabby his life, he was sure.

◆ ◆ ◆

At that same moment, Dieter Hoffman was racing into the Grand Central Terminal after leaving his supposedly disabled cab once more at the curb, this time along Vanderbilt Avenue, west of the terminal. His eyes scanned the crowd, especially the escalator to the old Pan Am Building. He saw no sign of Voorster, or of the two gunmen.

Of all the places in Grand Central that made the least sense for a hunted man to be, the information kiosk of Grand Central was it—but that was precisely where Dieter Hoffman spotted Jacob Voorster, standing with his briefcase in hand. Dieter began moving toward him, relieved at seeing

Jacob and half amused at his stance, which indicated frustration. Caution caused Dieter to slow his pace and take time to let his eyes wander along the sides and to the far end of the terminal, where his glance flickered across the faces of several people standing there. His eyes snapped back to two of them who looked familiar, and his heart leaped into his throat as he realized who they were.

Dieter's senses came to full alert. These men were killers. They had not yet sighted their target, but it was obvious they soon would. They were professionals, so they might try to kidnap the Dutchman quietly at gunpoint, rather than kill him here. That meant there was a chance to warn Voorster.

Dieter knew he was in the line of fire as well, but he broke into a run nevertheless. He wanted to yell, but the noise might alert the gunmen. Just in case they had noticed him too, he altered course to the south side of the kiosk to confuse them. Dieter let the structure's bulk mask him as he slid to the side of it and reached around, grabbing at Jacob Voorster's sleeve just as the two Germans spotted Voorster.

At first, Jacob Voorster was shocked and off balance as Dieter literally dragged him around the side of the kiosk. But he quickly recognized the cabby and allowed himself to be tugged toward him.

"The gunmen! They're here, and they're coming for you!" Dieter gasped to Jacob, whose eyes flared in fright as he turned and saw the two killers now running toward them.

There was no time. To dash in the clear across the terminal floor would give them an open shot, with no policemen in view to prevent it. To hide behind the kiosk was useless. There was nowhere else to go.

"When I hit them, run as fast as you can to the nearest exit."

Dieter left Jacob behind the kiosk and began moving at a rapid pace toward the two men like an ordinary passenger in a hurry, his head down. He was little more than an obstacle. As expected, they parted slightly to let him pass.

Dieter knew he had to time it just right, and he let instinct guide him. As they approached, he dropped to his knees and lunged forward with his arms out, catching the legs of both men as they charged forward, bringing them down hard on their faces.

He heard the sound of a heavy metal object hit the floor and skitter across it. A nearby passenger gasped as she saw it was a gun.

Dieter clambered to his feet before either of the killers could regain theirs. He kicked the side of the taller man's face with every ounce of strength he had, connecting just above the cheekbone and behind the eye. He could feel bone break and flesh tear as the man's head snapped to one side.

Dieter then turned toward the other one, who was crawling for his gun. Dieter, realizing the killer's intention, closed in on the weapon too, intending to kick it across the terminal and out of harm's way.

To Dieter's utter surprise, the gunman reached out at the last second and yanked the cabby's legs from under him. Dieter had no time to raise his hands to protect his head from crashing against the marble floor when he fell. Everything faded as he lay helpless on the terminal floor.

The killer got to his feet and scooped up his gun, verifying in a split second that Dieter was unconscious. There was no need to shoot the man. Hundreds of people were looking, and his accomplice, if not dead, was incapacitated as well. His neck appeared broken.

He whirled, looking for Voorster, wildly casting his eyes around the terminal. He spotted a police officer approaching from the vicinity of the south entrance. In the distance to the right he saw Voorster disappearing into the portal for track number 32. The assassin pocketed his gun and broke into a dead run toward the same portal. He looked back briefly, and saw the policeman leaning over one of the downed men by the kiosk.

There was still a chance to finish the job!

Jacob kept a death grip on his briefcase, realizing too late that he had missed finding an exit. He raced with all his might down the ramp between two waiting commuter trains in the great dark expanse of the terminal beneath the old Pan Am Building. He expected to hear bullets whizzing past his head at any second.

His eyes scanned ahead, taking in everything as quickly as possible. Commuter trains sat on either side of the platform, both of them with their doors open. Jacob darted in the second car of the train on his left.

The noise of a door opening behind him startled Jacob, and he turned just in time to see a conductor leaning out of the train on the opposite side from the platform. The man had opened the door to examine something on the adjacent track. Jacob moved instantly. The conductor didn't see him until he had brushed past, leaping out the open door into the gravel and dirt between the tracks.

The conductor yelled at him, startled. Jacob was sure the commotion would draw the gunman's interest, but he couldn't wait to see.

An oncoming train was less than a hundred feet away. If he timed it right, he could lose the gunman by appearing to go one way while darting another. The headlight was high off the track. He hoped it would blind the gunman and obscure his own desperate move.

Something pinged and whizzed above him. Then another bullet slammed into the concrete wall next to him.

He's shooting at me!

He would jump in front of the train when twenty feet remained.

NOW!

Jacob leaned low and darted to the left across the track, his right foot clearing the rail easily. His left shoe caught, however, and his entire body began to rotate downward. He grasped for balance as he felt himself rolling to the right, losing sight of the oncoming lead car as he fell.

The lights of the train seemed directly above him now, bearing down on him as time dilated and everything seemed to slow.

The huge oncoming machine was mere feet away. Jacob could see the operator looking down at him, half-standing in the control cab. He knew the man wouldn't be able to throw on the brake until it was too late. With one final effort, Jacob gathered his feet and legs under him and pushed with every ounce of energy he had, leaping to the right of the oncoming car. The right edge of the lead car brushed his feet and ankles as the trunk of his body cleared the edge of the track. The impact was mild and spun him into the gravel. Somehow he hung on to his briefcase. Jacob jumped up in an instant and darted in the opposite direction of the moving train, moving up the long black tunnel from which the train had come.

He could hear the cars screeching to a halt beside him as more shouts echoed behind. On impulse, he turned and crouched between the rails halfway underneath the edge of the train and looked back. His heart sank at what he saw.

The gunman hadn't been fooled! He was now on Jacob's side of the train, moving in his direction.

Jacob instantly crawled under the car to the other side of the track, resuming his dash to the relative safety of the feeder tunnel. He ran for what seemed like ten minutes, frequently glancing back. He ignored the increasingly distant shouts and the reflection of a bright electrical flash behind him before stopping in a small recessed doorway and listening. There were no more sounds of footsteps, but, looking back, he could see bright lights intermittently reflecting on someone coming his way.

Jacob turned and examined the door. It was ancient and wooden, and it smelled. He tried the handle, astounded when it responded. He pushed the door open slowly, trying to minimize the creaking sound. Then he turned and closed it behind him.

The sound of a male voice from the darkness caused him to jump in fright. He banged his elbow on the wall, almost dropping his briefcase.

"This is my hidey-hole, brother. But I guess there's room."

A foul stench of urine and rotting food permeated what looked like an old utility shed. The room was dimly lit, and a large man lounged along the opposite wall, regarding him carefully from beneath a frayed gray watch cap.

"I've . . ." Jacob hadn't realized he was panting for breath, his words coming hard. "Someone's . . . chasing me . . . with a gun. Is there a way out of here?"

"A *gun*? Lordy, my man, when you brings trouble, you brings trouble."

"Is this a closed room?"

"Nawsir. There's a way out. Hold on. I'll show you."

"He's not far . . ."

The homeless man got to his feet far more quickly than Jacob would have expected. He then motioned for Jacob to follow, and disappeared into a passageway that at first appeared to be a dead end. It wasn't. The man continued to lead Jacob through several foul-smelling passageways before showing him a rusted metal ladder, slick with seeping moisture from above.

"Okay. Climb up here and shoulder open the manhole cover, and you'll be out in a alley behind the station. You can get yo'self a cab there. Don't hang around here."

"Thank you . . . thank you," Jacob said huskily, looking the man in the eye and resting his free hand momentarily on his shoulder. He felt he should say more.

"Ain't no problem, brother. Have a nice day, as dey say."

Jacob clutched his briefcase securely to his chest. Then he began climbing. When he reached the manhole cover, he found it much harder to move with one hand than he had expected. But he finally shoved it up and to one side, and as promised, he climbed into daylight in an alleyway four blocks north of Grand Central.

Jacob Voorster stopped to dust himself off, then began running westward. He had to get away and find a phone.

35

Monday, March 27, 3:00 P.M.
Grand Central Station, New York

Elizabeth had bypassed the commotion by the main kiosk in Grand Central and descended to the next level down, moving to the bookstore where she was supposed to meet Jacob Voorster. She looked in every corner for a man with a briefcase and a gray overcoat. Creighton joined her a few minutes later, looking grim.

"Elizabeth. That mess upstairs? I think it involves our man."

They ascended to the main level and walked over to the kiosk where the police who were handling the investigation were located.

Creighton took an officer aside and spoke earnestly with him for a few moments before returning to Elizabeth.

"He says the man over there on the floor was carrying a gun with a silencer. He's dead. Looks like a broken neck. The other guy sitting up and holding his head is a cabdriver who tackled the dead guy and one other."

"The two gunmen Mr. Voorster mentioned! The two from the courthouse!"

Creighton nodded. "There's also been an accident on one of the tracks. The policeman doesn't know who, but someone touched the electric rail and fried himself. And this gunman's accomplice was seen running down to the platforms behind us."

"Oh God, if that's Voorster down there, we've got to get his briefcase. He said he had a report, Creighton! That's the key to everything!" Elizabeth's eyes were wide. Creighton nodded and returned to the officer.

It was twenty minutes before the body of the dead man was pulled from the tracks. They found no briefcase, and little ID. The word was relayed to Creighton that the man had died with a gun in his hand. Witnesses said he'd been shooting at another man, who'd disappeared behind one of the trains. That was as much information as Creighton could muster before federal investigators arrived and began clamping down the lid on any additional revelations.

"Then where is Voorster?" Elizabeth asked, tears of frustration hovering at the corner of her eyes. "He's carrying our salvation, and he's gone!"

"Do you have your cellular phone?" Creighton asked.

She nodded.

"Make sure it's on, and call Bill Phillips. If our Mr. Voorster called him once, he'll no doubt call him again."

Monday, March 27, 3:00 P.M
Clipper Fifteen, on approach to Kennedy Airport

Brian Murphy called for another increment of flaps and ordered the gear down as he settled Clipper Fifteen smoothly onto the glideslope for an instrument approach to Kennedy. The switch to tower and final landing clearance went as scheduled. Brian taxied off when he reached the end of the runway after an almost perfect touchdown.

The crew wore artificial smiles at the gate until all the passengers had disembarked. Then they cornered the station agent to hear the latest word on their company's fate.

"You see those men in trench coats through the terminal window?" she asked.

They nodded.

"They're all equipped with repossession papers. I understand the sheriff will be out here to seize this airplane at five-oh-one P.M. exactly."

"Any word from the legal team?" Brian asked. It had been three hours since he'd talked to Elizabeth. Maybe they'd been able to get a delay.

She shook her head. "I've heard nothing."

The crew was scheduled for a layover in New York. None of them wanted to go to the hotel until they knew what was going to happen. They reboarded the aircraft, deciding to wait for the outbound aircrew. They were fully aware that there might not be an outbound flight, despite the scheduled presence of the mayor and other dignitaries who were supposed to arrive at around 5:30 P.M. for the 6:00 P.M. departure of the round-the-world inaugural flight.

Brian left the others in the forward section of the plane and wandered back, wondering what he would do if the company folded. He was deep in thought when he glanced down at a particular row of seats near the tail of the aircraft. He realized he was looking at the video camcorder case of the man he had talked to during the flight.

The case was distinctive and easy to identify.

Wait a minute, didn't that fellow say he was getting off in New York? Brian thought. He reached down and snapped open the case, finding the camera and one extra battery still inside.

Brian closed the case and carried it to the rear, where the caterers were working, loading the galley for the flight to London.

He watched the caterers briefly and started to turn away, when something familiar about one of them caught his attention. He peered at the man more closely, thinking he'd seen him before—and recently.

With a shock, Brian remembered where he'd seen the caterer before. He was the passenger Brian had talked to, the one who owned the camcorder—the one he was holding right now!

"Hey! You there! Excuse me!" Brian saw the man's head snap up and his smile fade rapidly as he recognized the four stripes of the captain he had spoken to on the way in from Seattle.

"Yes?"

"Didn't you just come in on this flight? Isn't this camera yours?"

"I wish it was, mate," the man in the catering coveralls said, "but I can't afford one."

The accent was Australian, but it sounded false. Brian knew Aussies too well to buy the flawed inflection. Yet he still wasn't sure he'd identified the man correctly.

Before he could make a move, the man straightened up suddenly and turned his back to Brian. He simultaneously dropped something in the wastepaper slot of the galley.

"I think I've got it fixed," he said as he slid the cart back into position and turned on the internal heater.

One of the other caterers was arranging empty carts in the front of the truck body as it sat extended vertically at the level of the 747's doorway. Brian walked across the narrow metal bridge and tapped him on the shoulder.

"Have you ever seen that guy in the galley before?" Brian asked in a low voice as he gestured toward the airplane where the man was standing at the door.

"No, but he said he's one of our repairmen. He didn't come in with us."

Logic told Brian he had identified a saboteur. Instinct told him to hide that recognition. He turned to the man in the doorway and smiled, shrugging his shoulders. "Sorry to hassle you. Can't be too careful about security, you know."

"Quite all right, mate." The man looked at the other caterer in the back of the truck, gauging whether he'd been fingered as an unknown. He knew the Kennedy catering operation from previous surveillance. There were too many employees for them all to know each other. "Okay if I ride back with you guys?"

The caterer hesitated, then shrugged. "Sure."

Brian took the camcorder around the corner into the galley and opened the case again. Then it hit him.

The battery! When he had seen the case opened in flight, there had been two batteries. Now there was one.

He pulled out the remaining battery and slipped it into his pocket. Leaving the camcorder and case in the galley, Brian returned to the rear door. The driver had lowered the safety railings and was preparing to disengage the truck from the aircraft before lowering the lift-body. The passenger-cum-caterer was standing on the platform just inside the truck body when Brian waved him forward.

"Excuse me. One more thing."

The man walked forward, stopping on the bridge, which was now bare of its protective railings. Brian pulled the rectangular camcorder battery pack out of his pocket and held it up. He watched the man's expression freeze as he calculated what Brian was going to do with it.

If this is a bomb, Mr. Saboteur, you're not going to want it to hit the ground, are you?

"You left this behind."

Brian tossed the battery to the man, low and outside.

The man's eyes followed the battery in flight, calculating its trajectory as he realized it might hit the body of the truck. He began to move, lunging for it. The battery sailed through the door and off to one side of the truck as the man clawed after it before realizing that he had leaned too far and was falling. He reached for a handhold, but it was too late. His lower abdomen came down hard on the edge of the bridge and left him dangling over the thirty-foot abyss to the concrete below. He hung there momentarily, until gravity inexorably pulled him off.

The sound of the man's head hitting the concrete below was sickening. Brian climbed down the ladder on the outside of the truck and rushed to the body. The shocked caterers called for an ambulance. He found no pulse. The cranial damage was obviously extensive. Brian unzipped the top of the man's coveralls, revealing, as he expected, the shirt and tie he had seen him wearing earlier. As sirens approached, he located the man's billfold and looked inside. He found a Washington driver's license with the saboteur's picture, except that in the picture he had a mustache. His name was listed as Bart A. Richardson.

Several Pan Am mechanics had run to the scene. Brian turned to one of them now, his captain's uniform commanding attention.

"We've got a bomb on board, in the rear galley area! Clear the airplane immediately and call the bomb squad. Have them report to me!"

The mechanic nodded and pulled out his hand-held radio to relay the information as the paramedics arrived and began checking the body for vital signs. Brian continued to search through the man's suitcoat pockets for any additional clues. He was about to give up when his fingers contacted a plastic bag in one of the pockets. He removed it and found himself staring at a small piece of molded latex that was rounded and slightly ridged. At first it looked like a scrap, until he pulled it from the clear plastic bag and examined the rounded side of it, finding a perfect replica of a single fingerprint.

Brian slipped it in his pocket and stood up. He used his cellular phone to call Loren Miller, the FBI agent in Seattle. Brian hurriedly described the situation in New York and the name of the dead man before getting to the reason for his call.

"Loren, it's very important that the FBI sit on New York authorities not to release any information on this situation, the man, his alleged name, or the incident. Trust me, but don't ask me why yet. I'll be in late tonight, and I'd like you to meet me at the airport."

"I can't ask why?" Miller replied with a chuckle.

"No. I'll tell you tonight. I'll call you back with the time of the inbound flight. Trust me, Loren. This is important."

"You got it, Captain."

Monday, March 27, 3:30 P.M.
New York City

The receptionist at Jamison, Reed, Owen, and Phillips wasn't sure what to make of the disheveled man in the stained and dirty gray overcoat looming over her desk. His name had a familiar ring to it, so she called Bill Phillips on the intercom.

Phillips shot out of his chair. "Jacob Voorster is *here?*"

Phillips appeared within seconds, pumping Voorster's hand and assuring him he had found the right place at last. Jacob told him of escaping the tunnel and finding a taxi several blocks west of the terminal.

"Those men are still looking for me," he said.

"They're both dead, Mr. Voorster." Phillips filled him in as he walked him back to his office.

♦ ♦ ♦

Elizabeth's cellular phone suddenly rang in the middle of Grand Central. She quickly relayed the news to Creighton that Jacob Voorster—and his briefcase—had surfaced. Creighton pointed out that they had less than ninety minutes to halt the seizure of Pan Am aircraft worldwide, including Ship 609, the round-the-world inaugural 747 currently being swarmed over by a bomb squad at Kennedy Airport.

Elizabeth and Creighton dashed by cab to Phillips's office, while Bill Phillips requested a hearing before the three-judge panel at 4:15 P.M. Other members of his firm now labored to prepare new court orders for Judge Hayes to sign. When they arrived at Phillips's office, they were quickly filled in after a brief introduction of Jacob Voorster. Jack Rawly gave them a capsule account of how the hearing would be handled.

"Okay, here's the deal. Intertrust, the holder of the revolving loan, is still prevented from declaring a default because Judge Hayes's temporary restraining order is still in effect. Intertrust took us to court this morning to kill the TRO and, as you know, we were given until five P.M. to find new evidence, or the appeals court would sweep the TRO away. Thanks to our new-found best friend here, Jacob Voorster, we now have that new evidence. I expect the appeals court to deny Intertrust's motion. The problem is, the airplanes themselves are owned by Empire Leasing, not by Intertrust. To stop them from any cowboyish repossessions, we need Judge Hayes to slap an additional TRO on *them*. Judge Hayes has agreed by phone to do this for us immediately, but we have a major problem. Someone in authority is going to have to deliver the order in person at the gate at Kennedy while we do the appeals hearing. I don't see how anyone can get out there in time."

"You can't fax the court order?"

Jack Rawly had a disgusted look on his face. "Empire Leasing was so convinced they'd have the right to seize our 747 at five-oh-one P.M. that they briefed their man out at Kennedy to take no phone calls *or* faxes.

We can't even communicate with him. It's obvious he's been programmed to think the formal notice of default is going to take effect automatically. He plans to hand our station manager the repossession papers at that precise moment, and refuse any further access to the aircraft.''

"Good heavens, Jack, is that the case everywhere Pan Am has airplanes?'' Creighton asked.

"No. Everywhere else, the Empire representatives seem to be agreeing that they won't attempt any repossessions unless they get *positive* word the TRO has been thrown out—which it won't be.''

"But at Kennedy—'' Creighton continued.

"Well, at Kennedy,'' Jack replied, "the jerk representing Empire apparently has orders to disrupt the inaugural ceremony any way he can.''

"Let's call the sheriff,'' Elizabeth said.

"We already have. That's who I was talking to, the Queens County Sheriff—or one of his deputies. Unless we place a court order in his hands before five-oh-one P.M. ordering Empire to stand down, the sheriff will be helping Empire take the plane and destroy the inaugural. If that happens, all the public relations and advertising investment in this round-the-world kickoff—three months and fifteen million in expenses—will have been wasted. That flight has to go on schedule and in front of the cameras, or the damage to public confidence will probably be irrecoverable.''

Elizabeth sighed, got up, and headed for the phone on an adjacent desk.

"I've got an idea,'' she said. "Give me a second.''

A limousine had been ordered, and the receptionist reported that it was standing by now in front of the building. Within two minutes, Elizabeth was back with a strained smile.

"Okay. Creighton, you'll need to be at the hearing. But I don't have to be there, so I guess I'm elected to be the 'person in authority' to deliver the TRO. My former partner, Eric Knox, is going to fly me out in his helicopter.''

"To Kennedy?'' Creighton asked. "On this short notice?''

"His chopper's at the Wall Street Heliport, and he's already in motion. If you knew Eric, you'd know this isn't unusual. He loves last-minute challenges.''

Jack Rawly looked greatly relieved. "That's great! I had no idea how we were going to make it.''

They gathered Jacob and began moving to the elevator rapidly as Elizabeth turned to Jack Rawly. "Are the press already there?''

"They're hovering like vultures, though they're invited vultures. I talked with Ralph Basanji earlier. We expected good local and national coverage, but with all that's been happening, he's gambled big-time. This five-o'clock deadline will be played out before a live CNN audience. Several of the other networks may be there, too.''

Monday, March 27, 4:15 P.M.
Foley Square, Manhattan

Judge Walter Hayes had been monitoring the progress of events closely. He had listened carefully to Jack Rawly's update and request on the phone. He ushered the team in immediately, questioned Jacob Voorster for less than five minutes, and glanced over the report that had so disturbed Sol Moscowitz several hours earlier in the Pan Am Building.

''I knew my faith in your conclusions was well placed, but this is overkill. Where's the order?''

Jack Rawly slipped two court orders across the desk. One extended the TRO against a declaration of default by the revolving-loan lenders headed by Intertrust. The other ordered Empire Leasing not to repossess any Pan Am aircraft until the entire matter could be brought to a formal injunctive hearing.

As the judge's pen scratched along the signature line and a clerk stood by to emboss it with the court seal, Jacob Voorster's voice reached their ears.

''I left one thing out, sir.''

Judge Hayes looked up. ''Yes?''

Jacob turned to Jack. ''Mr. . . . Rawly, is it?''

''Yes. Jack Rawly.''

''Mr. Rawly here mentioned the name Empire Leasing just now. You may not be aware—I may not have mentioned this in all the confusion—but I know that company. It is owned by Bermuda Investments, Limited, which in turn is a wholly owned subsidiary of VZV. I didn't realize they owned Pan Am's aircraft. I just knew that we owned *them*, and that was a VZV secret, of course.''

Judge Hayes shook his head and took a deep breath before looking at Jack again. ''You've got a lot of work ahead of you, Counselor. Civil and criminal and multijurisdictional, I would think. You've got so many targets to sue, it boggles the mind. This is going to be a political thunderclap as well, if it turns out the motive of this Dutch company is what you think it is.''

"Excuse me, Your Honor, I don't understand," Jacob said.

Judge Hayes cocked his head and looked at Voorster.

"What I was referring to is Mr. Rawly's theory that your former employer has somehow secretly bought illicit majority interests in the big three airlines in North America, and manipulated their secretly controlled voting stock to decrease competition among them and produce ever higher profits. It's what we call over here 'combination in restraint of trade'—*if*, in fact, that's what has happened."

"Oh, I assure you, Judge, that is exactly what's happened," Jacob said quietly and in a manner Judge Hayes couldn't ignore. Hayes looked the Dutchman in the eye and studied his expression.

"How can you be sure, Mr. Voorster?"

Jacob Voorster reached out and gently placed the fingertips of his right hand on the judge's desk as he looked down, and then back up at the judge.

"Because, Your Honor, you are speaking with the architect of that plan. I spent the last five years putting it together very quietly from Amsterdam: setting up the intermediary corporations all over the world, transferring the money with great stealth from VZV to those holding corporations, and then arranging for them to buy the airline stock they were created to hold. Our lawyers found ways that were considered legal to circumvent the barriers against what we wanted to do. At the same time, others at VZV worked to hire board members who would serve our interests, without realizing in each case that the intermediary corporation they thought they were representing was owned in turn by a single, larger company overseas. It was never direct control in violation of U.S. laws, but it gave us effective control, and it was working. In a few years the profits would have been unbelievable—that is, if our managing director had not panicked and used criminal means to try to destroy a competitor."

The judge's chambers were electrified by this admission, which fully explained why a corporation such as VZV would want this man dead. But the distinction between what he had done and what his managing director had done—although presented by Jacob Voorster as a contrast of right against wrong—staggered them all. There was no time to consider the implications. That would come later, as they tried to help him in return for the cornucopia of damning information he had brought.

Judge Hayes broke the spell first. "I'm staggered, Mr. Voorster. But"—he turned to Elizabeth and inclined his head—"you've got a helicopter to catch, young lady." The clerk had finished stamping copies of both orders, and handed them to Elizabeth. She thanked him and flashed a smile at everyone, her eyes locking for a moment on Creighton's before she raced out the door.

♦ ♦ ♦

Eric was waiting when she reached the East Side Heliport at Thirty-fourth Street, by the East River. As soon as her door was closed, he lifted the turbine-powered helicopter into the air and headed for Kennedy.

"I've already arranged clearance to land right next to your 747 at the gate, Elizabeth. They think it's part of the celebration."

"How'd you do that?"

"Friend of mine in the FAA owes me. I called the favor, and he pulled the strings."

"In less than an hour? I'm impressed, as usual."

"We'll make it before five P.M., Elizabeth, but then what?"

"What do you mean?"

"Can Pan Am really make it?"

"Eric, the airline is a success, except for this incredible campaign against us, and we're about to blow that apart. You won't believe what we just heard! The fallout from this is going to shake Washington. And not just Washington—it's going to shake up the entire airline world."

She filled him in briefly on the saga of the previous two weeks and the revelations Jacob Voorster had brought with him. She was startled to see him glance at her, wide-eyed.

"VZV? You're kidding! I know they're powerful, but they did all that?"

She was nodding her head. "They paid for a sabotage campaign run by Nick Costas and Irwin Fairchild, seduced the idiot who was Pan Am's CFO before me to replace the loans and sell the airplanes, manipulated our stock, probably sabotaged our computers, and in Brian's opinion, they may have been responsible for the two near-fatal accidents we had."

"Really? He thinks Costas could have attempted mass murder?"

She nodded again. "We can't prove it yet, but he's working on it. The thing is, as much as Jacob Voorster knew about the operations of VZV, he knew nothing about any sabotage of airplanes or even computers, so there are still some missing links and unanswered questions."

John F. Kennedy Airport appeared in the distance as Elizabeth checked her watch. It was 4:46 P.M. Eric was already talking to Kennedy Tower, getting clearance into the terminal control area.

The radio quieted and Eric turned to Elizabeth again.

"You don't know any of the names of those dummy corporations, do you?"

She thought for a moment. The report Voorster had brought had a list of names. She could almost see a few of them in her mind's eye.

"I think I can remember two or three. Let's see, Great Circle Investments, Limited, and something called Condor Corporation, and one with a name that struck me as funny because I've always loved Groucho Marx, Marx Investments."

She felt the helicopter bobble for a second and assumed they had transited a bit of turbulence. She saw Eric looking at her again in surprise.

"Marx Investments? Of Tampa?"

"I think so. I only had a glance."

"Good Lord, I hope not!"

"Why, Eric? You know them?"

He was nodding and laughing and shaking his head from side to side all at the same time.

"Elizabeth, you may not remember, but you and I put together the deal that financed their purchase of fifteen percent of a certain American aviation concern called"—he looked at her—"AMR Corporation, otherwise known as American Airlines. Bob Crandal's airline! In 1990."

"Oh my God!"

"Innocently, of course!"

♦ ♦ ♦

Pan Am's station manager had hurried the TV crews to the departure lounge in time to catch Elizabeth's arrival as part of their coverage. With the bomb search of Pan Am Flight One now successfully completed, the cameramen focused on the Jet Ranger as Eric brought it delicately to the ground aft of the right wing of the giant Boeing.

Brian was there to open the right-hand door of the chopper to help Elizabeth out.

A grim-looking contingent of men stood adjacent to a large aircraft tow tractor while watching the proceedings. Brian gestured toward them now.

"If you've ever wanted to put a face on the grim reaper, there he is—along with his hired rent-a-cops."

"Empire's men?"

Brian nodded. "The station manager's already told them it's over. *I've* told them it's over, but they refuse to leave. They think they're going to hook up that tractor and tow our bird away in a few minutes."

Elizabeth smiled and showed Brian the court orders as he briefed her on the successful search for the bomb. They had talked earlier by cellular phone while she was headed to the courthouse. The incident at the aircraft still seemed surreal. She wasn't at all sure what it meant.

"It wasn't a bomb at all the guy planted. It was a firestarter—an incendiary device designed to catch the galley on fire in a hurry and cancel the flight. The man threw it in the wastebasket in the aft galley when I first confronted him."

The ringing of her cellular phone interrupted them. It was Jack Rawly, calling from the hallway outside the appeals court.

"All done, Elizabeth. The appeals judges dismissed the action, and you should have seen Sol Moscowitz. He hardly said anything. He had his jaw clamped down so tight I thought he was going to break a tooth. He hardly spoke to his client. And *then* he was asked outside the courtroom by a *New York Times* reporter if they might try again. He said, 'Ask someone else. I'm withdrawing as attorney of record for this client.' "

"Fascinating! And he didn't fight it?"

"Not at all. The TROs are as good as gold. How're *you* doing?"

She looked at her watch. Five minutes remained.

"I'm on the ramp by the airplane, Jack, about to stuff a turkey with a court order."

"Oh, by the way, Creighton's headed out there for the ceremony. He's going to be heading back to London tonight."

With Brian standing beside her, that news had to be stored, not absorbed, and she thanked Jack and rang off.

Brian briefed her as they walked slowly toward the small contingent from Empire Leasing.

"The man in the gray suit is Arthur Collins, executive vice-president of Empire. He's about as unfriendly as they come. Judy Schimmel, our station manager, had to ask him to leave the boarding lounge because he was talking to the passengers. He told them we were finished and they should go find alternate transportation."

"Hasn't anyone told him we have the court order?"

"Judy did, but he ignored her."

TV lights shone from behind the glass of the boarding lounge above them. Elizabeth resisted the temptation to look up and check whether the cameras were trained on her as she walked up to Collins.

"Mr. Collins, I'm Elizabeth Sterling, chief financial officer of Pan Am."

Collins kept an even expression as he checked his watch and raised his eyebrows. He extended his hand, and Elizabeth slapped the court order in it.

"I would suggest you read that. And then leave. Immediately."

The time was exactly 5:00 P.M.

♦ ♦ ♦

Elizabeth prudently omitted the details about the shocking revelations Jacob Voorster had brought from Amsterdam as she briefed the media in the boarding lounge.

"Our public affairs people will make the formal announcements," she said on camera, "but I can tell you that we have, today, utterly defeated what we can now legally *prove* has been a major coordinated campaign by offshore corporate interests to put Pan Am out of business. That campaign has failed. We're here to stay with the best service in the world, and the flying public is the beneficiary!"

She smiled and stepped away from a barrage of follow-up questions as the outbound crew appeared with Judy Schimmel, giving the reporters someone else to interview.

Elizabeth took the chance to slip away with Brian, who had already borrowed the key to a small VIP room down the concourse, with privacy in mind.

He locked the door behind them, then drew Elizabeth into his arms in a long embrace which evolved into a deep, passionate kiss filled with stored-up longing. She responded in kind. After a few long, dizzy moments, she could no longer control the trembling in her knees.

They sat on the couch then, Brian touching her cheek lightly with his fingertips. From the changing expressions on his face, she could tell he was in turmoil over something. He was trying to decide how much to say, and she could see he'd reached a decision as he suddenly repositioned himself on the couch and lightly touched her knee. His voice came out forceful, hopeful, and pleading all at once.

"Elizabeth, let's start over again. We got off to a rocky start with all the pressure, and I—"

She pulled him to her, speaking low in his ear. "After I see Mother and Kelly, the first night back in the condo is ours, and the phones will be turned off."

He laughed. "I'll look forward to that, but you don't have to do that. I just have to get used to things." He pulled back and looked her in the eye. "I *am* getting used to things, like the fact that you're the most capable executive we've got, and I'm proud of you . . . and I love you."

"I love you too, Brian."

The words almost caught in her throat, and she hoped Brian hadn't noticed. She sat back suddenly, remembering that he was heading back to Seattle prematurely.

"Now tell me why you're rushing back."

He sighed and nodded. "Okay. This isn't over yet, with the death of that impostor, I mean. There's at least one more rat in the woodwork."

"Rat?"

"I think the company's got a mole. I've thought so all along, and so does the FBI."

"You mean 'mole' as in espionage?" she asked, eyebrows raised.

"As in sabotage, from within the company."

"How high up?"

"I don't know!"

"But why do you have to go back so quickly? Can't the FBI handle it?"

He smiled and shook his head. "I found something on the body of that guy—something I recognized. A business card with a familiar logo that I've seen before, from a condominium rental agency in Seattle. In fact, I'd swear I've had a card from the same company given to me sometime in the past, but I just can't remember when, or by whom. If I'm right, though, that card—and the handwritten address on the back—could lead to whoever hired that bastard I caught on my plane today."

"You think he was a hired gun?"

Brian nodded solemnly. "I think he's the one behind the computer dirty tricks, all the sabotage, and that explosion. Remember my theory about the fingerprint?"

Elizabeth remembered the explanation of the rubber-stamp fingerprint, but it had seemed farfetched. Brian fished out the small plastic bag with the latex stamp. Elizabeth looked at it in complete surprise.

"Whose is it?"

"A thousand-to-one odds you're looking at the index fingerprint of the late Marvin Grade."

Her eyes returned to his, her memory mingling the chances Creighton had taken playing detective with her own frightening experience in Hong Kong.

"Promise me you won't take unnecessary risks!"

"I promise."

♦ ♦ ♦

Elizabeth had agreed to substitute for Ron Lamb at the formal initiation of the new service. Speaking to the crowd with a false-front smile was the last thing she wanted to do as she watched Brian wave her goodbye and hurry down the concourse toward his Seattle flight. She forced herself to say the appropriate words just before cutting the ribbon to launch Pan Am's first round-the-world flight service. But the sight of Clipper One, pushing back on time with a full complement of eager passengers on board, was beautiful, and she was teetering on the verge of tears when a large, gentle hand closed softly around her right shoulder.

"That 747 you've launched represents the salvation of your whole airline. You did it, Elizabeth! Congratulations!"

Creighton MacRae had a broad smile on his face as she turned into the sunshine of it, at once thrilled to see him and feeling guilty for reacting that way. Brian, she reminded herself, was probably not even away from his gate yet.

His hand had progressed from her shoulder to encircle her waist, and he kept his arm around her now as they both stared at the departing jumbo.

To the others in the departure lounge, they were two happy Pan Am people sharing a side-by-side victory hug.

To Elizabeth, his touch triggered a crisis of confused longings.

"I have a message for you from Jason Ing, by the way," he said.

She brightened as she looked around at him. "Oh?"

"He's recovering quite nicely. He thanked us for the small florist shop you sent, and he said to assure you that the papers for the one hundred forty million have already been faxed to Seattle as per your instructions. Jeremy expects they can transfer the funds by midnight our time. Jack Rawly tells me the suits he'll file tomorrow will make it unnecessary even to pay interest to Intertrust for the next few years while this stays in litigation."

"Good heavens, Creighton, do you realize that gives us a totally new five-hundred-million credit line?"

"I do. Jack says to tell you he doubts that we will—excuse me, that *you* will—ever have to pay a cent of that back. Four hundred thirty million in damages would sound about right under the organized-crime statutes."

Elizabeth was regarding him quietly, her eyes gazing into his.

"Creighton, you've been so invaluable to us, it almost scares me to have you leave."

"Jack Rawly and the rest of you can handle things from here. You've got the buggers dead to rights, and I've got to get back to Forres, Elizabeth. I have business to take care of, a meeting in London tomorrow that I was afraid I was going to have to cancel, and besides that"—he dropped his arm from her waist and held her elbow instead as she turned to face him—"I left my poor housekeeper on the doorstep stunned and speechless when I dashed out the door last week, and that's frightening. I've seen her stunned before, but I've never seen her speechless."

She looked down and placed her finger on his chest.

"I guess I also . . . hate to see you go personally."

She looked up at him, part of her mind screaming at her to consider the signals she was sending, while the other part urged her on.

Creighton was smiling. "Well, if you want me, just call. Of course, after you get my bill, I doubt you'll be calling anytime soon."

"I couldn't have done this without you, you know."

"Nonsense."

"How about your successful sleuthing around the other night? That gave us the extra time and kept us alive."

He cocked his head slightly, smiling a conspiratorial smile. "It did work out rather well, now that you mention it." He looked over his shoulder at the departing 747 before looking back at her.

"Well, we got that bloody beast from Boeing launched, at least," he said.

He let go of her elbow and gestured toward the concourse.

"Why don't you walk me to my gate, then, Elizabeth Sterling, CFO? Unless you've got something else you need to attend to . . ."

"I wouldn't think of letting you depart without waving goodbye."

She took his arm as she walked with him toward the adjacent terminal, both of them speaking rapidly of the things left undone.

"Jacob Voorster wants to see the cabdriver who saved his life, so Jack Rawly is planning to arrange police protection for Mr. Voorster and take him over to the hospital."

"How's the man doing?"

"Voorster?"

"No. The cabby."

Creighton nodded. "Brave fellow. Nothing wrong but a mild concussion, fortunately.'' He looked at her with a worried expression. "I warned Jack to find a safe house and keep Voorster guarded twenty-four hours a day until he's been fully debriefed on the record—until he's testified. He's agreed to stay here until it's all over.''

All too soon they were standing in another departure lounge, watching the last of the passengers board a British Airways 747 to London as Creighton took his boarding pass from the gate agent and walked with Elizabeth to the door.

She was having trouble meeting his gaze, and he gently raised her chin until their eyes were locked on each other.

"Scotland's rather beautiful in the early spring, you know.''

She smiled. "Yes, I do know.''

He looked at her in silence again, his smile slowly fading, his carefully guarded emotions finally overwhelming his resolve to stay thoroughly in control.

"Elizabeth, I . . . come with me.''

He saw the look of surprise and the startled turmoil in her eyes, but he was also aware that she hadn't pulled away.

"What . . . do you mean?'' Elizabeth asked softly.

He felt himself swallow hard. "I . . . just mean this shouldn't be goodbye.''

She smiled, a little too sadly, he thought. He knew a little about her history with Brian, and he could see she was struggling with herself.

"Creighton . . . I have a commitment in Seattle . . .''

"No strings, Elizabeth, just an open invitation.''

He had reached a truce with himself. She could see it in his eyes, and knew the invitation was permanent. He was okay alone, but he would be waiting.

She smiled. "Like our connecting doors in Vancouver, then.'' Her words formed no question. The image was clear, and they both knew.

He nodded, closing his eyes as he leaned down to kiss her.

EPILOGUE

Tuesday, March 28, 11:00 A.M.
Seattle

Brian Murphy sat quietly in a wooden rocking chair facing the door, listening to the sound of footsteps in the hallway of the condominium. He knew how long it would take to drive to the Redondo Beach area, a few miles to the southwest of Seatac Airport. The recipient of the single-page fax he had sent should be arriving any minute.

The sound of a distant door opening swallowed the footsteps. Quiet once again settled over the building.

Brian looked around at the expensive interior. For an attempted mass murderer, the renter of the condo had shown elegant taste in his choice of furniture and decor. It was hard to believe such a man would be careless enough to leave the handwritten address of his base of operations on the back of a card in his wallet. But he had done exactly that. It had been simple for Brian to obtain a key, using a carefully constructed lie to the rental firm.

He had entered gingerly, just as unsure of what to expect as he'd been in Marvin Grade's house—but here there was a world of difference. The condo was full of electronic equipment, computers, printers, scattered electronic components and tools, and a fax machine with ten memory buttons. Marvin Grade's little house had contained no such incriminating evidence. This must be the right man!

Brian had counted on finding a telephone with a dialer memory, or some record of who the renter normally called. But the fax memory provided something more: a record of all the numbers to whom documents had been sent in the previous few months—even local numbers. One number in particular kept reappearing time and again.

Its owner hadn't been difficult to trace, but the realization of who it was had provided quite a shock.

The distant slamming of a car door filtered into the darkened room. Brian felt himself tense slightly and feel for the switch on the power cord he'd connected to several floodlights on a stand.

The rubber-stamp fingerprint *had* been Marvin Grade's, after all. Loren Miller, the FBI agent, had apologized to Brian for his previous smug denial that the fingerprints could have been faked. They agreed that at worst, Grade had been only a co-conspirator. Less than an hour later, while searching the condo, he had found enough evidence to prove that Marvin Grade had been nothing more than an unwitting pawn.

Brian thought back to the lonely little house and the calendar with the birthdays of Grade's children so lovingly inscribed. For the first time he felt true compassion for the man. Apparently he was exactly what Brian had come to believe: an innocent victim.

There were new footsteps on the stairway.

The wording of the fax had taken some time, but he'd decided to keep it terse and simple, searching for the shortest number of words that would strike the greatest amount of terror into the heart of the unidentified co-conspirator—a co-conspirator who also carried a Pan Am ID.

> *We've got major problems that could lead right to your door-step. Meet me at the Redondo location at 11 A.M.! I'll leave the door unlocked. I'm not answering the phone, so just be there—or I'm heading south w/o a forward.*

Urgent, rapid footsteps thudded down the hallway, becoming louder with each report. Suddenly they stopped. He heard the sound of the doorknob turning.

The door to the condo opened and then slammed shut as the man moved angrily into the room, spotting no one until Brian snapped on the bright lights.

The man stood in the entryway, holding his hand over his forehead and trying to peer beyond the glare.

"Turn those fucking lights off!"

Brian altered his voice before speaking in an approximation of the saboteur's voice. "I've got a loaded, cocked Uzi aimed right at you. Don't move!"

"What is this with the lights, Hansen? What are you *doin'*?" he growled.

Okay, the man's name was Hansen, Brian thought.

Brian began again. "I'm watchin' your reactions. I want to see if you're going to lie to me again."

"What? About what? I haven't lied to you!"

"Answer me yes or no. You hired me to screw up your airplanes, cause delays, and make your airline look incompetent, right?"

"Christ! You've already been *paid* for all that, Hansen! The money's in the bank on Grand Cayman, just like you said. *Now* what do you want?"

"You didn't tell me your goddamned chief pilot was gonna play detective. I got jumped yesterday at Kennedy."

He seemed stunned. "What the fuck were you doing at Kennedy? I told you the job was over. You could go home to your island bank account and forget this ever happened. I told you we had gone too far with the airplanes. *What's with these damn lights?*"

Brian snapped the lights off and watched as Pan Am's vice-president of operations, Chad Jennings, stood in complete confusion, his eyes focusing at last on Brian Murphy, but his brain refusing to comprehend what had happened.

"You're right, Chad. It's all over."

Four FBI agents who had been waiting in the adjacent room entered, guns and handcuffs at the ready.

Wednesday afternoon, March 29
Washington, D.C.

Jack Rawly sat on the edge of a borrowed desk in the office of the Senate Foreign Relations Committee, giving a brief update to the board members in Seattle by speakerphone. With the formal announcement of the lawsuits Pan Am was filing, the company had suddenly found itself in the eye of an international political hurricane.

"Well, as Ralph Basanji can tell you," Brian said, "we're being beneficially portrayed as a giant-killer. The mouse that roared, if you will. Congressional hearings are pending into the illicit foreign control of our airlines. The Dutch government is moving rapidly against VZV. We've filed a stack of lawsuits. *And*—the most galvanizing news of all, I think—the Justice Department and the CIA believe Jacob Voorster has solved a long-running puzzle. Remember the billions of dollars missing from BCCI in the Bank of Credit and Commerce International scandal? No one in Washington could figure out where all of that money from Noriega, the Medellín Cartel, Saddam Hussein, and every other badass criminal on the planet ended up. Well, it's beginning to look like VZV was the conduit. The money went, in part, to buy up secret controlling interests in our big three airlines through that stack of holding corporations they created.

Justice has a grand jury working overtime on indictments this morning. As for Nick Costas, let me just say things are in motion.''

"Are . . . are w-we going to win those suits, Jack?" Ron Lamb's voice crackled over the connection to Washington, triggering a smile on Jack Rawly's face. Ron's voice was still hesitant, but getting stronger by the hour.

"Speaking as your highly conservative general counsel, Ron, the answer is an unqualified yes!"

Friday, March 31

FAX COVER SHEET

From: Jack Rawly
To: Ron Lamb
Subj.: Further newspaper clippings, as promised

Secret Airline Control Scheme Unravels

Indictments Prepared As Dutch and American Officials Press Investigations

---

(Washington, D.C.—Special to the Times) Pan American Airways, Inc., filed numerous federal lawsuits here this morning against a long list of defendants, including the principal lenders and the lessors of their air fleet, seeking damages that could theoretically run as high as $3 billion. The massive civil action charges the defendants with various acts of sabotage and criminal conspiracy designed to bring about the destruction of the year-old airline through purposeful financial interference and direct criminal acts against its aircraft and computer systems. The Pan Am move comes amid a burgeoning investigation of a giant Dutch multinational corporation, Van Zanten and Vetter, Ltd., which is suspected of illicitly and secretly trying to buy into and manipulate the North American airline market.

Van Zanten and Vetter, also known as VZV, is a two-hundred-year-old icon among Dutch trading firms which has historically enjoyed a reputation of unshakable honesty and incorruptibility. But that bastion of Dutch integrity stands accused this morning of having secretly designed and carried out a plan to circumvent U.S. laws that limit foreign investment in airlines. VZV, investigators allege, secretly purchased controlling interest in the three largest airlines in North America through "dummy" holding corporations set up for just that purpose. While there has been no reaction from VZV officials, the government of the Netherlands is said to be in an uproar as a result of the charges, with a major investigation of its own under way.

Tangled Web of Sabotage

Pan Am's general counsel, Mr. Jack Rawly of Seattle, Washington, held a media briefing yesterday in New York in which he used a series of charts to trace the Byzantine web of alliances and transactions which Pan Am believes resulted, among other things, in the following:

■ The March 8 bombing of a Pan Am Boeing 747 on a Seattle-Tokyo flight.

■ The March 14 sabotage of a computer system aboard a Pan Am Boeing 767, which led to an unprecedented engine-out landing on a frozen lake above the Arctic Circle.

■ The attempted firebombing on March 27 of Pan Am's inaugural round-the-world flight.

■ A highly effective scheme involving a network of banks and investors which led Pan Am to sell and lease back their aircraft and replace their critical revolving credit line, moves which made them dependent on the very corporate institution that was working to shut them down.

■ A massive and worldwide campaign to discourage financial institutions from lending money to Pan Am.

According to Mr. Rawly and court documents filed by Pan Am, the scheme went so far as to "plant" an insider in a high position at Pan Am to oversee an internal sabotage campaign that included tips of artificially created safety problems reported to the FAA, "dirty tricks" misprogramming of baggage and reservations computers, and the hiring of a professional terrorist. The vice-president of operations, Mr. Chad Jennings, the corporate officer allegedly responsible for the inside portion of the campaign, has been arrested and charged with numerous criminal violations, but is said to be cooperating with federal authorities. More arrests are pending within the United States and the Netherlands in a dragnet that is expected to result in indictments against several high-level financiers.

The Missing BCCI Link?

In addition to the likelihood of multinational criminal actions against VZV for its circumvention of U.S. laws, and its alleged commissioning of a sabotage campaign against Pan Am designed to stifle the growing threat of their competitive influence, there is a growing belief in Washington that VZV may have been the destination for several billion dollars in stolen funds from the bankrupt Bank of Credit and Commerce International. BCCI, the criminal enterprise disguised as a bank that for twenty years managed to stay in operation through bribery, was unmasked and shut down in 1990, but in the aftermath of the scandalous revelations of its operations, investigators for several governments were never able to uncover the repository of staggering amounts of missing funds.

Now, perhaps they have. A highly placed administration source speaking on condition of anonymity says that information being provided to the FBI and the Justice Department by a recently dismissed former employee of VZV validates the theory that when BCCI was shut down, VZV quietly and effectively picked up not only missing BCCI funds, but new deposits from Iraq, the Gulf Emirates, and other sources, which could include Iran. These funds were apparently invested in a brilliant long-range scheme to construct effective monopolies in various transportation markets around the world, and North America was to have been the crown jewel in that clandestine crown.

The Motive was Monopoly

Pan Am's Mr. Rawly explained the motivation for the attack on his airline as simple greed on a staggering international scale. While he was quick to say that none of the three major U.S.-based air carriers nor their executive teams had any knowledge of outside influence or criminal activity, the three dominant airlines were being subtly guided by directors representing the dummy corporations to disengage increasingly in city-pair markets where they compete. At the same time, similar quiet movement toward higher and higher domestic fares and lower operating costs were being urged. As a consequence, profits had been rising concurrently. As Mr. Rawly put it, "The big three have learned to make themselves very lean in terms of operating expense. They run cattle-car interiors now, with high-density seating, minimal food service, minimal salaries and benefits for their people, and tight control over every

penny spent on the passenger. Wherever those economies have diminished service, we attacked them wholesale, which is why passengers have flocked to Pan Am." Indeed, Pan Am has successfully attacked its far larger cousins with revolutionary concepts in cabin seating, airborne compartments, and many different service innovations. "In a nutshell," says Mr. Rawly, "Pan Am was threatening the increasingly profitable status quo, and the offshore interests who had invested billions in order to cash in on this monopoly saw the ugly head of competition looming in the near future. If they could stamp out Pan Am, they could stamp out that competition. That's what they tried to do illicitly, and that's what our various legal actions will prove."

Changing Fortunes

For Pan Am, the turnaround could not have been more dramatic. Just one week ago, it faced financial disaster, with its $500-million revolving credit line canceled, a payment demand of $140 million it couldn't raise, and the threat of being handed a declaration of default by its lenders—an act that would have triggered repossession of its entire fleet and an instant termination of service. All this followed a month of bad publicity for FAA safety violations, two near disasters in which heroic action by experienced Pan Am flight crews resulted in safe recoveries of both aircraft with no loss of life or injury, and various embarrassing episodes of lost bags, canceled reservations, canceled flights, and crashing public confidence.

In the blink of an eye—with the revelation of the alleged sabotage campaign—all that has changed. With a much-advertised and heralded resumption on March 27 of the famous round-the-world service abandoned some years back by the then-failing original Pan American World Airways, Pan Am's fortunes are soaring again. Chief Financial Officer Elizabeth Sterling sums it up this way: "Our load factors are astronomical, the public knows we've got the best pilots, the best aircraft, and the best product, we're motivated, *and* we've got new credit lines and the ability to retire our debt in record time. As a financial officer, I couldn't be happier."

Ms. Sterling adds that the freezing of any requirement to repay over $400 million in debt while litigation proceeds against Van Zanten and Vetter, Ltd., and others, will certainly assist Pan Am in continuing the growth and profitability that has astounded many observers on Wall Street.

Monday, April 3

Former Airline Chief Charged

(Washington, D.C.) The expanding Pan Am sabotage investigation has resulted in criminal charges against one of America's best-known corporate raiders and former airline chiefs. Nicolas Costas of Denver, Colorado, the former chairman and mastermind behind the expansion and eventual destruction of one of the nation's oldest air carriers, Columbia Airlines, has been charged by federal prosecutors in Washington with numerous counts of criminal conspiracy, attempted murder, theft, securities and monetary violations, and many additional counts. The move, according to sources in the Justice Department, is merely the beginning of what is expected to be a hurricane of civil and criminal legal actions marking the collapse of a scheme to exert illicit foreign control over North American airlines.

Mr. Costas, described after the collapse of Columbia Air as "the most hated man in America" for his vitriolic attitude toward airline unions, was said to be out of the country. The charges will be presented to a grand jury within the next few days.

Wednesday, April 12

UPI—(Miami) BULLETIN
Fugitive financier Nicolas Costas, former chairman of defunct Columbia Airline Systems, was arrested early this morning by federal drug agents after attempting to leave the United States in his private jet. Costas was forced down by Air Force fighters after his aircraft blundered through restricted airspace near Hurlburt Air Force Base, Florida.